EVERYBODY WANTS TO RULE THE WORLD

ALSO BY ACE ATKINS

White Shadow
Wicked City
Devil's Garden

Infamous
Don't Let the Devil Ride

QUINN COLSON SERIES

The Ranger
The Lost Ones
The Broken Places
The Forsaken
The Redeemers
The Innocents

The Fallen
The Sinners
The Shameless
The Revelators
The Heathens

ROBERT B. PARKER'S SPENSER SERIES

Lullaby
Wonderland
Cheap Shot
Kickback
Slow Burn
Little White Lies

Old Black Magic
Angel Eyes
Someone to Watch Over Me
Bye Bye Baby

NICK TRAVERS SERIES

Crossroad Blues
Leavin' Trunk Blues

Dark End of the Street
Dirty South

EVERYBODY WANTS TO RULE THE WORLD

A NOVEL

ACE ATKINS

WILLIAM MORROW
An Imprint of HarperCollinsPublishers

Without limiting the exclusive rights of any author, contributor or the publisher of this publication, any unauthorized use of this publication to train generative artificial intelligence (AI) technologies is expressly prohibited. HarperCollins also exercise their rights under Article 4(3) of the Digital Single Market Directive 2019/790 and expressly reserve this publication from the text and data mining exception.

This is a work of fiction. Names, characters, places, and incidents are products of the author's imagination or are used fictitiously and are not to be construed as real. Any resemblance to actual events, locales, organizations, or persons, living or dead, is entirely coincidental.

EVERYBODY WANTS TO RULE THE WORLD. Copyright © 2025 by Ace Atkins. All rights reserved. Printed in the United States of America. No part of this book may be used or reproduced in any manner whatsoever without written permission except in the case of brief quotations embodied in critical articles and reviews. For information, address HarperCollins Publishers, 195 Broadway, New York, NY 10007. In Europe, HarperCollins Publishers, Macken House, 39/40 Mayor Street Upper, Dublin 1, D01 C9W8, Ireland.

HarperCollins books may be purchased for educational, business, or sales promotional use. For information, please email the Special Markets Department at SPsales@harpercollins.com.

hc.com

FIRST EDITION

Designed by Nancy Singer

Library of Congress Cataloging-in-Publication Data has been applied for.

ISBN 978-0-06-329344-1

25 26 27 28 29 LBC 5 4 3 2 1

*For Doris Atkins, 1938–2025,
the Queen of Lenox Square*

Let me share with you a vision of the future which offers hope.
—Ronald Reagan

Never tell anyone your true feelings. Let them believe an illusion.
—Aldrich Ames, CIA officer and KGB spy

EVERYBODY WANTS TO RULE THE WORLD

1985

1

VITALY

He'd only been in Rome for a week when he walked into the Hotel Ambasciatore, found a bank of pay phones across the broad lobby, and dialed a number he'd memorized for the American embassy. It was early fall but still quite hot for a Russian, and Vitaly Yurchenko had already sweated through his white dress shirt and navy jacket as he'd strolled back and forth in the Borghese Gardens and up and down the Via Veneto trying to work up the courage to betray the Motherland.

"Yes," Vitaly said, cradling the phone close to his ear and scanning the lobby adorned in marble and gold. "Hello? I am Russian and wish to defect."

"Can you speak up?" a man said. "We have a bad connection."

"Do not be a stupid person," he said. "I am Russian here now. In Rome. And I wish to defect."

"Call back in ten minutes."

"Ten minutes?" Vitaly crashed the phone back onto the cradle. "Fuck your mother."

These foreign American agents didn't know ass from hole in ground. Their incompetence would get him killed as he tried to orchestrate a very professional and quiet defection. *Hello. Yes. I am Russian. Can I walk across the street and defect?* So very simple. Can you call back, the man had said. Vitaly wasn't surprised by incompetence everywhere. *Should this not be like McDonald's, where you talk in speaker and order the Big Mac and a piping-hot apple pie?* Leave with a smile for such good service like the happy purple monster and his milkshake.

Vitaly moved on to the hotel bar and ordered a double vodka. He'd already had a bit of Chianti that afternoon, becoming very fond of a little café in a narrow alley near the Trevi Fountain. He'd had thoughts of returning one day with his love, Zoya, when it was safe. He patted a handkerchief to his brow. Lovely, lovely Zoya, with her cunning mind and reflexes of the mongoose. Soon they would be reunited as the rest of the world went up in flames.

The bartender set down his drink. Vitaly raised the glass to Zoya but winced after taking only one sip.

The vodka was American, horrid Smirnoff, and smelled of embalming fluid. Good vodka and real caviar would be what he'd miss most. Certainly not his overbearing wife, Jeannette, with her love of sable coats, diamond necklaces, and Doktorskaya sausages. They'd met while he'd been stationed at Sevastopol submarine base, before the shy and petite young woman had grown so large and opinionated. It was not enough that he'd finally escaped the Third Directorate into the First; *she must know why was he still number two man and not number one. Why was their summer dacha so very small and bare? Why was their daughter not in the best schools, already being eyed for top positions in Moscow?* And their car. Don't get her started on the car. That stupid black Lada with the angry gear shifter. *This car. It sounds like a wounded cat.*

Vitaly smoothed down his brushy walrus mustache with his

thumb and index finger. It will not be so long. Zoya, my love. I will free you from such a boring life in America. So very strong, like that wild woman Sheena from the comic books. We will live in New York City or perhaps San Francisco. We will walk arm in arm and look at all the latest fashions in the store windows. We will visit museums and drink good wine from California. We will make much love.

The bartender asked if he would like another vodka and Vitaly shook his head. He must be clearheaded walking into the nest of the eagle. The CIA might become his new master, but that didn't mean he would trust them any more than he trusted the KGB. Since arriving in Rome, he'd wandered the ancient streets past buildings thousands of years old. Statues memorializing men long dead. Marcus Aurelius staring down with such judgment from atop the Capitoline Hill. *Memento mori*, as if just written for a middle-aged Russian spy.

Vitaly checked his old Majak watch (so Russian. Rarely keeping the proper time), paid the tab, and returned to the bank of pay phones. He inserted more lira and heard the *buzz, buzz, buzz* on the line until the same man answered. Again, Vitaly identified himself as a Russian defector.

This time, the man said hold on. He patched him through to another agent.

"Good evening, sir," this man said. "Have you been followed?"

"Earlier, yes," he said. "Two men. KGB. But now. No."

"Are you sure?"

"I am professional," Vitaly said. "Confident of my abilities."

"Ten minutes," the man said. "Walk around the palazzo and use the servants' entrance. You do know how to find us?"

"Do I sound like idiot?"

Vitaly hung up—*fuck your mother*—and walked back through the Ambasciatore lobby, where a little man in a tuxedo hunched over the grand piano, singing a sad song in English about a total eclipse of the heart. Women in colorful silk dresses with voluminous hair studied him as he passed, taking inventory of his worn blazer, wrinkled gray pants, and sad government shoes. He pushed through the hotel doors and out into the humid Roman night.

The American embassy sat behind a tall iron gate in the old Margherita Palazzo, three stories of stucco and red tile among tall, stately palms. An obvious spoil of the big war. A Black man in a US Marine uniform stood at attention as Vitaly walked straight through the open gates toward what looked like a servants' entrance. Vitaly wiped the back of his neck with his handkerchief as the Marine followed. *All this walking. All this heat.*

A rear metal door buzzed and another Marine held it open. The man waved a metal detecting wand over Vitaly's body. Vitaly waited a beat, took a long breath, and stepped across the threshold. Somehow this reminded him of his childhood in Leningrad and his grandmother's talk of inviting in bad spirits. Is that what he'd become, a bad spirit roaming the earth looking for refuge? Oh, *dorogoy*. A fierce pinch of the cheek and a smile on a face shrunken as an old apple.

Vitaly followed the efficient Marine into a sprawling entryway filled with marble statues of gods and conquerors. A life-size nude Venus greeted him with a foot placed high on a pedestal, one hand modestly covering a perfect breast, a robe dropped low around her wide hips.

"Giambalogna carved that," said a young white American. He was dressed in a khaki suit and wore big, round tortoiseshell glasses. His hair longish around the ears, uncombed and free. "He was a Frenchman who changed his name. The Medicis thought he was the cat's ass."

"You are CIA?" Vitaly said.

"Just a friend."

"Ha," Vitaly said. "That is bullshit. CIA has no friends. Talking to me of a cat's ass. Where is head of station? I wish to speak to him now. It is urgent."

"It may have to wait until morning."

"Morning?" Vitaly said. "Fuck your mother. I see him now or I go."

"Or we can see her now." The man spoke into a radio he'd held carefully against his leg and led the way.

They climbed a dramatic marble staircase up to a massive ballroom, the floor reminding Vitaly of a sprawling chessboard of black and white. A stout woman with a helmet of red hair leaned against a long dining table. She wore a black silk dress and long diamond earrings that sparkled in their decadence. Just one earring would pay for all of his retirement.

"So many defectors this summer," the woman said. She checked her watch and then took in a deep, dramatic breath. "So little time."

"You are head of station?"

"Sorry to disappoint, comrade," she said. "We were fresh out of peckers this year. My name is Gibson. Like the cocktail. What's yours?"

"First I would like drink," Vitaly said, taking a seat at the head of the table. "Do you have the Jack Daniel's?"

"Do we have the Jack Daniel's?" This woman Gibson looked to the CIA man and nodded her approval. The man disappeared across the chessboard, his government shoes—much nicer than his own, fashioned of rich brown leather—clacking against the marble floor. The room was cool as a crypt. Vitaly removed his worn navy blazer, folded it carefully, and set it across the back of a chair. His back wet with perspiration.

"I apologize." Gibson sat down, opened a black leather folder, and clicked open a pen. "The prime minister is hosting Sophia Loren at the Moderno. He'll be late. She'll be late. The goddamn Italians just can't help themselves. It's in their blood. Okay. So, what is your name, comrade?"

"Vitaly Surgeyavich Yurchenko."

She scribbled down some notes. His name apparently meant nothing to her.

"And what is your position with the Soviet government?"

Yurchenko sat up taller in the hard chair. He smoothed down his thick mustache. "I am deputy director of First Directorate of KGB."

Agent Gibson stopped writing, her mouth as wide open as a cattle gate. She looked across the table at Yurchenko. He nodded. *Yes, lady. It is true.* She looked over his shoulder at the CIA man, bustling back into the room with a tall whiskey dripping onto the floor, and told him that she'd be late for the prime minister. And goddamn Sophia Loren.

"Hold on," she said, holding up the flat of her hand. "First I have to ask if you're aware of any imminent threat or attack upon the United States."

"Imminent?" Vitaly said, shrugging. "No."

"Are you aware of any American officials currently spying for the Soviet Union?"

"Ha." Vitaly smiled. "So many."

"What is it that we can do for you?" she asked. "Mr. Yurchenko."

"No leaks to press," Vitaly said. "And I wish to be brought to America, to Washington, immediately by military jet."

The CIA man set down his whiskey. He'd added ice. Vitaly didn't care for ice—ice reminded him of Moscow winters and gray skies—but complaining now would be considered rude. He picked up the overfilled glass and toasted them both.

"That might take a few phone calls," the woman said, smiling. She had the feet of the crow along her pale blue eyes.

"No," Vitaly said. "For this you will bounce a code off your satellite to Langley. There your message may only be read by six of your top people. I was once stationed in Washington. They have a large file on me and will confirm everything I have told you."

Vitaly took a large sip of the American whiskey. So much more sweetness than the vodka. He drew in a deep breath and for the first time relaxed his shoulders. He'd made it inside the gates of the embassy. He was safe now and could breathe much easier, but still somehow felt as if a target had been painted on his back. The KGB had thousands of spies in America. Most likely, one would find him someday and place a bullet in his head.

"Why did you come here now?" this woman Gibson said. "Tonight?"

Vitaly shrugged. He looked up at the ornate glass ceiling and pointed his fingers at the heavens. "World annihilation is such a tedious business. Don't you think?"

"That's it?" The head of station folded her arms across her chest, smiling. "You have information that can save the world?"

"Has this not been the summer of spies?" Vitaly asked, refusing to comment. "That's what I have read in the American newspapers. And the *Time* and the *Newsweek*. So many of my comrades dead. Your intelligence service is nothing but a sieve."

"Win some," she said. "Lose some."

"In nearly two months, Reagan and Gorbachev will meet in Geneva."

"Pardon my French," the woman said. "But no shit, comrade."

"Reagan is cocky," Vitaly replied. "The lone gunfighter come to town to find the order. But his gun is empty. There are not bullets in it."

"Yeah?" she said. "I know for a damn fact the Gipper is packing more heat than Milton Berle at a burlesque show."

"I have already said too much," Vitaly said. "Does any of it matter anymore? Only possible peace and détente to last for the ages. Or we both blow ourselves out of existence and set the world on fire. It's quite simple."

"Okay," Agent Gibson said. "Go on, comrade. Tell me everything you know."

"Everything?" Vitaly asked, rattling the glass. "First, more whiskey. No ice. And then the jet. *Whoosh*. We must leave as soon as possible."

2

PETER

His room was a total mess, bedspread on the floor, no sheets on the mattress. The walls covered in concert and movie posters—*Conan the Barbarian*, *The Last Starfighter*, Prince in *Purple Rain*—along with cut-out pictures from *BMX Plus* and the *Sports Illustrated Swimsuit* issue. Carol Alt. *Paulina Porizkova is in the pink in Aruba.* A small wooden bookshelf held a couple of old *Guinness Book of World Records*, novels by Forsyth and Ludlum, and an incomplete set of ragged paperbacks by a guy named Dennis Hotchner. Peter hadn't read one in months, ever since his shrink said they weren't good for a boy his age. *Too much sex and violence.* "Total trash," his mother said.

Peter lay in bed flipping through a year-old copy of *Front Page Detective*. Some perv in a checkered shirt tying up a woman in a bikini with rope. The woman looked freaked out but the man smirked with pleasure. CAROLE'S LUST KILLER USED A WEIRD

WEAPON! *Probers Search for the Hooker Smothered in Cat Food!* And a headline in red above the magazine's name: KGB SPIES LIVING NEXT DOOR!

His mom knocked on his door and Peter quickly slid off the bed and tucked the magazine between the mattress and box spring. "Coming."

"Gary's here," she said. "He wants to say hello before we leave."

"*Cool*," Peter said. "*Awesome.* I'll be right there."

"Peter?" she asked from the other side of the door. "Where are you going tonight?"

"Scott's," he said. "We're going to the dollar movie."

"Does Mrs. Adams know?"

"Of course she knows," he said. "Jesus."

Peter had been asking a lot of questions lately about his mom's new boyfriend, to the point of his mom sitting him down last weekend, after a rare service at the Methodist church, and telling him that no one could take the place of his father. "Gary just wants to be your buddy." *Terrific.*

His name was Gary Powers. A real "stud muffin," according to Connie Bennett—Peter winced every time she said it—that she'd met one night at a singles bar off Powers Ferry. The place where they'd filmed that movie *Six Pack*, right across the street from the Holiday Inn. He was in his mid-thirties, maybe early forties. A real all-American kind of guy with curly Matt Houston–style hair but without the mustache. He liked ragged blue jeans and V-neck sweaters without undershirts, chest hair and gold medallion spilling out. Gary wore pointy-toe cowboy boots and liked to talk about pro football, saying he'd been drafted by the Dolphins out of college. (Always vague about where he went to school.) He also had a weird European accent sometimes, especially, Peter noticed, after his second Scotch. When he asked his mother about it, she'd just give a dismissive wave and talk about Gary's dear dead grandmother from

Germany, who'd raised him. *Don't say anything, Pete. He's really self-conscious about it.* Why? Peter asked. *Because the poor woman is dead! The war was hard on her! She had to eat a rat.*

"Peter!"

"Coming!" he said. "Shit, Mom."

The thing was, Peter really—*no, seriously*—wanted to like Gary and accept this new man in their crazy, nomadic life. They'd lived in multiple cities and he'd gone to a dozen different schools. Of course, there had been lots of other men since moving to Atlanta. The vice principal/football coach at Sprayberry High, the married guy who sold used Rolls-Royces in Buckhead, more than a few real estate agents, and an older guy who owned a chain of restaurants where you ordered burgers and shakes from private booths with telephones. Connie Bennett liked the company of men. And just because she had a teenage son (all this Peter had overheard on a phone call to one of her coworkers), she didn't have to become a goddamn nun.

Gary was nice enough to Peter. *But who was he? Really?* He talked about dabbling in commercial real estate. And that previous investments afforded him a life of leisure. *What the hell did that even mean?* Peter couldn't even find the right Gary Powers in the Greater Atlanta White Pages. One was a Pentecostal preacher and the other had died five years ago. And then there was that time in July—the first time Gary had stayed overnight—and Peter snuck out to snoop through his 911 convertible parked in their driveway. Inside the glove compartment, he found a loaded .38 Special and two unmarked Maxell cassettes. The first one he played sounded like computer gibberish from *War Games*, beeps and boops that helped computers speak to each other, and the other tape was filled with this crazy bombastic marching music. *Sung in Russian!* This according to Fat Sam, who worked the back room at Ole Sarge's military surplus. "Where the hell did you get this?" Sam had asked. "Holy shit, kid. This is the goddamn 'Invincible and Legendary.' The theme song of the fucking Soviet Army."

"Peter!"

"Coming, Mom."

Peter pulled on an old green Adidas T-shirt and his worn-out Nikes, reached under the mattress, and stuffed the rolled-up *Front Page Detective* into his back pocket. He'd already torn out a page from the Yellow Pages last week, his first lead on where he might find Dennis Hotchner. *Dennis X. Hotchner, a former muckraker, current raconteur, and internationally bestselling writer of men's fiction, lives in Atlanta.* A little more work at the public library found Peter an old profile in *Atlanta* magazine with Hotchner explaining that the publishing business was a crock of shit and Hotchner was forced to write freelance articles and work at a used bookstore. Dennis X. Hotchner shelving books! Hard for Pete to imagine.

But Peter had been worried about his mom since June. Now it was October, and his mom was already talking about going on a vacation with Gary somewhere out west. *Oh, you know how much Gary likes cowboys.* That was the other thing Hotchner had written about: Russians fucking loved Westerns! Especially some movie called *Mackenna's Gold*. This guy had KGB written all over him, hiding in plain sight in the Atlanta suburbs.

Peter walked down the hall of their basic but failing ranch house in the sad Woodland Hills subdivision, with its fake wooden paneling and corroded brass light fixtures, and into the living room and kitchen. Gary was holding court at their glass-topped gold kitchenette. He leaned back in the chair, wearing an eye-blinding white V-neck, a glass of his mom's cheap red wine in his left hand. "Peter, Peter," he said. "Pumpkin eater."

Peter had heard him say that about a million times. And now it was starting to sound less dirty and more condescending, as if Peter was still a kid. Peter was fourteen. He was a freshman in high school and soon he'd be driving Connie's stupid worn-out Mazda RX-7. He'd been over nursery rhymes for a long time.

"Big movie night?" Gary asked. He was swirling the wine around the glass, like he was in some expensive restaurant.

Peter shrugged.

"What are you boys seeing?" his mom asked. "Tell Gary. He just loves movies."

"*Invasion U.S.A.*," Peter said. "I guess."

"I saw the trailer," Gary said. "Chuck Norris takes on hundreds of scumbag terrorists. I think he kills five hundred guys. Sounds really cool, Pete. Have fun."

Peter could smell Gary's aftershave from six feet away. *Brut.* He could also smell the Scotch (his personal gallon of J&B kept in the cabinet over the refrigerator). The man's eyes were unsteady and bloodshot. They must've hit happy hour at the country-western place where they two-stepped and listened to fucking Kenny Rogers. How his mother loved Kenny Rogers. If he had to hear "Islands in the Stream" or "The Gambler" one more time, he thought he might puke. She once dated a real estate agent who wore this totally gross cowboy hat ringed in bird feathers with a real bird's head in the center. *Bubba from Sandy Springs.*

Gary, still seated, stuck out his right hand. Peter dutifully stepped forward and shook it, feeling his knuckles cracking under Gary's weighted stare. *He knows. The fucking commie knows I'm onto him.* Peter didn't often say *fucking*, but Fat Sam's words came to him.

"I have something for you," Gary said, the accent showing. "And all your buddies."

Gary stood up and reached into his ridiculously tight jeans. He opened his hand and pawned off a stack of business cards all stamped with a logo for some place called the Muscle Factory. The logo featured a disembodied red arm curling a dumbbell. Even the arm was red!

"Gary's opening up next month," Connie said, beaming. "Right across from the Chuck E. Cheese."

"Yeah," Peter said. "Cool."

"You and your friends stop by sometime after schools," Gary said. "I can help you boys really bulk up."

"Wow," Peter said, noting *school* with an *s*. "Gee, thanks, Gary."

"Be safe," his mom said. "Love you."

Peter nodded and headed to the back kitchen door and the carport where he kept the white PK Ripper he'd built from parts mail-ordered from California. It had taken him two years to cobble together an exact replica of his favorite freestyler's bike.

"Call if you need us," his mom said.

But Peter knew that was all just another polite lie. Gary and his mother would be gone until the early hours or maybe she wouldn't come home at all. If she did, she'd complain of a splitting headache she'd gotten from a busy week at the office. She'd still reek of booze and Gary's cheap cologne, and then there were the bruises on her neck.

Peter really hated seeing the bruises. *One way or another, Gary had to go.*

• • •

Peter was on his bike, riding through Woodland Hills, zipping down past the subdivision's nearly identical squat ranch houses, the same shingle roofs, fake window shutters, and black iron lampposts just now flickering to life. Tall transformers towered behind the homes like enormous Erector sets. Woodland Hills was one of the older neighborhoods in East Cobb County, with so many houses needing paint or new roofs, the asphalt broken and cracked. Peter swept a wide left into Twin Lakes, where Scott Adams lived. The broken concrete became smooth asphalt as he pedaled uphill past two, three, four houses and then up onto the dead grass and behind Scott's house, jumping off his bike and carefully laying it down in the yard.

He ran up under the back patio and knocked on the basement

window, where he spotted Scott's neighbor Brenda Yee watching television. Brenda was his age but looked older, at least a foot taller and twenty pounds heavier than Peter. Her parents owned the Chinese restaurant—China Palace—in the strip mall near National Video, and Brenda usually hung out at the Adamses' house until her mother picked her up to run the register.

The worn-out old basement door was unlocked, the brass knob loose and busted, as he walked inside and said hello to Brenda, Martha Quinn on MTV in some kind of crazy big-shouldered jacket introducing the weekend video countdown. *Stay tuned for number one . . . You don't want to miss it.*

"What's up, dipshit?" Brenda asked.

Peter didn't answer. He wandered into the disheveled basement, which Scott's parents had never entered as far as Peter knew. There were old Domino's pizza boxes and half-empty plastic bottles of warm Pepsi. *People* magazines and board games that no one ever played. A cable box from Scientific Atlanta, the company where his mom worked, sat on top of the big, square TV.

"Scott's in the bathroom," she said, taking a drink from a can of Pepsi.

"Okay."

"Probably whacking off."

"Why do you have to be so gross, Brenda?"

"I'm gross?" she said. "Isn't that all you boys do? Whack off?"

The sofa was a brownish-beige-ish mess, as rough as burlap, that somehow had withstood years of punishment. The horrors of Pepsi spills and cigarette burns (although no one admitted to smoking), pizza stains, and worst of all, being used as a trampoline launch pad. Not to mention the kinky shit that happened when Scott's older sister, Liz, came down into the basement with her boyfriend to watch movies. Peter and Brenda spied on them once and witnessed what they believed was a hand job but later realized was just the stupid remote control up under a blanket.

Liz changing channels during a network showing of *Superman II*. *Kneel before Zod!*

"Hey, Brenda," Peter said. "Did you ever talk to Stacey?"

"Get over it, Pete," she said. "She dumped your ass."

"Because she believed a bunch of crap about me."

"What?" she said. "Didn't you make out with Laurie Saye? People saw you in the Monster Plantation at Six Flags giving her the tongue."

"That's bullshit," he said. "That's not what happened."

"Maybe not," Brenda said. "But Stacey's telling everyone you're a total pillow humper."

Scott came bounding down the basement steps and jumped up and over the couch, landing right next to Brenda and knocking the Pepsi out of her hand. "What the hell, Scott?"

"Brenda said Stacey says I'm a pillow humper."

"A *total* pillow humper," Brenda said, standing up and wiping the Pepsi off her jeans. She had on a gray Mickey Mouse sweatshirt, now stained. "I saw her after school with Mitch Siegel. He was giving her a ride on that stupid moped."

"No way," Scott said. "Shit, man. I'm so sorry, Pete. A fucking moped. How embarrassing."

Scott was still in his school clothes, a faded blue polo, jeans, and Docksiders. The shirt smeared with sauce from the crappy pizza they had for lunch. He was about the same height as Pete, only skinnier and with light brown, super-curly hair. They'd been friends since seventh grade and had gone on a lot of adventures together and rented thousands of movies. Scott and his mom had been working on a script they were going to send to Steven Spielberg someday. *Indiana Jones meets E.T.* Peter wasn't sure if that meant Indiana Jones actually meets E.T. or if it was just a mash-up.

"Forget all that shit," Peter said. "Who cares? Listen, man. I need a big favor. I need your sister to give me a ride somewhere."

"She's taking us to the movies," Scott said. "On the way to wherever the hell she's headed."

"What about after the movies?"

"You can ask," he said. "Where are we going?"

"Downtown."

"Downtown?" Scott said. "Are you nuts? We can't go downtown. We'll get killed. Or worse."

"The address is more midtown on Peachtree," Peter said. "Listen, it's not a big deal. It won't take long and I promise to pay for her gas."

"My mom would totally shit if we went downtown," Scott said. "If we don't die, she'd murder me. Remember when we went out to Cumberland Mall to get you those nunchucks? I couldn't leave the house for two weeks. My mom made me read these stupid self-improvement books. Guy's name was Zig Ziglar. *It's not how high you fall but how far you bounce.*"

"You don't have to come," Peter said. "I just need to find someone and then I'll come right back here. No one will even know I'm gone. My mom is out somewhere disco dancing with Gary. She doesn't give a shit what I do."

"Why don't you ask Brenda?" Scott said. "She's the one who sends out deliveries. Maybe one of her cousins can drop you off?"

"Downtown?" Brenda said, both boys surprised she'd even been listening. She'd acted like she'd been engrossed in a commercial for Lee Press On Nails. A fancy woman with big hair about to shit a brick because she broke a nail before an important dinner with her husband. "We don't deliver to downtown. My dad's the one who sends out the orders. Not me. And you know my dad."

Brenda's father was a hot-tempered man allegedly from Hong Kong who could swear in seven different languages (at least according to Brenda). Last spring, after Brenda got into a fight with Tommy Hicks on the school bus, Mr. Yee hopped on board with Brenda one morning and tried to interrogate Tommy and some of the other kids on the way to school. He was dressed in a serious dark suit and tie with a tan raincoat. He looked like a cop and spoke in broken English, wanting to know who'd messed with his darling Brenda. The true story was Brenda could've beaten Tommy's ass any day of the week. It had taken three kids to hold her back.

"What's the movie tonight?" Brenda asked.

"*Invasion U.S.A.*," Peter said.

"That looks like something you dorks would watch," she said. "One man taking on an army in a stupid shopping mall. I remember when you two idiots cried at the end of *Red Dawn*."

"That's complete bullshit, Brenda," Scott said. "And you know it."

"Oh, is it?" Brenda said, reaching for the remote and turning down MTV. "*Wolverines! Wolverines!* You stupid pillow humpers."

• • •

Scott's sister, Liz, dropped them at the Parkaire Mall—refusing to speak to them during the five-minute ride—for the dollar movie. For ninety restless minutes, they watched Chuck Norris kick people in the crotch and shoot down bad guys with an Uzi. During the movie, Peter couldn't stop thinking about Gary and how Gary knew so much about *Invasion U.S.A.* It must've seemed like a training film to him, how to take over America in five easy steps . . . "*Niko was easy*," Peter said, quoting Chuck Norris as the credits rolled. "*Now it's your turn. One night you're going to close your eyes, and when they open, I'll be there. It will be time to die.*"

"*Now we can destroy the Americans and crush their struggling nation*," Scott said in an equally terrible Russian accent.

They walked out of the run-down theater and into the chilly night, turning up the hill to the bright blinking sign of Sparkles roller-skating rink. It was pretty much understood that after the movie you'd meet up at Sparkles, play some video games, and talk to girls. Peter hadn't rented a pair of skates in two years.

"So that was it?" Peter said. "Chuck Norris just shoots the Russian with that big rocket launcher and everything is over? Freeze frame and fuck it. Credits!"

"He killed pretty much everyone else," Scott said. "He shot like twelve guys in the shopping mall."

"I still don't get it," Peter said. "A bunch of terrorists jump off a boat in Miami and think they can take over the United States? What a bunch of crap. It doesn't work that way. When the Russians come for us, we won't even know it. They're already living all around us."

"You're nuts."

"Am I?"

"What's going on, man?"

"Nothing."

"Is this about your mom's stupid boyfriend again?" Scott said. "You seriously think he's KGB?"

Peter didn't answer as they walked into the skating rink, "Kids in America" blaring from the speakers. The lights pulsing and flashing across the floor with the smell of weed floating out of the bathrooms. The DJ changed up the songs, announcing a couples' skate to "Heaven," and for a moment, Peter caught a glimpse of his ex, Stacey, holding hands with Mitch Siegel. The thought of her riding on the back of the moped, hands lashed around Mitch's waist, made his face flush.

"Forget her," Scott said. "You can't compete with the moped, man. Mitch's parents let him ride it everywhere. He got it for his bar mitzvah."

Peter turned to see a couple of seniors he knew in the farthest booth by the snack bar. A boy in a leather jacket with spiky black hair and eye makeup had his arm around a girl with wild blond hair and dangly earrings. You could see her black bra under her fishnet top, dozens of jelly bracelets down her left arm. Chad Summers and his girlfriend, Tracy. Chad was a complete asshole but Tracy was cool. A good friend of Scott's sister, Liz.

"Wait a second."

"Don't even think about it," Scott said. "They're a bunch of freaks."

Freaks were okay by Peter, they just smoked a lot and did doobs in the high school bathroom. Most had tragic, fucked-up family lives. Lots of divorces and dead parents and maybe an arrest or two. Peter had heard Chad Summers had been arrested at Six Flags for getting into a fight at a Cheap Trick concert. He punched some guy who went to Wheeler right in the dick.

"How much money do you have left?"

"I don't know," Scott said, reaching into his pockets. "Ten bucks."

"Let me borrow it."

"No way," he said. "I'm still hungry."

"Come on," Peter said. "I promise to pay you back."

"If you go downtown, you're on your own."

"I know. I know."

Scott walked off as Peter took a deep breath and scooted into the booth across from Chad and Tracy. Tracy smiled at him while Chad just leveled his eyes at Peter. The couples' skate ended and the DJ started to play "The Power of Love." The red lights flashing, disco ball spinning as dozens of kids sped around in circles. The strobe effect passed over Chad and Tracy's faces.

"Are you lost, kid?" Chad asked.

"I need a ride."

"I wouldn't give a ride to a maggot like you if I had a gun to my head."

"Good," Peter said. "Because I don't own a gun."

"Don't be a dick, Chad," Tracy said.

Somewhere he'd heard that when Chad was twelve he'd pitched in the Little League World Series and everyone at school believed he was going to be the next Phil Niekro. But then his dad took off, Chad pulled something in his throwing arm, and he traded out the baseball uniform for black jeans, T-shirts, and crazy-ass fuzzy boots that looked like they'd been made out of yeti fur.

"Just to midtown," Peter said. "To a bookstore."

"A bookstore?" Chad said. "What a dork."

"Come on, Chad," Tracy said.

"I'll give you twenty bucks."

Chad looked to Tracy and Tracy kind of shrugged. Chad sunk down into the booth as if he was weighing a transport job to Alderaan. He scratched at his cheek and tilted his head. "And what else?"

"What do you mean, what else?" Peter said, tossing some crumpled bills onto the table. "It's all I got."

"When someone says it's all they got, they're usually holding something back."

Peter stood up and pulled his pockets inside out, the stack of gym passes Gary had forced upon him scattering onto the candy- and gum-stained carpet. He stooped down and started picking them up. Chad held open his palm. Peter handed a few over.

"*The Muscle Factory?*" Chad asked. "What the fuck is that?"

"Real cool club that's opening by Chuck E. Cheese," Peter said. "You wouldn't be interested."

"Sounds like a gym," Tracy said.

"It's not a gym," Peter said. "More of a club. I know the owner. He's from Europe or something. It's going to be really cool. A place for real men and hot women in tights and stuff."

Tracy stared at Chad's face in the flashing strobes, kids on skates whizzing by and sometimes crashing into the wall. No one spoke for a while, Chad looking away until all of a sudden, he turned back and said, "What the hell is this about, Petey?"

Peter shrugged and took a long breath. "You ever know something so true and real and still no one believes you?"

Chad shuffled through the passes and glanced over at Tracy. He shrugged back. "All the fucking time," he said. "This place sucks anyway. I hate roller-skating. I hate this music. If I hear goddamn Huey Lewis or Michael Jackson one more time, I'm going to shoot myself."

3

DAN

Armed with a dozen red roses in the passenger seat of his Chrysler LeBaron, Daniel J. Rafferty headed straight to M Street in Georgetown and Joanna's 1819 Club. Miss Trinity Velvet was working a happy hour shift for a bunch of DC lobbyists, horny tourists, and government hacks, and he couldn't dare be late. He'd been coming to the club since the night of a coworker's bachelor party last year, where in the VIP room he'd been taken by Trinity's immense knowledge of theology—her father had been a snake-handling Baptist minister who'd forced her to read the Bible front to back. Twice!—and understanding of geopolitical events.

Trinity, actually just plain old Wanda Tarpley of Wheeling, West Virginia, said she'd come to Washington with hopes of work in government service but ended up doing a phone sex job through her roommate. It had been the most tedious damn thing she'd ever done, having to describe complicated details of love acts for special clients. Whips, chains, even a donkey or two. But Dan saw so much promise in her and knew if he could expose her to a larger world, the finer things like smooth jazz and fondue, or maybe introduce her to the right people, she could really make something of herself. After all, there'd been a reason why God had sent him to Joanna's 1819 Club and it sure as hell wasn't about godless Bob Davis getting married for the third time.

Joanna's was nearly hidden in a narrow three-story building sandwiched between two brownstone storefronts. You'd barely notice the place with the discreet brass signage outside, like Universal Exports fronting for MI6 in a Bond film. Dan found a spot by the main stage. A rainbow of neon ran along the far wall and up and around the stage, Trinity swinging up and around the brass pole to "All She Wants to Do Is Dance." She really liked that song, explaining to Dan one night in his foggy-windowed car out on M Street that Don Henley was very political, motivated to write that song as an affront to the Reagan administration's policies in Central America. *Or maybe*, Dan grumbled, *he was just some long-haired hippie with an axe to grind.*

Things went like that with her. She liked to kid him about being old. She thought his thick gold glasses, neatly trimmed mustache, and Members Only jacket were square. But he thought she was just terrific. Maybe the most beautiful woman he'd ever seen outside the pages of *Penthouse* or *Playboy*. Another Candy Loving if she got the breaks.

Dan's glasses fogged up watching Trinity descend the gold pole in an expert twirl and he took them off to clean with a cocktail napkin. When he slid the glasses back on, Trinity was on all fours and staring right at him. "Well, hello there. Ain't you a sight for sore eyes."

Dan reached into his jacket pocket, extracted a twenty, and slid it across the stage. Several other young ladies in varying stages of undress danced under the neon glow and scattering light. In a large booth by the bar, two women in bikinis entertained a half dozen Japanese men, nodding along but not seeming to understand a word.

None could compare to his one and only Miss Trinity Velvet, with her short Lady Di hair and cute little pug nose.

She wore only pink bikini bottoms and the half-karat diamond studs he'd bought for her at the Pavilion. As Trinity bent down to pick up the twenty with her teeth, Dan whispered into her ear. "We're on," he said. "Meet me at the Roy Rogers at eight. And, oh, wear the black wig this time."

...

Dan ate two Double R Bar Burgers with his Diet Coke before Wanda showed up. She had on a khaki trench coat, the long black wig, and enormous dark sunglasses. The sunglasses were a bit much, but he knew she was just getting into the spirit of the mission. Wanda never asked him a lot about these missions around DC, what they were for or why they were doing it. She was mainly happy with the money, always delivered in cash in a neat white envelope. The amount varied based on the length of the mission and the danger factor. There had been trips outside the Beltway, to New York and Chicago. Once he'd even arranged for Wanda to fly all the way to Vienna for a very special assignment. They'd strolled the Ringstrasse, learned how to waltz, and took on a dangerous operation at the Volksoper.

"Are you gonna eat all them fries?" she asked, taking a seat across from him.

"You must be hungry," he said. "I'm so sorry. Let me get you something."

"Naw," she said. "My nerves are jumbled up plenty. I'd just throw it all up. What are we doing tonight, daddy?"

"Please don't call me that."

She reached under the table and placed a hand on his knee. "I'll call you whatever you'd like."

"Just my name will suffice."

"Well, it's no fun to say Winfield Legate," she said. "Winfield. If that's not the most stuck-up sort of name I ever heard in my life."

To Wanda, Dan Rafferty had always been Winfield Legate, International Man of Mystery, with a specially made State Department ID to confirm her suspicions.

Wanda loved to tease him. She knew it absolutely tortured him. But Dan did his dead-level best to keep their interactions professional and chaste. They'd never consummated their relationship by any legal terms. He didn't count the time in Chicago at the Drake Hotel when he'd allowed her to take him in her mouth. Dan hadn't finished and told himself he hadn't enjoyed it. Humming "The Battle Hymn of the Republic" while staring at the blinking red light atop the Sears Tower.

"You'll have to drive your own car," he said. "If you're stopped or caught, you know I don't exist."

"Yes, sir."

"I'll be there watching," he said. "It's the same as before. The park in Fairfax County."

"That little ole bridge?"

"Yes," he said. "Look under that little ole bridge."

"Ooh wee," she said. "I get goose bumps just thinking about it. Winfield, you are so much dang fun."

"Don't take this lightly, my dear," Dan said. "These so-called games are how you learn the art of tradecraft."

"Will you carry a gun?"

"Of course." Dan smiled, reached into his Members Only jacket, and slid across the envelope with cash. "You must believe and prepare for any situation. So when the time comes, you'll be ready."

• • •

Okay. So Dan was married. And he might have four children. Three boys and a girl. Ages six to sixteen. The middle boy—Blake—just going through confirmation class at St. Catherine's. But did that make him a creep? Absolutely not. He felt working with women like Wanda was all part of God's grand plan. The little acorn that he could plant, water, and watch grow into a giant oak. A wonderful little *Pygmalion* thing about the adventure. Even if he didn't know a damn thing about George Bernard Shaw. He'd seen *My Fair Lady* in the original Broadway run after he and Delores had just gotten married. But thought the movie with Audrey Hepburn was a crock. She didn't even do her own singing.

Maybe that's what drew him to Wanda. She was completely authentic, holding the world in wide-eyed wonder like some kind of Elly May Clampett, and swearing like George S. Patton. *All God's creatures eat and fuck. Just what are you, Winfield?*

Somedays he just wasn't sure.

Father. Husband. Family man. Computer nerd. Villain. Hero. Wasn't it all pretty much the same these days? The one word that he hated most of all was *liar*. Dan was many things, but he wasn't a liar. He just chose to get at the truth from a unique perspective.

He drove past the White House, the Lincoln Memorial, over the Potomac.

In Arlington, Dan stopped off the interstate and changed cars at a Safeway parking lot. He opened the trunk of a Chevy Citation and donned an old army jacket and a Redskins Super Bowl cap. He was no longer Dan Rafferty. Or Winfield Legate. But plain ole Joe Pappas from Silver Springs. As he drove, it started to rain and he turned on the windshield wipers and radio.

"We Are the World" blasted from the tinny speakers. *Jesus H. Christ.*

That song continued to torture him. As if a bunch of morons from MTV could stop what was going on in Africa or the rest of the damn planet. Sometimes he wished he didn't know so much about global politics and international relations. It was a lot of water to carry.

• • •

Dan parked where he always did, a little gravel lot across the street from the entrance to Foxstone Park. He killed the lights and waited, already getting that little adrenaline thrill after leaving the go signal (a diagonal line of medical tape) on a nearby stop sign, letting Wanda know they were on. Even more thrilling was knowing that Delores and his kids were less than a mile away, settled in for the night watching *Dallas* while he played spy games with Miss Velvet. *Who the hell cared who J. R. Ewing was fucking over tonight?*

Dan got out of the Citation, the asphalt slick with rain. He waited for a few cars to pass, headlights blinding him, before he jogged across the street and entered by the old wooden sign to the park. He and Delores used to take the kids there when they were younger. When he'd gotten on a jogging kick some years ago, two years after he gave up handball, he used to run the trails and imagine he was back in Vietnam and in the fighting shape of a much younger man. The first heart attack put a stop to all of that, along with the Scotch and the pack of Benson & Hedges a day, but he had slimmed down, losing the belly and a lot of the stress. All thanks to his little spitfire muse.

The rain and wind picked up a bit as he followed the asphalt trail marked with wooden pilings every five or so yards. The mission he'd given Wanda was to make it into the park without her or her car (a nifty red Mercedes coupe he'd bought her for Christmas) being seen and to make it to the drop site to retrieve the special package.

Dan had laid out the package two nights ago while walking Delores's poodle, Miss Sadie, a stack of four *Newsweek* magazines and two *TV Guide*s in a plain brown wrapper. But Wanda didn't know if the package was real or imaginary, which all lent an edge of danger to their little training. He'd told her long ago that he worked for the US government but couldn't share any details. Wanda thought he was CIA, because when he couldn't shake free of his family responsibilities, he made up stories about being in London or Paris, Helsinki once or twice. That's how he'd gotten the idea for the Big Op in Vienna. He'd had to go to Vienna anyway—that was a long and boring story about a computer conference—and so he'd bought her a round-trip ticket to Austria and a room at a hotel next to his.

It had been nothing but fun and games, cloak-and-dagger, for a blissful forty-eight hours.

Tonight, he had a mild sense of panic that somewhere there were other people in the park watching their maneuvers. No, he hadn't heard or seen anything, just that sixth sense of something amiss, someone else wandering about in the dark and the rain and possibly watching him from the shadows. He'd had feelings like this, that tingle, ever since Vietnam. And besides once being shot through the left buttocks and receiving a Purple Heart, the instinct had served him well.

Dan unbuttoned the old army jacket and felt for the .357, snug in the holster. He stepped out of the intermittent lights spaced along the path. He listened for footsteps and voices but could only hear the patter of rain. The worst part was that fucking "We Are the World" anthem, which still rang in his ears. That nutso Cyndi Lauper, who influenced his daughter, Mary, to take his clippers and shave the right side of her head, warbling and wailing.

The footbridge over the Foxstone River wasn't far and Dan kept walking, listening, and watching. He wanted to beat Wanda there, or where was the fun? Tonight, he planned to catch her removing the package, arrest her, and go straight to the Ramada Inn in Arlington for a heated interrogation. *Why are you here? What were you doing? Do you work for an unfriendly foreign government? Who told you to pick up this package?*

Winfield Legate! Winfield!

But she wouldn't break. She'd hold fast. That woman was made out of tough West Virginia hardwood. Maybe she'd make it to government work after all, if she could do something about her education, arrest record, and the questionable moral and ethical choices she'd made for most of her adult life.

Soon he spotted not Trinity Velvet but virginal Wanda Tarpley emerging from the woods. A lovely vision of Little Red Riding Hood coming to mind, moving wobbly legged and ginger-footed out into the open in that black wig and trench coat. She glanced behind her and then stared in his direction, Dan in full shadow, silently admonishing her for being exposed and under a lamp. Did the tradecraft he taught mean nothing to her! The rain slanted sideways through the warm yellow light.

Wanda soon left the path and moved into the darkness, where she'd go down the slick hill and under the bridge, feeling up and around the rusted girders until she came across the special package. She'd do about anything to prove she was a woman worth more than just brass poles and satin G-strings.

It seemed she was down that hill an eternity, maybe five minutes, when she reappeared crawling up on all fours and holding the package in her teeth. Her teeth! *What a woman.* She got to her feet, adjusted her black wig, and placed the package under her arm, smartly walking in the opposite direction. If Dan hustled, he could get to her before she got to her Mercedes coupe and bluff his way through the next bit. He was a new man, a local policeman maybe, who'd take her by gunpoint, in her own vehicle, back to Arlington. After the interrogation and all the fun, she could drop him back at the park and he'd only be five minutes from Delores and the kids.

He'd be home in time for the nightly news, maybe Carson, and he could put his feet up and talk about the hell of the day he'd just had at the office.

Dan kept his head down, a jogger appearing out of nowhere and nearly giving him another heart attack, until the footpath branched off to the right and narrowed Wanda's lead, Wanda not looking back once, following the trail in the dark and the rain until she was nearly gone. Just then, Dan saw a man emerge from the shadows and grab Wanda by the upper arms and start to shake her. The manila envelope tumbled to the asphalt as Dan's walk became a jog—God, he was still winded. He got within maybe ten yards when he pulled the

.357, aimed it at the man, and said, "Let her go, punk, or I'll shoot your nuts off."

The man did indeed look like a punk. In his mid-twenties, with shaggy hair, narrow eyes, and a pinched nose. When he turned, his denim jacket opened to show a bright red COKE IS IT! T-shirt. "This ain't none of your business, old man."

Old man? Dan didn't answer the ridiculous insult. He leveled the gun and circled him and Wanda, waiting for the man to make a stupid move. Dan wouldn't hesitate. Oh, what a mess this would be. How would he explain it all to dutiful Delores, his boss, and the kids? *Daddy's little stripper friend needed help, kids.*

The man shoved Wanda onto the ground and ran fast down the trail into the darkness. Dan got onto his knees, the rain streaking down Wanda's face and making a goddamn mess of her mascara. He picked up the package and lifted her to her feet, Wanda exposing a bare leg from the trench coat, her knee skinned and bleeding.

"Oh, shit, daddy," she said. "I'm so sorry."

Soon they were safe in her Mercedes, circling around the park back to where he'd left the Citation. He kept an emergency kit in the trunk and tended to her knee, Wanda crying and apologizing for making a complete mess of the mission. "I'm so damn sorry, Winfield," she said. "Shit, shit, shit."

"You got mugged," he said. "People get mugged, for Christ's sake."

Dan reached for more gauze to wipe away the mess under her eyes and across her cheeks. *Everything was going to be okay.* The windshield wipers were slapping back and forth. He took a deep breath and told her maybe it was best they didn't play these little games anymore.

"That man wasn't just some mugger," she said. "That's Larry, my ex, and he told me the next time he saw me that he'd kill me."

"Oh."

"Can I ask you something?" she said.

Dan nodded. "Anything."

"Just who on God's green earth are you?" she said, leaning into him and laying her head on his shoulder. The rain tapped across the Citation's windshield. "The truth this time. 'Cause if you really work for the government, you can help me. Right? Please tell me that you're the real deal. I sure could use a true friend right now. I'm in one hell of a fucking pickle."

4

HOTCH

Dennis X. Hotchner had once been a famous writer. Maybe not internationally famous, as his press release read (although three of his books had been published in Japan and two in France), but at least regionally famous. (Two profiles in the *Atlanta Journal-Constitution* and one in *Creative Loafing*, the last in 1979 when Ben Jones was briefly attached to shoot an ABC Movie of the Week.) The movie would've been crap anyway, not befitting of an author who reinvigorated the American detective genre after it had been taken over by goofy conspiracy thrillers and stupid humorless spy novels. *The Parallax View?* What a crock of shit. He'd been the very first to bring together a white hero and a Black heavy (unlicensed PI Bud Everett and his head-busting partner, Brutus) two years before Robert B. Parker got all the credit.

Hotch sat at the long bar of George's, near the corner of Virginia and Highland, where the owner, George Najour, set down another gin martini with three olives. George was a short, stocky Syrian guy who'd played and managed baseball in the minor leagues before getting shipped out to the Philippines during the war. He'd been running the bar for about twenty-five years and liked to tell jokes between orders. "You heard the one about the screwdriver who walked in the bar?"

"No," Hotch said. "But I have the feeling I'm about to."

"The bartender says, 'Hey, we've got a drink named after you,'" George said, tossing the bar towel over his shoulder. "The screwdriver looks up and smiles. 'You've got a drink called Phillip?'"

George laughed. Hotch went back to his martini.

He'd been drinking at George's since the dawn of time; more so since Janet (wife number three) had left him last year. Lately, he'd been taking his yellow legal pads with him, finding some special magic in that back booth at George's to write a new kind of adventure novel. He'd quit writing about Bud Everett six years ago when his contract with Popular Library ran out. The last phone call he'd had with his agent, Maury Brillstein—of Brillstein and Associates—was about tracking down royalties from Japan with Maury asking about the World War II novel he'd been writing for "five goddamn years." *You know what I could sell, Hotch? A contemporary spy caper. Something with sexy Russian broads, killer snipers, and amnesia. Fucking Bob Ludlum is killing it out there. Have you read the goddamn* Matarese Circle *yet? So exciting I nearly soiled myself. That old hard-boiled Mickey Spillane stuff is dead.*

"How's the book coming?" George asked, moving on from screwdrivers.

"Like my goddamn prostate," he said. "Fits and starts. Something's choking my creativity."

"Maybe it's all these new people," George said. "The damn yuppies are trying to take over the neighborhood. They don't wear socks with their loafers. Who the fuck does that?"

The bar was getting more crowded, mostly regulars. Postal workers, cops, local politicians, and a few working girls nursing strong cocktails before hitting Peachtree Plaza and the downtown Marriott. A couple young guys sauntered in wearing white linen suits with T-shirts and huarache sandals. *Miami Vice* shit. Hotch couldn't pull off a white suit in a million years. He was short, fat, and balding, with a bad eye after nearly having it shot out at Yongdong. He wore an old black leather trench coat over a wide-lapeled black shirt, the right pocket weighted down with a pack of Pall Malls and a hefty silver Zippo.

With his good eye, Hotch glanced up at the television and watched a grown man in a black Trans Am talking to his fucking car. The sound was off but there was something going on with a homicidal trucker and a fancy-looking guy on a private jet. The guy in the car hit a big red button on his dash and the Trans Am flew over the 18-wheeler. Maybe Maury was right. The hard-boiled hero was dead. *No untarnished man to walk down the mean streets.*

Hotch watched the show for a bit, finishing off the third martini. George soon delivered his burger and Hotch cut it in half with a knife. He'd take the second half back home and maybe have it for breakfast. He'd had a full day at work starting at 9 a.m., rifling through trades at Oxford, Too used bookshop. The pay was shit, but at least he got half price on all books and a special look at first editions before they went out to the shelves. That's how he scored a copy of *Celebrated Criminal Cases of America* just like Nick Charles owned in *The Thin Man*.

The front door opened, cold air blowing in, and a big, muscular Black woman in a gold-sequined minidress wandered up to the bar. She had broad shoulders, thick muscular legs, and a square jaw. A wild, spiky Tina Turner wig affixed on her head. "Thank God for happy hour," Jackie Demure said, sidling up to Hotch at the bar. "Grenadine, gin, and juice, Mr. Najour. Heavy on that grenadine."

"What do you call that?" Hotch asked.

"A Sweet Jesus."

George shrugged. "Most folks call it a Sunrise."

"Most folks ain't Jackie Demure."

Hotch had known Jackie since the dirty old days in Atlanta, back in the seventies when Jackie had been a recently retired Falcons defensive end working as a bouncer at a club in Underground Atlanta. Back then he'd been known as "Big Time" Jackie Johnson. But then disco and cocaine came along and Jackie got big on the drag scene, strutting out from the closet and not giving a damn who knew. (Even Hotch, as straight as a fucking arrow, had to admit Jackie had great legs.) Jackie Johnson had become Miss Jackie Demure, a star of the weekend drag shows at Illusions, where he worked alongside such luminaries as Brigitte Bidet and Cherry Jubilee.

"How we looking against Seattle this week?" Hotch asked.

"Shiiit," Jackie said, adjusting his spiked blond wig and checking his makeup in a compact mirror. "Hadn't won a damn game all year. And that Seahawks defense is mean. Whole thing gonna come down to that new kid Archer not getting his panties in a twist and hitting Billy 'White Shoes' Johnson long. That happens and the Falcons might have a shot."

"Maybe you could suit up."

"Baby," Jackie said. "My ass may be made of gold, but my knees have turned to shit."

Hotch nodded and slid his empty martini glass toward George. George looked down, shook his head, but took it anyway.

"How many's that?" Jackie said.

"Not enough."

"You okay on money?" Jackie asked.

Hotch reached under his jacket and patted his shirt pocket for his paycheck. George always cashed it for him on Fridays. He felt into the pocket and into his pants, but couldn't find it, finally remembering he'd forgotten to pick it up. *Son of a damn bitch.*

"Ain't no shame in it," Jackie said. "Borrowed from you plenty of times."

Hotch shook his head and handed over the keys to his old Cadillac. "Run me by the bookstore later? I need to pick up my check."

"Hell of a thing to be stocking your own books," Jackie said. "Do people know who you used to be?"

"Last customer who came in looking for Bud and Brutus books informed me the series ended because the author had died," Hotch said. "I told him that was a great relief. I thought the son of a bitch had just given up."

"Any progress on the new one?"

"Yeah." Hotch smiled. "I kidnapped Hitler last week."

"Goddamn," Jackie said, raising his Sweet Jesus. "That's some progress. Cheers, baby."

• • •

They drove north on Highland in Hotch's baby blue '63 DeVille, Jackie behind the wheel since Hotch had his license suspended back in June. A complete and absolute misunderstanding about traveling down a one-way street when Hotch was simply attempting to make a U-turn. The damn thing about it was that Hotch had only had two—two!—martinis that night and was headed home early from George's. The young officer didn't give a shit that Hotch happened to know a few detectives with APD—sources for his Bud Everett novels—and looked disgusted as Hotch tried in vain to pass him a five-dollar bill.

The stereo played "Ain't That a Shame" from a 45 on a record player nestled under the dash. A real novelty to anyone who'd ridden in the car he called Big Bertha, a little gift to himself after he'd gotten a decent advance on Bud and Brutus #5, *No Prayers for the Dead*. A story about police corruption that ran deep in Atlanta, with ties all the way to the Philadelphia mob's smack dealers. Everett left for dead in the final chapter, Brutus picking up his gun. Ready to avenge him.

"I still don't understand it."

"What's not to get," Jackie said. "It's a goddamn computer in the car. And it can talk. End of story. Like that shit in *2001*. *I'm afraid, Dave. My mind is going.*"

"*Knight Rider*," Hotch said, arm hanging out the window and hand patting the door in time with Fats Domino. "Because the guy's name is Michael Knight. Remember when the Everett movie was canceled because that suit at ABC said there was no way that an ex-cop in Atlanta would partner up with a 'colored guy.' He also didn't think it was sexy enough because Everett didn't get laid. That was the whole point of the book. Bud was too damn busy to get laid. It was nonstop action."

"Ancient history, Hotch," Jackie said, weaving the boat in and out of cars on Morningside. "The question is, what the fuck are you going to do with Hitler?"

"Hell," he said. "I don't know."

"You kidnapped goddamn Hitler, but you don't know what you're going to do with him?"

"You can't kill Hitler," Hotch said. "Not yet. It's 1943. Besides, who gives a shit? Maury doesn't want to sell it anyway."

"Maybe you can torture Adolf a little," Jackie said. "I read a story one time about a guy picked up in Tijuana by the cops. He wouldn't talk, so they hooked up his balls to an old car battery. Motherfucker shot bolt upright, smoke pouring out of his ears."

"Sounds like something in *Front Page Detective*."

"How much do they pay you to write that shit?"

"Ten cents a word."

"Makes sense," Jackie said. "I thought you'd been slipping. Using all those adjectives and adverbs. Wasn't like your books at all."

"That's the motherfucker of invention," Hotch said. "Goddamn need."

• • •

Jackie parked Big Bertha behind Oxford, Too. Hotch used the metal staircase up to the back entrance. Oxford, Too was open every day until midnight including New Year's, Christmas, and Rosh Hashanah.

BARGAINS, USED, COMICS. The old brick house was properly broken in and worn, like a bookstore should be, with creaky wooden floors and the delightful smell—to Hotch anyway—of old paper and glue. He headed through the fiction section and past the rare book room to the main cash register, where they sold old comics and vintage nudie books.

Before he could even ask, Keith opened up the till and pulled out the envelope with Hotch's paycheck. "We thought maybe you died," said Keith, a skinny hippie with stringy hair and something that may have been a mustache above his upper lip. "Linda wanted to take up a collection to bury you. But I said you'd be back as soon as you ran out of Manhattans."

"Martinis, Keith," Hotch said. "Gin martinis. Beefeater and three olives."

"Very Fleming of you, Hotch," he said, handing over the check. "Hey, by the way, I didn't know you had a kid."

"Neither did I."

"Well," Keith said, eyes red-rimmed and glazed over. A frequent toker on the delivery dock. "Some kid's been over in mystery and thrillers for the last half hour. He came and asked about you. I figured you were his father or something. Maybe you'd skipped out on the child support."

"Your belief in me is what keeps me going, Keith," Hotch said. "I really can't thank you enough."

"The kid asked me why we didn't stock the great and mythical Hotchner backlist," Keith said, shrugging. "I had to explain to him that you were out of print."

"Only temporarily," Hotch said. "Only temporarily."

Hotch folded the envelope and stuck it into the inside pocket of his black leather jacket. Another relic of headier times, a gift from his second wife, Margaret, the spoiled daughter of a Coca-Cola exec who kept imagining him writing the great American novel on the side, when he wasn't loafing around writing about bullets and cheap broads. He amused her for a bit, writing some crap about star-crossed lovers in Montmartre. Goddamn Toulouse-Lautrec. Midgets, absinthe. All of that shit.

Hotch headed toward the back door, his shoes finding every creak and moan in the sagging floors of the bookstore, already thinking about having the second half of his burger early, maybe opening up that bottle of Calvados he'd been saving for a special occasion.

"Mr. Hotchner?"

Hotch had his hand on the exit door handle as he glanced over his shoulder. A teenage kid in a green Adidas shirt was standing before him holding a copy of *The Atlanta Underground* in his hand. Hotch recognized the cover illustration of Bud Everett brandishing a gun with a gorgeous woman in a thin, baby blue nightgown. The side art showed Brutus knocking a faceless man onto his back.

"Look, kid," Hotch said. "I have a hot date with Johnny Carson and a bottle of Calvados. I'm glad to sign the book, but if you want something else, you'll need to check with my social secretary."

"It is you," he said. "You are Dennis X. Hotchner."

"Sure."

"I just thought you'd be," he said, "you know?"

"Taller?"

"Maybe not so old."

"How old do I look?"

"I'd rather not say," the kid said, looking nervous and frozen. Goddamn it. Maybe the kid was his after all. He looked to be about fifteen; that would've put him back teaching at Chapel Hill. There'd been an undergrad named Violet. She'd been a redhead and wore white pantyhose. Always with false eyelashes and lots of green eyeshadow. But the kid wasn't a redhead and not nearly as pale as Violet.

"I need your help, Mr. Hotchner," he said. "I've read everything you've written."

Some of the lackeys from the bookstore had started to snoop about the travel section, acting as if they were restocking and organizing.

Keith wandered up to a table stacked with James Michener remainders, thick as phone books, flicking about a fucking feather duster. "Yes," Hotch said. "This is my child. Can a man not have a moment of peace bonding with his son?"

"I'm not," said the kid. "I just thought—"

Hotch turned to Keith and offered him his middle finger. Keith huffed off as the kid struggled with something he'd tucked into his back pocket. He flashed a copy of a shitty old *Front Page Detective*, a woman being lassoed by some crazy perv.

"You wrote this?"

"I can neither confirm nor deny."

The kid handed over the magazine and Hotch reached into his shirt pocket for his reading glasses, flipping to the index. "KGB Spies Living Next Door." By Dennis X. Hotchner.

"It appears so," Hotch said. "I sincerely apologize."

The kid looked crestfallen as Hotch handed it back, glancing down at the magazine and then back up at him. He tucked the magazine into his back pocket again, clutching the old paperback in his right hand. "But it's true," he said. "Every word."

"Nope," Hotch said. "It's just some bullshit I wrote to fill the coffers, kid. Thanks for stopping by. Remember to always keep your nose clean, and like the former Nancy Davis, star of *Donovan's Brain*, says, *Just say no*."

"I don't think you're listening to me, Mr. Hotchner," the kid said. "I just walked two miles after this dickwad kicked me out of his stupid station wagon. All because I told him that Van Halen's last album sucked ass."

"I don't know what you're talking about," Hotch said. "I stopped caring about music when Elvis died."

"Can we talk?" the kid said. "I want to hire you."

"Hire me?" Hotch held up the flat of his hand and looked at a few of the other book folks listening in. "Christ. Who put you up to this? We're way past April Fool's."

"I think my mother's life is in danger," the kid said. "And I think you're the only one who can help."

• • •

"Rooty Tooty Fresh 'N Fruity," Jackie said, snapping the laminated menu shut. "You just know I'm having that shit."

The kid—Hotch now knew his name was Peter (no last name yet)—couldn't stop staring at Jackie Demure. He looked at Jackie like Richard Dreyfuss looked at those big-headed aliens in *Close Encounters*. A confused but silent respect for something he'd never witnessed on God's green earth. Hotch guessed the burbs were a long way from the city.

They sat in the IHOP at the corner of East Paces and Peachtree in Buckhead, Jackie announcing to all of them that he was treating them to breakfast at 10 p.m. "You know, I can eat breakfast anytime," Jackie said. "Especially since I haven't eaten all goddamn day. I woke up this morning with a white pastor from Waycross trying to repent for all he'd done last night. I couldn't do a thing to help him but grab my wig and head on into work."

"Where do you work?" Peter asked.

"Ever hear of a world-renowned club called Illusions?"

The kid shook his head. He had a glass of water, ice melting and untouched, and seemed too nervous to look at the menu. He'd been babbling something about finding some computer cassette tapes of Russian music in a Porsche.

"I do what they call a 'Tribute to Tina,'" Jackie said. "I know folks expect me to do all that new shit. *I'm a private dancer. A dancer for money.* And all that. But I like the old Tina. The original Tina. God knows Ike beat the damn hell out of her. But is there a better song than 'Nutbush City Limits'? Or 'River Deep, Mountain High'?"

The kid shrugged. The waitress came over and Hotch ordered

hash and eggs. Jackie had that Rooty Tooty thing and the kid wanted toast. Dry white toast.

"What are you doing up so late?" Jackie asked. "On a school night in Buckhead?"

"It's Friday," the kid said, explaining where he lived and why he'd come so far. Looking for Hotch because of that crap article he'd written for *Front Page Detective* or whatever it was. He also breathlessly said he was a big fan of Bud and Brutus, looking to Hotch and then Jackie, confused as hell.

"Yeah, don't I know," Jackie said. "He'll deny it until Christ comes home. But you and I both know that Brutus is based on my Black ass. And what the fuck's his name?"

"Bud Everett."

"Goddamn Bud is supposed to be Hotch's alter ego," he said. "Only taller, handsomer, and with two good eyes. I guess that's the thing about fiction. Every writer wants to give himself a big ole swinging dick."

"Jackie."

"Shit, don't you want to be that Bud Everett?" Jackie said. "Tell me I'm lying."

"My mom," Peter said. "She started dating a man this summer named Gary Powers."

"Gary Powers?" Hotch said, raising an eyebrow and snorting. "Francis Gary Powers who flew the U-2 plane over Russia? I thought he was dead."

"No," Peter said. "This Gary says he's from Pennsylvania. But he's got this weird accent. My mom says it's because he had a German grandmother who ate rats in the war. But I don't buy it. He's a Russian. Fat Sam said it has to be true."

"Fat," Jackie said, clicking his long red nails on the IHOP table. "Sam."

"Sam works at Ole Sarge on Buford Highway," Peter said. "He's the one who identified the second tape as definitely Russian in origin. I mean, who drives around in Atlanta listening to Soviet fight songs?"

"Old liberals like Hotch here," Jackie said. "Ain't that right, Hotch? Former adjunct professor of journalism. Did some sit-ins up in Chapel Hill, always supporting unions, workers' rights, and all that."

"Okay," Peter said. "I know this is crazy. And it sounds crazy in my head as I'm saying it. But I think Gary Powers is an agent of the Soviet Union. I think he's trying to get close to my mom because she works at this company called Scientific Atlanta. They work on satellites and top-secret government shit. I swear to God that if we don't expose him for what he really is he might really hurt her. I mean, I can't go to the cops. And what am I going to do, call the CIA? You said in your article that you had sources connected to the CIA?"

Jackie snorted so loud, a table of three old women turned and glared.

"I may know some people," Hotch said, giving the side-eye to Jackie, "who used to work for the State Department. From back when I was a reporter. But I got to be honest, kid. I wrote that article while flying half blind on Maui Wowie and Beefeaters. All of it is complete bullshit. Just page filler for perverts who want to get to the good parts of women in bikinis attacked by psycho killers."

"But you believe me," the kid said. "Right? No one else will listen to me."

"What about your daddy?" Jackie said. "You got a daddy somewhere?"

"My father is dead," Peter said.

"Well, fuck a goddamn duck," Jackie said. "You got to help the boy now, Hotch. Kid showing up talking about some fucking Russian on a spy plane coming in to do the nasty with his momma. And he's driving with some freaks and geeks out to Oxford, Too to find your broke-down ass. I mean, come on. You brought this bullshit on your own damn self. Writing about KGB killers among us and all that. Help out poor Peter, Peter Pumpkin Eater."

"Please don't call me that."

Jackie looked at the kid and then over at Hotch.

"Gary calls me that," Peter said. "Like I'm a kid."

"Oh, I meant it as dirty," Jackie said. "I meant it like, you know, eating pussy."

"Goddamn it, Jackie," Hotch said.

The trio of old women turned to stare at their table. One big woman in a frilly, flowered dress stood up and made a beeline over to them. "If you don't mind, we are having a meal after Bible study."

Jackie looked up at the woman and pushed at his Tina Turner wig. "Well, I sure do apologize, lady," he said in a deep voice. "I guess I better excuse myself while I go untie my dick from this big ole knot."

The woman's mouth widened as she stared at Hotch, the drag queen, and the kid. The waitress thankfully arrived with their food and set down the hot platters in front of them. "If you don't mind," Jackie said.

The woman huffed off as Jackie cut into his pancake platter slathered in berry sauce red as blood. Hotch took a bite of his hash and then pointed to the kid with an empty fork. "Just how are you planning to get home?"

"I hoped you could give me a ride."

"I figured," Hotch said. "But that's the end. I don't care what Auntie Entity over here says. We are not Bud and Brutus. And this Gary Powers is not some Soviet spy. I get it. I swear to God that I get it. When I was a kid, I thought I was Lash LaRue and the folks who worked cattle on the farm near us were a bunch of rustlers. It's just hormones, kid. Messing with your brain. I promise it will all go away."

"What if it doesn't?" Peter asked.

"Gin martinis," Hotch said. "Trust me. Martinis cure all. The hallucinations don't stand a chance."

5

LISICA

So many names and so many identities. It was very hard for Lisica to keep track of them all. Driver's licenses, passports, library cards, fake business cards and résumés. Lisica had been in America for nearly twenty years and memories of any true identity had started to fade. Once there'd been a hardened child of the war in East Berlin. An orphan who lived in half-bombed houses, cooking potato soup in old coffee cans and making their way picking pockets. Those were wonderful times of freedom until Lisica picked the pocket of the Kommissar and was banished to an orphanage in Dresden. Hell upon this earth. A smart child, a child of promise, the record would show. Lisica was soon sent to special schools in Moscow to learn proper Russian, English, Italian. Perhaps a great athlete or an Olympian? Lisica trained so very hard in gymnastics and judo. But no, it was in a cold, empty airplane hangar outside Moscow when the first mention of the Illegals program was heard. *You will live as an American from now on. You will eat as an American, sleep as an American, talk like an American.* Lisica still didn't know what it meant to sleep as an American.

First came university in Chicago, an early job in New York, and then being filtered back to Moscow for two years. A dormant spy until a very complicated matter led to a new identity, a new résumé, and back to the States to live a life of lying, cheating, and bribing assets. Americans could be tricked into anything with either sex or money. Lisica could provide both, being even better with sex, having attended a class at the KGB center that taught the many ways to please both a man and a woman. Lisica had been violated so many times as a child, the act meant nothing. Between picking pockets, Lisica would perform oral pleasure for perverted Russian soldiers for nothing more than a candy bar.

Lisica didn't have a real family or friends, spending the most time attempting to gain trust. Like the woman Lisica was meeting tonight. A very plain, very unremarkable secretary from a tech company that supplied spy satellites from the CIA. This one had been tricky. She had many hang-ups with the sex and turned down so many gifts until she finally accepted an incredible floor-length sable Lisica had bought her.

That's when Lisica owned the woman. The soft and luxurious sable meant everything. They planned to meet at a fondue restaurant across from Lenox Square, Dante's Down the Hatch, always furtive adventures as the woman believed Lisica was married. A strange place that vaguely reminded Lisica of being in the old city of Kalingrad, with the fishnets, diving helmets, and wheels of ships hung on the walls. Lisica wanted this to be a special night and reserved a table aboard the pirate ship, where you had to enter over a gangplank. Two live crocodiles huddled in the stagnant water below.

Lisica was surprised when the woman arrived. She looked less homely tonight in an elegant red dress with tiny straps across her bony shoulders. Lisica welcomed her, and they ordered champagne, perhaps the Mandarin platter with the shrimp, chicken, and beef to fry in their personal vat of boiling oil.

There was a jazz band and much frivolity and Lisica truly hoped that the evening wouldn't end in death. Killing an asset that you worked so hard to cultivate was always a sad thing. Much like training a dog that wouldn't take commands and must be put down.

Did the woman not know that Lisica knew what she'd done? Did the woman think Lisica was so foolish not to see that the painstakingly copied floppy disk was missing? The treachery didn't bother Lisica as much as the arrogance.

"Where's your fur?"

"Oh, it had a stain," she said. "I sent it to the cleaners."

"You'll freeze in that dress."

"I thought we might go dancing later," she said. "At the Limelight? It gets so hot."

Lisica considered the Limelight to be an inner circle of hell, a place only the real Dante could appreciate. An aging disco next to a grocery market filled with cavorting homosexuals and pulsing electronica. Lisica much preferred English music, adored Genesis, and anything sung by Phil Collins. *No Jacket Required* a true masterpiece.

They listened to the American jazz as Lisica laughed at the woman's stories of her boss. The dreaded professor who tried so hard to take her to bed. He'd ogle her breasts in low-cut sweaters when she'd bring him files, comment on the shape of her thighs, and once even grabbed her backside.

"You should report him," Lisica said.

"Do you know how hard it was to get a job there?" she said. "I can't afford it."

"How do you feel about melted cheese?" Lisica said. "With the good bread? They say it's made by Indians in the cellar."

"I don't think anything here is real," the woman said. The lights above them cast a soft blue glow in the room. "It's like a movie set."

Lisica felt they could be in Marseilles, Casablanca, Buenos Aires.

Maybe when all this was done, Lisica could return to Moscow. Or maybe one day Germany. *Where was Lisica's home anyway? Who was Lisica beyond just the assassin the KGB handlers called the White Fox?*

They stuffed themselves on the fried meats and gooey cheese. More champagne and chocolate fondue for dessert. The dance club was only five minutes from the restaurant, and Lisica drove with the top down on the Porsche 911 Carrera. How Lisica loved shifting the Porsche in and out of Atlanta traffic. The cassette radio played the theme to *Against All Odds*.

Lisica reached for a tin of skinny Dunhill cigars in the dash and mashed the cigarette lighter. "Do you find Phil Collins attractive?" Lisica said.

"The singer?" she said. "I can't say I really ever thought about it."

"It's true he's short and balding," Lisica said. "But some women find him quite humorous."

"Quite humorous," the woman said, giggling. "Sometimes your accent creeps me out in funny ways."

"What would you say?"

"Funny," the woman said. "Some people think Phil Collins can be funny."

"*Funny*," Lisica said, making a mental note.

The Limelight was packed on a Friday night. The woman was cold, and Lisica offered a spare leather jacket from the trunk, stuffed among a tarp, rubber gloves, and a shovel.

They entered the club to pulsing music, Human League, and descended the grand Roman steps to the dance floor. Bubbles floated down from the ceiling, the room smelling of sweat, cigarettes, and sex. In the bathroom, Lisica saw a couple copulating in a stall, two women snorting cocaine across a towel dispenser.

"Don't you love this?" the woman said. She raised her hands and combed through her ash-blond hair, working her hips toward Lisica and offering her mouth. Lisica kissed her as she turned and worked her buttocks in time with the music.

The flashing colored lights turned to a strobe and soon they were caught in the flickering images of a black-and-white film. Moment by moment caught in blinding white light. Lisica pulled the woman close, smelling her cheap perfume, and wrapped an arm around her throat. "You shouldn't have stolen from me."

The woman turned hard, breaking Lisica's grip.

"I did it for you," she said. "I'm protecting you."

The crowd kept on dancing. "Don't You Want Me Baby." Lisica and the woman had stopped, the strobe stopped, and they were back in real time. Standing inches apart and looking right at each other.

"Where is it?"

"I threw it away," the woman said. "Let's dance. Forget it. I should've never taken you into the Vault. It was my mistake. Okay? Leave it."

Lisica knew she was lying. *Who was she? Who had she told?* Everything Lisica had built in Atlanta would be burned to the ground. Control would be furious. And then another move, another name, another assignment in a city that was less hospitable.

"I can't breathe," Lisica said.

The air so thick with the smoke and the sweat.

"It's okay," the woman said. "I handled it."

"Can we go?" Lisica said. "I need air."

. . .

The woman rested her head on Lisica's shoulder as Lisica downshifted and headed along the crooked road back to the river.

"Why would you do that?"

"What?"

"Protect what I've done?"

"Don't you know?" The woman squeezed Lisica's arm. "I think I'm falling in love with you."

Lisica's face tightened, and she shifted into a higher gear and took a turn north toward the deep, muddy river. There was a secluded spot, not far from the road, where everything would end. Lisica turned up the Phil Collins. "In the Air Tonight," the fuzzy guitar rattling the speakers.

There was no going back now. *Zakanchavit*.

6

VITALY

Vitaly had spent the last twenty-four hours as the lone passenger strapped inside the back of a C-130 from Frankfurt to Andrews Air Force Base. He still wore the same worn navy blazer, white shirt, and gray trousers he'd had on when he'd defected. He carried no personal items, no photographs, only the seven hundred dollars he'd had in his pockets in Rome and a shoulder bag filled with toiletries. Compliments of the CIA. But nothing for his stomach, his stomach aching since he'd left Italy. Most of the flight over the Atlantic he'd spent thinking of his poor mother who'd died of stomach cancer and the incompetent Soviet doctors who could find nothing wrong with her. *Perhaps the nerves? Something you ate disagreed with you, comrade?* It was so much the shit of the horse.

And now he was seated in the back of a black car, one of three that pulled onto the tarmac to welcome him to America with seven men in suits. They patted his back. They shook his hand. Like the old traveling circuses of his youth. *Look! A Real Live Defector from the USSR. What secrets will he tell? What surprises might he divulge?* But his stomach, the gripping pain. His aching stomach.

Vitaly had been taken to an office, where he signed many papers. He was given entrance in the name of Robert Rodman of Virginia, USA. Robert. Perhaps a Bobby like the Kennedy? A new man, born just minutes ago, and now hustled into the back of an FBI car with another identical car driving in front and two in back. They would not lose him to the KGB. He would not be shot, garroted, or poisoned. Not on this day, anyway.

They crossed the Potomac and headed south. Yes, Vitaly knew the District well from when he'd been former security chief at the rezidentura, and believed they'd be taking him straight to Langley for a long debriefing. He sat in silence as they passed Burger Kings and Kentucky Fried Chickens, gas stations without a single line at the pumps. Shopping malls and grocery stores. So many riches that the Americans were blind to. Bright white marquees and the curve of neon. Freedom for the masses, not just the party elite.

"Are you okay, sir?" asked the man sitting up front with the driver.

"Yes," Vitaly said. "Yes. My stomach sometimes gives me pain. Is there a store where I might find ginseng or turmeric? I left my remedies back in Rome."

"No, sir," the man, not much more than a shadow before him, said. "Turmeric? Not that I know of. But I can check."

Vitaly didn't answer. There was little left to say and he focused on his pain and the decision he had made. What would his wife say? His daughter? Would the KGB cause them much distress before sending them off to Siberian work camps or fishing boats in the Bering Sea? What had he done? Was it the wine and the golden loveliness of Rome that had made him such a romantic fool?

He fell asleep for a while, the first time since the journey started, and he dreamed of Zoya in a field of wheat. She was dressed as a Young Pioneer, her freshly scrubbed face smiling, in a white blouse and red kerchief around her neck. Standing at attention, she saluted him, the wheat flowing endlessly around her. Vitaly going to her, waist-deep in the wheat, his hands touching the tips, his walk now a run, but suddenly she was gone. As fast as a coin trick of a magician. He wandered and stumbled through the field, the scent of the grass so strong in his nostrils, until the car hit a bump and his dream and sleep were broken.

"We're here, sir."

"We are where?" Vitaly said, rubbing his eyes.

"The safe house."

"Yes," Vitaly said. "Of course. The safe house."

The safe house did not look very safe or secure to him, just one of those town houses now fashionable about the capital. A tan-and-brick structure, dull and shuffled between others nearly indistinguishable from the next. A federal agent waved him forward and offered Vitaly the flimsy canvas bag filled with a toothbrush, toothpaste, a razor, shaving cream, and a small and most insignificant bar of soap.

They walked up the steps, the morning still and silent around them, two agents standing by the door and letting him into a short foyer. The little narrow home smelling to him of a dacha with cinnamon and spices, and more men in suits waiting for him. More handshaking and backslapping and men calling him comrade, welcoming him to America. Land of the Free and the Home of the Brave. Elvis Presley. Ronald Reagan. Daffy Duck. One man in particular seemed to tower over the rest, a man who said he was from the Agency and called himself Charlie. A name that Vitaly did not believe in the least.

The agents who had brought him left, and he was taken to a living room, where Charlie walked down into a sunken pit. The carpet was thick and shaggy and of a deep brown color. He could see more men behind an opening to a kitchen and there were the sounds and smells of cooking. Just the thought of food made him both hungry and sick to his stomach.

"I bet you're hungry," Charlie said. He was tall, thin, and possessed the air and the dress of a man who had attended premiere schools, as he knew CIA men often did. His hair was jet black but quite gray at the temples, and he had a nose and narrow face that gave him the appearance of a hawk. His eyes the lightest of blue, almost translucent and colorless. "You must be tired, Vitaly."

Vitaly found the familiarity interesting.

"Yes," he said. "Yes. I am very tired."

"We have made a bed for you upstairs," Charlie said. "We will talk soon enough. Get some rest."

"No," Vitaly said. "I am tired. But I can't sleep because I have much to say. I cannot rest until I tell all that I know. Isn't that the price of my passage?"

"You tell me, Comrade Yurchenko."

"I love Mother Russia, but I am physically sick at what we have become," he said. "So many legitimate investigations dropped. The favors to so many Kremlin leaders suppressed. This is not socialism. This is greed for few and tyranny for all. My life—and I fear it might be coming to an end—has all been wasted. A dirty, disrespectable lie."

"That must be one hell of a burden."

A young man in a white dress shirt splattered with grease and wearing a yellow tie brought out a large platter of scrambled eggs and fried meat. A pot of coffee sat on an octagonal table inlaid with bronze bowls that appeared to be ready for hot soup. Vitaly smelled the bacon and eggs and again his stomach seized. He stood and asked for the toilet, an agent taking him to a tiny bathroom where he turned on the faucet and took down his pants. His insides emptied quickly but he must have sat there for many minutes because an agent knocked on his door and asked if he was okay.

"Yes, yes," Vitaly said, and then under his breath, "Fuck your mother."

When he returned to the living room—as large and decadent as the apartment of a family of six in Moscow—he noticed the presence of yet another man. This new man stood at the front door speaking to the other dark-suited agents. He had on thick gold glasses and wore a sporty and quite handsome black windbreaker with the collar raised.

The man showed his credentials to the men at the door and then exchanged a few words with Charlie. Charlie didn't look pleased to see him and the men argued a bit. Vitaly had yet to sit and could make out a bit of the conversation. This man was FBI and objected to all the CIA agents lurking about.

"Would you rather he be killed?" Charlie said. "Or protected?"

"Mr. Yurchenko is our guest," the FBI man said, adjusting his bulky gold glasses. "Not our prisoner."

Someone had thankfully removed the bacon and the eggs from the table and Vitaly took a seat again. The man bounded down the steps into the sunken pit and offered him a large smile and a strong handshake. "Boy, am I glad to see you," the man said, removing his sporty jacket and tossing it with little care onto the sofa. He leaned toward Vitaly and whispered, "These guys wanted to put four agents upstairs by your bedroom. You couldn't even fart without them knowing. Don't you worry a bit, Vitaly. I've worked it all out."

Vitaly tilted his head, seeing his own reflection in the man's large gold glasses.

"Hello, Daniel." Vitaly reached out to wrap him in a bear hug. "It has been many years."

7

SYLVIA

Sylvia Weaver didn't have a problem with the carpooling, or that she still hadn't been given her own vehicle as she'd been promised. It was the damn day after day, week after week fight on who would control the radio on the morning drive into downtown. They'd decided a few months ago that the driver should choose, since the driver was busting their butt through the morning commute while the other three could sleep or look out the window as the Atlanta skyline appeared heading south on 75. The big Coca-Cola sign, the Varsity drive-in, the final jockeying for position until they were on the off-ramp downtown and headed deep into Hades beneath their office building. Today it was Irv Ravetch at the wheel, a fellow rookie fresh from law school, cursed with a Jersey accent and a rotation of two of the ugliest off-the-rack suits Sylvia had ever seen.

Irv preferred, God help her, Peach 94.9 FM on the dial. Goddamn easy listening versions of all the hated classics. *Is "Raindrops Keep*

Fallin' on My Head" too harsh for you? Well, you're gonna love this smooth cover version with all kinds of flutes and shit. The worst part of it was Irv humming along, patting the wheel, and damn well knowing he was annoying the hell out of everybody in the company car.

Jimmy Caruso rode shotgun and Bill "Bulldog" Drummond sat in back with Sylvia. Drummond was a husky guy (hence the name) who took up a lot of space, even more as he spread out to eat a microwaved Jimmy Dean sausage biscuit. Caruso damn near invisible up front with his head tilted back, sunglasses on, softly snoring until they slowed to a stop in traffic. They were a hell of a crew, a Jew, an Italian, maybe an Irishman (what kind of name was Drummond?), and a Black woman from Grabtown, North Carolina, rolling on through the Atlanta traffic.

They all lived within a few miles of each other. She and Bill Drummond both in the Akers Mill Apartments at the cross section of 75 and 285, a goddamn rabbit warren of young professionals new to the city. There was a pool and a Nautilus gym, a walking trail down by the ruins of the old mill by Rottenwood Creek. The apartments advertised with a massive mill wheel that was visible from the interstate. Sylvia used the gym nearly every day and the pool during the summer but seldom walked down the creek trail. The last time she had, during a drought when the water had receded, she'd found two arrowheads and some old Civil War minié balls. Like the man said, the past was never past.

"Did you know there might be water on Mars?" Caruso said, waking up to unfold the *Journal-Constitution* in his lap.

"Glad to hear it, Jimmy," Drummond said.

"Do you understand what that would mean to NASA and space exploration?" Caruso asked. "Not to mention eventual colonization."

"Who would want to live on fucking Mars?" Drummond said. "Sylvia, would you want to live on Mars?"

"Depends," Sylvia said. "Do they have music like this on Mars?

Oh, man. What is this, Irv? Hall and Oates by way of your momma's dentist office?"

"What can I say?" Ravetch said, slowly hitting his blinker and taking his own sweet time to merge and head off 75 and up onto Peachtree Street. "Puts me in a good frame of mind before I get to work. If you don't like it, then one of you guys drive. What about that shit you like, Sylvia? Whoever heard of a Black woman listening to all that country-fried nonsense?"

"Um, you mean Linda Ronstadt?" Sylvia asked. "Irv, you got the soul of an eighty-year-old. And Linda Ronstadt is the great poet of our times."

"Fucking Monday," Drummond said. "I got six reports to file and I hear the typing pool is backed up all week."

"Here's a crazy idea, Bill," Sylvia said. "Why don't you type up your own damn reports?"

"You realize those nice women in the typing pool rely on us to be completely incompetent at a keyboard," Caruso said. "Where would we be without them? It would take me a week to hunt and peck three pages."

"Yeah?" Sylvia said. "I type ninety words a minute."

"Bullshit," Drummond said.

"Time me," Sylvia said.

"Keep it up and we're all fucked," Irv said, taking a slow turn onto Peachtree Street and passing the flickering marquee of the Fox Theatre. "You get more competent and who knows what might happen?"

"Equality in the workplace?" Sylvia asked.

"This water thing is incredible," Caruso said. "Scientists say it's like in permafrost beneath the surface in caverns and shit. They say if you look at the surface of Mars, you can actually tell where water has eroded rocks and made canals."

Irv headed up Peachtree Street and took a left down into their building's garage. The tires squealed on the concrete until he turned onto the level with their assigned parking spaces. Most of the slots already taken as men in suits and women in brightly colored skirts and tops hustled toward the elevators or into the labyrinth of tunnels running to other office buildings. Another big day to hustle in Hot Lanta. The tunnels always reminded Sylvia of those tubes that connected play sets for gerbils.

"Ninety words a minute," Drummond said. "Ha. Then what the fuck are you working here for?"

"Well," Sylvia said. "Maybe I like carrying a badge and a gun, too."

Sylvia Weaver got out of the gray Chrysler and straightened her black coat over the bulge of her .357 Magnum. This was her eighth month on the counterintelligence squad for the Atlanta office of the FBI.

• • •

The squad shared a car, several battered metal desks on the fifth floor, and even had to share a damn telephone—a beaten tan push dial—that had a ten-foot cord. Sylvia removed her jacket and sorted through the pink message slips piled on her desk before spotting the name of a man she'd been trying to connect with all week. The fact that he'd called her back was a good sign. Five years ago, he'd been a damn purple wizard for the KKK in Forsyth County before getting right with Jesus and starting up a Pentecostal church in a trailer. Some of his former associates had recently regrouped and the Feds were curious about the current lineup of shitbirds.

Sylvia had no problem talking with these people. She had an advantage over most of the Yankee agents. She'd been dealing with racist peckerwoods her whole life. Thankfully she'd gotten the hell out of Johnston County, went to college, and did law school at UNC, where one of her professors had been in the Bureau. He'd pulled her aside one day after class, given her a nice pitch, and then she thought, what the hell. The Bureau sounded like a lot more fun than clerking for some fat-ass judge in Raleigh.

Irv Ravetch, his off-the-rack suit looking two sizes too big, walked up with a Styrofoam cup of that bad coffee they sold down in the lobby. He slid his blue tie up to his neck, complying with standards in place since Melvin Purvis was in diapers, and took a seat at his desk, mashed up against hers. He had a piece of toilet paper stuck to where he'd nicked his neck.

"I need to borrow the car," Sylvia said.

"I just get the keys and already you want the car," Irv said. "Bulldog and I were going to ride out to Stone Mountain to do some more interviews on the Parham thing. You know that loony private eye and the crooked cop?"

"Can it wait?"

"Well," he said. "I guess. It's not like we don't have a mile of audio and video explaining how the son of a bitch planned to blow up that couple in South Carolina. It's just if we don't get it done this week . . . Well, you know the way shit rolls."

"Guess who called me back?"

"Pat Sajak?"

"Almost as good," Sylvia said. "How 'bout Barabbas Johnson."

"Bullshit."

Sylvia reached down and showed him the pink message slip. "He may have actually gotten right with the Lord."

"Sure," Irving said. He scratched at his neck, found the toilet paper, and tossed it into the can. "No offense. But have you two met in person yet? You know, face-to-face?"

"Not yet."

"Well, please excuse me if I withhold congratulations."

"I hear Barabbas is a new man," she said. "And he wants to talk. Even if it is to a Black woman."

"Keep dreaming, baby," Irv said. "I know I wasn't born down

south with grits in my mouth, but these turds don't change their spots."

"Lovely sentiment, Irv," Sylvia said.

"What can I say?" he said. "I do my best to class the place up."

Sylvia reached into her battered metal desk, broken fluorescent lights winking on and off overhead, to find her Forsyth County street finder. Johnson's trailer church was way the hell out in Cumming, about an hour from downtown. She'd just cross-referenced the street when she noticed Ella—their squad supervisor's secretary—standing over her desk. "Old man wants to see you and Jimmy."

"Does he know you call him that?" Irv asked.

"Old man?" Ella said, hand on her hip. "Sure. Y'all rookies started that shit five years ago and it ain't ever going away."

• • •

Their squad supervisor was a tall, rawboned guy from Texas named Jeremiah Sullivan. He had premature gray hair and a ramrod demeanor, one of those guys who probably gave J. Edgar wet dreams back in the day. He looked like one of those Hathaway shirt ads, only without the eye patch and the mustache. More in the way he held himself, his posture speaking of a quiet confidence. She'd heard Sullivan worked on both the MLK assassination and the killings of those three civil rights workers down in Mississippi. But rarely, if ever, spoke of it.

Sullivan looked up from his desk and told them both to sit. A long cigarette smoldered in his ashtray as the old man tapped at a blue file splayed across his desk. "We got a dead woman, an asset, dumped out by the Chattahoochee River. Christ on a cross. What a mess. Buck Revell called me personally this morning. Just in case we all needed a fire lit under our asses."

"Who was she?" Sylvia asked.

"A secretary at a place called Scientific Atlanta," he said. "With top-secret clearance."

"Access to DOD files?" Sylvia asked.

"Access to pretty much everything," Sullivan said. "Someone broke her neck and dumped her in the woods. Somebody tried to bury her but a man walking his dog found her. Dog wouldn't quit digging."

"Top-secret clearance, huh?" Sylvia said.

Sullivan held up the flat of his hand. "Don't get too excited," he said. "Could be personal or a random nut."

"Is she married?" Irv asked. "Does she have a family?"

"You better find out," Sullivan said. "Check in with Fisher on the way out. He's got the ticket to Sci Atlanta and can put you in touch with their security guy."

Sylvia reached for the blue file and Sullivan rested his hand on top of it, pointing to the name. "Sylvia, have you ever heard of this woman?"

"No, sir."

"Well, she apparently knew you," Sullivan said. "Your business card was in her purse along with some photocopies of top-secret files."

8

PETER

His mother had left a note. Peter had to give her that much. *Gone off to Mexico with Gary! Surprise trip. Loves and kisses, baby. Cash in the cookie jar!* Peter spent the rest of the weekend ordering Domino's and eating Cap'n Crunch, watching MTV and renting movies Saturday night at Scott's. They wanted to rent *Sixteen Candles* for the fifteenth time—a real milestone for both boys—but Liz insisted they watch an old movie called *Vertigo* with Jimmy Stewart. He didn't want to admit it, but he really thought it was terrific, something wonderful and unsettling about it.

Jimmy Stewart came off like a total perv, forcing this woman to bleach her hair and dress like his dead girlfriend. Miss Ellie from *Dallas* was in it, too. Only much younger and much hotter with cute little cat's-eye glasses. Is this the way adults acted? Haunted and obsessed, doing anything for sex. He didn't like to think about what stud muffin Gary and his mom were doing in Cancún. Disco dancing and back rubs. She'd come home with a sombrero and maybe a piñata for him. There'd be a big fuss about what a grown-up young man he was, holding down the fort while Mommy got a little rest and relaxation. She'd say it just like that, calling herself Mommy again as if Peter was still seven.

That Monday, he set his AM/FM radio alarm, blasted awake by Huey Lewis and the News, "Back in Time," got himself showered and dressed, an Eggo waffle clamped between his teeth as he ran out to meet the bus. Brenda Yee was seated at the front, refusing to look at him as he sat across from her. "What's the matter with you?"

"I heard you went downtown and got loaded."

"Yep," Peter said. "That's exactly what happened."

"Scott said you rode home with some drunk guy and a prostitute."

"He wasn't a prostitute," Scott said. "He was a drag queen. Believe me, I learned all about the difference. He could sing just like Tina Turner."

Some kids in the back started blasting Cheap Trick from their boombox. "She's Tight" played as Peter stared out the school bus window, hoping his mom would get back soon. He only had two bucks left and the refrigerator was nearly empty. Scott's mom would understand and take him in, but he hated to rat out his mom like that. He hadn't mentioned to anybody that she'd just flown off to Mexico with her sketchy boyfriend. Nobody wanted to think of their mother as a loser.

• • •

School was a blur. All of ninth grade was a goddamn blur. So many kids in the halls, shoving and jostling Peter as he tried to get from English to math. It didn't help at all that the English teacher—Mr. Farrell—had some kind of fucking meltdown. He'd been reading a passage from a book called *A Day No Pigs Would Die* that got into this crazy fighting sex scene with pigs, blood, and fluids and biting all around, and everyone started cracking up. Who the hell could help themselves, it was pigs getting it on. The stupid kid in the book crying "Pinky, Pinky!" as his beloved pet piglet was getting jackhammered. Between the giggles and the comments, all of a sudden Mr. Farrell slammed down his paperback and stormed out, saying *these kids don't know jack shit about any goddamn thing.* Peter was pretty sure he'd started to cry. Christ, what had gotten into him?

He'd eaten lunch, gone to gym class, and rolled out to the temporary trailers where he took world history from his wrestling coach, a florid-faced redneck named Coach Ryan. The coach diverged from the history textbook to give an impromptu talk about how God had promised Israel wouldn't exist for nearly two millennia. Peter nearly dozed off before a cute girl named Ashley smiled over at him, flashing the greenest eyes he'd ever seen. They had to be contacts, looking so bright with her tan skin. He didn't know much about her. She was cute, maybe even cuter than Stacey. To hell with her and Mitch's stupid moped.

"Peter?" Coach Ryan said. "Mr. Bennett? Have you heard a damn word I've been saying?"

• • •

Coach hadn't forgotten and took it out on him at wrestling practice, pairing him up with this disgusting country kid who smelled like cooking oil and farts. The kid kept on muttering how he was going to beat Peter's rich ass—*since when was he rich?*—attempting a double takedown with Peter easily gripping his head and twisting him onto his back like a steer. They did this over and over again until Coach blew the whistle and ordered them to roll up the mats. On the way out, Peter begged an older kid to give him a ride home. He didn't give a damn if his mom was home yet. He didn't really care if she ever came home. Peter remembered he had a box of Eggos in the refrigerator and a few extra slices of pizza. He'd survive. Let her continue to rut around with her stud muffin like Pinky the goddamn pig.

On the way back home, he spotted a big banner hanging up in a space next to the new grocery store. It was a new strip mall, most of the storefronts not even occupied yet. More shops and malls popping up all the damn time. "You can let me out here," Peter said. The kid stopped in front of the space with the banner reading THE MUSCLE FACTORY COMING SOON. Peter wandered up to the plate-glass window and looked inside. Mirrors lined half the walls, with collapsed ladders and paint cans bunched up by a counter. He could see shiny silver pieces of workout equipment and rows of empty dumbbell racks. Lots of unopened boxes and the lights were off. What the hell, he thought, trying the door and finding it unlocked, pushing into the space, which smelled new and fresh like poured concrete and paint fumes. There was a pile of pamphlets on the unpainted counter. JOIN NOW FOR AS LOW AS $9 A MONTH. A WHOLE NEW YOU IS WAITING!

The room echoed with its emptiness as he walked around the boxes and exercise equipment, heading toward a back room filled with a glass wall and more mirrors. The space had floors like a basketball court, dead neon tubes wrapping around the ceiling, and two huge speakers up on a raised platform. He found another hallway and followed it, bathrooms without fixtures and then two closed doors. The first one was locked, but the second opened up into what must've been an office. Besides two beaten metal desks and some filing cabinets, the office also had a cot and a push rack filled with clothes. Faded jeans, a few white suits, and V-neck sweaters that smelled like fucking Brut.

How damn successful could Gary Powers be if he was living in his own office? Peter started to look through the desk, finding endless flyers for the gym, more of those stupid passes that he'd given to Chad Summers, and binders filled with workout plans, aerobic routines, and résumés. Some woman named Mona had applied to be an aerobics instructor and called the job her Christian calling in life, to bring health, happiness, and peace of mind to her clients. Yeah. That sounded like the kind of person to work at the ole Muscle Factory. Peter went through two gym bags holding a can of some shit called BIG protein powder and a bunch of vitamin pills. He checked through the pockets of Gary's gross tight jeans and down into two pairs of pointy-toe boots. There was a footlocker that was—of course—locked, and Peter went back to the desk to look for a paper clip. He tried for twenty minutes to open the fucking thing with the paper clip, but it wouldn't budge until he went back into the workout room and found a screwdriver one of the workers had left. He broke into it within two seconds.

Gary's personal stash.

Peter, exhausted from practice, got down on his knees and shuffled through piles of gross satin underwear and loads of tank tops, finding a pile of books about weight lifting. He didn't think much of them until he tossed them to the floor and saw one cover with a weird illustration and symbols that looked very foreign. He flipped through the book with a big-muscle mustached man demonstrating squats and curls and noticed everything appeared to be in fucking Russian! *Come on, Gary. You got to try a little harder.* He was making this too damn easy. He also found a deck of weirdo nude playing cards. He couldn't be sure, but the women looked odd, lots of eye makeup and bearskin rugs. Their signature printed upon each card. The queen card was a woman with her hands behind her head, showing off a pair of huge breasts. He could barely make out her signature, and although he couldn't be sure, it didn't appear to be English.

He heard pounding on the wall, some voices coming from inside the space. Probably some workers come back to finish up. If they found him, he'd just tell them he'd come to see Gary. After all, it was true. He'd like to know when his mother was coming back and how did a dirty, disgusting commie go parading around as the owner of a gym.

Peter hurried up, tossing the underwear and T-shirts to the side until he found this really weird but cool-looking machine. It could be a radio. It could be a dick stretcher. Who knew. It was definitely larger than a bread box, with dials and buttons, a couple of meters with needles, and a pair of big, oversize headphones. This was it. A goddamn Russian radio, how Gary contacted his superiors back in Moscow. Now Hotch had to believe him! The breath left him as he sat back and looked at the stash of Russian nudies and this contraption. He could call the police right now and tell them. It would be the end of Gary. The end of the stinky cologne and V-neck sweaters and mysterious cassette tapes. A radio. A spy radio right here in his hands.

"Peter, Peter," a voice said.

Peter looked back over his shoulder to see Gary standing in the doorway with two young women in shiny leotards and tights. One pink and one blue, neither his mother. Gary was tan, with more scruff on his face, wearing a Hawaiian shirt and shorts.

"Where the hell is my mother, you Russian son of a bitch?"

9

DAN

His supervisor at the Bureau gave him Monday off after he'd debriefed Yurchenko all weekend. So Dan spent the afternoon with Father Rick at St. Catherine's collecting little blue donor boxes from the church members, kiddies, and businessmen who'd passed the collection around the office. Even some of the OWLS—Older, Wiser, Livelier Souls—had managed to putter about and scratch up a few bucks in change. Dan and Father Rick rolling the money and placing the rolls into boxes as his beeper went off, Dan figuring it could only be two things: Yurchenko wanted to talk more or Delores's father had wandered away from the home again. Her father had been in the D-Day landing and had a steel plate in his head, which helped him know when the weather changed, but lately he said he'd started getting signals from both Eisenhower and, for some reason, Clayton Moore.

Dan didn't recognize the number on the beeper and asked Father

Rick to use his office, punching up the number. It rang once, and then: "Winfield?"

Dan didn't say anything. She was only supposed to call his beeper number in case of a serious emergency. "Please don't be upset," she said. "Larry's on my ass again. I watched my rearview mirror like you taught me and saw his Firebird. I know damn well it was that son of a bitch. I tried to shake him, daddy. I really did."

"Where are you?"

"The Americana Hotel," she said. "It's in Crystal City right by the airport."

"Why'd you go to a hotel?"

"I couldn't go home," she said. "He'd be waiting on me. I tried calling you. At both them numbers."

"You need money?"

"Oh, God," she said. "I see his car outside the window now. He's just sitting behind the wheel, smoking marijuana cigarettes and watching the hotel with binoculars. Should I call the police?"

"Don't call the police," Dan said, checking his digital Seiko. "Not yet. I can be there in less than an hour. I'll get this whole damn thing straightened out. Once and for all."

Dan stepped back into the rec room, where Father Rick looked up from a table as he rolled more change. Father Rick had on a black vest over a starched white shirt and a cleric's collar. Priest-casual today, looking all of eighteen. "No rest for the wicked?" Father Rick said, stroking his black beard. A big, dumb smile on his face.

Dan stared back, sliding into his Members Only jacket. He started to speak but could think of nothing to say to the young priest who'd been so kind to his family.

"Just joshing with you, Dan," the priest said. "Looks like some important Bureau business. May God bless you and keep you."

• • •

Dan stopped by a Bank of Virginia near the interstate and pulled out three hundred dollars from one of his secret accounts. He called Delores at a pay phone, explaining he had to head back to the office (never mentioning Bureau business on an open line) and wouldn't be home in time for dinner. *Oh, what a shame*, she said. She was making Dan's favorite, cowboy stew with hamburgers and franks all mixed up in a tangy barbecue sauce. Dan never had the heart to tell her that he thought the stuff was god-awful, one step above what they fed their damn dog.

The sun was setting in his rearview as he made it to the outskirts of the District, radio tuned to drive time on 97.1 WASH FM, starting off the next hour with "Peaceful Easy Feeling." Dan had always loved that line about how her sparkling earrings lay. It reminded him of the day after the encounter with Wanda in Chicago, the night he'd rebuffed her advances over and over. He brought her breakfast in bed, embarrassed to learn she slept in only her cotton undies, sitting up topless and startled by his red face. "Baby, you've seen me with a lot less on at Joanna's."

Dan parked up under the motel and took the elevator to the third floor. The hotel had been a nice family place twenty years ago but now looked as if it rented rooms by the hour. The hallway was a faded and sad yellow, the green carpet stained and torn. He knocked two quick and three long. A little variation on a shave and a haircut.

Dan was about to identify himself with one of his aliases when the bolt snicked and she threw open the door. "Baby," she said, jumping up into his arms and wrapping her legs around his waist. "I was so scared, I was about to hop out of my skin. He told me he'd kill me the next time he found me, and I dang well believe him."

He let her down and walked into the dark, cool room. The drapes drawn and the wall unit humming. The room smelled musty, dank, and of thousands of cigarettes. Dan walked to the windows and pulled back the drapes, staring onto the interstate and down into a small parking lot. "Well, I don't see him."

"Wait," she said. "Maybe you scared him off."

"You said he drove a Pontiac Firebird?"

Wanda had on a curly red wig and some kind of gold metallic jumpsuit that looked as if it had been made from a parachute. She wore tall white stilettos and a flowery silk scarf knotted about her throat.

"Baby blue," she said, walking up behind his shoulder as he turned back to the empty lot. "A big blue eagle on the hood. Larry loved that damn car more than me. But guess who's been stuck making the goddamn payments?"

Wanda pulled him in close and wrapped her arms around his neck. He stayed still. She felt so soft and smelled so good, but he couldn't touch her. He must never, ever touch her again. Just to focus on something else, he tried to concentrate on Mrs. Johnson, one of the kindly silver-haired OWLS at St. Catherine's who'd brought coffee to him and Father Rick as they counted out the change. "Thank you," she said, her moist mouth close to his ear. "I don't know what I'd do without you."

"I brought money," he said. "Let me get out my money belt and you can get home. Then let's talk about getting a patrol unit out past your apartment. A baby blue Firebird can't be too hard to spot."

"A real waste of a motel," she said. "Don't you think?"

"Wanda."

"Winfield."

"I must never, ever touch you again," he said. "I made a solemn vow. Is this why you brought me here? You promised not to tempt me."

Wanda reached up and started to rub her little hand with bright red nails over his chest, unbuttoning his shirt. She smiled up with those big blue eyes and said, "What if I know of a way where you don't lay a hand on me? And I do all the work. That wouldn't be a sin. Now, would it?"

Dan couldn't move, visualizing a smug look from Father Rick. His mouth felt dry. Cowboy stew would have to wait.

• • •

Wanda had brought two thick rolls of the hospital tape he'd given her for signal exchanges at the park. She made Dan lie down with his shirt unbuttoned and his slacks down to his knees and raise his hands above his head. She began to bind his wrists to the motel bed headboard, Dan closing his eyes and trying to focus away from Wanda's wonderful, sensuous perfume. He tried to imagine the kind and thoughtful Mrs. Johnson rolling pennies, but instead Clayton Moore and Silver came to mind, *hi-ho*-ing across the plains. Six-shooters firing and arrows flying. "Winfield."

She pulled down his Jockey shorts and began to bind him at the ankles, like a cowboy with a calf before branding. That was it, the red-hot fire poker coming down upon him, marking him forever as dark and black as the mark on Cain's face. How could he ever explain this to Father Rick at confession? "Wanda," he said. "Wait."

But it was too late, Clayton Moore was hidden high on a rocky mountain, shooting silver bullets from behind a boulder. Bad men approaching from the foothills below. She'd wrapped her perfumed scarf across his eyes, adding to the whole Lone Ranger scenario, Dan refusing to give in, trying to think of a way to escape. He had to escape. But then a most wondrous thing happened: Trinity Velvet had found him in her hand and started off in a rough motion like a country woman doing the wash or shucking corn. "My God," he said. "Easy. Easy."

Dan heard a loud pounding on the door. She stopped what she'd been doing, and he heard the bed ease from her weight. "Wait," he said. "Cut me loose. Cut me loose now."

Wanda yelled that she was going to call the cops and then he heard a hard thud against the door and then another, and then a rough jangle of metal as it sounded like a security chain had been yanked from the wall. Dan squirmed on the bed and tried to bite through the tape at his wrists. "You goddamn liar," a man said. "Is this the fella from the park? I'll skin his ass alive."

Dan chewed at the tape, the perfumed silk scarf coming loose from one eye, and he spotted little Wanda standing in front of Larry—the Coke Is It! hippie—with Dan's black service revolver in her shaky outstretched hands. "Wait," Dan said. "Stop. Let's talk this thing through."

"Buddy," Larry said, looking down at the bed. "You look more excited than a sundial at high noon."

And then Wanda shot him. And shot him again.

The sheer blast of it in the shabby little motel room was enough to wake up the entire Americana Hotel and all of Crystal City. Larry fell to the ground and Wanda rushed up to Dan, tearing at the tape with her long fingernails, freeing one wrist and then the other. He finally broke free to find his Case knife down in his dropped slacks and cut away the rest of the tape binding him at the ankles.

"Oh, God," he said. "Oh, God."

"God ain't here, Winfield," she said. "Pray later. We need to go."

Dan was up on his feet but unsteady as the blood had gone from his legs. He reached for the nightstand, pulled up his Jockey shorts and trousers, his sensible rubber-soled Hush Puppies still firmly tied. He looked around the room for any evidence, taking his service revolver from where she'd set it on the bed. "Gather your things," he said. "I'll wipe everything down. God. Oh, God."

He looked down to see the front of Larry's T-shirt—Molly Hatchet, Take No Prisoners '82 tour—stained with blood. Blood leaking from the corner of Larry's stupid mouth, his eyes staring straight ahead.

"What name did you use?"

"One of them crazy names you told me to," she said. "I don't know. Torchy Blane. Right? Isn't that right?"

"Good girl," he said, finally able to take a breath. Dan smiled at her as he took a towel from the bathroom and wiped down the telephone and the headboard. *Had he touched the plate-glass window? What would the desk clerk remember?* He moved on to the bathroom to wipe down all the fixtures.

He shouldn't have come. He should have gone home and rested until it was time to return to the Russian's safe house. More complaints from Yurchenko about his aching stomach and ambitious wife and the stupid bureaucrats but going quiet, just a mischievous spark in his eye, when the agents asked him about T sector. *What did T sector know about the new ground-based lasers? Did T sector have new information?*

In time, Yurchenko would say. *In time. First I need the Alka-Seltzer.*

Dan had composed himself and grabbed Wanda's hand to leave when two men pushed open the splintered door. One man was short and stout wearing a black winter jacket with a black fur collar, an old-fashioned fedora on his head. The other man was taller and much younger, wearing a Members Only jacket nearly identical to Dan's. He had a lollipop hanging out the side of his mouth like Kojak.

"Who are you?" Dan asked.

The older man smiled and removed his fedora to show a gleaming bald head. "You do not know us, but we know you, Agent Rafferty," he said in a Slavic accent. He flicked his fingers across the brim of the hat. "We were following you, as is our business, and heard the sound of a gunshot. Perhaps we may be of service before police arrive?"

"Fucking Russians," Dan said. "Son of a bitch, Wanda. What the hell have you done?"

10

PETER

Gary gave him a ride home in his Porsche, top down with its Blaupunkt stereo being humiliated by a Kenny Rogers cassette. He didn't speak to Peter as he downshifted along Johnson Ferry Road with some agitation, not saying a word since he'd seen Peter going through all his shit at the gym. He couldn't tell if Gary was pissed off or embarrassed. Stupid Kenny Rogers singing some corny song about "This Woman" making him lose control. Gary in his Muscle Factory sweatshirt and crazy-short red satin shorts. Gary sped up as they passed Peter's old middle school and rounded toward the Parkaire Mall. Peter had so many questions but didn't know where to begin or how to ask. The big secret he'd been keeping to himself had already been shot out of the box and into the open. Gary would either say he was crazy or threaten to kill him if he told a living soul. At this point, Peter figured, it was pretty much all fifty-fifty.

"I am not Russian," Gary said, talking against the wind and music. "My father was in the air force. In Germany. My mother was German. I lived there until I was eight and then my father brought me to Georgia. That's why I still have a little accent."

"Sounds Russian to me," Peter said, holding on to the door handle. Gary took a tight, hard left turn onto Roswell Road, maybe trying to beat the yellow light or maybe trying to scare the crap out of him.

"I don't like to talk about it, because my parents weren't married," he said. "My father was married to an American woman and had another family here. When he finally brought me over, kids made fun of my accent. They called me Little Dutch Boy."

"You just said you were German."

"Kids can be stupid," he said. "And mean. One boy called me Hans Strudel Anderson."

"That doesn't make any sense."

"My father's name was Anderson," Gary said. "That was the name I used until he sent me away. I lived with his mother, my nana, in Pennsylvania until college."

They passed the Kroger, the dollar movie theater, Sparkles, and the strip mall with the Radio Shack, National Video, and China Palace. He wondered if Brenda was working or back down in Scott's basement. He didn't have much money left but figured maybe Brenda could send a delivery this one time. She'd do that. Better than letting Scott's mom know his mom was a complete deadbeat.

"Where's my mom?" Peter said.

"I told you," Gary said, driving at what felt like sixty, crossing into the oncoming lane and then back around an old VW bus. "She's running late at work. She'll meet you at home."

"Where were you guys?" Peter said. "What the hell is going on?"

"It was a surprise," Gary said. "A special trip for your mom. I thought she had it all worked out. We tried to call you from Cancún but couldn't get through."

"Bullshit," Peter said. "You were drinking margaritas, disco dancing, and screwing her. Just like you're probably screwing those trashy aerobics bunnies at your stupid gym."

Gary raced forward, then slowed, downshifting. He pulled onto the side of the road, right across the street from the entrance sign to Woodland Hills. Peter sunk down into his seat with shame. If any of his friends saw him with this mega asshole giving him a stupid man-to-man talk, they'd never let him hear the end of it.

"*Man to man*," Gary said, raising his finger at him. "You don't speak of your mother that way. Ever. Your mother—"

"Is a special lady?" Peter asked, saying it with a bit of whatever kind of accent Gary had.

"That's fine," Gary said. "Make fun of me all you want and go through my things. I have no secrets."

"You have a goddamn Russian radio in that big metal trunk," Peter said. "Don't give me that shit, Gary."

Gary shook his head, Kenny Rogers still singing about how special his woman was and how he wanted to love her all his life. She meant a lot more to ole Kenny than some buried treasure.

"This music makes me want to puke."

Gary shrugged. A car passed and for a moment, Peter thought he spotted Mitch Siegel in the passenger seat, smirking at Peter and some weirdo in a Porsche. It must've looked like some total pervert situation. *Hey, kid, want to ride in my little car before I pull out my wiener?* Completely gross.

"I have more music," Gary said, nodding to his glove box. "Go ahead. Help yourself."

"You really want me to open it, Gary?" Peter said. "Or whatever your name is."

"Yes," Gary said. "And I promise my name is Gary."

"Then why aren't you in the phone book?" Peter said. "Gary Powers."

Gary shrugged. "Because my number is unlisted. You can do that, you know. It cost ten bucks."

Peter nodded to the glove box. "I'm opening it."

"Help yourself."

"I am," Peter said. "Comrade."

Peter opened the glove box and a dozen or more cassettes spilled onto his legs and down into the floor of the Porsche. More Kenny Rogers and Dolly. And then also some new ones like the Power Station, Robert Palmer, Dire Straits. Peter really liked Dire Straits, especially the guitar work of Jack Sonni on some of the live bootlegs. He rummaged into the box, only finding a 911 instruction manual and more of those goddamn Muscle Factory passes. Gary must've printed off a million of those things. But no gun. No Russian military music.

"Where's the gun?"

"Yes," Gary said. "I have a gun. I used to work downtown. I had it for protection. If finding it upset you—"

"And the spy radio?" Peter said. "Come on, man."

Gary shook his head and ejected Kenny Rogers. He snatched the *Brothers in Arms* cassette from Peter's hand and snicked it into the player. "Have you ever heard of biofeedback, Peter?"

"What?"

"It's like music for your body," Gary said. "It can help you recover faster, breathe better. Even manage your mood. You should try it sometime."

"Sounds like more bullshit."

Gary started the engine and looked back into his rearview before cutting across Roswell Road and into Woodland Hills. He didn't speak as Dire Straits played "Walk of Life," Peter silently embarrassed that he and Gary liked the same kind of music. This day was just getting worse and worse.

"Like I said, your mom is working late," Gary said. "She wanted me to make sure you're all settled before I leave."

"I'm fine."

"I promised," Gary said, staring straight ahead, alone with his secret thoughts as he turned down Peter's street and rolled up into the stained driveway covered in old pine needles. The house looked empty and dark as Peter grabbed his backpack and trudged to the front door. What a shit day. He didn't believe this guy in the damn least. Gary was definitely cheating on his mom with those aerobics bimbos, working more of his lies on them, too.

He looked back to see Gary still behind the wheel, head tilted back and smoking a cigarette. He blew smoke up into the air and then reached down for something under his seat.

• • •

Peter unlocked the front door and walked into the living room, slipping off his Nikes and heading into the kitchen to grab a Coke. With any luck, Gary the stud muffin would get tired of waiting and go the hell away. Maybe he was a Russian. Maybe he wasn't. Maybe he was a spy. Or a cheater. Or maybe, most surely, he was a complete and total dick. Peter reached for a Coke and popped the top, listening to the humming of the fridge. Maybe he'd call Brenda up at China Palace and see if she could spot him some moo goo gai pan and throw in a few egg rolls.

He was so damn mad that his mom had not only left him all weekend but again tonight. There wasn't shit in the refrigerator but freezer-burned Eggos, he had two dollars in change, and would rather eat cat poop than ask Gary for some money. On second thought, he walked back to the front door and locked it behind him. Fuck that guy.

Peter was headed back to his room when he heard the voices. It sounded like someone was out on their crappy back deck. Had fucking Gary walked around the house? Nobody went on the back deck; most of the wood had rotted through, leaving big soft spots or gaping holes, the only thing out there a sad, rusted charcoal grill they'd been carting all over the country but never used. He set down his Coke and circled back to the living room, with its flowery furniture and a framed print of some model in a big black hat covering one eye, a red gloved hand propping up her face. Brittle yellow curtains left by the last owner covered up the sliding glass doors to the porch.

Peter peeked out and didn't see anything. He slipped between the curtains and unlocked the door, walking out on the deck with bare feet. Just then he heard the Porsche start up and pull out of the driveway. Tires squelching on the asphalt.

Connie Bennett, nominee for worst mother of the year, was out on the deck in her business clothes drinking tea or coffee or some shit with a young Black woman wearing a dark, official-looking suit. They both turned to stare at him.

"Hey there, Peter," Connie said, smiling brightly. "I'd like you to meet Sylvia Weaver. She came by to ask me some questions about a woman I used to work with. Wait inside and I'll be right there."

"I've been waiting all weekend," Peter said. "The fridge is empty. Hope the fiesta was worth it."

11

HOTCH

His third ex-wife, Janet, woke him up at ten thirty, knocking until he cracked open his apartment door and commented on her new hat. It was one of those safari numbers, like Indiana Jones or Charlton Heston in *Secret of the Incas*, and he told her so. "Ha-ha," Janet said. "You're a riot, Hotch. I miss your wit like a case of the piles."

"I don't have your check, Janet," Hotch said, letting the chain guard fall. "Would you settle for a cup of Sanka?"

"You're so full of shit," Janet said, brushing past him and into the apartment overlooking Orme Park that they'd once shared. He hadn't done much with the place after she'd taken pretty much everything except for the mattress, a rickety old dresser, an unknown quantity of rare and first-edition books, and a console Magnavox he'd owned since '67. Sometimes on a very clear day he might get two stations. "God," she said. "Did you get robbed?"

"Well," he said. "It appears you're doing your damnedest."

Janet was pretty, maybe even beautiful after two martinis, a wannabe poet moonlighting as a perfume girl at the downtown Rich's. She was fifteen years younger than Hotch, and they'd met at the Stein Club, bonding over their love for Ella Fitzgerald and Walter Mondale. Hotch had, God please forgive him, encouraged her work. She was an atrocious poet, but he introduced her to Pound and Hughes, a selection of Robert Penn Warren, before pulling out some old longhand crap he'd published in *Carolina Quarterly*. There was a time when she believed he was a true and underrated genius.

Hotch lit up his first Pall Mall of the day, set a teakettle to boil, and pulled out a jar of Sanka.

"I was fired," she said. "Nobody goes downtown anymore."

"I'm sorry," he said. "I'd offer you a seat. But you took the dinette set."

"You said you didn't want it."

"I didn't want anything," Hotch said. "I was broke when you met me. And I'm even more broke now. Two lumps or three?"

"You don't remember?"

"I do like the dress," Hotch said. "Goes with the hat."

The dress was red, fitted through the waist, and fluttered above her knees. The big shoulder pads made her look like Joan Crawford or maybe Jackie after hitting the gym. He thought about making a crack about the shoulders—there was once a time when Janet found him clever and funny—but didn't have the energy for it. He'd finished the bottle of Calvados last night and felt like his head was wrapped in a wool blanket.

Janet plopped down into his ratty old reading chair held together with duct tape, taking off her hat and twirling it onto her fingers. She looked good and smelled nice, probably from a sample of some expensive French perfume, and for a moment Hotch wondered if she'd come back to try to make amends. He couldn't really remember what their last fight had been about, only that she'd tossed a wineglass at his head and missed, soaking a toreador painting of Elvis Presley he'd bought in Tijuana.

The kettle soon whistled. He made the coffee, handing her a mug.

"You keep coming back," Hotch said. "My second wife just called me a talentless idiot and took the cat."

"She had money."

Hotch nodded and began to mix his own Sanka. It was true, Margaret had come into their marriage—and left it—with loads of money. She'd mainly married him as an affront to all her Buckhead friends. He'd met the second Mrs. Hotchner in '79 at a wrap party for *Murder in Moonshine County*, a CBS Movie of the Week starring Ben Jones—Cooter from *The Dukes of Hazzard*—as some kind of Buford Pusser–like character busting up stills and shooting down baddies.

"What am I going to do?" Janet asked.

She had on a lot of makeup that morning, like maybe she had more important business today than just shaking down her ex. She had a heart-shaped face, plump little cheeks with pinkish rouge that matched her lipstick. Her eyes were brown and quick and stared at him the way you would a dog that had gone through your trash.

"I could get you a job at the bookstore."

"You'd do that?"

"Sure," he said. "Why not? It's like hanging out in a library, only you get paid for it."

Janet covered half of her face with the flat of her hand and let out a long breath, explaining that she was about to interview at the Macy's makeup counter at Perimeter Mall. She was running down the pros and cons of Estée Lauder versus Clinique when the sliding window over the sink creaked.

His black cat, Beelzebub, squeezed inside and headed straight to the dish he'd filled last night and gobbled Cat Chow while glaring at both of them.

"Can I ask you something, Hotch?"

"Why the hell not?"

"If something doesn't work, why keep on banging your damn head against the wall?" she said. "Isn't there a time when we all have to quit?"

"Interesting," Hotch said, carefully scratching Beelzebub's ears while the cat growled. "You know, the thought never really occurred to me."

• • •

Hotch wrote till one and then treated himself to a club sandwich with two cups of decaf at the Majestic. He spent the rest of the afternoon at the library across the street, rummaging through bargain book bins and reading through the Sunday *AJC*. Sometime in the early afternoon, he'd fallen asleep at a research table with a big fat copy of *Jane's Fighting Ships of World War II* sprawled out in front of him, a fresh and unmarked yellow legal pad as a pillow. A librarian shook him awake and wanted to know if he was all right.

Hotch brushed the old woman off and walked over to George's Bar.

He returned to his favorite booth, the bar nearly empty except for George himself setting up, and soon lost himself in *Save Hell for Tomorrow*. That was the working title, although he knew Maury Brillstein would have plenty to say about it. Hotch went right back to his stopping point, writing everything in longhand, the Merry Marauders capturing Hitler on a daring mission to the Eagle's Nest. Lots of blood and the clatter of machine guns. The war was nearly lost for the Germans and a hoard of Nazi gold and plundered art was on a transport train bound for a cave in Poland. Hotch had already decided that the Nazis would replace Hitler with his double, a kindly and timid jazz trumpet player named Klaus, while the Marauders kept the real one. Hotch decided to keep that his little secret from his readers, doubling back to a racy bed scene with Eva Braun in a black nightie discovering Klaus had both testicles. *But* mein Führer, *now there are two?*

"George," Hotch said, moving from the booth to the bar. "Ever hear any personal stories about Hitler? Back when you were in the service?"

"I know he was a prick," George said, pouring the draft High Life. "Ever see the cartoon of Daffy Duck when he dressed up like him? The slobber flying all over the place. What a riot."

"I just figured you might have heard a thing or two."

"I was too busy ducking fucking Japs in the Philippines," George said.

"You know, the Soviets say Hitler faked his death."

"Like Elvis?" George said. "Interesting. Is that what you're writing about?"

Hotch didn't answer, taking a long swallow of cold Miller High Life, already thinking about how he could get lovely Lilli, the beautiful yet resourceful Resistance leader, onto that train before they buried the loot.

The bar's door burst open and a cold wind blew through the long narrow space of George's. Jackie Johnson sauntered in and took a seat beside Hotch. He was dressed in a fishnet top and tiger-print tights, some kind of fuzzy blond Mohawk wig on his head. He tossed down his purse and told George to turn on the fucking television. George tossed a damp towel over his shoulder and glowered at Jackie.

"Where the hell you been, Hotch?"

"Working," Hotch said.

"Bullshit," Jackie said. "Didn't you see the paper? Been trying to call you all goddamn day."

"I read Sunday's paper front to back," he said. "Even the ads with the women in their underwear. I'll get to today's news tomorrow."

George got up on a footstool and futzed around with the television, finding 11Alive and helmet-haired Wes Sarginson announcing a shocking and grisly—*did he really need both adjectives?*—discovery in Cobb County. George played with the antennae until the wavy lines and static subsided. *The body of a woman was discovered by a man walking his dog late Sunday when . . .*

Hotch hunched around his beer, playing with the edges of a cocktail napkin. "What time's the show?"

"No show tonight."

"Them don't look like street clothes."

"You don't live on my street," Jackie said. "Now shut the fuck up and listen to the nice white man on television."

Hotch shrugged and glanced up at the big glowing box above all the bottles of liquor. He reached into his shirt pocket for his Pall Malls and tapped one loose. The great thing about Pall Malls, as the old commercial went, you could light 'em from either side. "Want to give me a hint?"

Jackie's big, made-up eyes were glued to Wes Sarginson saying something over the B-roll of cops shuffling about a wooded area, a jogger saying they usually felt safe along the river. A police spokesman offered up the Crime Stoppers number. And then Wes Sarginson mentioned something about the police saying where the woman worked. Hotch's damn hearing was playing tricks on him lately, and a bunch of asshole yuppies guffawing from the booth back by the toilets made it hard to hear.

"What?"

"Scientific Atlanta," Jackie said, showing his palms. "The dead woman was employed at Scientific Atlanta."

"So what?"

"Isn't that where the kid said his momma worked?"

"Coincidence." Hotch lit his cigarette and snapped shut his Zippo.

"You always say coincidences are for dumbasses."

Hotch shrugged.

"You were that little boy's last hope."

"For Christ's sake, Jackie."

"I mean it, Hotch," Jackie said. "About time you got off your ass and did something nice. That kid's done lost his momma."

Hotch turned his head and blew out some smoke. "Okay," he said. "Okay. But at least let me finish my damn beer. I can't be a hero sober."

12

SYLVIA

She ran down a mental checklist of everyone they'd spoken to after being assigned the case: the distressed dog walker who'd found the body, the local detectives first on the scene down by the river, and eight different coworkers and three friends of the dead woman. None of them seemed to know a damn thing. Her name was Jennifer Buckner, a UGA grad from Newnan, Georgia. She was twenty-seven and white, living alone in an apartment maybe two miles from Sylvia, another rabbit warren of young professionals and horny divorcés. A college roommate recalled a string of breakups with bad boyfriends. She liked to travel, France last summer, and had been planning Spain in the spring. Sylvia's squad supervisor wouldn't say what Buckner had done for the Bureau. Only that she'd reported on security concerns at her place of work.

Sylvia and Irv Ravetch took the Chrysler sedan north on I-85 that afternoon, catching the ticket from Bart Fisher, who did background checks for the folks at Scientific Atlanta. It was raining, a light drizzle misting their windshield as they exited off the interstate and down onto a commercial drive, searching for the address Sylvia had marked on her StreetFinder. The rain tapped at the glass as Irv tuned in for more of his sweet Peach FM.

"Sorry you had to ditch your meeting with Barabbas Johnson," Ravetch said. "I hear he's a regular Prince Charming."

"I would've brought him around."

"I heard he stinks," Ravetch said, adjusting his big black glasses. "Really stinks. Like a boxcar full of elephant shit. I didn't like the idea of you going anyway. A guy like that doesn't all of a sudden up and grow a conscience. I think he was setting you up."

"Maybe," Sylvia said, pointing to a small concrete sign on the left. SCIENTIFIC ATLANTA. "But maybe his ass would've come across. You know how these people are, like damn water moccasins. Not happy unless they're turning on their own kind."

"Any idea why this dead woman kept your card in her purse?"

"Like I told the old man, I have no idea," Sylvia said, pointing to the radio in disgust. "*Jesus.* They're really murdering that song. And it's one of my favorites, Irv. Shit. I never heard 'Blue Bayou' like that. Pull over while I puke. If Linda ever heard this, it just might kill her."

Ravetch grinned and turned up the volume and drove onto a private road bordered by a thick forest of tall, skinny pine trees. They drove for about a mile with no buildings or signage until she made out several tall concrete buildings topped with antennae and satellite dishes. Ravetch continued for another half mile before turning left toward a guard shack set up by the entrance of what looked like a junior college campus.

The guard checked Ravetch's ID as Sylvia reached for hers. The guard, a beefy-faced white guy, looked down at Sylvia's ID and then back at her face twice, making sure that he'd got it right. *A Black woman Fed?* There was the ever-so-subtle shake of the head as he handed back their IDs, and Sylvia couldn't help herself. "Something wrong, Bubba?"

"How'd you know my name?" the guard asked.

Ravetch grinned until the guard wandered back into the shack and raised the arm.

• • •

The head of security was a tall, very handsome Black man named Coleman Vaughn. He seemed to know Bart Fisher pretty well, so well that he seemed confused as to why Bart hadn't come out himself instead of two rookie agents. "Bart does background checks," Sylvia said. "We wanted to talk to some folks who knew Jennifer Buckner."

Vaughn had a big, shaved head as slick as a seal's back. When he shook Irv's hand, Sylvia saw Irv wince a little. "Oh, man," Vaughn said. "Jenny. She was real sweet. Already talked to the cops about what happened. I heard something about a boyfriend."

"Boyfriend?" Sylvia said.

"Oh, I don't know," Vaughn said. "Just something I heard them ask. I promise I know a lot less than you do."

Ever since she'd walked into that cop shop in Cobb County yesterday, Sylvia felt no one was being straight. Those boys were either playing dumb or were the real deal. Hard to tell. She and Ravetch gave Vaughn a rundown about providing assistance to the police department and the GBI.

"She worked for Dr. Keyes," Vaughn said. "Let me see if he's still around."

She raised her eyebrows at Ravetch, knowing Vaughn knew if the doctor was in or not, and turned back to look at the wide, bland lobby. The whole place had as much personality as a nuclear bunker, concrete walls and floors, big plate-glass windows looking out onto other concrete buildings and a grassy atrium filled with empty picnic tables. Red and blue lights blinked on top of several buildings.

"You're in luck," Vaughn said. "The doctor's in."

• • •

Dr. Keyes was a thin, craggy white man with longish graying black hair and a mustache-goatee combo. He wore a tattered brown corduroy jacket over a checked shirt and kept a pair of reading glasses hung around his neck. The man looked pleasant and weathered to Sylvia, kind of like an old dog. Or some of her English lit professors at UNC. "Jenny was a wonderful secretary," he said. "Damn near impossible to replace. But I don't think I can really help you. We never discussed her personal life."

"Did you hear something about a boyfriend?" Sylvia asked.

Keyes shook his head. "I didn't know anything about Jenny's personal life."

"But she had friends here?" Ravetch asked.

"Of course," Keyes said. "I'm sure Mr. Vaughn can help you with a list. But I was told this was just a random event. Jenny was attacked."

"Nobody really knows," Sylvia said. "That's why we drove all the way to Lawrenceville to find out."

Dr. Keyes's office was big and impressive but looked more cluttered than Fred Sanford's garage. Keyes had shit piled up damn near everywhere: in bookcases, on drafting tables, even in boxes stacked up on the windowsill. There were oversize framed photos of big satellites in tropical and arctic locations, a ribbon cutting with three white men in suits in front of the building they had just entered. Each of them with crew cuts and thick, black glasses.

"What exactly were Miss Buckner's duties?" Sylvia said. "On a day-to-day basis."

"She took longhand for me, typed up my notes, and helped with correspondence," Keyes said. "Made coffee, picked up my dry cleaning. Often reminded me of people I'd already met and was about to meet again."

Basically, wiped your damn ass.

"I'm sorry," Keyes said, rubbing at the graying whiskers on his chin. "We're all sick with the news. Just absolutely awful. She was such a lovely and bright young lady. Would either of you like some coffee?"

Sylvia shook her head, wondering who the hell was going to fetch it for him. "Can you tell me what exactly y'all do here?"

"Scientific Atlanta is a pioneer in satellite communication," Keyes said. "Our three founders came from Georgia Tech in the late fifties. They started this business with seven hundred dollars. Another partner joined later after working at Oak Ridge."

Ravetch leaned over and whispered to Sylvia, "That means nuclear shit."

Sylvia subtly rolled her eyes. Yeah, she knew the Oak Ridge project.

"They went on to sell breakthrough designs of television antennas before the idea of connecting satellites to earth-based stations," he said. "That, of course, led to the miracle that is now cable television."

"I can't afford it," Sylvia said. "Got those old rabbit ears on my RCA. But Agent Ravetch here can't live without his Cinemax After Dark."

Irv shook his head and grinned. All part of loosening up a subject. Keyes leaned back in his chair, satisfied with giving the same compact story he'd told a million times, sure that less intelligent people couldn't be bothered with any more details. "Do you mind if I ask how Jenny died?" he asked.

"The police haven't released that information," Ravetch said.

"This may be an awful question to ask," he said. "But do you know if she suffered?"

Sylvia wanted to say, *Goddamn right, the woman suffered. Some son of a bitch snatched her up and broke her goddamn neck.* But instead, she just slowly shook her head and offered a pleasant smile to the good professor.

"I understand Jenny had top-security clearance," Sylvia said.

Keyes looked as if someone had turned up the heat under his ass. He moved around a bit and then nodded. The lights kept on blinking in a two-, three-second rhythm on the building behind him. "That's correct."

"I guess that means she handled some pretty high-level plans for y'all," Sylvia said, straightening her black blazer over her gun, looking the man directly in the eye.

"Jenny went through an exhaustive process with the DOD," Keyes said. "Why does that matter now? She was attacked by some random psycho."

"If you guys just make television satellites," Ravetch asked, "why does the DOD get involved with security clearances?"

Keyes again shuffled a bit more in his chair, pursing his mouth, and nodded. "We build satellites and hardware for a variety of clients. I'm sure our list of clients is well known by the FBI."

"How about you just get me started a little?" Sylvia said. "Y'all do military-grade spy shit? Is that right?"

"Sounds like you are on a need-to-know basis, Agent Weaver," Keyes said, stroking his professor goatee some more. "And I guess your superiors don't think you need to know."

"We want to do our best," Ravetch said. "To provide the locals with assistance."

"Atlanta is a dangerous city," Keyes said, standing up. "I don't need to explain that to the FBI. And Miss Buckner was a beautiful young woman. The idea of what happened to her makes me physically ill."

Ravetch felt into his jacket and handed Keyes his card. Sylvia did the same, but then held her card out of reach of Keyes's waiting hand. "Miss Buckner had my card in her personal belongings," she said. "Any idea why?"

"We've known you people have been spying on us for a long time," Keyes said. "We've been under your microscope since this company was founded. Maybe you need to ask your boss, young lady."

"Young lady?" Sylvia said.

Irv Ravetch reached out and touched Sylvia's elbow. She felt her face heating up and turned to her partner. "We appreciate your time, Dr. Keyes," Ravetch said. "We'll be in touch."

13

LISICA

Lisica parked the Porsche 911 on the upper deck at Lenox Square and entered by the Magic Pan. The air smelled of hot crepes and burning sugar, a reminder of another time, another assignment, back in those early days of training in Paris. Lisica had been French back then, barely passable, one with German parents. There was always the backstory of German parents just in case someone noted a trace of an accent. Lisica walked past the glowing map of the massive shopping mall—the largest in the South—and over to the B. Dalton bookstore with its big displays full of the latest bestsellers. John Irving. James Michener. Jackie Collins with more of her trash! *Hollywood Wives* in red and gold. Lee Iacocca, the gaudy, unapologetic capitalist, with his life story. Louis L'Amour. Robert Ludlum. A book called *The Hunt for Red October*, a personal favorite of the maniac Ronald Reagan.

A large rack held hundreds and hundreds of magazines for sports, hunting, home repair, beauty, cars, and celebrity worship. Tom Cruise.

Liz Taylor. *Simon Le Bon's Brush with Death at Sea!* And pornography. So much pornography, free and wild for everyone to check out and examine as if they were at a supermarket. *Playboy*, *Penthouse*, and *Hustler.* Big, teased hair and lace, Vaseline smothered across the camera lens to soften the pouty expressions and legs spread so wide. *Madonna: Unlike a Virgin for the Very First Time . . .*

Lisica pushed up the sleeves on a white sweater, tight designer jeans stuffed into cowboy boots, and headed to the center of the mall, toward the Macy's and the new mall expansion to meet Mr. and Mrs. X. Handlers for the Center. Lisica didn't know their real names or any of their false ones, but they appeared to be a nice, middle-aged American couple, and perhaps they even were. Lisica passed the Camelot Music with its shiny mirrored walls, a new store called Banana Republic with a full-size Jeep parked in the center amid mountains of African safari clothes, and a Sharper Image with enough espionage fakery and techno gear to make a Muscovite blush. The mall was huge and airy with skylights above.

Lisica remembered first arriving in Atlanta when there had been organ grinders in the mall with monkeys on chains. The monkeys would smile and tip their little hats for a quarter but would stick out their tongue for a penny. *Sad American monkeys.* Now they were all monkeys, worshipping at the golden altar of capitalism. *Sales! Buy Now! Electronics! Fashion!*

Lisica stepped outside to make sure no one had followed, smoked a short, thin Dunhill cigar, and then walked briskly toward the new mall expansion with its skylights and smooth railings painted white. A glass elevator dropped down to the food court while its twin shot upward past yet another record store to the third level.

Mr. and Mrs. X were already seated in the open air of the California Pizza Kitchen, arguing about whether to order the Thai or the Jamaican jerk chicken pizza. Mrs. X might've been in her late forties or early fifties. So hard to tell with American women. Her skin had been deeply tanned, her face looking a bit unnatural with blue eyeshadow and pink frosted lips. Her bleached blond hair was secured in a hairdo the film star Doris Day would've found very stylish twenty years ago. Mr. X seemed much older, balding and dull, in a red sweater vest pulled over a white dress shirt with a wide collar.

"There's a man on the second floor," Mrs. X said. "He has a camera and I don't like the looks of him."

"He's no one," Mr. X said. "You can tell from his shoes."

Lisica casually glanced up to the railing and then back to Mrs. X. As promised, under the table sat a red Rich's shopping bag. Mr. X whispered so that the next table couldn't hear, a young mother with her toddler son. The boy wore a *Star Wars* T-shirt and aimed a space blaster at Lisica. *Pew-pew.*

Lisica glared at the boy and the boy turned away to hide his face in his mother's arm.

"Leave it under the table," Mr. X said. "And take the bag."

"I have nothing for you," Lisica said. "Not today."

An energetic young woman in a yellow apron approached the table. She brought out a pad and pen. Her name tag read *Suzie*. "We're having a special today on our duck sausage with arugula and—"

"Suzie," Mrs. X said. "Give us a goddamn minute. Our head is just spinning from the choices."

The girl's smile dropped, and she walked off as Mr. X leaned into the table. "You were given instructions."

"I followed instructions."

"Then where's the goddamn package?" Mrs. X asked.

"An asset interfered with the delivery."

"What the fuck does that mean?"

"It means the package was lost," Lisica said. "And the asset was dealt with."

"Dealt with?" Mr. X said. "What in the hell did you do?"

Lisica shrugged again. "Only what was needed."

"Control won't be happy," Mrs. X said. "Control will be pissed. You royally fucked up."

Lisica took in a long breath and reached under the table for the large shopping bag. Lisica stood and nodded to Mr. and Mrs. X. "Enjoy your meal."

"Don't you even think about it," Mrs. X said.

"Who's going to stop me?" Lisica asked, raising an eyebrow. "You?"

As Lisica turned to leave, Mr. X muttered, "Fucking sociopath."

14

VITALY

The day had been long and filled with many questions. The CIA men, all with false names like Charlie and John, drove him a few miles from the safe house for his second debriefing. A bland office building, a sign outside selling insurance, so that he would not associate the safe house with negative feelings. KGB did the same. Do not shit on the place where you dine.

What do you know about the agents spying for the Soviet Union? How do they communicate with you? Even the tiniest detail will help. Vitaly agreed. Of course, that's why he was here. But first he'd demanded a kettle of hot water to mix herbs to settle his stomach while explaining he'd only been second at the First Directorate since April. However, he did recall one spy in the CIA, thirty-eight, thirty-nine years old. The man had been fired for being a drug addict and an alcoholic. "I do not know his real name, no one did, but he communicated as Robert."

The agents leaned forward to listen.

"I learned about him from a telegram from Vienna residency when I was in Directorate K," Vitaly said. "Robert gave KGB three important pieces of information; two were penetrations of KGB by your CIA."

The men all stared at each other, aware of those who'd been recently executed in the Soviet Union. Vitaly shrugged. *Such is the way of this dirty business.* He drank his tasteless dandelion tea and felt his stomach relax.

"And one of these," one of the faceless, nameless men asked, "led to the arrest of our agent, Stombaugh, in Moscow?"

Vitaly sighed and took a sip of tea. "I am afraid so," he said. "But such an ingenious drop. You gave our agent from Moscow Station phony dog poop to hide so many technical plans. Who would wish to walk through a park and check under every dog dropping they see?"

"KGB has their own dirty tricks," said another man at the end of the conference table. "Your dog-in-heat spray? One of our couriers in Istanbul had to climb the gates of the embassy to get away from a pack of horny hounds. If they caught him, they might've humped him to death."

Vitaly had to laugh. So much boyish humor in the spy game.

"I was there when they brought in Stombaugh," Vitaly said. "Major General Krasilnikov pounded the table hard with his fist. Like a hammer. *You are spy not a diplomat!* Your man, I am sorry to report, had one hundred twenty-five thousand rubles on him. Stashed in a hollow brick. Perhaps CIA should have fashioned larger dog turd."

No one laughed. The Stombaugh case was still fresh to the Americans.

A platter of sandwiches was brought in later with a large urn of hot coffee. Americans always with their acrid coffee. Just the thought made Vitaly's stomach clench. The sandwiches made of white bread, cold cuts, and soft cheese. He declined and asked the handlers if they might bring him some hot soup. A young agent was dispatched as the

CIA men ate, looked at their thin files, and asked more questions. *Operation Ivy Bells? Did the KGB use Bulgarians to try to assassinate the Pope?*

"Perhaps," Vitaly said, shrugging. "I do not trust them. But didn't this man, the one who shot the Pope, not also claim to be Jesus Christ?"

The men all nodded. He was being recorded by a video camera yet no one took notes. The questioning went on for hours and hours. He had no idea of the time; the hands on Vitaly's old Majak had frozen. *Fuck your mother.*

...

Dan Rafferty returned to the safe house just as the sky began to darken. Vitaly's old friend seemed to sense his foul mood, tossed him an overcoat—new with tags!—and said they'd been approved to go for a little stroll. "Thank you," Vitaly said. "I could use some fresh air. All day long with surly spies and the cold cut meats."

They walked side by side, two FBI agents trailing on foot, two teams in cars as they headed toward a large school and a small stadium situated nearby. Oakton High. Home of the Cougars!

"How's it going, pal?"

"They wanted to know about our people in the Agency," Vitaly said. "Some talk about Stombaugh. But what else is there to know? They know how the game is played. The man was caught with the red hand."

"And there were others?"

"Of course," he said. "Of course. I told them about a man called Robert who'd identified the penetrations at KGB. I gave them his age and some background. I could tell they already knew this man but that he hadn't been caught. Nonsense about the KGB and the Pope. Georgi in London. Raskatov in Paris."

"Those were KGB hits?"

"Bulgarian secret service," Vitaly said. "But they used an umbrella gun with poisoned pellets developed by KGB. More games. More deaths."

"Raskatov lived."

"Very sick with fever," Vitaly said. "He should not have survived."

As they walked, Rafferty seemed lost in a dream, distracted, as if he wanted to discuss something more important and was simply making time. They arrived at an open gate to the school's stadium and entered, Vitaly noting two men from the safe house up in the stands watching.

"I have something to admit to you," Vitaly said. "It has bothered me since I left Washington."

Rafferty had his hands in the pockets of his sporty windbreaker. He stared straight ahead behind his thick gold glasses, expressionless, as they walked.

"When I left, I presented you with some cognac and tins of caviar."

"I remember," Rafferty said. "Very generous of you."

"Not so generous," Vitaly said. "The wrapping was powdered with something KGB developed. In English, they call it spy dust. This powder could have made you and your lovely wife very sick."

"We were fine," Rafferty said. "And the caviar was delicious."

"The dust was developed to track you," he said. "It could be seen for many weeks under a blue light we developed."

"Am I still being tracked?" Rafferty asked, stopping and turning to Vitaly. The man's face seemed waxed and stiff. His glasses smudged and tarnished in the fading light.

"I don't know," Vitaly said. "I am sorry, Daniel. I hope this has not ruined our friendship. I thought of you and Delores often after I returned to Moscow. I trust your family is well?"

"Very well," Rafferty said. "They're fantastic. If Delores knew you were here, she would send her regards."

The men walked in silence for nearly a half lap around the track, something still nudging Rafferty's mind, winded as they walked.

Vitaly watched as a black sedan parked near the school, two more agents watching them. If KGB came for him today, it would be a suicide mission.

"I didn't want to ask but—"

"Jeannette?" Vitaly said. "And my daughter? That is why I have told CIA to say nothing of my defection. Nothing official is to be known. If KGB finds out what happened to me and that I am in America, Jeannette will be assigned to a bear canning factory in Ukraine."

"And your daughter?"

"She has plans to marry a man high in the party," Vitaly said, smoothing down his mustache. "He will protect her."

"Everything comes with a cost," Rafferty said.

"Yes," Vitaly said. "Even love."

"What's that supposed to mean?"

"I will explain later," Vitaly said. The lights in the stadium coming to life, brightening the green on the field as they left the track and headed back to the safe house. "It is such a long story that began long before Rome. But I will need a favor."

"Anything," Rafferty said. "We haven't much time together, old friend. I have something to ask you that can't be shared with the Agency. Do you understand?"

Vitaly did not. But he nodded anyway.

"What have you told the Americans about your knowledge of our missile defense system?"

"You mean the folly with the space lasers?" Vitaly asked. "Reagan's war in the stars?"

"I understand it's not all folly," Rafferty said. "What have you told the Agency about what Moscow knows about the Strategic Defense Initiative?"

It was quite cold for this time of year; a sharp breeze whipped at their coats as they walked back down the road toward the safe house. But Dan Rafferty had the faintest trace of sweat on his brow.

"Are you okay, my friend?" Vitaly said. "What have they done with you?"

Rafferty smiled and laughed as if Vitaly had made a big joke. But this was no joke. Not now.

"I've grown so tired of the talk of spies and nuclear war," Vitaly said. "My heart, head, and stomach ache with no end. I have nothing to do but boil potatoes and watch a television show about an old woman who works as a maid. Her name is Hazel. Do you know this show?"

"It's a rerun."

"What is *rerun*?"

"Something you've seen before but pass off as new."

"I have something new for you, Daniel," Vitaly said. "I must get to the city of Atlanta to see an old friend. Very important. This is why I am here. I have spoken to the man they call Charlie, but he won't listen. I have been debriefed. I have been run through your ringer. Now I have this one favor to ask."

"Are you having second thoughts, Vitaly?"

"This isn't about ideology, Daniel," Vitaly said. "This is about love. A woman named Zoya. Let me tell you about her. In strictest of confidence."

15

HOTCH

"On the upside," Hotch said, "at least your mother is still alive."

"But for how long?" Peter said. "I don't believe that Russian son of a bitch for one goddamn minute. You know he killed her friend."

They were seated across from each other in a booth at the Majestic Diner, looking out on Ponce de Leon Avenue and across to the old Plaza Theatre. The diner was a big, fat slice of Americana that served breakfast and burgers late into the night from a hot griddle and had been around since the twenties. Lots of Formica inside and neon outside, the food and service passable when the bums didn't come in and start tap-dancing on the tables. That had happened more times than Hotch could recall, having to tell the bums to please take the fucking show elsewhere so he could enjoy his lemon meringue in peace.

"It's getting dark," Hotch said. "Maybe I should run you home?"

"And miss your reporter friend?"

"He said he might be running late," Hotch said. "And if your mother starts getting worried, she's going to tell her muscled friend Gary. I'd rather him not be onto us. You know what I'm saying? We got to be careful about this stuff, kid."

Peter put down his cheeseburger and stared at Hotch. "You don't believe me."

"If I didn't believe you, Jackie and I wouldn't have hauled ass to the burbs the other night," Hotch said. "If I didn't believe you, I wouldn't have sat my fat ass down in the basement of the public library going through reels of microfilm on Scientific Atlanta until my eyes crossed. Did you know they've been chamber of commerce award winners in Lawrenceville for three years in a row? Digging way back, there was a lot of ribbon cutting and big talk about the World of Tomorrow. Real Disneyland shit. TV antennas, satellites, cable TV, but I didn't see a damn thing about something a Russian would kill to get their hands on. Or maybe those Russkis really want their MTV."

"My mother never talks about work," Peter said. "When we first moved here, she once dragged me to one of their lame Christmas parties. I met her boss."

"Dr. Keyes."

"I guess," Peter said, picking up the cheeseburger again but not taking a bite. The kid hadn't even touched his fries. What kind of kid doesn't eat his fries? "I don't remember names. I never really thought what she did was that important."

"Dr. Keyes is pretty damn important," Hotch said, lighting up a Pall Mall and reaching for an ashtray. "I read up a load on him. A genius with three degrees. Two doctorates from MIT. Did your mom tell you what her coworker did? The woman who got killed?"

"She told me she didn't want to talk about it."

"Maybe you can ask her again tonight?"

The kid gave Hotch a look like maybe he'd gone simple or had insulted him even by asking. But he didn't want to mess this up. This one thing, a real-life spy case playing out in Atlanta, might be a nice poker chip back into the game. Maury Brillstein would shit his pants if Hotch served him up a nonfiction project he could take out to the major publishers. Not to mention sub rights on foreign, maybe an excerpt in *Playboy*. Hotch had always wanted to be in *Playboy* or *Esquire*, plucked from obscurity and the pulps to discuss his views on race, politics, and religion. *What was the purpose of you creating a white and Black hero to duke it out in modern-day Atlanta? Were you trying to make a point about racial harmony or is this what you know by living in such a hard-boiled Southern city?*

"In that 'KGB Spies Living Next Door' article, you said the KGB were masters of disguises and emotional manipulation, right?"

"Yeah, sure." Hotch leaned back into the booth and blew out a stream of smoke. "Same could be said about my second wife. But the Russians? That's probably, maybe even definitely, mostly entirely true."

"Why would you write it if you don't know it?"

"Don't you watch movies, kid?" Hotch asked.

"I watch nothing but movies."

"Then you know fiction often holds more facts than truth."

"That sounds like bullshit."

Hotch tapped the ash from his cigarette into the tin tray. He looked outside the plate-glass window just in time to see Fred Willard crawling out of his raggedy maroon Oldsmobile. He was a medium-size guy with prematurely gray hair, dressed in khaki pants, a wrinkled white dress shirt, and loose tie. He had on a pair of cheap sunglasses and a reporter's notebook hung from his back pocket. Willard and Hotch went way back, to grad school at UNC, when Willard was young and eager, writing scathing stories about the Chapel Hill town council. Once writing a column calling them all fascists. He still covered politics for the *AJC* but was more general assignment these days. Hotch had to scan through all the sections, from Sports to Living, to find his byline.

Willard walked through the front door and looked about the

Majestic. Hotch held up his hand and waved him over to their booth. He wasted little time, bounding over and scooting in beside Peter. "I didn't know you had a kid."

"Ha." Hotch rolled his eyes and shook his head. He introduced Peter to Willard and Willard to Peter and then thanked him for digging into Scientific Atlanta for them. Willard signaled the waitress, ordered a club sandwich, and then pointed at Hotch for the tab.

"Don't thank me yet," Willard said, reaching for the notebook. "I didn't find much. I talked to the woman who covers science and tech and even she was a little in the dark about what these people actually do. We know they sell satellites and cable boxes. They've made a fortune on it. I think every cable box in the South has their name on it."

"That's it?" Hotch said.

"Sorry to disappoint you," Willard said, giving a sour look at Peter. "I go out and bust my hump for my old friend here and he's upset I can't deliver a top-secret dossier on some company out in fucking Lawrenceville. Sorry, kid. I didn't mean to cuss. But you know what I mean."

"What about the morgue?" Hotch asked.

"Gee," Willard said, rolling his eyes. "Wish I'd thought about that. Is that where we keep the fucking clippings and old photos? Sorry, again. Cussing is a newspaperman's cross to bear."

"Don't worry about it," Peter said. "My mom is dating a fucking KGB goon."

Willard's eyebrows raised. "Whoa," he said. "You're holding out on me, Hotch. This is 1-A stuff. Please tell me more."

Willard reached across to Peter's plate and snagged a few fries. Hotch held up the flat of his hand. "Ha-ha," Hotch said. "This kid's full of all kinds of jokes. He's a big reader. Loves spy books from the store. He wanted to tag along with a regionally known author of supposed cult classics of the last decade. Thought he might learn a thing or two. He may even want to be a writer one day."

"God help him," Willard said. "I did go down to the morgue and find three files on Scientific Atlanta. Each one is marked with dates going back to 1959. The last entry I saw was sometime last year."

"Great."

"Nope," he said. "Not so great. Someone checked them out but never returned the clippings."

"I thought the clippings couldn't leave the damn morgue," Hotch said. "Shit. What kind of Mickey Mouse bullshit are you guys running over on Marietta Street?"

"Whoever got those clips either kept them at their desk or tossed them," Willard said. "I don't give in to happenstance. I'd say someone wanted all this shit erased from our institutional knowledge."

"*Institution* sounds about right for the paper," Hotch said. "Can you still ask around?"

"Christ, Hotch," Willard said. "What do you take me for? Of course, I'll ask around. By the way, how's 'Big Time' Jackie doing? The last time I saw him was at Illusions doing an impression of Eartha Kitt as Catwoman. Leather whip and the whole shebang. I was covering that big AIDS benefit."

"Truth be told, I don't mind Jackie's dancing," Hotch said. "But goddamn, he sure can't sing."

Willard smiled. "I'll make sure to tell him you said that. God knows he could still line up for the Falcons."

Hotch stared out the window, not sure what to tell the kid. He'd been looking forward to getting some quick, direct line on the place his mom worked. Maybe enough for an article in better than just *Front Page Detective*. And if he didn't have that, he didn't have much to rub in Maury's face. What kind of self-respecting KGB agent wanted to steal cable box designs for their superiors in Moscow? All this reminded Hotch of when he was younger and more ambitious and dug into the story of a Florida company buying conveniently burned-up properties around Sweet Auburn. Most had been arson cases tied to vagrants building fires during the winter. He got a Livingston Award for that one and a Pulitzer nomination. *Years gone by.*

"So, no one knows what this company really does?" Peter said.

"I've heard some rumors."

"Okay," Hotch said.

"Maybe they got some big DOD contract," Willard said. "Doing some work on Reagan's Star Wars shit. And I'm not talking about a galaxy far, far away, kid."

"I know about Star Wars," Peter said. "I watched a whole *3-2-1 Contact* about it in seventh grade."

"It's Reagan's wet dream," Willard said. "To crisscross the skies of the continental US with laser beams to knock down nuclear missiles. The government has spent twice as much on this shit as the Manhattan Project."

"You don't have to tell me," Hotch said. "The goddamn Russians hate it. The whole idea of mutually assured destruction would be moot. A first strike by the Russians wouldn't be a deterrent."

"Nope," Willard said. "The government has spent something over twenty billion so far. Peace through strength, my friend. Meet all threats, according to the Gipper. Can you believe a man who made a movie with a fucking monkey is president?"

"My mom might know something."

"Yeah?" Hotch said. "But you don't trust your mother."

"I trust my mother," Peter said. "She just never talks about work with me. Like you said, if I ask too much, she might get suspicious."

"There is one thing that might help," Willard said. "The cops reporter covering the homicide said he saw Feds digging around the scene."

Hotch leaned back and lit a cigarette. "Oh, we know," he said. "Peter here saw his mom being interviewed by some woman from the local office. What was her name again?"

"Agent Weaver," Peter said.

"Oh, come on, Hotch," Willard said. "You know the Feds won't say shit if their mouths are full of it. Again, my apologies to the wayward youth."

"Who said I was wayward?" Peter asked.

"All youth are wayward," Hotch said. "I was wayward as hell. If you're not wayward, something's a' matter with you."

Willard flipped to an open page of his notebook. "Want to tell me a little more about this KGB theory, kid? Sounds interesting. If I could connect the dots."

"How about off the record?" Hotch asked.

Willard shook his head just as his club sandwich arrived. Hotch blew him off with a dismissive wave. The last thing he needed was fucking Fred Willard trying to muscle in on his possible big break.

"Would be nice to have someone inside the company," Willard said. "You know?"

Peter looked up. "I can get inside."

"I think my esteemed ex-colleague meant that figuratively," Hotch said. "Maybe an ex-employee willing to talk?"

"But if there was a way," Peter said, "to get past security and into the offices, we'd have to know more than we do now."

Willard took a big mouthful of the sandwich and nodded his approval. Hotch shook his head. What a terrible, awful idea. "No way," Hotch said. "The last time I got arrested was in Charlotte in sixty-eight. And I promise, jail and Dennis X. Hotchner do not mix."

"I wasn't talking about you," Peter said.

16

DAN

For Dan to get the damn thing over and finished, he'd have to wait until Delores and the kids were off to bed. At the moment, they were all lazing about the RCA watching some insipid show called *Hardcastle and McCormick* about a retired judge who teams up with a hotshot car thief to right the wrongs of the criminal justice system. The old judge was played by the guy who played the father on *Family Affair* and although Dan couldn't recall the actor's name, he could remember his daughter's silly doll on the show. *Mrs. Beasley*. Delores had even bought a damn Mrs. Beasley doll when she'd first gotten pregnant, believing they were having a girl. But instead, they ended up with moody and sullen Mark with his infatuation with rock music, playing an electric guitar and idolizing some long-haired hippie named Eddie Van Halen.

Mark was home tonight, sprawled out in front of the TV, grounded for returning from an Anthrax concert—whoever they were—reeking of marijuana although he denied smoking it. He watched the thief race around Los Angeles in a tiny red sports car. Blake and Mary were on the couch and their youngest, Phillip, sat in Delores's lap eating a box of Nilla Wafers.

The sports car crashed through an alley, sending garbage cans flying. Delores turned to Dan and said, "Did you remember to take the trash out?"

Dan nodded and waited for what felt like an eternity for a Burger King commercial to head to his study, where he opened his safe and removed a brown wig, a glue-on beard, and a wallet filled with new identity cards. The beard matched the wig but not his mustache. He'd have to use a little mascara to make sure it blended in. He stuffed a change of clothes and a Redskins cap into a gym bag and headed to the door.

"Work," he said on the way to the garage.

No one even glanced up from the television. He was invisible to them.

Dan drove toward the city and the parking garage near Dupont Circle where he'd stashed the Citation. Everything so damn crazy and upsetting after his encounter with Wanda at the Americana Hotel. Those Russians said they'd been tailing him ever since Yurchenko landed, saying they only wanted to help after hearing the gunshot. What else could he do but accept? Was he supposed to call the police? The Bureau? How would he explain what had happened? *So sorry, I was restrained with hospital tape when Wanda shot the son of a bitch.* His life and career would be in the toilet. Maybe, just maybe, he could get out of this shit show with a little dignity.

He changed clothes in the new car and carefully pulled on the wig and beard. He removed his big clunky glasses and put in a pair of contacts that he absolutely hated. They felt like dinner plates against his eyeballs. But no one could recognize Dan if the embassy was being watched.

That's where the men had told him to go tonight. The goddamn Russian embassy.

• • •

Dan parked two blocks away and walked up Sixteenth Street. The Russian embassy had always looked like a haunted house to him, built shortly after the turn of the century in that over-the-top Beaux Arts style with bowed windows and a flat Roman roof. The building appeared lifeless and cold from the street, a mausoleum oddity with countless antennae up on the sloped roof to listen in on communications from the Pentagon and the White House, probably the Hoover Building, too. But that wasn't his worry. Tonight, he'd pass along what he'd learned from their defector, his old friend Vitaly, and tell them he was done.

As he walked along Embassy Row, he couldn't shake the image of little Mrs. Beasley's creepy doll eyes watching him. He saw her staring down from office windows, judgmental in her poofy bonnet and tiny little reading glasses. He wondered what Delores had done with the goddamn doll after Mark was born. Did she give it away or box it up? He certainly didn't see the damn thing when Mary was born. A couple years ago, she'd been all about those godforsaken Cabbage Patch dolls with their chubby little hands and farmer grins, plump little faces stitched into pantyhose.

Dan kept his hands in his pockets, Redskins cap down over his eyes as he headed toward the imposing gates to meet those two Russians again. They'd kept to their word by not contacting him after he'd left the hotel with Wanda. Wanda, an absolute wreck that night, with blood splattered across her neck and chest, hands shaking as they drove down by the Potomac to throw away his service revolver. He'd already reported it stolen from his vehicle, a true embarrassment for any agent.

As he looked up at the piked iron fence, there was Mrs. Beasley again, watching. Goddamn that little doll. Her head turning as he waited by an intercom and pressed the button. *Dan Rafferty works for the Russians! Agent Rafferty is a dirty, filthy spy!*

By God, he wasn't working for them. He was trading with them. Perhaps he could use this contact later for his advantage. *Yes.* He would grow closer to this man Dimitri, the older, more seasoned of the two in his black suit and black fedora. The larger man, the one he'd called Zub, seemed like an ox, barely able to speak English. A good head taller than both of them, with thick black eyebrows and a black brush military hairstyle.

Dan glanced up to see the winking red button under a camera lens. He lifted the bill of the cap and nodded. No one spoke or said a word as the chains on the gate started to move.

• • •

The embassy smelled of mildew and mothballs, few Americans stepping inside since the birth of the Soviet Union. After the guard let him in, he was alone, walking into a wide marble lobby with a marble staircase sweeping up to the second floor. A massive portrait of Lenin at the landing. Dan had read most of their agents worked up on a fourth floor, listening to communications and typing reports. KGB agents who masqueraded as journalists or representatives of Aeroflot. The lobby was mostly for formal meetings and parties, where they served rivers of vodka and mountains of caviar. A facade of respectability under the buzzing beehive up above.

Dan soon heard the sounds of clapping and cheering. Without anyone to guide him, he followed the sounds out of the lobby and around a corridor to what looked to be a large, dark banquet room. A dozen or so men sat in folding chairs watching the flickering images of a Western up on a big screen. Dan remembered seeing the film on the late show years ago. *Mackenna's Gold* or some such nonsense.

Not knowing what else to do, Dan walked into the darkened room and took a seat. Below a Pueblo village, a woman clung to the wall of a canyon made entirely of gold. Gregory Peck—*yes, he remembered now*—stoic and tall, pulled the woman covered in gold dust from a creek. *"I don't care if there's all the gold in the world here, we have to go now."*

Dan removed his Redskins cap. And soon someone took a seat behind him. Dan turned to see a hulking shape in the shadows; a meaty hand reached out and touched his shoulder. "You would like the popcorn?"

"No," Dan said. It was the big goon, Zub. "No, thank you."

"Vodka?" Zub said. "Very good. Very cold."

"I don't drink," Dan said, trying to whisper as Telly Savalas got himself killed. A big tomahawk thrown by an equally large Apache shaman.

A side door cracked open and he saw the short, bulky shape of a man Dan assumed to be Dimitri. He wasn't wearing the black fedora, his bald head glowing like a bulb as he passed in front of the projector.

"No popcorn," Zub said.

"Please," Dimitri said, taking a seat right next to Dan. "You are our special guest."

"What do you want from me?"

"Did you speak to Yurchenko?" Dimitri said, whispering. He had a tiny bag of popcorn in his lap. His eyes on the big Indian as he picked a few kernels from the bag.

"Yes."

"And what does he say?"

"He's counterintelligence," Dan said. "Like me. He said he doesn't know anything about your missile technology."

"He brought nothing with him?" Dimitri said. "Usually a gift is customary. Anatoliy, bring this man vodka."

"No," Dan said. "I'm fine. And no, Yurchenko only arrived with seven hundred dollars, a toothbrush, razor, and a bar of soap. He helped us with some internal matters. But I can't discuss any of that. That wasn't our arrangement. May I leave now?"

Dimitri sat silent, eating tiny bits of popcorn as the standoff in the golden canyon played out. "That is Camilla Sparv," Dimitri said. "Have you ever seen a woman so beautiful?"

"Where is your friend, Agent Rafferty? The angry naked woman with the gun?"

"Why?" Dan said. "Is she yours?"

Dimitri pulled out a handkerchief to wipe his bald head as Omar Sharif backed up from the Indian and drew his six-shooter. He clicked through all six empty chambers.

"*I removed your bullets,*" said the big Indian. Jesus. Was that fucking Chuck Connors in a long black wig?

"*Why?*" Omar said.

"*The Great Spirit warned me of your treachery.*"

"I have to know," Dan said. "Does Wanda work for you?"

Dimitri shook his head. "I never saw your friend before," he said. "But I'd be very careful. Prostitutes only cause misery."

"She's not a prostitute."

"Go back to your family, Dan," Dimitri said. "Go back to the Bureau. Return to your life. We will call you when we need you again."

"Again?" Dan asked. "This was a one-time-only deal, buster."

"Buster?" Dimitri said. "What is a *buster*?"

"Yurchenko hasn't passed on anything of military value," Dan said. "Okay?"

Dan stood up, momentarily blocking the projector. A few angry Russians turned around to boo him and tell him to sit. Or at least that's what he thought he heard them say. He felt the vise grip on his forearm and again turned to the man called Zub. "You don't like the *Mackenna's Gold*?"

"Thank you, but I've seen this picture before."

Dan picked up his hat to try to leave when Dimitri said, "One last thing, my friend. A very important file has been misplaced. We fear it may be with your agents."

"What kind of file?"

"What does it matter?" Dimitri asked. "But it may have ended up with your people. We must know."

"I'm not asking anyone about something you people lost."

"Zub."

Zub stood up, a good foot taller than Dan, and reached deep into his pocket and pulled out a plastic baggie filled with two bullets. Dan didn't even need to ask. He knew they'd been cut out of Wanda's ex-boyfriend, Larry. Dan Rafferty was fucked six ways from Sunday.

"Shit."

"This file," Dimitri said, "was lost in the city of Atlanta."

17

SYLVIA

She met up with Coleman Vaughn at the Busy Bee in Vine City.

The Bee had been one of her favorites since moving to Atlanta. The chicken, neck bones, and collard greens reminded her of being back in Grabtown eating her grandmomma's home cooking. The atmosphere down-home and relaxed, a beaten long shot of duct-taped booths stacked along the far wall, air smelling of grease and cornbread with what had to be one of the best jukeboxes in the city. Some new Luther, old Isaac Hayes, Gladys Knight, and Natalie Cole. There was no Linda on there yet, but maybe she could persuade Tracy, the owner's daughter, to mix it up a little.

Coleman Vaughn looked a little nervous when he walked through the door and took off his black overcoat, dressed casual in a black sweater and khaki pants. She knew he'd probably been thinking there was more to the message on his machine. The way he'd been flirting with her in the lobby in Scientific Atlanta, wanting to know if there was a Mr. Weaver, how'd she handle that gun, and all that nonsense. She hadn't lied to him. She just left a message asking if he'd like to meet up on his day off. And now here they were.

"Ms. Weaver," he said, sliding into the booth. "I have to admit, I was a bit taken aback by your phone call. I didn't think federal agents had private lives."

"We don't."

Vaughn picked up a napkin to wipe the water off his head and face. "I guess you figured out why I wrote my personal number on the back of my card."

"Oh, yes," Sylvia said. "I learned little tricks like that at Quantico."

"This is a personal meet?" he said. "Right?"

Sylvia was about to answer when Vaughn spotted Irv Ravetch behind her in the last booth. Vaughn had been so intent on making eye contact with Sylvia he hadn't noticed the skinny white guy in his funeral-black suit and tie trying to eat fried chicken with a knife and fork. A knife and a damn fork. Come on, now.

"Okay," Vaughn said. "But I can't talk about my job."

"Wouldn't dream of it."

"But you inferred that you wanted to see *me*."

"I did want to see you," Sylvia said. "Why else would I have called you?"

"Because Dr. Keyes didn't tell y'all shit," he said. "He told me to make sure you and Ichabod Crane back there were escorted to the parking lot and out the security gate. And weren't invited back."

"I know you, Coleman," she said. "You're a good man. *Marine. Morehouse.* Wear that wedding ring from time to time."

The statement provoked the exact response she wanted. He adjusted himself in the booth as if a burner had been turned up under his ass. "My wife and I are separated."

"Ain't that a shame."

"How about you?" he asked, motioning with his chin. "Got to be a lot more to Agent Weaver here than just that badge and gun."

"It's a hell of a gun."

"You carrying now?"

Sylvia opened her navy blazer and flashed him the .357. The big gun seemed to always impress folks for some reason. It was a bit of overkill left over from J. Edgar's time. A man who may have had big-gun issues.

"Got-damn," he said. "Could stop a Mack truck. How'd you do with it?"

"Not great," she said. "I handle a hunting rifle just fine. But this elephant gun about tripped me up in training. Took a lot of target practice."

"You got a boyfriend?"

"Okay," she said. "Look at you. You don't waste no time getting on with it. I'd say that's also on a need-to-know basis."

"Like knowing I live down the block from the Busy Bee?"

"You do?" Sylvia said, a little smile showing. "Ain't that a coincidence."

"So, Agent Sylvia Weaver isn't married," Coleman Vaughn said, leaning forward with a confident, steady gaze. "What about family?"

So now the subject wanted to be the interrogator. Okay. That was fine by her. Like she'd been taught, she'd give out just enough to be friendly and open, get them talking about themselves. Men like Coleman Vaughn always liked talking about themselves.

"Daddy still in Grabtown, North Carolina," she said. "Home of Ava Gardner. You know that old movie star? The kind of woman that made powerful men run around buckass naked with their hair on fire."

"Momma?"

"Dead."

"I'm sorry."

"Long time back," she said, shrugging. "Two half sisters and a younger brother. He's a Marine just like you. One of those jarhead-fool motherfuckers."

"I'll take that as a compliment."

Sylvia smiled as Tracy walked up to take their order. Sylvia glanced over her shoulder at Irv finishing up his plate, not wasting any time while she waited patiently for her contact to show up. Coleman Vaughn raised his eyebrows at her, wanting to know, "You sure you don't want your friend to join us?"

"Nah," she said. "He'd only slow me down."

"We headed somewhere?"

"I like you," Sylvia said. "I really do. If I weren't doing my job, maybe I'd walk over and put some Luther on the jukebox. Maybe that new song, 'The Night I Fell in Love,' they play on V-103 all the time and I'd tell you all about my daddy. How he brought me up a country girl, fishing in the creek, hunting, driving an old Ford pickup when I was only ten. But I ain't got much time. Something about Jenny Buckner being strangled down by the Chattahoochee and not knowing what happened has been messing with my mind."

"I still don't understand what y'all Feds have to do with it."

"The woman was found with my business card in her purse."

"So?"

"So," Sylvia said. "I never knew any Jenny Buckner. And y'all ain't exactly working at Kmart. You've got to have top DOD clearance, run through us, to work at Scientific Atlanta. Top-secret tech. Satellites and lasers beams is what I'm hearing."

"Not my job," he said. "I'm security. Not a scientist." Vaughn nodded and self-consciously ran a hand over his smooth head. She didn't believe for a hot second that he and his wife were getting a divorce. She'd heard that story too many damn times. But she liked the way the man presented himself, ramrod straight, cashmere sweater, mustache perfectly trimmed. Looked like he'd stepped right out of a *GQ* ad.

"Just meeting with you could get me fired."

"That's what threw me," Sylvia said. "Why doesn't Scientific

Atlanta want to cooperate? Seems like they'd be doing everything they could to find out what happened to one of their own. Especially one that's a big security risk."

"Is that what Jenny was?" he asked. "A security risk?"

"You tell me."

"Look," Vaughn said, gazing about the Busy Bee, smiling up at Tracy as she passed. "Keyes and some of the partners don't think this is about Jenny. They think this an excuse for you people to be looking into their business. Trying to make trouble for them."

"Okay."

"I'm not stupid," he said. "I know you didn't leave that breathy message on my voicemail because you liked my style. I agreed to come here because I liked Jenny. I didn't know her well, but she was smart and sweet. Some days we ate together in the cafeteria. Even went on a couple dates, if you must know."

"Oh, I must."

"Kind of woman that would walk arm in arm with a Black man right down the middle of Cumberland Mall," he said. "Sit out by the fountain and enjoy a cool Orange Julius. Even bought me the latest Cameo LP."

"Folks out in Cobb County must've loved that shit."

"We were just friends," Vaughn said. "But something had been weighing on her lately. Moody, depressed. She'd barely speak to me when I'd see her in the lobby or the cafeteria. About a month or two back, she asked if we could talk in private and I walked her out to her car. She told me she'd been seeing a man who she thought was a spy. She said he'd been asking her lots of questions about Dr. Keyes, even giving her a little Minolta camera to take pictures of documents and certain files."

"Did she?"

"She said she didn't," Vaughn said. "But her body language told me she did. She wanted to know how much trouble she'd be in for knowing someone like that. Wanted to know if Keyes would fire her. If she could go to jail. When I started to ask her more questions about this guy, she started to cry, got in her car, and drove off."

"Did you report her?"

Vaughn just stared across the table. "I'd be pretty damn sorry at my job if I didn't."

"But they didn't fire her?"

"Hell, this was a few weeks ago," Vaughn said. "Some outside folks came in for an internal review."

"You weren't invited?"

"Above my pay grade."

"Any idea who might've given her my card?"

Vaughn shrugged. Tracy returned with two steaming-hot plates of today's special: meat loaf, collards, and cornbread. "I do like a woman who likes to eat."

"What's your take on all this, Coleman Vaughn?"

Vaughn cut off a piece of meat loaf and started to chew, thinking on things. "Your people come out to Sci Atlanta every year to give us a rah-rah security pep talk. Loose lips fuck up ships, and all that shit. They got the same ole talk every year, telling us ancient history about the Rosenbergs and nuclear secrets. The damn slide show always puts me to sleep."

"And Jenny?"

"I think this mystery man got to her," he said. "I really do. And turned her world upside down and inside out. You got anything on a boyfriend?"

"Her friends and family never heard about anyone special."

"Way of the damn world," Vaughn said. "Say. You gonna eat your cornbread?"

"Don't you even think about it," she said, moving her plate close. "Have you lost your damn mind?"

Vaughn laughed and showed the palms of his hands. He knew he'd overstepped trying to eat off her plate.

"I've worked at Sci Atlanta for six years but still don't really understand what Keyes and his team do over in Building Three," Vaughn said. "He's brilliant but crazy as hell. You know the type. They don't discuss their research. I do know I get to pick up plenty of folks from Hartsfield flying in from Washington."

"DOD?"

Vaughn shook his head. "Motherfucking CIA."

"Come on, now."

"I'm going to tell you something that you're going to find out sooner or later," Vaughn said. "Sci Atlanta just landed a big-ass deal. Biggest contract in the company's history. And I promise you it ain't about building more cable boxes."

"Spy satellites?"

"Keep on digging, Special Agent Weaver," he said. "I don't want to make this shit easy on you."

"Bart Fisher from our office give those annual talks?"

"Yep."

"He say anything more than just talk about loose lips?"

"Your man told us privately Atlanta was full of damn Russians," he said. "With us, Lockheed, and Dobbins, they've been diverting agents from New York and the West Coast for years."

"Shit," she said. "And you think that was Jenny's man?"

"You tell me, G-Woman."

18

HOTCH

Back at the Battle of Yongdong, the first wave of troops came up on Hotch's unit fast. He remembered emptying four clips, hot and sweaty in the Korean summer, until his rifle jammed. He picked up another, but it didn't work either, and his sergeant saw him struggling behind the sandbags. The sergeant handed over a bayonet, but Hotch saw in the man's face that they'd all be dead soon. So Hotch reached for the only thing that gave him some comfort. A goddamn can of fruit cocktail from his ruck.

"That's when my sergeant asked, *Are you ready to die?*" he told Jackie.

Hotch and Jackie had been parked outside the Muscle Factory for nearly an hour, Jackie having to use the bathroom at the Harris Teeter once and Hotch three times. The last trip, he bought a six-pack of Heineken and cracked open a bottle off the bumper of the Cadillac, waiting for Peter Bennett's mystery man to lock up for the night.

Jackie had heard the story many times but for some reason wanted to hear it again.

"What the hell else was I going to say?" Hotch asked. "I opened that can with the bayonet and said, *Sure. Why not?* And Sarge called in mortar fire. The mortars came in so close, it singed my hair and busted one of my eardrums, but damn, if it didn't take out most of those commies over the hill. I got cocky and raised up, holding the bayonet dripping with fruit cocktail syrup, and a sniper hit me dead in the eye. I fell onto my back. Real Audie Murphy shit."

"How was that fruit cocktail?"

"Like everything else GI," Hotch said. "Tasted like crap."

An OPENING SOON banner hung over the gym door, where Hotch had caught a glimpse of Gary Powers thirty minutes back demonstrating squats to two heavyset women. Powers had on a pair of red-and-white-striped silk shorts and a red tank top, not taking note of the portly man strolling by. Jackie glanced over from behind the wheel, staring at the side of Hotch's disfigured profile. Jackie was dressed down tonight in a pair of ripped jeans, flip-flops, and a sleeveless Madonna *Like a Virgin* T-shirt. No wig. No makeup.

"Can we please talk about something else?" Hotch asked. "You seemed to be more interested in the geishas I met during my R and R in Tokyo."

"You must've been just a kid."

"I was almost nineteen," Hotch said. "But I was an old nineteen. You know?"

"You bet your ass, Kemo Sabe."

Hotch never had been one to think back on things, dredging up all the muck that had filtered down to the lowest parts of his reptilian brain. He'd much rather think about his characters, his stories: *Lilli the Resistance leader. Bud and Brutus on a stakeout at Underground Atlanta.* His own history wasn't very pretty. What could you say about being born during the height of the Depression, your parents so damn poor that they gave you and your kid sister away to an orphanage in Fayetteville, North Carolina? Hotch and his sister bounced from foster home to foster home, sometimes separated and then reunited. Hotch had been beaten black and blue. His sister molested. Hotch had taken about all he could, the last one a foster home in Nash County. They put him to work with all the other castoffs, picking tobacco from sunup until the sticky leaves sweated into his skin and he became so nauseated and sick that he thought he would die. He joined up with the army a few weeks later, lying about his age. You could do those kinds of things back then. He hadn't been much older than Peter Bennett.

"Don't look now," Jackie said, pointing to the storefront. "But here comes Boris."

"Boris?"

"Yep," Jackie said. "That's what I call his Russian ass. And that makes you Moose and me Squirrel. What in the fuck is that son of a bitch wearing? Looks like he's headed out to rustle some steers."

Gary Powers walked across the dark parking lot, changed from gym clothes into a red snap-button shirt, jeans, boots, and brown cowboy hat. Hotch and Jackie had a good laugh watching him try to get into the Porsche in a pair of dark jeans that appeared to have been spray-painted on. The man could barely bend his knees. The top was down on the DeVille and they could hear the man's stereo blasting that new song "Money for Nothing."

"Kid told us Russians loved cowboy movies."

"I'm the one who wrote that," Hotch said. "In my article. 'KGB Spies Living Next Door.'"

"You told Peter that was all bullshit."

"Maybe I was wrong," Hotch said. "What the fuck do I know? Give me a bottle of Jack Daniel's and a few hours on the typewriter and I might just find the truth for a sentence or two."

Jackie tried to crank the Cadillac. After the third try, the engine turned over and he backed up. "I give Boris about thirty seconds before he sees this goddamn U-boat."

"Next time I'll check out something more conservative from the motor pool."

"You know, I didn't have to haul my ass out to motherfucking Cobb County to be your chauffeur," Jackie said. "I was supposed to work the early shift at Weekends as a go-go dancer."

"Go-go dancer?" Hotch said. "That's a hoot. What is this, sixty-eight? Nancy Sinatra and her white walkin' boots?"

"I wear a leather jockstrap, too," Jackie said. "So shit doesn't fly out like *Bwana Devil* in 3D."

"Bwana," Hotch said, firing up a Pall Mall and clicking closed his Zippo. "Yeah. I saw that movie. Never will forget those red eyes jumping out at you."

• • •

Jackie drove three to four cars back from the Porsche while Hotch turned on the record player, switching out a Fats Domino 45 for a Little Richard. "Long Tall Sally" played and skipped as they hit a bump while they followed the Porsche to Parkaire Mall, where Powers turned right onto Lower Roswell and hopefully the hell out of Cobb County. The burbs gave Hotch the creeps. Every house looking the same, all the strip malls the same, all the same Hardee's and McDonald's. The endless twists and turns inside the subdivisions. You could get lost just trying to find yourself. The county had probably been good farmland back in the day, filled with dog trots and big red barns. Now it was a wasteland of ranch houses and fake Colonials. Like Faulkner said, nothing gives an uncivilized man more comfort than hearing the sound of his neighbor's toilet flush. His Southern lit professor at Chapel Hill would've been impressed he remembered.

"Long Tall Sally" was over before it had barely started, Hotch reaching into the record player and flipping to the B-side, "Slippin' and Slidin'." The fall air was crisp and cool, flowing through the big

Cadillac, the Porsche's twin red brake lights clicking off and on around the turns.

What if the son of a bitch was leading them into a trap? This might be just as dumb as trying to eat some fruit cocktail in the middle of the Battle of Yongdong. Jackie was right, they had to look like part of the White Star Line trailing behind Powers in the baby blue DeVille with Miss Jackie Demure driving a white man across Cobb County. Not to mention, they were playing oldies, smoking cigarettes, Hotch riding shotgun with an open beer. If this guy was really KGB, and that was a hell of a big *if*, he'd lure them down somewhere by the river and slit both their throats. Maybe he should've bought a gun. He had a snub-nose .38 pistol he kept in his cookie jar back at his apartment, but he hadn't shot the damn thing since celebrating Hank Aaron breaking Babe Ruth's record.

"Man's headed to Dobbins," Hotch said.

"The air force base?"

"Probably to meet his contact."

"Dressed as Roy Fucking Rogers?" Jackie said.

"Maybe it's a disguise."

"Come on, Hotch," Jackie said. "Man's Russian. Not retarded."

The Porsche took a fast turn south onto Franklin Road, nearly coming around on two wheels past a lonely stretch of old warehouses, run-down businesses, and fast-food restaurants. Jackie had to push Big Bertha to the limits, the front of the Cadillac lifting up like a speedboat until Gary Powers squealed into the gravel lot of a red two-story building that resembled a tobacco barn with neon beer signs in the windows. An old-fashioned sign above a tin-roof porch read MISS KITTY'S SALOON.

"What in the damn hell?"

"Don't you watch *Gunsmoke*?"

"Sure, I watch *Gunsmoke*," Jackie said. "My auntie loved her some *Gunsmoke*. She always said Miss Kitty wasn't no can-can girl. She sure as shit was selling pussy upstairs."

Jacked-up pickup trucks, most with gun racks and Confederate flag stickers, filled the gravel parking lot. The sound of lap steel came from the front door while a bunch of good ole boys and gals wandered the porch. Some of the heads turned to stare, but it appeared they were more interested in the convertible Caddy than him and Jackie. "Wait here."

"And miss all the fun?" Jackie asked. "I will have you know I did a tribute to Dolly last year at Illusions and goddamn near brought the house down with my 'Jolene.' Not to mention '9 to 5' dressed up as an uptight secretary. High heels. Cute little glasses."

Hotch reached into his left-hand pocket for his cigarettes and shook one loose. "This would be a good place to make a brush pass. Lots of activity. Loud and busy so that no one would notice. So close to Dobbins. It all makes sense now. The kid was right."

"Good," Jackie said. "But fuck me. I sure wish I'd brought my cowboy hat."

"You have a cowboy hat?"

"Bitch," Jackie said. "I got a dozen."

• • •

Hotch couldn't find Gary upstairs or downstairs in the ramshackle building, not at the long bar or on the dance floor, where a bunch of peckerwoods were slow dancing to "A Country Boy Can Survive," Bic lighters held high as Hotch made his way through the neon light and cigarette smoke. Jackie had already found a spot on a barstool and had borrowed, or stolen, a white cowboy hat ringed in pink feathers. He had a tall cocktail in his hand and seemed to be telling an animated story to two white women dressed up like Dale Rogers. As Hotch passed all he heard was Jackie saying, "Not if you tie it up right, it don't."

Hotch knew he didn't have long. Jackie was the man you wanted with you in a fight, but keeping a low profile wasn't exactly his thing. Hotch moved through the crowd, getting a few side-eyes himself. His bald head shining under the blazing bar signs and looking like a damn Yankee in his black leather trench coat, knotted at the waist. If any of those rednecks bothered to look at his shoes, they'd have been appalled—if any of them knew that word. He was wearing scuffed Florsheim loafers his second wife bought him for church. Church! She believed she could actually reform him. Save Dennis X. Hotchner's damned soul.

Hotch glanced around again, thinking about heading back out to the parking lot, when that third Heineken hit him. He headed to the bathroom, standing in line for a few minutes before having to saddle up to a latrine that looked like it used to be a horse trough. Up on the wall, some enterprising soul had shellacked nude pictures of women, most of them Playmates, so you could enjoy the view while relieving yourself. Hotch had half a cigarette bobbing in his mouth and was about to zip it up when Gary Powers, still a hell of a name for a Russki to choose, saddled up next to him. The man was a good head taller than Hotch, his fancy cowboy hat tipped way far back on his head.

"Whew," Gary Powers said. "I love this music."

Hotch didn't know what to say. He just nodded as he zipped up his pants and buckled his belt.

"You looking for someone?"

Hotch shook his head. He left the urinal and began to wash his hands. Powers stood right behind him as he ran the water. Reflected in the mirror, the man was big as an ape, staring down and waiting. Hotch felt that old fight-or-flight flow through him in a way he hadn't felt for years.

"If you like the scene," Powers said, "might want to run out to Horsetown and get some duds. Women sure do love a cowboy."

"Thanks," Hotch said. "*Horsetown.* I'll keep that in mind."

"One of the bartenders picked you out when you walked through the door," he said. "Figured you for a narc."

Hotch laughed and tried to walk around the big man. Powers put the flat of his hand on Hotch's chest and stopped him cold. Hotch looked up into his unsmiling face. "Haven't I seen you around?" he said. "Were you grocery shopping out in East Cobb today?"

"Where?"

Powers stared at him some more, looked down at his scuffed loafers and then up to his bald head. He reached out and plucked the cigarette from Hotch's mouth and ground it under a pointy-toed boot. If Hotch could just get free from the restroom, he could maybe get Jackie's attention and Jackie could whip this beet-eater's ass.

Powers reached out and gripped Hotch's right upper arm.

"I know who you are."

Hotch opened his mouth, about to really give it to the guy, put the fear of God into him. Let him know he'd announce to every one of these God-fearing, Confederate flag–waving rednecks that they had a true and authentic KGB spy in Miss Kitty's Saloon.

Powers reached under his fringed jacket, Hotch closing his good eye.

"But you can change," Powers said. His hard face went soft. "You can get off the cigarettes and booze. Become a new man. Start a new life."

Gary Powers produced a business card and pressed it into Hotch's hand. *The Muscle Factory! Gary Powers, manager/personal trainer. We Build Bodies.*

"That's very generous of you."

Powers touched the brim of his cowboy hat and headed out the door. Hotch took a breath and followed him back into the sea of cowboy hats and tight jeans. Jackie was still at the bar but now arguing with two white men with mustaches who wore what looked to be identical outfits. Black jeans, black boots, red jackets over white cowboy shirts. One of the men had his right hand on his hip as if searching for a six-shooter. The other stepped in front of him and spit on the floor in front of Jackie.

"Boys here don't like me at the watering hole," Jackie said. "Said I might be giving everyone AIDS."

"Nice," Hotch said. "Come on, let's go."

"I told them you can only catch it from fucking," he said. "But with those faces, the only thing they looked to be fucking was themselves."

Hotch had little doubt that Jackie could break those good ole boys in half. He stood a head taller than both, his arms veined and muscular in the cutout Madonna T-shirt. Jackie had asked Hotch to go to her concert with him, but Hotch had declined, telling Jackie to let him know when Rosemary Clooney was in town. Jackie said Rosemary Clooney was dead, but Hotch pointed out she was alive and selling paper towels on TV. Jackie said, *Worse than dead.*

"How about I buy you boys a round of drinks?" Hotch asked.

"This your date?"

Hotch looked at the man and shrugged. He lit up a cigarette, reached into his pocket for a few crinkled bills, and nodded. "Yep."

"Saw you walk out of the bathroom with that muscleman," one of the mustached men said. "You know who he is?"

Hotch blew some smoke into the man's face. "A KGB agent."

The men all laughed and shook their heads. The bartender appeared and Hotch bought a round of Budweisers.

"He's selling steroids to the flyboys."

"How do you know that?" Jackie said.

"Because he's always in here on a Friday night at the exact same time," the other mustached man said. "He comes in, sits down at that table over yonder, and hands off a gym bag. This is the longest I've ever seen him stay."

"He's gone?" Jackie said.

The two men nodded over toward the front door, where they saw Gary Powers's broad back and big cowboy hat leaving Miss Kitty's.

"Don't hate me because I'm pretty, boys," Jackie said, turning to follow Hotch back outside. "And don't be so stupid to get your ass stomped by Miss Jackie Demure."

19

PETER

He'd found the neatly folded note, written in purple ink on pink paper, inside his locker after fifth period. A faint whiff of perfume as he unfolded the pages in the high school hallway, looking about to see if anyone was watching. The note was short and sweet, maybe even a little bit flirty.

> *Peter. You don't know me but I know you. You were at the dollar movie watching Chuck Norris on Friday with Scott Adams. I know you are worried about your mom. And her creep of a boyfriend. I want to meet and explain everything. I'll be at Kicks tonight. Don't tell anyone and come alone. By the way, I'm much cuter than your old girlfriend. Let's be friends. XOXO*

Okay. Maybe this was bullshit. But maybe it was an honest attempt at helping Peter figure this all out. Maybe this girl had been having problems with Gary Powers, too. The man had a cocky swagger about him like an unneutered cat. The way he'd paw at his mom, put his hands on her shoulders and lower back, whispering dumb stupid shit in her ear. *Oh, Gary!* Barf. You just knew there had to be other women. All the adults Peter knew were so damn horny, only caring about dancing, drinking, and screwing each other instead of actually being parents. *Be back late tonight, sweetheart.*

"What's wrong?" Scott said, reading the note over his shoulder. Peter folded it up quickly and stashed it in his back pocket.

"You think your sister might actually give me a ride somewhere tonight?"

"Where?"

"Kicks."

"Come on, man," Scott said. "I knew a kid who went to Kicks and saw a bunch of freaks sniffing coke off a toilet seat. And some kid getting a handy while he was playing Ms. Pac-Man. A nightclub for kids? Who the hell came up with that stupid idea? My mom read about it in the paper and said if I ever even thought about going there, she'd melt down my Mongoose. And she meant it, too."

"What else are we going to do? Rent *Nightmare on Elm Street* for the millionth time? I'm so sick of Freddy fucking Krueger, I could barf. He's just a gross old perv."

"Does this have something to do with your mom?"

"No."

"You're lying again, man," Scott said. "You know your left eye twitches when you lie. You'd really suck at poker."

The hallway was bustling, endlessly sad and tired with its stained industrial carpet and buzzing fluorescent lights. All the girls seemed to be trying to overdo their hair this fall, teased up stiff and tall, wearing bright-colored tops with faded jeans safety pinned to the ankles. Rubber bracelets and Swatch watches. They smelled like bubble gum and perfume, hustling past to get to the last class of the day, before heading back home on the buses or jumping into the cars parked out by the football field.

"It's some hot girl that wants to meet up," Peter said. "She wanted to see if I could bring a friend. I think she goes to Wheeler or something. I heard they were cheerleaders."

"Then why wouldn't they be at the game?" Scott asked. "Don't be a nerd. You do realize tonight is Friday?"

Peter slammed the locker door and snicked on the lock. He leaned his back against the lockers and let out a long, dramatic sigh.

"You were a lot more fun before your mom started dating this dick."

"One time."

"Okay," Scott said. "My sister does owe me."

• • •

It cost two bucks to get inside Kicks, the line stretching out in front of the strip mall from a spot that Peter recalled had once been a comedy club, called something really lame like Yuks or Sidesplitters. Kicks had opened at the start of the summer, so many parents dropping off their stupid kids they were turning away people out on Roswell Road. The asshole who owned the place announced the grand opening with dance contests and spotlights like some kind of Hollywood premiere. Kids from all over the Atlanta burbs wanted to get inside, not for the cheap cherry Coca-Cola and fake cocktails, but because this was a chance to break beyond the boundaries of your stupid school. You could meet up with kids from Lassiter or Marist or even Pace. There were Catholic school kids and Jewish kids, even a few Black kids who could part the lighted dance floor, trying out some break dancing.

Peter and Scott pushed inside the club, seeming a lot emptier than he'd expected. Just a dozen or so kids on the dance floor looking ridiculous trying to keep up with Prince and "When Doves Cry." Man, Peter loved Prince. He had all his albums going back to *For You* and on into *Controversy* and his favorite, *1999*. He was obsessed with *Purple Rain* and had even seen Prince at the Omni earlier that year. His friend Troy's older brother had driven them downtown in his deluxe conversion van. When they returned to the parking lot, they found some homeless guy had camped out inside during the show and taken a shit in the van's sink.

"That's gross," Scott said.

"But that's what happened."

"What did you guys do?"

"Rode home with the windows open," Peter said. "It was awful."

Peter had to give it to the folks who opened Kicks: the club's dance floor flashed on and off like the ones he'd seen in movies with a spinning disco ball and colorful lights over the DJ booth. The song faded into "A View to a Kill" by Duran Duran, the electric drum pulsing hard with the fuzzy synthesizer as Peter made his way through the kids, a few smoking cigarettes by the bathrooms, yellow and red neon washing over their faces. He smelled pot and alcohol in the air.

"How will you know her?" Scott said. He'd worn jeans and his best Polo shirt that day, bright green with the collar up. Peter had on jeans and a jean jacket over an EPCOT T-shirt he'd gotten two years ago. It was about the only thing clean in his closet, his room a complete mess even by his own standards.

"She said she'll know me," Peter said. "She obviously knows you. Because she said it in her note. She said she saw us at *Invasion U.S.A.*"

"If she's that hot, then why don't we know who she is?" Scott said. "And what about her friends?"

"Well," Peter said, heading up to the bar and showing two fingers to some pimply faced kid at the counter. "I may have exaggerated that point a little bit."

"Shit," Scott said. "I knew it was too good to be true."

Peter and Scott stood at the counter, Simon Le Bon going off on the Bond song, until they got their drinks and moved over to a black leather couch under a mirrored wall. The couch sat alone and off to the side like some kind of penalty booth. The DJ released some fog from a machine, and it spread out over the pulsing dance floor.

"I'd rather cut my nuts off than go out there and make a fool out of myself," Scott said.

Peter wasn't listening. Stacey Brand had walked in with her crew of friends, passing Peter and Scott on the dumb-loser couch. She was talking and laughing and didn't stop to acknowledge Peter's presence, pushing her long black hair over her right ear. He started to stand but Scott grabbed his wrist. "Be cool. Don't go chase after her."

"Everything she heard is crap," Peter said. "I want her to know the truth."

But there was the real truth, and then there was Peter's truth. And maybe he had invited Laurie Saye to go into the Monster Plantation. And maybe as they hit the last turn in the fake river, the monster sheriff giving them a stern warning about coming to his town, Peter may have leaned in and kissed her. It was just a moment, over so fast that he barely remembered it happening. So did it even happen at all?

"Didn't we come here to find out about that fuckhead who's with your mom?" Scott asked. "Just let Stacey go. The Monster Plantation? That's just weird. That's a dumb place to go make out. Monsters dressed up like the Civil War?"

The Monster Plantation was pretty fucked up if you really thought about it. Like some kind of wacko version of It's a Small World with animatronic monsters singing and dancing to the backdrop of fucking *Gone With the Wind*. Monsters with crazy Southern accents.

Peter caught Stacey's eye from across Kicks. She was tall and skinny, with straight black hair and large, dark eyes. He remembered all the times they'd hung out at her house, listening to records. She was the first one to play U2 for him, and the Clash. She wore this awesome perfume that made him crazy and once had pressed one of her earrings into his hand after they'd gone to see a sneak preview of *The Breakfast Club*.

"I still like her, man," Peter said.

"No shit," Scott said.

Peter got up, and Scott didn't try to stop him this time. It all looked like something in a video with the strobe lights and the fog machine, "Crazy for You" playing as Peter walked toward her. He remembered being so nervous at the eighth-grade dance, worried that she'd be going off to private school. Maybe they'd never see each other again. Peter looked across at her and waved and she held his look for a moment before fucking Mitch Siegel rounded the corner with a few of his cheeseball friends. She ran over and hugged Mitch, looking over his shoulder at Pete. And then she did something so bold and out of character it was like a damn gut punch.

Stacey flipped him the fucking bird.

"That sucks, Pete," Brenda Yee said. She'd walked up right next to him, and he hadn't even noticed. Brenda held a big soda cup in both hands, slurping on the straw.

"Shit, Brenda," Peter said. "You can't just sneak up on a person like that. What the hell are you doing here?"

"I come here every Friday to party," Brenda said. "Duh. I don't sit around on the couch watching horror movies like you two losers. I'm looking for some action."

"Gross, Brenda," Peter said. "Seriously."

Peter walked back to the long black sofa by the toilets, the smell of pot roiling out into the main room. He and Scott sat for a long time, forty minutes—*two hours?*—watching everyone dance. They started talking to some girl from St. Pius who pointed out all the losers on the dance floor and how much she hated the music. She started telling them all about the Cure and the Sex Pistols and how she believed that Phil Collins might seriously be the Antichrist. She was short, with bleached hair tied up in a big black bow. She had on a lot of eye makeup and her lips and fingernails had been painted black. Peter looked out on the floor to find Stacey, but she was long gone.

The dance floor parted and some kid in a red leather jacket with chains, like Michael Jackson wore in the "Beat It" video, was really showing off his moves. He must've been a regular because everyone was clapping and yelling watching the stupid kid perform a fucking moonwalk. "His name is Gabe," the gloomy girl said. "He goes to Marist and thinks he's hot shit."

"The moonwalk?" Scott asked.

"I know," the gloomy girl said. "He thinks he's hot shit."

"This place sucks balls," Scott said.

The gloomy girl agreed, and Peter was about to add to his dislike of all things Kicks, from the smoke to the hair spray to the sweat to the boozy kids, when he saw the white-haired girl walk in.

The girl's hair probably wasn't really white, just super blond, the way he'd seen Sabrina the Teenage Witch drawn in the comic books. She was thin and kind of tall for a teenager. She had on a fuzzy red sweater, worn off one shoulder, patterned with checks and circles. Lots of gold studs in her left ear. She seemed to spot Peter right away, heading straight to the sad sofa where he and Scott sat with the girl from St. Pius.

Scott looked to Peter. And Peter back to Scott. Neither of them spoke.

The girl had the most precise, interesting face, with delicate features and a wide mouth. Her eyes were a bright, icy blue and she had just a little bit of makeup on her cheeks. She looked like she'd hopped straight out of a Benetton catalog.

She stuck out her long slim hand, and the formality struck Peter as weird. But he took it and stood from the couch as if he'd been summoned. Her nails were cut short and painted a bright red. She was chewing gum and for a long time just stared at him without saying a word. Peter's mouth felt very dry.

"Hello, Peter Bennett," she said. "I'm Ana. Is there somewhere we can talk?"

Peter motioned to the sad leather couch. He and Scott exchanged looks. The gloomy girl with the black nail polish rolled her eyes, stood up, and left. "Fags," she said, parting.

"I mean in private," Ana said.

20

VITALY

The CIA men were outside the new safe house grilling steaks.

Vitaly had had more than enough of the rich American food. They'd even tried to hire a Black woman, such a racist country, to do his cooking and cleaning, promising she'd make real Southern-style fried chicken. Vitaly had declined. No more of that. He would do his own wash. And he'd given the agents, part of his new team, a list of food he would require, including the black tea and alfalfa pills for his aching stomach. He'd just got his chicken and potatoes to boil, an embarrassment of riches in this new house on a man-made lake, when Dan Rafferty walked inside carrying a brown paper bag.

"You're a hard man to find, Vitaly Yurchenko," Dan said, hugging Vitaly like a bear and handing him the paper bag. "Stoli. I remember you telling me how bad the vodka was in Rome. There's a wine store in Georgetown that sells it by the caseload. You can thank the good folks at PepsiCo. They trade Pepsi to your comrades for vodka."

"I shouldn't," Vitaly said, admiring the clear bottle in the warm late-afternoon light. A familiar reminder of home. "I have this ailment. *Is it ulcer? Is it cancer?* I don't know. It's a mystery sickness. A spin of the mortal wheel."

"How about one glass, pal?" Dan said. "Just among friends."

"Of course," Vitaly said. "Of course. To friendship. How can I refuse you, Daniel Rafferty?"

Rafferty could only find something he called jelly jars in the cabinet, squat glasses with threaded tops like you used to store pickles and beets. He poured them both a generous amount, the kitchen already smelling of the simmering chicken and potatoes. A bit of salt and paprika, maybe some dill. Simple food. Nothing fried or grilled. He would only make simple food to settle his angry stomach. Just one day. Just one day without the aches and pains of the living.

"The CIA took me furniture shopping today," Vitaly said, finding a seat at his brand-new kitchen table. What the salesman called top of the line. He knocked on it with his knuckles. "Walnut. Strong as iron. I never shop for furniture in my life. You earn furniture when family dies. My uncle left me a china cabinet that belonged to my great-great-grandmother. Or maybe you move into new apartment and furniture still there. People in such a hurry. No one buys furniture. Furniture finds you."

"Welcome to our consumer culture, comrade," Dan said, lifting the jelly jar and offering him a toast. From where Vitaly sat, he could see Dan's large, gold-framed glasses were dirty and smudged. He hadn't shaved in some time, his clothes wrinkled and fitting loose about his shoulders. His old friend stared into the transparent vodka as if something weighed on his mind.

"I'm just glad they're treating you better," Dan said. "I made a real fuss of it at the Bureau. Those spooks don't operate like us. They don't understand the courage it took to defect. Or how you put your life at risk."

"They think of me as a traitor."

"Someone said that?" Dan said, his eyes lit up. "Who?"

"No," Vitaly said, taking a large swallow of the Stoli. A bit of home. "I see it in their eye. They treat me as outcast. Expecting me to act like prince. They want to find me servants and play golf during the day. Why the obsession with the golf? Hitting little ball with sticks. Seems like much work for such little point. All they do is scare the goose."

"What do Russians do for relaxation?"

Vitaly shrugged. "Take a steam," he said. "Drink much vodka. Find a good woman. We are simple people."

"More debriefing?"

Vitaly shook his head. "Just once before we came to this place."

"It's called Bealeton," Dan said. "You're now in Bealeton, Virginia."

"They call it something else," Vitaly said. "'The convent'? I figured it must be holy place on the water."

"Coventry is the development," Dan said. "This was some old spook's retirement house that he rented to the Agency. God knows for how much. It's all a scam. And now they're buying you furniture? This must be your new home. Congratulations."

"So many pots and pans," Vitaly said, taking another sip of the Stolichnaya. Dan reached for the bottle and tried to pour him more. But Vitaly held up his hand to stop him. Still more flowed. The sun began to set outside the patio windows, a soft orange-red glow over the lake. Geese flying into the orange orb. One CIA agent hitting more balls into the lake to make them scatter.

"You don't have to do anything you don't want to do."

"Ha," Vitaly said, standing and moving over to the red iron pot where he boiled his chicken. He wore an apron—*KISS THE COOK*—over the khaki pants and white T-shirt they'd bought for him. Still with the creases and smelling of a plastic wrapper. He stirred the chicken parts with a wooden spoon and then tasted the broth. Perhaps tomorrow he'd try borscht. But none of the sour cream. Dairy turned the stomach.

Dan glanced back out the sliding doors, smoke rising from a metal grill, two agents removing slabs of meat. Just the charred smell made Vitaly nauseous, reminding him of the massive crematorium outside Moscow. If he ever returned, that's where he'd end up, piled high with the traitors and thieves, their ashes used to fertilize wheat fields. "You do know you asked for the impossible," Dan said. "The CIA will barely let you leave the compound. A trip to Atlanta might not happen, old friend."

"I was made promises," Vitaly said. "About my freedom. And personal reasons for my defection."

"Did you tell them it was love?"

"Of course not," Vitaly said. "Men do not speak of such things."

Vitaly sat back down at the big kitchen table. The chicken would need another hour at least. Perhaps two. But what was time now? Things must take time to simmer, give them flavor, character. He slept little, having to listen to the sounds of agents watching television, the *Johnny Carson*, the late-night movie with the yelling and the shooting. A fat man who solved crimes named Cannon. Later, the CIA men came to the bathroom near where he slept, expelling gas like out-of-tune trumpet.

"I promise to make a case for this meeting," Dan said. "But I agree. It's best to not mention a lover. Okay? They might not sign off for that. Do you know anybody else in Atlanta?"

"Of course," Vitaly said. "I know people there. I know many Russians across America. Would you like to stay for the chicken?"

Dan shook his head. Could Daniel not smell the simple deliciousness coming from the pot? In Russia, this would've elicited every neighbor poking noses from their apartment doorways. Boiling a whole chicken? An embarrassment of the riches. *Perhaps you might save the bones for me to make another broth?* He looked over at Daniel, slumped in his chair and pouring out more vodka. His gray raincoat loose around his wrinkled suit.

Vitaly's eyes wandered over a beaten man. "You look troubled, Daniel."

"I'm fine and dandy," Daniel said. "Although I do appreciate your concern. I just have a lot at my office. And with Delores and the kids. Peewee football practice. Dance recitals. Lot of responsibility at my church. Meals on Wheels. Outreach to at-risk youth. The damn OWLS. Folks we call Older Wiser Livelier Souls but are really just a pain in the ass."

"Nothing is bad enough to let them control you."

"No one is controlling me," Dan said. "Who do you mean? Why would you say that?"

"All the questions about what Russians know about the STDs."

Dan laughed and rubbed his eyes with his fists. "Ha," he said. "You mean SDI. That's pretty much on everybody's minds these days. Not to mention stockpiling the biggest nuclear arsenal the world has ever seen. The best we can hope for is that we don't produce more. Not that we eliminate what could already blow up this planet hundreds of times."

"It keeps peace," Vitaly said, smiling. "Good fences make good neighbors."

"Fences don't incinerate millions," Daniel said. "The Strategic Defense Initiative is the game changer."

"But does it work?" Vitaly said. "That is hundred-dollar question."

"You tell me," Dan said. "Old friend."

The conversation had veered off course and taken the rocky road, Vitaly noticing the dark circles under Daniel's eyes. He'd already consumed nearly half the bottle of Stoli. Vitaly didn't touch the little jelly jar again. He wanted his mind to stay focused and sharp to see what kind of game Daniel had come to play. Outside, the CIA men had set up at a picnic table, laughing and making jokes to the man who'd hit golf balls into the lake. They appeared as jovial and distracted as young boys. Only, these boys carried guns on their hips and had installed many cameras and trip wires across the property. Just in case the KGB wanted Vitaly back. It made him laugh, watching all the trouble they'd gone to. *For what? Spying was such a silly game.*

"Is it money?" Vitaly asked.

"What?" Dan said. "No. Damn it, Vitaly."

"Are you a Marxist?"

"That's a laugh."

"Then it's a woman," Vitaly said. "Is she Russian? Russian women can be very persuasive. And quite strong in their thighs."

"I don't know any Russian women," he said. "Now pass me the fucking bottle and stir your chicken."

"I think I have stirred enough."

"Funny you mention Atlanta," Daniel said. "There's an outfit down there doing top-secret research into SDI. A woman was recently killed, and some vital information went missing. If the Russians were to have it, it might upset damn near everything we have prepped for Geneva. It might send the Gipper off script, and no one wants to go back to his whole 'evil empire' strategy."

"That was not so popular in Russia," Vitaly said, nodding to the men outside the sliding glass door. "If there is intelligence to be known in Atlanta, perhaps you speak to the Agency about a trip. I could make meetings with old Russian friends who have ears to ground. Two birds and a stone."

Daniel looked out at the lake to watch the men from the Agency sit down to dinner. "No promises, pal," he said. "But I'll do my damn level best."

The golfer, who lied and still said his name was Charlie, had joined the other three and sat down to a large piece of charred meat and baked potato. A fork and knife in hand. They all wore flawless blue suits, crisp white shirts, and colorful ties. This Charlie was older, with black hair that had gone white at the temples. He wore some kind of skull and crossbones tie clip. When Vitaly had inquired about the clip, he said he'd been a Yale man like the vice president.

"There may not be another chance after Geneva," Dan said. "This intel could be a game changer. We haven't had both sides at the table for three years."

"America moved the long-range missiles and the Pershings into Western Europe," Vitaly said. "What did you expect?"

"What was it that made this man Gorbachev come back?" Dan said. "What is the one thing that made him want to sit down to bargain again?"

Both men knew it was the lasers in outer space that could shoot down missiles and create a safety net over all of America. They called it the Star Wars. *But was this all a Hollywood fantasy, peddled by the old actor from Westerns? Or something quite real?*

"Pass the paprika, Daniel Rafferty," Vitaly said. "The chicken is almost ready to eat."

21

SYLVIA

Sylvia didn't approach Bart Fisher until her squad supervisor had left for the day. She watched as Jeremiah Sullivan tucked his London Fog overcoat in the crook of his arm and slapped a houndstooth hat on his head before heading toward the elevators. He simply nodded as he passed Sylvia's desk, Sylvia hammering out what he'd assumed was a report but was really her just typing *ALL WORK AND NO PLAY MAKES AGENT WEAVER ONE DULL BITCH* over and over for the last twenty minutes, until Sullivan disappeared. She didn't waste a single moment in pushing back her chair and wandering over to Fisher's desk, a half-burned-up cigarette smoldering in his tin ashtray alongside a cup of cold coffee from McDonald's.

Agent Bart Fisher had to be in his late forties going on seventy, short and silver-haired, wearing the same company navy blue suit with a pair of thick Sears, Roebuck glasses. He had all the proper family photos on his desk. Wife, kid, a dog of some sort. A faded photo of a bunch of army boys with buzz cuts and cigarettes from decades ago. And for some reason a framed eight-by-ten of him and Burt Reynolds. He looked up at Sylvia staring at the pic.

"I helped with security when they shot *Sharky's Machine*," Fisher said. "Reynolds's manager gave me some vouchers for that crappy Po'Folks restaurant. It's like Cracker Barrel but much worse. They print up menus in all this illiterate writing. I think I still have 'em in my desk somewhere if you're into soggy turnip greens."

"I need to talk to you about Sci Atlanta."

"Hm." Fisher picked up the cigarette and took a long pull, letting out a stream of smoke overhead. "I wondered how long it would take you."

"The head guy out there has been jamming me up," Sylvia said. "He won't let me and Irv work. Wouldn't answer any of my questions."

"Keyes?" he said. "He may be a genius, but he's also a real-deal asshole. Keyes doesn't mean to be rude. He just thinks he's above everyone. He's also completely paranoid, convinced we or the damn CIA have a leak somewhere. All because of some kind of high-tech gizmo that ended up on a Russian satellite ten years ago."

"His personal secretary was killed."

"Oh, I know," Fisher said. Sylvia noticed the hair scraped over his bald spot was darker than the silver sides, like he'd only thought to dye the strands. "Jenny Buckner. Real nice young lady."

"Any theories?" Sylvia asked, crossing her arms over her chest, feeling a little nervous going around this FBI chain of command. "She had my business card in her purse. I never even heard of Jenny Buckner until last week. I got to say that makes me a little nervous."

"And Sullivan didn't explain this all to you?"

"If he had," Sylvia said, "I wouldn't have missed my damn ride home tonight. You know how much it costs to take a cab back to Akers Mill?"

Fisher ashed the cigarette and took another draw. He reached over his desk and closed the thick file he'd been studying. Sylvia didn't mean to snoop, but she couldn't help but notice the grainy surveillance photos of that bank job out in Marietta by the Big Chicken. A security guard shot and thirty grand taken.

"Only person out there worth a shit is a guy named Coleman Vaughn," Fisher said. "Man's too smart to be sitting at reception checking IDs and looking in ladies' purses."

"I met Vaughn," she said. "He told me you had some concerns about their security?"

"Glad to know someone was actually listening." Fisher squashed out the cigarette and pushed back his rolling chair. "Wait until you have to do these damn slide shows and pep talks. What all did he tell you?"

"Russians," Sylvia said. "Soviet devils that went down to Georgia and all that."

Fisher nodded. "Not exactly something we advertise," he said. "But this town is lousy with them."

"You know that ole bullshit about 'need to know'?" Sylvia said. "Don't you think it's about damn time I need to goddamn know?"

Bart Fisher looked down at his gold Timex, a twisty Speidel band on his wrist, and nodded to himself. A little smile on his face. "How about we take a little stroll downtown?" Fisher said. "There's something I want you to see. And a hell of a lot you need to know, Agent Weaver."

• • •

"Remarkable," Bart Fisher said. "Isn't it?"

"It's a Hyatt."

"Not just a regular Hyatt," Fisher said. "This place is unique. Man named John C. Portman designed a bunch of these buildings for the whole rebuilding of Atlanta. You know this town hasn't been right since Sherman burned it. Not an original quote. I heard that on *The Dukes of Hazzard.*"

"Oh," Sylvia said. "I think General Sherman did just fine. Only he missed a spot or two."

Fisher laughed. They were high up on the seventeenth floor looking into a massive atrium topped by a glass ceiling and ringed by balconies, plants spilling from every corner and four glass elevators lit up with tiny white bulbs going up and down from the lobby. From their perch above, they could watch the little folks, smaller than ants, going about their business at the concierge stand, at the front desk, and over at a bar covered by what looked like a huge glass umbrella. A jazz trio was playing to what seemed to be a convention of some type. Lots of drunken noise coming from below.

"See, this Portman was kind of a nut," Fisher said. "He wanted to design a brand-new centerpiece to downtown. So he did the AmericasMart, Peachtree Center, and this place. All this artsy-fartsy open-air design with ferns and palms. He said architecture is something you don't live with but live in. Or something like that. It was his idea to pull elevators out of hidden shafts. Said he got tired of watching folks push buttons and only being able to stare at their shoes."

"Ain't that something," Sylvia said. "Now, are we going to talk about Russians or are we just going to dance about the architecture?"

Fisher smiled and ran a hand over his loose black strands of hair. "Well," he said. "They're all around you. Russians tend to stay at the Hyatt but eat across the street at the Hilton. That place is a knockoff of Portman's work. Same atrium, glass elevators, and all that. Not as harmonious, in my personal opinion. But they do have the finest Russian restaurant outside New York. Nikolai's Roof. Ever had caviar?"

"Russians?" she asked. "Where?"

"Don't stare," Fisher said. "And don't look for furry caps or heavy boots. You see those two gentlemen sitting across from each other by the fountain? A grouping of four leather chairs with only two occupied?"

Sylvia spotted the two men but couldn't see their faces, only the tops of their heads. They looked to be white, clean-shaven, both wearing business suits and of middle age. Like everyone else in the lobby. How the hell had Fisher made them out to be Russians?

"Fucking Aleksei Sokolov," Fisher said, resting his elbows on the ledge. "He's officially an executive for Aeroflot. The Russian airline. But in truth he's the number two spy for the KGB in DC. The man across from him is Sergey Shumovich. We call him the Schmoo. You know, like that crazy cartoon blob that can change into all kinds of different shapes? My kids used to watch it on Saturday morning with the fucking *Flintstones*. That's Sergey. He can change into damn near anything. Right now, he's running a tire center out in Sandy Springs. He's like a local unofficial minister of Russian culture and godfather to Russian immigrants. I can't say if he's KGB, but he definitely greets them when they're here. Sokolov notified the State Department on Monday he'd be driving outside his twenty-five-mile radius from DC with his family."

"For what?"

"Same bullshit," Fisher said. "What else? Going to fucking Disney World to see the great mouse. Funny how these Russians can't find an airport with a map. This is all official business. Aleksei is checking in with the locals, catching up on the latest from Dobbins and Lockheed. And on the good folks at Scientific Atlanta, whether they want to admit it or not."

"Goddamn."

"I don't like to take the Lord's name in vain," Fisher said. "Unless you really mean it."

"Oh, I mean it, sir."

Sylvia felt pissed off and humbled at the same time. She'd always been so good at seeing the details, knowing when there was something she'd missed. So much of growing up back in Grabtown, being a Black woman, had been knowing the unsaid. The facial gestures, the body language. Folks almost never talked straight, and she got real good at reading between the lines. But Fisher was shooting at her straight while her own supervisor had kept her on the grind of doing interviews and figuring things out on her own. Either he was testing her or didn't think she was qualified to know everything yet.

"Let's all go to the lobby," Fisher said, offering his arm. "Shall we? Time to meet the neighbors."

"You're just gonna walk up to those Russians and say hello?"

"No," Fisher said. "*We* are going up to those damn Russians and saying hello. Didn't they teach you about a bump and a smile at the academy? Or I do have to teach all you rookies myself?"

"I know a bump and a smile," Sylvia said. "Let 'em know we're watching."

"Exactly."

They took the great glass elevator down to the lobby, the whir of it, the speed, making Sylvia feel like she'd left her stomach back on the seventeenth floor. She took a deep breath and watched as the small people grew larger, until it felt like a giant parachute had unfurled to glide them safely down to the earth.

Before the elevator doors opened, Fisher turned to Sylvia and said, "Jenny Buckner wasn't just Keyes's secretary. She was a civilian on our payroll. She came to us and volunteered. I was her point person. And with me retiring, you were about to take my place."

"Why didn't Sullivan tell me?"

"Because he wanted you to ask," Fisher said. "That's why she had your card. She'd been right under Keyes's nose without him knowing. Meanwhile we had her pushing off a ton of horseshit intel to the Russians. We think that's what got her killed."

The elevator door slid open with a ding and Sylvia followed the older man out into the lobby. As they crossed the atrium, one of the Russians turned, recognizing Fisher, and stood.

"Aleksei," Fisher said. "What are the chances of seeing you here? Off to EPCOT again?"

22

LISICA

Okay. Lisica could admit it. Mistakes were made. The boy and the man, the writer of paperback adventures, had become troublesome. And the Black man who wore the dress and the wigs had gotten too close. At least now Control had confirmed the man, the one called Hotchner, would no longer be a problem, and that Lisica could get back to what mattered—finding what Jenny Buckner had taken.

Without access to the Vault, Lisica would have to break into the next best thing, Dr. Keyes's mythical glass house. A rumored wonder of technology and capitalism, unlisted and unknown to most. The house hidden in a forest like something from *Aesop's*. A rumor, maybe even a little fanciful to some, but now Lisica knew it was all true. A four-story house made of nothing but windows located down a twisty, narrow road and situated among the tall, dark pines.

Lisica had whores—*oh, what a horrible word but the only one that came to mind*—for such purposes. And tonight, as Lisica waited in the tall, dark trees, the professional woman appeared and soon found the three hundred dollars under the windshield wipers of her Toyota. They had never met and never would meet, but the woman would've poured the special bottle of Johnnie Walker once she'd gotten Keyes home, an easily ridiculous pickup from a bar for sad, lonely men called Johnny's Hideaway. Such awkward disco dancing and groping in the shadows Lisica had never seen. Not even on a Friday night outside the Vilnius station in Minsk.

Control had known about Dr. Keyes's proclivities for some time and finally put the plan in motion tonight.

As the prostitute's car drove away, Lisica found the front door open, no need for a security code or worry of the cameras. Still, precautions were taken with black clothing and a ski mask, Lisica not feeling secure until coming upon Dr. Keyes, vulnerable and naked, snoring soundly in a strange round bed. On the same floor, the furniture faced a blank projection television and a tower of stereo components, a broad equalizer floating up and down to the sounds of smooth jazz. Lisica saw an empty whiskey tumbler and a wineglass on an enormous coffee table.

Two speakers as tall as a grown man played cloying music until Lisica turned off the radio and reached into a pocket for a cassette of Phil Collins's latest, *No Jacket Required*. The cassette player door snicked closed, and Lisica was finally able to pull up the mask and breathe, wandering the glass house to joyous "Sussudio."

Lisica checked the Rolex. The chloral hydrate would wear off in two hours. There was much work to do until then, and not a piece of lint could be out of place. Dr. Keyes had been drunk, gone home with a loose woman, and woken up naked hours later. A good time had by all, as the Americans might say. Lisica went back to where Dr. Keyes slept in disgrace and removed the man's socks and pulled the silk sheets over his flaccid *struchok*.

Lisica danced to Phil Collins as rugs were pulled back from nail studs, drawers dismantled and reassembled, cabinets opened, and paintings and framed prints pulled from walls. A few dull files were found, blueprints for a new building, and Lisica snapped pictures with the mini camera.

As the search continued, Lisica started to wonder what "Sussudio" meant. Was it some kind of English slang, the song about a woman who doesn't even know Collins's name? But Collins thinks he must have her with his great lust. So elusive. So secret. Like Jenny Buckner. Full of lies and deceit until her last gasping breath. *Ot sud'by ne ubezhish.* "One can't run from fate."

Soon the cassette was over, and Lisica flipped it to the B-side, now going to the top floor of the glass house, another small sitting area with white leather furniture and a large circular mirror, a kitchen, and a railed patio that looked out over the tops of the skinny pines. Moonlight and a carpet of brown pine needles. Lisica would listen to *No Jacket Required* twice, all the way through, and then it would be time to leave. But when "Don't Lose My Number" played downstairs for the second time, Lisica knew there was nothing of value. Dr. Keyes had kept a clean house. *A clean home for an unclean mind*, as Lisica's instructor would've said.

Lisica left Dr. Keyes and the house as found, a great glowing box deep in the woods, following the ancient creek that wandered down the meandering hill from a giant white church on Peachtree Road and a lone Amoco station. Only one of four battered pay phones worked, and Lisica rang the line five times and then hung up.

The phone soon sputtered to life with a weak ring. Lisica picked up the receiver.

"Sussudio," Lisica said, and quickly hung up before heading to the pickup point.

23

HOTCH

"Have you killed Hitler yet?" George said, yelling from the bar to the back booth, where Hotch sat among scribbled yellow legal pads and empty martini glasses. A Tiffany-style pendant lamp advertising Coca-Cola hung overhead. George Najour continued to polish the scarred and cigarette-scorched top of his wooden bar.

"Working on it," Hotch said. "Give me a break. Christ."

The whole Hitler thing had become a big joke in the last week after Jackie happened to mention something about Hotch having writer's block about killing the son of a bitch. It wasn't that Hotch had writer's block; it was that he'd been so preoccupied helping the kid, he'd barely had time to work on his damn book between bookstore shifts. Who cares about killing fucking Adolf Hitler forty years late when you had some KGB kook tooling around Marietta in his Porsche. Killing women and passing off intel right outside the gates of Dobbins. *Holy shit.*

George's Bar was dim and mostly empty fifteen minutes before closing time. Hotch had been there since happy hour, trying to be responsible and pace himself with only one gin martini on the hour. Every hour. Sometimes it helped with the creative flow, sliding into the thought process and time traveling back to 1944. But goddamn it, all he could think about was that big galoot Gary Fucking Powers, his sour breath, and Peter's pretty but naïve mother, Connie, falling for the muscles, the chrome, and the cowboy boots. If they could just find something on the son of a bitch, maybe he could hand it over to Fred Willard and get a piece in the *AJC*. Or call up his old buddy Wes Sarginson at 11Alive and hand off the proof live and on camera! *Top story tonight. Suburban mayhem! Soviets running amuck!*

Amuck. Christ, Hotch hated that word. *Amuck.* So corny.

All week, Hotch had been reading the morning and afternoon paper for anything in the City section about that dead woman Jenny Buckner. So far, there'd only been the first story about that unlucky son of a bitch and his dog discovering the body along the Chattahoochee. What a tragedy. Buckner was a quiet, single woman barely known at her apartment complex.

"Where's Jackie?" George asked.

"What do you mean, where's Jackie?" Hotch said. "He's working like always. Double shift at Illusions."

"Eartha Kitt?"

"Still on Tina Turner," Hotch said. "I think Tina works with Jackie's legs. He also invested two hundred bucks in a new wig. He talks to the thing like it's his pet. Cooing while he holds it and combs through the spiky blond hair. You should hear him do 'Private Dancer.' It would truly break your heart."

"Why don't you go?" George said, dipping some pint glasses into the sudsy sink. "Check out the show?"

"I've seen his act," Hotch said, lighting up a Pall Mall. "He's good. But Illusions ain't exactly my scene."

"During the war, I got stuck on this island for six months," George said. "Some of the guys put on a show with grass skirts and coconut bras and all that mess. No harm in it."

"How about one for the road?"

"I think you're good, Hotch," George said, putting up the gin and vermouth for the night. The tinkling of the bottles sounding like the closing door of Edmond Dantès's cell. "I tell you what. You kill Hitler and the next one's on me."

"Kill Hitler?" Hotch said. "I'm doing better with my liver."

Hotch scooted out of the booth, tucked the scattered notebooks and pens into his old leather satchel, along with *Jane's Airships* and two dog-eared Cornelius Ryan books he'd been reading. The truth was he'd been doing more reading than writing, the rabbit hole of World War II, those heroes of his youth, so damn fascinating. A few of the older boys he'd known at the orphan homes in North Carolina had joined up. One of them had been blown up in the Battle of the Bulge and the other got shipped out to the Pacific and wrote sappy postcards to Hotch's sister. He'd sent her seashell necklaces he'd made in the Philippines, waiting to attack the Japs on the next island. Hotch never knew what happened to the kid. Or the necklaces. What the hell was his name? Johnny? Jim? Sam?

Hotch stood and walked over to the bar, reached into his pocket, and counted out what he thought he owed. He laid down the cash and George looked down, rifled through the bills, and only took half. "You sure you can find your way home?"

"That, my good man, is a question for the ages."

Hotch made it to the front door, sliding into the leather trench coat he'd hung on the rack, and stepped out into the brisk cold of Highland Avenue. He lit up another Pall Mall and started the crooked walk home, along the old storefronts that used to be drug and hardware stores and now had turned into bars and restaurants, down toward the turn to his apartment in Orme Park. The night seemed even colder than usual and he lifted the collar on the coat. He had his head down, still deep in thought about Gary Powers and the nonsense Peter had told him about being able to get into Scientific Atlanta on his own. He'd told the kid that it was a terrible idea, too fucking dangerous, and that he wanted no part of it. No aiding and abetting a crazy minor. He told Peter to keep an eye on his mom, ask her lots of questions, and watch his back for that son of a bitch Gary Powers. Hotch had given him the phone numbers to his apartment, the front desk at the library, the bookstore, and most important, the pay phone at George's just behind his favorite booth. *If the shit hits the fan, Hotch and Jackie will haul ass to you.*

Dry leaves scattered at Hotch's feet as he walked along, whistling the Big Bopper's "Chantilly Lace." Memories of being deep into a foxhole along the 38th Parallel with only a tin of Vienna sausages and a pack of smokes. A MARTA bus passed, blowing diesel fumes in his face. Hotch kept walking, keeping his eye on the steeple of the Church of Our Saviour, the light shining down from the stained glass and onto the opening arms of Jesus like a nautical beacon. Hotch was almost to where he'd cross Highland when he heard a car start. He glanced back to see the headlights turn on and the car pull out onto the street.

Hotch paid it little mind until the damn car sideswiped him, the sideview mirror knocking him flat on his ass. Already feeling unsteady, he took a moment to get to his feet and brush himself off. Goddamn it, he'd broken his cigarette in half. Hotch shook his head, tossed it, and reached into his coat for another just in time to see the car stop in the middle of Highland. Hotch didn't know much about cars but instantly recognized the boxy shape of an Audi, or maybe a Volvo, make a hard U-turn and speed right back toward him. The gin hadn't pickled his brain enough that he believed the bastard was coming back to apologize. This was it. This was fucking cowboy Gary Powers returning to skin his damn ass.

Hotch clutched his satchel and ran behind several cars parked along Highland to duck down behind some trash cans. The Audi—yes, it was an Audi, black or maybe gray—slowed down and then passed by the old bungalows. The car stopped again, and Hotch heard two doors pop open. Hotch watched as another MARTA bus came barreling down Highland and took the opportunity to sprint across at the last minute, the bus nearly flattening him. He was out of breath and tripping across the lawn of the Church of Our Saviour, running to the big front doors and trying to open them, only rattling the chains inside. "Christ Almighty," Hotch said, more of a plea than a curse as he ran away. The boys in the Audi—*who's fooling who?*—Gary and his Russian goons, had turned down the side street after him. Hotch kept to the shadows and the shrubs around the church. He could see the Audi slow; someone with a fucking flashlight shone a beam into the hedges and up into the porches of the bungalows along the neighborhood street. The church parking lot was empty, the next house too far away and surrounded by a chain-link fence. Somewhere a dog was barking its head off. He spotted the dirty hulking shape of a city dumpster. *Would the indignity never end?* Hotch suddenly recalled chapter ten of *Save Hell for Tomorrow* when Lilli and Francois had to hide themselves in an ox cart filled with manure to escape from the Gestapo. The scene was like a hellscape of the senses, Lilli wanting to scream while *being suffocated under the dung, Nazi pitchforks stabbing all around her.*

Okay. A dumpster would do. Hotch ran for it and performed an inexpert leap into the open lid and down into the wet trash bags smelling of sour milk and rotting food. *Just lovely.* Hotch burrowed deep into the plastic bags, not being able to catch his damn breath. If he could just get through this, just two more minutes, without his wheezing alerting the commies, he'd quit smoking forever. Here he was in a church dumpster, and that promise had to damn well mean something.

His wheezing was awful. Hotch didn't think he'd actually sprinted since basic training down in Biloxi. *Why on earth would a grown man need to run that fast?*

Hotch heard the car, voices. The sound of shoes on asphalt. Just like Lilli in the dung. But he could stand the smell of wet plastic, the decaying meat, what he hoped was a mushy old banana in his hand. His paranoia steadied into resolve as he heard a man speaking Russian. Hotch listened to him cursing. A flashlight shone into the dumpster and Hotch could see the narrow beams of light through the wet black bags and hear more Russian cursing before the dumpster lid closed with a thud.

Were they going to lock him inside? Maybe shoot into the dumpster like he'd mapped out for Lilli in chapter thirty-one in the quaint German village Obersalzberg?

Hotch placed his hand over his mouth. He waited. His breathing reminded him of goddamn Secretariat on the final stretch of Churchill Downs. Just a minute. Just another minute.

Then the Audi motor revved and tires squealed. As Hotch tried to stand, he felt a sharp pain in his ankle. *Goddamn it.* If these boys were after him, that would sure as hell lead them back to Peter. And without Hotch around, that kid would be in real trouble.

Hotch gritted his teeth, pushed open the lid, tossed his satchel out of the dumpster, and lifted himself up and out.

24

PETER

It had been the most incredible night of his life. He'd left Kicks with Ana at nearly midnight, leaving Scott to ride back with Brenda Yee and her cousin, the delivery guy from China Palace. Ana was a year older and had been given a white Volkswagen Rabbit for her sweet sixteen, a convertible that felt exciting and free as they roamed back over the river and around a few subdivisions. Her bobbed blond hair whipped across her face as she shifted gears and worked the radio, punching in Wham! and "Everything She Wants." Peter wasn't really into Wham!, their whole act seemed totally lame, but he was having such a good time that he didn't care. It felt like he'd finally broken free, out of the house, away from Connie and Gary, being driven around by the most beautiful girl he'd ever seen.

Every so often Ana would cut her eyes over at him and smile. She had very wide-set, exotic eyes and perfect bow lips. Her red sweater was big and baggy with a wide neck that would sometimes fall off her shoulder as she shifted gears. This girl was headed somewhere fast, and Peter didn't need to know where. Only that he was with her. He just smiled, arm hung over the car door, cold wind rippling his hair and cutting through his jean jacket.

They hadn't really spoken since leaving Kicks. Finally idling at a stoplight, she turned to him and asked, "How old are you?"

"Sixteen," Peter said, lying.

"Do you have a car?"

"Sure," he said. "A 911 Carrera."

"Bullshit," Ana said. "You mean Gary's car?"

Peter laughed. "Yeah," he said. "But I can borrow it whenever I like."

Ana parked out front of Sparkles skating rink, long since closed, the glittering white lights now cold and dark and the lot empty. Ana shut off the engine and reached over to Peter. His breath caught in his throat, thinking she was about to kiss him, but instead she opened the glove compartment and pulled out a pint bottle of Bacardi. "The only way to get through a night at Kicks is to get shit-faced."

"Totally."

"And after all we've been through," she said, unscrewing the cap and taking a swig. "With fucking Gary."

"Tell me about it."

Peter had so many questions about who Ana was, where she went to school, and what she knew about Gary. But he couldn't even seem to form the right words. It was like his stupid brain had shut off as the parking lot lights shone on Ana's bare shoulder. Her mouth wet from the rum.

"How come I've never seen you at school?"

She shrugged and passed the rum to Peter. He'd never had a drink in his life. Actually, that wasn't true. He'd once tried a little bit of his mom's vodka and replaced it with water. He'd been reading Ian Fleming the summer before last, and Fleming made cold vodka sound like the best thing in the world. But it was actually terrible.

He ended up mixing it with Minute Maid Lemonade and then passed out while watching *Punky Brewster* after a football game. His mom out with the luxury car salesman from Buckhead who smelled like boiled peanuts.

"It was my mom's idea that he open up that gym," Ana said. "Before that, he'd been selling ladies' shoes at the Rich's at Perimeter. That's where she met him, the hunky shoe salesman complimenting my mother on her crazy-big feet. He told her she should wear open-toed shoes more often."

"Gross."

"Right?"

"I think he's worse than that," Peter said, kind of blurting it out. "I think he's a Soviet plant."

Ana laughed and spit out a little rum. She nearly choked as she wiped her face. The radio was playing soft and low, "Careless Whisper," the parking lot cold and quiet. Peter wished he'd never said something to this girl that sounded so damn crazy out loud. Now she'd know he was just a stupid kid.

"His mother is German," she said. "I met her. Listen, I had to call Gary 'Dad' for nearly a year. My mom made me buy him some crap from the Sharper Image last Christmas. A revolving tie rack. He doesn't even wear ties. Only jogging suits."

"I don't even know who he is."

"Why do you think he's a spy?"

And Peter went into the whole thing about his accent, the Soviet fight music, the gun, the computer sounds on cassette. And finding the spy radio that Gary swore up and down was actually just a biofeedback machine to strap to his nuts or whatever while he was working out. Not to mention the dead woman at Scientific Atlanta and how his mom had been interviewed by the goddamn FBI.

"You know that's crazy?"

"Some people believe me."

"Like who?"

"Respected journalists."

Her blue eyes widened. "You know journalists?"

"Well, I know a guy who used to be a journalist," Peter said. "Now he writes adventure books. You ever heard of *Death of a Debutante*? Book two in the Bud and Brutus series?"

Ana didn't seem to be listening, looking far out into the empty parking lot. After a few moments, she glanced over at Peter and he realized he'd been holding the rum. Embarrassed, he tilted the rum to his lips and took the tiniest of sips.

"You don't like it?"

"I prefer vodka."

"Vodka," she said. "Right."

She reached up and hit the flip on the cassette and then pressed rewind. Back to more Wham! "Forget about Gary," she said. "It's not your mom's fault. Apparently, he can screw like a jackrabbit. Sorry, but girls hear things. I had to put on earmuffs at night. But he'll be gone before you know it. He's totally gross and totally annoying. Just hang in there. The more you complain about him to your mom, the more she'll hold on to him. That's what happened to me. He's just a gross horndog."

"What if he stays?"

Ana shrugged. Peter really wanted to lean over and kiss her mouth and shoulder. His heart beating so damn fast. Ana finally turned to Peter, leaning into his ear and whispering, "That's why you have me now, silly. Forget about all that crap."

Her breath was hot and moist in his ear, and he unconsciously raised his shoulders as the hair stood up on his neck. He started to giggle—a really uncool response—as Ana touched his chin, turned his face toward hers, and kissed him hard on the mouth. *I don't want your freedom.* He heard the words so strong. The world seemed to freeze while they made out in the little white Rabbit in the Sparkles parking lot at 1 a.m. Like a broken pocket watch that could stop time, something he'd once seen in a movie.

• • •

Now it was late Saturday morning, and he was awake on the couch watching *Kidd Video*, a crazy cartoon about a teenage band caught in a bizarro world called the Flipside. The animation totally sucked, but the music wasn't half bad. The drummer was the little fat dork from *The Brady Brunch*, Cousin Oliver. Peter had, as always, made his own breakfast. Dry Froot Loops smothered in a squirt bottle of Hershey's syrup with a can of warm Coke.

Peter sat in the big chair pulled up a few feet in front of their crappy console RCA. He didn't know quite how to feel this morning.

There was this little pixie character in the cartoon, an obvious rip-off of Tinker Bell that would always appear and help Kidd Video get out of jams. The pixie character wore leotards and leg warmers and a headband, and in a weird way made him think of Ana. Of course, everything since he woke up reminded him of Ana. She'd written her phone number in the palm of his hand and he'd yet to wash it.

Maybe he could see her tonight. Maybe he could see her every night. She had her little convertible and all that freedom and maybe now he didn't need a damn thing from Connie. His mom had yet to wake up from her hard night out partying with Gary.

The wall phone rang in the kitchen and Peter got up to answer. If it was fucking Gary, he'd just hang up. But maybe it was Ana.

"What's up, pillow humper?"

"Hell, Brenda."

"Hope you had fun sucking face last night."

"I'm busy," he said. "What do you want?"

"Oh," she said. "Nothing. Just totally saving your ass from embarrassing yourself again. That girl you left with last night doesn't go to our school."

"How do you know?"

"Because she's not in the yearbook," Brenda said. "And because I'm such a good friend, I made a few calls this morning on your behalf.

Nobody knows a girl named Ana that looks like that. I checked with my friends at Wheeler and Sprayberry, too. I mean, that girl was hot stuff, and nobody knows her? That's weird."

"Wait," Peter said, closing his eyes. "You have friends?"

"Fuck you, dipwad," Brenda said. "Scott said she left you a note in your locker to meet up. How'd she get to a locker in our high school? How does she know you even exist? I mean, let's be honest, Peter, she's a lot out of your league. She looks like a Benetton ad. You still have braces."

"Sounds like you're just jealous."

"Of a pillow humper like you?" Brenda said. "Oh, right. Why don't you come on over and give me some tongue action."

Peter shook his head and hung up the phone. He walked back to the TV, grabbed his empty bowl, and started to refill it when the phone rang again. He reached up to the wall and picked it up, pissed that Brenda was looking into his personal life. Scott probably told her all about his worries about Gary and now Brenda thought he'd gone totally nuts. "You've got to stop it," he said. "Last night is none of your business."

"What happened last night?" Hotch asked. "And where the hell have you been, kid? I've been trying to reach you all morning."

"You have?"

"There's been some trouble," Hotch said. "I'm fine. I'm fine. But I twisted my goddamn ankle and I'm at the hospital. A couple of goddamn Russkis tried to take me out last night as I was whistling home in the moonlight."

"Wait," Peter said. "What?"

"I was walking home from the bar and two Russian freaks in an Audi tried to kill me," Hotch said. "You were right. You were right about everything, kid. That big son of a bitch your mom is seeing wants us to stop asking questions."

"How do you know they were Russian?"

"Because they were speaking fucking Russian," Hotch said.

"Come on. Keep up. Can you get over to Grady? You need to get out of there now. Your house has been compromised."

"I don't know," Peter said. "I met a girl."

Peter was about to explain but had to hang up as Connie walked barefoot into the kitchen in her sad old pink terry-cloth robe. She yawned, very dramatic, stretching her arms to the ceiling, and then walked over to give Peter an unwanted hug. "How's it going, kiddo?" she said. "I got in late last night and didn't want to wake you."

"No shit."

"Come on, Peter," she said. "Watch your language."

She said it half-heartedly, like a mom on a sitcom going through the motions but not really giving a shit. She opened the pantry and took out the can of Maxwell House and went about making her coffee. Peter reached for the chocolate syrup, the bottle making a disgusting slurping sound that made him happy as she winced.

Maybe that's where he really lived, on the set of a sitcom. The wallpaper with old-timey drawings of flowers, baskets full of fruit, silver ladles, and china teacups. The curling linoleum floor, popcorn ceiling, and musty carpet smell from the living room nothing but a video dream.

"Are you okay, Peter?" she said. "Are you sick?"

He shook his head.

"Good," she said. "I called Mrs. Adams and she said it's okay for you to spend the night over there. Tonight's Barry Manilow at the Omni. I'm sorry, but Gary got tickets for my birthday. He's been planning it for months."

"Where was Gary last night?"

"We went to see a movie," she said. "Since when are you the parent?"

"For as long as I can remember," Peter said, slamming the full bowl of cereal mixed with chocolate syrup into the sink. He stormed out of the kitchen and past the gleeful television and out to their broken-down old wooden deck. The deck faced a narrow stretch of woods, separating them from the identical row of houses on the adjacent street. Sometimes he felt he could pass right through the woods, walk into another house, and he'd find a nearly identical situation. Or maybe something much better.

He sunk down into a patio chair and tilted his head up at the tree branches overhead. One of the trees had died, its brown leaves floating down in the wind and adding to the crap on the deck. The old grill they'd had forever covered in a fine layer of green algae, already going back to nature. Peter stayed there for what felt like hours, dozing off and then coming back. He dreamed for a bit about following a rabbit down deep into a hole with lots of locked doors and mystery rooms and then startled awake. He'd been dreaming about chasing a cherry red Porsche up and over a hill and only seeing the back of a man and a woman's head as they sped off and disappeared into thin air.

Peter pushed himself up and walked back into the house. He thought about maybe apologizing, the idea of losing his mother making him feel uneasy. He knocked on her door but could only hear the shower running. When he got back to the kitchen, he wondered if it was too early to call Ana and looked down at his hand to see the ink had smudged and smeared until it was just a blur.

He gritted his teeth and yelled and kicked the cabinets under the sink. Son of a bitch. *Son of a bitch.* Maybe she hadn't been real either. Maybe he was going nuts.

All he knew was that Gary had made a fucking mess of his life. And tonight, he'd be off with his mother dancing to "Copacabana" while Peter was sitting in the basement with Brenda and Scott watching goddamn *Fantasy Island.* "Da' plane! Da' plane!"

Peter walked back to his mom's door and knocked again. He heard the shower.

In the kitchen, he saw her big brown leather purse carelessly slung over a chair. Peter looked back down the hall and then reached into her purse for her wallet and checkbook. The wallet was thick with twenty-dollar bills and Peter took two. He thumbed through her driver's license, Rich's card, Mastercard, and membership to—yuck!—the Muscle Factory. He finally found what he was searching for, deep within the bottomless purse along with a clown car of junk—keys, tissues, Virginia Slims, lipstick (*Moisture Whip!*), compact—a security badge on a lanyard for Scientific Atlanta. On the back a magnetic strip for security entry.

Peter stuffed the bills and the badge down into his jeans, slipped on his Nikes, and headed out to his PK Ripper and over to Scott's.

Somehow, someway, he'd get out to Lawrenceville to break into those offices and find out exactly what the hell everyone was so excited about.

25

DAN

Dimitri Kostov and his ape Zub had asked the impossible. They wanted everything the FBI had on Vitaly Yurchenko since the defection and everything they had on this tech company in Atlanta contracted with the CIA. He seriously doubted Vitaly's proposed visit to Atlanta was about a romantic getaway. But if this would facilitate an end to this circus, why the hell not. He'd argued with the Russians that he wasn't in the damn CIA, but they'd insisted, Kostov standing up at the credits of *Mackenna's Gold* and pointing to his watch. *Geneva*, he said. *We must have our information before the summit. Or* . . .

Dan hated dramatics, and Kostov was the master. Dan hadn't slept a wink since their meeting at the embassy, nearly falling asleep on the way home from the FBI annex, when he'd spotted the lateral line of tape on the stop sign near his house, signaling a meet. Dan gathered everything he had so far before this first live drop with the goddamn Russians at a family park just down the road from where he lived with Delores and the kids. The same place he'd practiced drops with Wanda. He'd thought about giving up, going right to the deputy director and explaining how he'd witnessed a murder while trying to proclaim Christ's love to a fallen angel. But everything Dan could think of sounded so stupid and ended in humiliation. He figured it was best to do as these bastards said for now. After this dog-and-pony show in Geneva with Reagan and Gorbachev, it would all be over.

Dan picked up Wanda at her new apartment the morning of the drop, off Georgia Avenue in a big brick complex on Blair Road. Not the best address. He'd already had a pot of coffee at home but thoughtfully stopped off for an Egg McMuffin for Wanda. Wanda waited for him at the curb (Dan always warned her about getting mugged while alone) in the most wonderful yet outrageous gym outfit. She had on a satin blue scoop-neck leotard with a gray Redskins midriff underneath and gray tights.

"You'll have to change."

"Why?" Wanda said, wide-eyed and smiling. "I think I look cute."

"You look like that goddamn commie Jane Fonda."

"Jane Fonda is a communist?"

"Come on," Dan said, unlocking the door to the Citation. "Get in."

Dan had on a brown Adidas tracksuit zipped up to the neck and a new pair of New Balance shoes that were supposed to help with his high arches. If he needed to run, he could do it. In the console between them was the yellow waterproof Walkman Dan had brought with him. The Walkman had been empty when the Russians gave it to him. But last night, he'd unscrewed it and stuffed in negatives with pictures of the files on Scientific Atlanta and two pages he'd typed on Yurchenko. He decided to photograph his notes and burn the pages just in case he got caught and his colleagues tried to match his printer with the message about Vitaly's new safe house and their latest conversations.

"Neat," Wanda said, reaching for the Walkman, putting on the headset and trying to get it to work.

Dan let her try to play it for a while until she slammed it down and said the gosh-dang thing was broken.

"Wear it while you run," Dan said. "You can run in that getup. Can't you?"

"I saw Kelly LeBrock wearing it in *People* magazine and bought it for one of my acts," she said. "I do an amazing number to Oingo Boingo. Oh, should I have worn a bra?"

Dan didn't answer nor did he ask exactly what was an Oingo Boingo. He circled back in the direction he'd come that morning and passed along the warm McDonald's bag and coffee. Four sugars with extra cream.

"Aren't you the gentleman."

Dan drove, the early morning light hard in his eyes. He reached for his clip-on dark lenses that went over his prescription glasses. The morning news was on, a story about that fruitcake in Nicaragua, Daniel Ortega, saying President Reagan's speech to the United Nations was a crock of shit. Reagan had only stated the truth that there were thousands of fucking Soviets and red Cubans stationed in Nicaragua. Ortega called them all medical personnel and . . .

Disgusted, Dan turned off the radio. He looked over at Wanda, admiring her shapely legs. "Where we going today, daddy?"

"Something important has come up," Dan said, flipping up the dark frames on his thick glasses. "I want you to listen to me very closely. This is what we've been training for."

. . .

Of course, Dan had given a passing thought about Wanda being a Russian asset. The setup and the execution at the Americana Hotel had truly been textbook. But the idea of Wanda being an agent of the

USSR or even a Russian herself was downright laughable. She was an innocent woman, a good American, caught up in the silly machinations of the two most powerful nations in the world. Dan would share more with her one day, but today it was too much for anybody over the morning news and Egg McMuffins.

Dan had a game plan.

1. Wanda must never acknowledge she knew Dan. Even if caught.
2. Wanda must stick to her story. Just exercising in the park.
3. If she were to be arrested, she'd say she found the Walkman that very morning. And planned to turn it in to local police.
4. If anyone tried to accost her at gunpoint or otherwise, she had to scream her head off. Never let a foreign enemy capture you.

"A foreign enemy?" Wanda said. "Does this have something to do with those two men with the funny accents? The ones that helped us get rid of Larry's body."

"Goddamn it, Wanda."

"I know you told me never to mention it again," Wanda said. "But sometimes I feel bad about what I did to Larry. I didn't mean to kill him. I was just aiming for his pecker and the damn thing jumped up and shot him in the chest."

"When this is all over," Dan said, resting his hand on Wanda's knee, "we may need to go off somewhere together. Leave the country."

"Like where?"

"I don't know," Dan said. "Tahiti. Bora Bora."

"Wow," Wanda said. "I've never been to France."

• • •

Dan could see everything, a curse of his training at Quantico. He could take in 360 degrees, truly feeling he had eyes in the back of his head, of everything at Foxstone Park that perfect autumn day. The leaves fell along the jogging paths and around the little play areas for the kids. The creek rolled over the jagged rocks and under the footbridge, where a middle-aged man in an Irish cap smoked a cigar. *Was he KGB? Was he a cop?* Maybe the FBI was onto him. When he'd gone into the archive to pull the Atlanta files, he didn't care at all for that nitwit Ted Bergen's tone. An archivist didn't need to question a senior agent with Dan's credentials.

Dan watched Wanda as she circled the jogging path for a second time. She wore the counterfeit Walkman headset, not once making eye contact. *Good girl.*

He tried not to think about Delores and the kids being right down the street, huddled in front of the TV to watch the Fightin' Irish. It wasn't that he didn't care for Delores. He still loved her and even found her attractive when she wasn't handing him a massive chore list. *Fix the gutters. Mow the grass. Paint the garage.* Painting the garage had been a bridge too far. It was almost as if she was thinking of something, absolutely anything, to keep him on task and away from her. Her days were filled with parent-teacher conferences, frequent trips to the Safeway for the middling food she made, and her goddamn stupid book club. Right now, they were reading some insufferable feminist tome called *The Handmaid's Tale* that Dan believed was only increasing her hatred of men. That was the thing about Wanda. She was always positive, always glad to see him, and not afraid to let a man step in and be in charge. It took some guts to kill that bastard Larry and then hand over Dan's .357, still quite warm, and allow him to dispense with the matter.

And continue to pay for it. A leaden albatross hung from his neck.

Dan stood a good forty, fifty yards from the footbridge. He watched two joggers pass by, ruling both out as agents. A skinny middle-aged woman in men's workout shorts and a baggy sweatshirt and then a professorial-looking man—did Dan know him from their cul-de-sac Fourth of July party?—jogging in place just off the bridge and checking his watch for time.

"Dan?" the man said as they crossed paths. "I thought you'd be at home watching football."

"Just taking in a little fresh air," Dan said. What the hell was this guy's name? Jimmy? Jack? Frank? He was the manager of the local Chevy dealership. He thought he was real hot shit in the neighborhood, tooling about in a silver Camaro.

"Hope the Skins keep it up tomorrow," the man said. "The Giants won't whip our ass like the Bears did. That one hurt. But if Theismann can just step up, I think he's gonna have his best season ever."

"Theismann," Dan said. "Sure. Right. Thanks."

"Good to see you, Dan," the man said, shaking his hand. "Stop by tomorrow if you can. I'm grilling some brats and icing down some Heineken. Even G-Men need to take a Sunday off."

Dan nodded. The man saluted and started walking away from the bridge.

Dan didn't see the other woman until Wanda's third pass (boy, would she be exhausted). A large, muscular woman in a snow white jogging suit stepped out from the woods, entered the jogging path, and ran straight into Wanda. Wanda toppled to the ground and Dan sprinted toward her, but in the confusion, he watched as the woman in white switched the yellow Walkman for an identical unit. She reached down, helped Wanda to her feet, and apologized. Wanda looked dazed but okay and slowly walked from the bridge toward Dan as the wide-shouldered woman disappeared down the trail. Something so damn familiar about that woman. Dan recognized the stubbled jaw and the thick neck and then knew it had been that big ape Zub in a wig and makeup.

Fifteen minutes later, Dan drove the Citation back to the main entrance of the park and Wanda got into the passenger seat.

"Sorry, daddy," Wanda said. "Some big old heifer knocked me flat on my ass. Never did meet up with that fella I was supposed to see."

Dan didn't answer, looking into his side and rearview mirrors. He was careful to drive just below the speed limit and take his time before heading onto the interstate and back into the city.

Wanda stared straight ahead, futzing around with the Walkman. He could hear some kind of tinny pop music coming from the little headphones.

"Well, I'll be dog," she said. "That big bitch must've jostled something. I can hear the radio just fine now. Coming in loud and clear."

26

SYLVIA

"That took some real balls," Irv Ravetch said. "Going over to Sullivan's house and interrupting his Saturday. *Jesus.* I never really even thought about the guy having a family. I thought he just went back to his crypt or slept upside down from the rafters."

"He's got a family," Sylvia said. "Wife. Three boys. The oldest one was home from Athens for the weekend. They were all eating pancakes and Sullivan was in his robe."

Irv had picked her up in the company car, heading out to Vinings again and Jenny Buckner's apartment. There had been two neighbors they hadn't been able to interview yet. One was a flight attendant for Delta named Maxine Reed. Reed had finally called Irv back and said she'd be in town for the next forty-eight hours.

"Was he pissed?"

"Only that I saw his skinny white legs," Sylvia said. "His wife got me some coffee and we went into his study. I was straight with him.

I told him I didn't understand why he didn't give me access to Jenny Buckner's file. He said it contained some high-level, secret squirrel shit and he wanted to keep me focused on who might've killed her. The part about her having my card was true and made a decent explanation for the locals."

"And the fucking Russians?" Irv said. "Only Russians I ever met in Atlanta were some fellow Jews who run a sandwich shop out on Buford Highway. They make some good sturgeon."

"Sturgeon?"

"Fish."

"How do you eat it?"

"Brined and smoked."

"Only fish I like is deep-fried with a side of hush puppies," Sylvia said. Irv reached up to fiddle with the radio, but she swatted away his hand. She'd already gotten on him twice about letting the dial drift from Casey Kasem's countdown to the damn easy listening. "Sullivan said most of the Russians were just passing through. He admitted some suspected Illegals are living here but nothing definite. But he's pretty sure the Buckner woman's work handing over bad intel was what got her killed."

"All we got to do this week was grill her grieving mother and knock on doors at her apartment," Irv said. "That sucked. The mother was the worst. Sitting there for four hours while she planned for the funeral. The old man off with his second wife and she got stuck with picking out dresses to bury Jenny in. I felt like a creep asking the poor woman about her daughter's personal life."

"I know she'd been seeing Coleman Vaughn."

"The security guy?" Irv said. "But he's Black."

"Damn, Irv," she said. "You are one hell of an investigator."

"I don't mean nothing by it," Irv said. "But you know how these Southern people are. They aren't into mixing."

"What about you?" Sylvia said. "Would you date a Black woman?"

"Is she Jewish?" Irv asked. "If not, my mother would kill me."

• • •

Jenny Buckner had lived in a pleasant two-bedroom apartment at a complex in Vinings called the Woods. Heated pools, Jacuzzi, and a big clubhouse situated in a dense forest with mountain views all the way to downtown. Sylvia had been out there four times already. She knew the woman didn't like to cook. Her refrigerator was nearly empty except for cans of Fresca and a few containers of Yoplait. Most of the clothes in her closet were basic office attire, long skirts and blazers, bright satin tops, and lots and lots of scarfs. Jenny did not keep a diary. Neither Sylvia nor the locals could locate a daybook and she figured the folks at Scientific Atlanta had it. They only found old letters from her father, a reformed drunk who begged for forgiveness after he'd found Jesus.

Irv stepped up and knocked on the door. Maxine Reed, a buxom frosted blonde, opened the door and invited them in. *Poor Jenny. Poor Jenny. The sweetest woman you'd ever meet.*

She stepped out into the hallway, some kind of party going on inside.

"I'd invite you both in," Maxine said, "but I'm having a little gathering."

"Would you like us to come back later?" Sylvia asked.

"This is fine," Maxine said. "I have a side job selling unmentionables in my downtime."

Irv's mouth hung open. Sylvia turned to him and said, "That's underwear, Irv."

"I know what unmentionables are."

Maxine had on a blue-and-white sailor's top and high-waisted pleated jeans, her makeup damn near perfect with frosted eyeshadow and bright red lipstick. Her nails long and an even deeper red. As she spoke, she had a nervous tic of clicking her nails together like castanets.

"If you're interested," Maxine said, "you're welcome to come on in. Are either of you married?"

They both shook their heads.

"Good," Maxine said. "Some of this stuff is a little racy. Things you can't find in stores. I sell it for an outfit called Undercover Wear. Sounds like something both of you might appreciate. I have some really hot models today. The Pleasure Seeker, Heat Wave, Bare Essence—that's basically just string—and some ass-less panties we call Bottoms Up."

"What's this, like Amway?" Irv asked.

"Or Tupperware," Maxine said. "Flying around the country and talking to women, you'd be surprised how many don't know how to find good lingerie. I mean, all they know is a slip like their grandmothers wore or maybe a Playtex bra sold by big ole Jane Russell."

Irv started to speak. Sylvia held up her hand.

"I'll get right to it, Miss Reed," Sylvia said. "We're looking for any information you can give us on Jenny Buckner. Did you know her well?"

"I can't say I knew her at all," she said. "I passed her in the hall. I gave her an Undercover Wear catalog one day. She didn't seem that interested but later ordered a whole bunch of stuff. What size are you, Miss Weaver? If you don't mind me asking."

"Have you ever heard of a company called Scientific Atlanta?"

"The people who make the cable boxes?" Maxine said. "Sure. I pay for all that crap. HBO, Showtime, Cinemax. But I'm never here. I hear *The Slugger's Wife* is coming on soon. They shot the damn thing right here in Atlanta. Some of my girlfriends were extras in the nightclub scenes."

"Jenny Buckner worked for Scientific Atlanta," Irv said.

"Ever meet any of her friends?" Sylvia asked. "Anyone else in the apartments Jenny was friendly with?"

Maxine shook her head. She clicked her nails together some more, thinking on it. It reminded Sylvia of that time in college when she'd seen a cut-rate version of *Carmen*. That bullfighter song and that crazy Spanish woman who drove them all wild.

"Did you hear anything odd coming from her apartment?" Irv asked. "Maybe as you passed by in the hall? Or see anyone you didn't recognize coming and going?"

Lots of laughs and screams came from inside Maxine's apartment. Another woman stepped into the hall, short and squat with frizzy brown hair and massive tortoiseshell glasses.

"They just opened up the men's stuff," the woman said. "I showed them how the front flap worked. Oh, hello. Is there something a-matter?"

Maxine introduced them both as the police, asking questions about Jenny Buckner. The short woman had on a starched white shirt clasped with an old-fashioned brooch, a long blue jacket over a pair of matching blue pants. "That's so awful," she said. "Oh, my God. I hope you catch the guy who did it."

"Did you know her?"

"I met her once," the woman said. "When I was over visiting Maxine. I didn't even know her name until Maxine told me what had happened. Looked like she'd had a long night. It was very late."

Sylvia caught a little glance between the woman and Maxine. Maxine was either trying to hide something or just get them gone and back to their peek-a-boo panty party.

Sylvia nodded to Irv, and Irv stepped between the new woman and Maxine. He asked her if she wouldn't mind getting him a catalog for Undercover Wear. Maxine grinned and disappeared into the apartment. More squeals of delight. Damn, sometimes women got on Sylvia's nerves.

"Was she with anyone?"

The woman shook her head. "Not anyone that I saw."

"What is your name, miss?"

"Wendy Jo Johnson," she said. "I'm not in trouble or anything?"

"Not at all," Sylvia said. "You didn't see anyone? Does that mean she was with someone?"

"She was being dropped off," Wendy Jo said. "Or at least that's what it looked like. It was dark and I just noticed how pretty she was. She had on a beautiful purple satin dress, cut all the way up her thigh. I noticed her stiletto heels as she stepped out of a car."

Sylvia nodded. "And what kind of car?"

"Oh, I remember that," Wendy Jo said. "That's what made me turn around. It was a damn convertible Porsche."

"But you didn't see the driver?"

She shook her head. Maxine Reed popped back into the hall, proudly handing off an underwear catalog to Irv. Irv smiled at her, gave her his card, and made a little small talk.

"Wendy Jo?" Maxine said.

"I'm sure you didn't see a license tag?" Sylvia asked.

Wendy Jo shook her head. "I just remember the car looked brand new and was a dark red color. Like ruby red or maroon. The top was up, but it was a soft top. Windows were down and I could smell a cigar."

"How'd you know it was a cigar?"

"My daddy smoked them," Wendy Jo said. "I just love to smell 'em."

Sylvia handed off her cards to the women and walked back to the elevator with Irv. As they waited, she looked out the hall window to spot a massive blue Cadillac pull into the parking lot. A large Black woman behind the wheel and a short, fat man crawling from the passenger seat. It appeared he was having some trouble walking.

"So she liked rich guys," Irv said.

"Newish Porsche convertible," Sylvia said. "Ragtop. Dark red. How many of those do you think are in the Atlanta area?"

"I dunno," Irv said. "Hundreds?"

"You still friendly with that woman at the DMV?" Sylvia said. "I know it's the weekend. But this can't wait."

27

HOTCH

Jackie knew how to break in. Hotch didn't ask, only watched as he did his thing with a little lockpick kit he pulled from his blue suede purse. This might be a stretch, coming out to the dead woman's apartment, breaking and entering and potentially getting arrested. But for the first time in a long while, Hotch was onto something big. Even if the kid's interest had fallen off, saying something about meeting a girl before hanging up on him earlier, Hotch had to know what the hell was going on. And if he got a book idea from it, so much the better.

"Voilà," Jackie said, pushing open the door.

"Only doubted you for a second."

They pushed inside Jenny Buckner's apartment, creeping about and turning on a few brass lamps. Jackie standing back and taking in the living room. "Goddamn, that woman sure loved pink."

The carpet, the furniture, the walls were all different shades of pink. Soft pink. Hot pink. Bubblegum. Fuchsia. Some wicker and lots of brass. Jenny Buckner also kept a couple of little palm trees and potted pothos. Hotch was a plant man. He couldn't seem to keep a job or a girlfriend but give him a fern and it would flourish.

"Like being inside a pussy," Jackie said.

"What do you know about pussy?"

"Hell, I was straight once," Jackie said. "I had so much pussy I got sick and tired of it."

The Buckner woman had a trio of those Patrick Nagel prints, porcelain ladies with jet black hair and full red lips. He'd read a profile of the artist in the *Times* last year; the poor guy died in his thirties and never lived to make a dime. "Nagel," Hotch said. "Guy had a heart attack after being in a fucking aerobathon."

"A what?"

"Like a marathon, only you do aerobics."

"I didn't know you were an art lover, Hotch," Jackie said. "You with your velvet Elvis and those dogs playing poker."

"Ever hear of irony?"

Jackie glared at him, threw his purse over his shoulder, and placed a hand on his hip.

"Guess you have," Hotch said. "Okay. You take the bedroom, and I'll go through the living room and kitchen."

"And what if we get caught?"

"We won't get caught," Hotch said. "But if we do, I'll blame it all on you. I'll say I was minding my own business when this big colored guy carjacked me and took me on a panty raid."

Jackie gave Hotch the finger and sauntered back to the bedroom. Hotch looked around the kitchen, not knowing where to start. The most he knew about rummaging through a victim's house was shit he'd seen on *Columbo* or *Streets of San Francisco*. He'd once been a decent newspaperman but couldn't recall a single time he'd had to break in anywhere. But desperate times called for true desperation.

"Did you call me colored?" Jackie asked from the other room. "What the damn hell?"

The kitchen didn't take long. The refrigerator held a few cans of Fresca and cartons of yogurt. She kept the bare minimum of cutlery and china, a few mismatched coffee cups. One emblazoned with the Scientific Atlanta logo. The globe adorned with a rabbit ear antenna. Hotch thought it too simplistic. He might've gone with Prometheus bringing forth fire.

Hotch hobbled back into the living room, where he spotted one of those faux-wood television/stereo cabinets with glass doors and a few compartments for books and assorted crap. A few more plants and a stack of ragged paperbacks. Hotchner couldn't help but read through the spines and thumb through each one looking for a clue. Jackie Collins, Belva Plain, Jeffrey Archer, and fucking Susan Sontag. *Under the Sign of Saturn.* His first wife loved that book. Hotch found Sontag's essays completely insufferable. And then . . . Eureka.

A tattered UK paperback of *And Quiet Flows the Don* by Mikhail Sholokhov. Hotch pulled it from the stack and looked through the pages, struck by lots of passages underlined in blue ink. *Life scatters into innumerable streams. It is difficult to foresee which it will take in its treacherous and winding course.* Had Jenny Buckner been a closet Russian lit fan or had someone given it to her?

Hotch was about to call Jackie when Jackie called for him.

"This woman's got more lacy drawers than Pia Zadora."

"Don't steal any."

"No joke," Jackie said.

"I found a book," Hotch said. "Something really odd."

"Me knee-deep in satin panties and you sniffing around ten-cent paperbacks."

"It's Russian."

"So what?"

"Like really fucking Russian," Hotch said. "Not Dostoyevsky or *Zhivago*. But like official Soviet literature."

"Is that a crime?"

"Maybe not a crime," Hotch said. "But might be a clue."

Hotch walked over to the bank of windows and peered through the vertical blinds out into the parking lot. He saw a tall, skinny white man and a Black woman standing beside a flat gray Chrysler. Definitely government-issue wheels. They appeared to be arguing. The woman pointing up in his direction. Hotch quickly stepped back and closed the blinds. "Okay, Jackie," he said. "Time to go."

"What the fuck is it?" Jackie said. "Just getting to the good stuff. A big ole stack of bills in the nightstand. Got credit card charges. Personal letters and shit. Now, that's what I call a fucking clue, Columbo. So quit sorting those goddamn books. You ain't at Oxford, Too today."

Hotch went back to the window, fingered the blinds, and saw the man and the woman walking back to the apartment entrance. "I wasn't joking," he said. "It's the goddamn cops."

"What about all this shit?" Jackie said, holding up the bills and receipts.

"Stick the papers in your purse," Hotch said. "And for the first time, please act casual."

• • •

They took a back exit, out by the pool and Jacuzzis, and circled back to the DeVille. Hotch drove using his good, right foot while Jackie leafed through the credit card statements and receipts he'd taken from Jenny Buckner's nightstand. Halfway back to Hotch's place, Jackie screamed.

"You break a goddamn nail?"

"This woman just put her sable in storage at Rich's."

"Lots of women have furs," Hotch said. "Wait. Isn't a sable from Siberia or something?"

"You don't get it," Jackie said, top up on the DeVille, wind blowing hard through the cab and making it tough to hear. "The Buckner woman just put her mink *in* storage. You don't put your goddamn fur coat *into* storage in the fall. That's when you take it *out*."

"Maybe it had to be repaired."

"Nope," Jackie said, holding up the ticket. "Says cold storage, baby. Why you think a woman would do something like that?"

"To hide it?"

"To hide that motherfucker," Jackie said. "Damn. Here we go now. Just like Bud and Brutus, we're on the case."

• • •

They made a few phone calls at an Old Hickory House out by the interstate and then headed to the old downtown Rich's. Hotch hadn't been there since meeting Janet at the perfume counter. The downtown Rich's had once been a jewel, an old 1920s building with a big clock facing Broad. Not a lot of folks came downtown anymore, the fucking malls killing business. He knew they still did the big tree at Christmas every year but wondered if they still set up that pig-shaped monorail in the kid's department. The Pink Pig had been a hell of a draw back in the day.

The cold storage was up on the eighth floor and a security guard directed them to a freight elevator. They were met by a harried, gray-headed man in a pin-striped suit with a red corsage. He had a thin mustache, like actors from the thirties, and wore a great deal of gold jewelry. He didn't give his name, but Hotch just thought of him as Mr. Fancy. Jackie handed over the claim ticket to Mr. Fancy and told him there'd been some mistake. "My maid wasn't thinking," Jackie said. "Dumb bitch didn't know what season it was."

"I see," Mr. Fancy said. "We'll still have to bill you for the month."

"Of course," Hotch said.

"Thanks, big daddy," Jackie said. "You sure do spoil me."

Mr. Fancy gave them both a sour look as they walked down a dim hallway to an industrial door sealed with two big-ass locks. The man looked down at the ticket and then back to Jackie. "I will have to see some ID, Ms. Buckner."

"Oh," Jackie said. "I must've left it in the Mercedes. Big daddy, would you be good enough to retrieve it for your sweetie?"

"I would," Hotch said, but pulled up his pant leg. "But I busted my ankle yesterday. Playing golf at the club. I'd be glad to pay for the monthly storage in cash."

Mr. Fancy forced a smile and nodded. "I don't think that will be necessary. Can you at least identify the coat?"

Jackie looked over to Hotch. Hotch raised his eyebrows and grinned.

"You bet, baby," he said. "It's slick sable and it's the damn cat's ass."

Mr. Fancy turned both locks and slid open the massive door. A hard chill greeted them as they entered the endless vault filled with thousands of coats. A labyrinth of mink, sable, and fox. Who knew? Maybe some polecats in there, too. Mr. Fancy walked into the maze; the coats hung from several levels of steel piping. He excused himself again and returned with a stepladder, moving on to a deeper row, Hotch and Jackie losing sight of him, until he returned with a dark brown fur coat laid over his forearm.

"Like I said," Jackie said. "The cat's ass."

The man studied Jackie as he reluctantly opened up the coat and offered it to him.

"I'll just carry it."

"I insist."

Hotch covered his hand with his mouth. Jackie was a 46 long and this coat looked like a women's medium at best. But Jackie did a hell of a job, only allowing the man to fit it over his broad shoulders like a cape, as he cooed and fretted about being so happy to have it back. "Oh, baby," Jackie said. "Mommy sure missed you."

Mr. Fancy stood at the elevators as Hotch paid him the forty bucks. Giving up the forty bucks hurt like hell, but what else were they going to do. Mr. Fancy held the elevator door and complimented Jackie on such a fine coat.

"That's what you get," Jackie said, smiling, "when you fuck like a Super Bowl champ."

The door closed with a snap, and on the first level, Hotch and Jackie made a quick escape to Broad Street, where they'd parked the DeVille.

"Can you even get one arm in there?"

"Woman's dead," he said. "No need to bust her goddamn seams."

Jackie tried anyway, for some kind of comical effect. He looked like a stuffed sausage, not even able to close the coat halfway over his big chest. Jackie patted the sides and did a little turn like a model as he dug into the pockets. "Not jack shit."

He searched the coat pockets for a moment longer but then suddenly stopped. He told Hotch to help him out of the goddamn thing, wriggling free. A few onlookers watched as they stood by the big blue Cadillac. "You feel that?"

"Feel what?"

"Something's in the lining," Jackie said. "I can feel the damn thing in my armpit."

Hotch pulled out an old Case knife, something he'd carried since he was fifteen, and took the coat from Jackie. He set the sable on the Cadillac's hood, found the obstruction, and then traced the lining's seam with the sharp point of the knife. He slid his hand inside and found something flat and plastic.

"Shit," Jackie said as Hotch handed it over to him.

"Looks like a computer disk."

"You got a fucking computer?"

"I've got my old Smith Corona."

"Better find us someone who does," Jackie said. "That Buckner woman went to a lot of trouble to hide this little son of a bitch."

28

PETER

"Are you nuts?" Brenda said. "I can't break into your mom's work computer. Do I look like fucking Matthew Broderick?"

"You have a computer like his," Scott said. "I heard your dad paid over a grand for it."

"Maybe," Brenda said. "But it's not as easy as it looks. You'd have to find me the interface number from Scientific Atlanta. And then I can't guarantee what I'd find. It's probably just boring shit like payroll and hours. They're not going to upload the most sensitive stuff. That's crazy."

Peter and Scott stood behind Brenda's office chair and stared into the monitor for her Commodore 64 complete with brand-new 1660 modem. Brenda was being modest; she'd already set up a nice business of changing grades at their high school. Twenty bucks for every letter. Changing a C to an A would cost you forty. She factored in a certain amount of risk for each job. Not exactly what Mr.

Yee had intended, only wanting to ensure his golden daughter got into the best colleges.

"What are you looking for anyway?" Brenda said.

"No one knows what they really do out there," Peter said. "Even this reporter that Hotch introduced me to said cable boxes and satellites were only part of their business. He says they might do work for the government. Like designing stuff for SDI."

"Strategic Defense Initiative," Scott said. "The Star Wars program. The laser grid over America."

"I know what the stupid Star Wars program is," Brenda said. "My parents get *Time*. What does your mom say?"

"My mom doesn't tell me anything," Peter said. "She called Mrs. Adams without even asking me. She says she doesn't trust me to be home alone anymore. What a crock of shit."

"Watch out, Scott," Brenda said. "And hide your pillows."

"Very funny, Brenda," Scott said. "I guess you don't want to sneak out with us tonight."

Brenda turned around in her swivel chair and crossed her arms over her chest. "I'm in," she said. "Don't even think of leaving without me. Who's driving?"

• • •

At two minutes past midnight, Chad Summers and Tracy pulled up in his crappy Country Squire station wagon. The exhaust chugged out black fumes as the windows rattled with Metallica. The driver's-side window rolled down and weed smoke poured out, Chad looking at them in his mirrored sunglasses and jean jacket. "Three?" he said. "You said it was just you and the Adams kid. Who the hell's the girl?"

They didn't answer, only piled into the back seat, Scott scooting into the way back as Peter leaned up between the front seats. The music was so loud, he had to raise his voice. "Can you get to Lawrenceville?"

"Where the fuck is Lawrenceville?"

Peter pulled out a folding Rand McNally from his jacket and passed it up to Chad. He'd drawn on the map with a fat red Magic Marker, leading them all the way to the address he'd seen on her pay stubs, Sugarloaf Parkway.

"This is gonna cost extra, Petey," Chad said, knocking the Country Squire into gear. "This is way the fuck out in the boonies. Like some goddamn redneck *Deliverance* shit."

"Can you turn it down?" Peter asked.

"*What?*"

"Turn it down," Peter said louder. "I can't hear a word you're saying."

Chad reached over and turned up the metal as he hit the gas and the car lurched forward, sending all the kids in the back toppling over. "Don't ever interrupt a Kirk Hammett solo."

Summers sped onto Roswell Road and into the unknown.

• • •

It was nearly 1 a.m. when they made it out to Lawrenceville and Sugarloaf Parkway.

"Okay," Summers said, slowing the car and stopping somewhere along a stretch of dark pine woods. "Pay me."

"Not until you pick us up," Peter said. "The last time I paid you, you dropped me off on the side of fucking Peachtree Street. I had to walk another mile to the bookstore."

"You know some say that metal is about anger or evil or even madness," Chad said, turning to talk to Tracy. "Society created labels out of fear. Metal is about freedom, aliveness, and strength to face life with power in your heart."

"Awesome," Peter said. "But I'm still not paying you jack shit until we're headed home."

"What if I decide to leave you kiddos anyway?"

Tracy punched Chad in the shoulder. She hadn't said much the whole ride, mainly checking her makeup in the visor mirror and applying more bubblegum lip gloss. As soon as Peter had told Scott that Tracy might be going, too, he was in. Even though he was two years younger, he thought he actually had a chance with her. Especially since it was widely known Chad Summers fucked up nearly everything in his life. It was only a matter of time.

"You can do what you want," Peter said, pointing to Chad's dashboard. "But I hope you have the money to get more gas, pecker breath."

Scott had fallen asleep in the far back of the station wagon and woke up when they'd stopped to argue. "Where are we?"

"The flip side, kid," Chad said. "The Cedar Woods. Siberia. Fangorn fucking Forest, Endor. It's all the same."

"Lawrenceville," Brenda Yee said, pointing to the glowing white halo of light deeper into the pines. "Keep driving, numb nuts, and get Peter where he wants to go."

"Who the hell are you?" Chad asked.

"Who are you talking to, man?" Scott said. "Are you hearing voices, Chad? It's just me and Pete."

• • •

Okay. They were fucked. The only way into Scientific Atlanta was along a private road closed off by a security shack and a guard. Peter told Chad to slow down as they passed but then they sped up when they saw the shadowed shape of a guard inside the shack. The man had turned to stare, a dark figure holding a coffee mug.

"I could hop the fence," Peter said.

"Like Steve Austin?" Scott said, making bionic sounds. "Good luck."

"I could climb the fence."

"You'd mangle yourself," Brenda said. "There's that spindly razor stuff on top. You'd shred your hands."

"What else can we do?" Peter asked.

"I can ram the fucking gate," Chad said. "And we can storm the fucking castle."

"Are you high?" Tracy said.

"Yeah," Chad said. "So?"

"Keep driving," Brenda said. "Look for another way."

"What's so important in there?" Tracy said. Only thinking to ask the obvious question after more than an hour in the car together. Scott had a crush on her, but Peter had never found Tracy that bright. She continued to check her makeup in the visor, dabbing at the corner of her mouth.

Peter would not give, and did not feel as if he owed anyone, any more explanations for his actions. There was a fee involved and he'd pay the forty bucks once they were headed back to Scott's house in Twin Lakes.

"That guitar is sharp as a dagger," Chad said, hitting his right hand on the dash.

Peter really, really wanted to tell Chad that Metallica sucked balls. But he knew that would end with him, Scott, and Brenda stranded in the woods. An hour of Metallica was worse than any torture he could imagine.

"There," Brenda said. "There. Stop."

Chad hit the brakes, the Country Squire skidding, headlight beams scattering up over the weeds and toward a chain-link fence as he left the road. They stopped and then Chad tried to move forward, his back wheels spinning in the muck.

"I said stop, genius," Brenda said. "I didn't say fucking run us into the goddamn mud."

Chad hit his head against the steering wheel as an angry drum solo came to a final beat. "Shit."

"You can cross there," Brenda said.

Scott opened the back door and stepped out, the headlights shining up onto a ten-foot fence without any razor wire. In the distance, he could see the blocky outlines of four concrete buildings and the blinking red lights of satellites and antennae.

"You guys get unstuck," Peter said, hopping onto the hood of the Country Squire and then grabbing a handful of chain-link fence to climb. In his best Arnold, he looked down at Scott and Brenda and said, "I'll be back."

"Oh, Jesus Christ," Brenda said.

. . .

He was on his own, walking alone through the skinny pine trees and headed toward the flashing red beacons. The ground was wet and mucky, and the mud and grass sucked at his Nikes as he marched through what looked like a matchstick forest. As he walked, Peter waited any moment for a big spotlight to hit him and a dozen army guys to train their rifles on him. Hands up in shame.

He nervously played with the key card in his hand, hoping it would get him in the building and, with any luck, into his mom's office. Maybe, just maybe, he'd find something in there that might help him and Hotch make sense of everything. *Gary. The dead woman. The Russians who'd tried to take out Hotch.* What exactly did they do at Scientific Atlanta? Nobody could be desperate enough to kill for basic cable.

As he walked, he hummed some Dire Straits to himself, "Walk of Life," making him feel a little lighter and more buoyant in the darkness. He hit the tree line, looking out into the empty parking lot that separated him from an office building. WARNING. RESTRICTED AREA. PHOTOGRAPHY OF THIS AREA IS PROHIBITED. Blah, blah, blah.

The guard shack was probably a quarter mile back and he decided to just go for it and sprint toward the glass doors of the concrete bunker. There were probably security cameras, and he knew he'd be exposed for a good thirty seconds, but there really wasn't any other way. He pulled his jean jacket up over his head and sprinted for the door, key card in hand. The door had a speaker and a button to talk. He looked around but couldn't see a card reader. He pulled at the door, but it was, of course, locked. He ran around the side of the bunker until he found another door and saw a little card reader. Holding his breath, Peter swiped the card and heard a long beep and the snick of the lock opening.

He was in.

Peter crossed a broad marble lobby. A big logo for Scientific Atlanta took up most of the concrete wall at the back, silver metal in the shape of the world with a rabbit ear antenna shooting beams on top. He walked toward a marble front desk and several turnstiles. He again used his mom's key card and spun right through. He didn't see or hear anything. He looked up and around and saw a few security cameras but held his breath and tried to ignore them. Hopefully by the time they figured out he'd been inside, he'd be halfway back home.

The hallway was flanked by big plate-glass windows and concrete and he soon found four elevators. He pushed the button, the door opened, and he was finally able to breathe. Five floors. Five fucking floors. Where would Connie Bennett work? He hadn't even thought about how hard it might be to find her office. But even just looking around, Peter thought he might find something.

He shook his head and punched four. The button wouldn't light up. He punched five. It still wouldn't light up. Peter saw another key slot and fumbled with the badge but still the buttons wouldn't work. So what the hell, he mashed five again. Peter was really sweating now, a little out of breath, until the button lit up and the elevator moved. If he could find his mom's office, he planned to go through her desk, maybe even try and steal her fucking computer. He could carry it back to the fence and maybe get it up and over to Scott and Brenda. Brenda could get into it. Or if she couldn't, he'd take the damn thing out to Fat Sam at Old Sarge's and tell him this was a matter of national security. Fat Sam was a patriot, always talking about his three tours of 'Nam, and would definitely help.

This sort of reminded him of the scene with Bud and Brutus in *Gridiron Gamble*, book number eight, Popular Library 1977, when Bud had to sneak into the football team office and get the evidence about the nasty owner who'd been betting against his own team. The owner had kept his black book inside a rare vase and Brutus had kicked it in frustration, shattering the vase and exposing the contents. If Peter needed to, he'd be glad to make a mess of Connie's office. Bringing in Gary had definitely messed up his whole life.

The elevator stopped and the doors opened.

A big Black man with a shaved head, in a black suit and tie, stood with two white security guards in tan uniforms holding walkie-talkies. Peter stepped back and mashed the down button over and over. But the big Black guy had stepped halfway into the elevator to hold the door from closing.

"You lost, kid?"

29

SYLVIA

"Sorry to wake you," Coleman Vaughn said. "But we have a little situation out here I thought you should know about."

Sylvia propped herself up on her right side and cradled the phone to her ear. Damn 4:56 on a Sunday morning. She'd been cozy down deep in her flowered bedspread and sheets, a light rain tapping at her window. "You finally catch some Russians?"

"I caught a kid," Vaughn said. "He climbed the fence and used his mom's key card to get into the offices. I'd usually just call the cops, but this kid is saying some crazy shit I think you need to hear."

"Who's the kid?"

"Fourteen-year-old boy," Vaughn said. "His mom is a receptionist for us, does some secretarial work. Been here almost two years."

Sylvia ran her hand over her face. She'd been looking forward to just one day off, maybe treating herself to brunch up at Baby Doe's and then hiking along Rottenwood Creek down toward the old mill.

"I don't see what this has to do with me."

"His mom is Connie Bennett," Vaughn said. "She was on the list of employees we gave you to interview. A friend of Jenny Buckner's."

"I remember," Sylvia said. "And I think I met her kid."

"Like I said," he said. "Kid's been saying some wild shit. I plan to report the break-in this morning. But if you were to get here first . . ."

"On my way," Sylvia said.

. . .

Coleman Vaughn met her outside the Scientific Atlanta main office building. It had been raining the whole drive and he had on a black trench coat and rubbers over his dress shoes. He offered an umbrella as she dashed from her car and held it above her head as they walked toward the lobby.

"What do you mean, wild shit?" she said.

"If I told you, that would kind of ruin the surprise."

"I can't talk to a juvenile without their parent," she said. "That's against the law. I could lose my job."

"You're not questioning the kid," Vaughn said, holding the glass door open wide. "But there's no harm in just listening to what he has to say."

Vaughn took her up to the fifth floor and into a small office with several gray cubicles. She saw the kid from across the room in an office with a glass wall, seated with his shaggy head down in his hands.

Vaughn opened the door. "This is Agent Weaver with the FBI," he said. "She's going to stay with you while I run down to the cafeteria for some coffee. Would you like a Coke, Peter?"

The kid shook his head. But he straightened up in the chair as soon as he was introduced to Sylvia. Sylvia had the feeling Coleman had told the kid she was on the way. She removed her coat and hung it up on a hat rack by the door. The conference room bare and sterile, six different chairs around an oblong desk.

"First off," she said. "I'm not here to question you, Peter. Trespassing on private property isn't a federal crime."

"Why did you question my mother?"

"Because she was a friend of a woman who'd been killed."

"Jenny Buckner."

"Did you know Jenny?"

The kid shook his head. "No," he said. "But I read about her in the paper. Some maniac strangled her and dumped her lifeless body down by the Chattahoochee."

Sylvia nodded to agree that was pretty much the situation and took a seat close to Peter. She looked down at her watch: 6:42. Vaughn would have to be calling this in to the locals real soon to report what had happened.

"Aren't you going to ask me why I broke in?"

Sylvia shook her head. She tilted up her chin and widened her eyes, taking a deep breath. She'd inherited the look from her aunt; a little bit of scorn and silence went a hell of a long way.

"I'm worried my mom is next," Peter said. "I think that maniac is going to kill her, too."

This is the part when the investigator would immediately ask, *What maniac?* but she let Peter continue with whatever tale he wanted to tell. After all, it was standard that an agent would be sent out when a facility with DOD clearance was breached. Even if it was breached by just a fourteen-year-old boy.

"I tried telling my mom," Peter said. "I even tried to call the cops. They thought it was a prank. But this is real. I swear to you. You have to listen to me."

Sylvia gave a subtle nod.

"His name is Gary Powers," the kid said. "Or at least that's the name he's going under. I found some kind of spy radio in his stuff at the gym. And my friends saw him passing intel at some hick bar out by the air force base. Yesterday morning, he and some other Russian came for my friend and tried to run him over. Are you listening?

Fucking Russians are running loose in Atlanta, and one of them is dating my mother."

Sylvia turned to see Coleman Vaughn walking back into the empty office suite. He held a couple of Styrofoam cups that he set down at a receptionist's desk. He picked up a phone, cradled it to his ear, and began to speak. He met Sylvia's eye and tapped his watch.

"What does your mom say?"

"She wants me to see a shrink."

"You know I can't be talking to you without a parent."

"It's only my mom, and she's fucked in the head," Peter said. "She's in love with this son of a bitch, and after he gets what he wants, he's going to break her goddamn neck."

The kid started to cry and buried his face in his hands. She patted the kid's back and made small circles on his shoulder.

"Where did you see this spy radio?"

The kid told her all about some fancy-ass gym that hadn't opened up yet in East Cobb. He said the Powers guy had found him snooping around and threatened him on a ride home in his Porsche.

"Come again?" Sylvia asked.

"Yeah," Peter said. "This dickless wonder drives a convertible 911. He thinks he's really hot shit."

• • •

Sylvia and Coleman Vaughn were back in the lobby, heading toward the glass doors. She saw a couple Gwinnett County Sheriff's Office cruisers pull up close to the curb. Two beefy white guys crawled out and started making their way to the big concrete building.

"I thought Keyes hated the Feds snooping around."

"I cleared it with Keyes."

"Say what?"

"Someone got to Dr. Keyes the other night," Vaughn said. "He won't discuss it with you or anyone. But he picked up some woman at

Johnny's Hideaway, or some woman picked him up. He thinks he was drugged and then his house searched. If it got on the news, it would make the whole company look bad. You know what I'm saying?"

"They get anything?"

"Keyes is too smart for that," Vaughn said. "But it will make him more compliant with y'all."

"Do you know the kid's mother?"

"Not really."

"Did the kid tell you why he broke in?"

"He said he wanted to find out what the hell we made out here."

"And what did you tell him?"

Vaughn smiled. He had a nice smile, slight and mischievous. "Cable boxes and satellites."

"Now, that's some bullshit."

Vaughn shrugged and motioned toward one of the big glass doors, where a deputy knocked.

"What about Peter?"

"Trespassing on private property," Vaughn said. "I advised the kid to keep his mouth shut to these here bubbas. It was all just some stupid prank."

"Can you get me the file on Constance Bennett?"

"With Keyes's dick twisted into a knot?" he said. "Yes, I can."

"I'm damn interested to meet this new boyfriend of hers."

30

VITALY

Vitaly wanted to shop for underwear, but Dan insisted on taking him to church instead. It had been many, many years since Vitaly had been inside a church. His grandmother had been a religious woman, taking him to Christmas and Easter mass as a boy and telling him of her beloved Church of the Savior on Spilled Blood. A magical place in Leningrad with colorful mosaics comparing the murdered tsar to Jesus Christ himself and intricate domes in the style of Saint Basil's. He knew it became a morgue during the war and smelled of decomposing bodies and then later a warehouse filled with vegetables to distribute to the starving poor. His father always called it Our Holy Savior of Potatoes. Vitaly had never found religion as an adult, something a rising young star in the KGB couldn't afford. Mystical, unscientific, nothing more than a tool to control the masses.

But anything to leave his imprisonment at the safe house was a welcome change. And so Vitaly had dressed in his old Soviet suit, cleaned, pressed, and broken seams fixed, along with a new pair of black-laced shoes that had appeared in his closet last week. A gift from "Charlie," who often made jokes about the thin, cheap soles on Vitaly's Russian footwear.

Vitaly sat with the entire Rafferty family that morning in the second pew of St. Catherine's, a more pleasant name than those old churches back in Russia. The church much smaller, new but more modest, an A-frame of varnished wood ceilings and a kaleidoscope mosaic of stained glass, a white dove seeming to be breaking through the mosaic into the sanctuary. The priest told a very long-winded story about the apostle Thomas. The man who thought his own eyes deceived him, the Doubting Thomas. *It's like when we see the old house needs paint. A child's hair needs to be brushed. Or the deep sadness and age on Abraham Lincoln's face in old photographs.* Lincoln? Why Lincoln?

"But eyes," the young priest said, "cannot see truth."

Vitaly looked up at the priest.

Thomas saw Christ a second time, the priest said, when Christ asked Thomas to touch the wound in his side. Christ had said, *Be not faithless, but believing.*

Dan leaned forward and glanced down the row, past his wife, three boys, and daughter, and met Vitaly's eye. Dan looked at his old friend and smiled. Vitaly nodded and returned the gesture.

Such distrust among good friends.

• • •

After church, there was a feast at the T.G.I. Fridays in Falls Church. All the many choices on the menu made Vitaly dizzy. He had to decide between more than twenty types of hamburgers, Steak on a Stick, Ultimate Nachos, and something called the skin of the potato. Why would a restaurant only serve the skin of the potato? The whole point of the potato was eating the hot matter inside. Were Americans so rich they discarded the insides for something they found more delicious? The cheeses and the bacon. Sour cream with chives.

"Vitaly?" Delores asked. "Have you decided?"

"I am sorry," Vitaly said. "My stomach does not allow me to make such bold choices. Perhaps I might just have the onion soup and tea."

The Rafferty kids all looked up at him as if he was a circus oddity. A boisterous young man who seemed to be on Benzedrine came back to the table. He wore suspenders over a T-shirt, many medals on his chest as if he was perhaps a hero of culinary excellence.

"After we eat, I'll take you to the mall," Daniel said, beaming. "If you think this menu is complex, wait until you see the underwear."

They all laughed, sharing an uncomfortable joke, Vitaly not wishing to discuss his underwear with women and children. If the underwear was anything like he'd seen in the shop windows in Rome, it would be scandalous. Orders were placed, with considerable confusion over hot tea versus cold tea, and Vitaly asked if he might be excused for a moment. Dan said of course, but then caught the eye of the two minders who'd followed them to the church, watched the service on Doubting Thomas, and then stayed with them at the bar drinking Coca-Cola.

Vitaly made his way through the tables and past the bar, one of the CIA men following him to a narrow hallway marked for the toilets. The CIA still refused to let only Daniel and the FBI watch him. As he was about to enter, he stopped, the agent nearly running into him. Vitaly held up his hand and whispered. "Please," he said. "My stomach is not well. I must have privacy."

The nameless, faceless agent was all too familiar with Vitaly's maladies and nodded, walking back to the end of the hall facing the dining area, on the lookout for nonexistent KGB assassins. The real assassins would be waiting for Vitaly if he ever was to return to Moscow.

The bathroom was empty, two stalls and four urinals. He checked under the stall doors and entered the last one at the end. A rectangular window waited, partially cracked and held open with a brick.

Vitaly removed his suit jacket, hung it on the door hook, and loosened his tie. He stepped up in his new American shoes and stood on top of the toilet. It had been many years since he'd attempted such acrobatics, but he was able to hoist himself to eye level with the window and pull it fully open. The cold air rushed inside as he found purchase on the brick sill and lifted himself to the small ledge, peering out at the parking lot and the Roy Rogers hamburgers next door. The wind bringing smells of fried meat.

His dismount onto the ground was not graceful, and had anyone been watching, they might've laughed at the middle-aged man, a bit paunchy, barely able to land on his feet. But he steadied himself, straightened his tie, and walked over to the Roy Rogers.

He slid a twenty-five-cent piece into the pay phone. It rang five times. He was about to hang up, already muttering "Fuck your mother," when a familiar voice answered.

Vitaly Yurchenko simply said, "Sussudio," and hung up.

Vitaly then walked briskly back across the parking lot, an impatient woman in a Mercedes laying on her horn as he passed. Very carefully, looking across the parking lot, he jumped up to clasp the window ledge and hoisted himself up and back inside to the toilet stall. The floor thankfully tidier than that of a public restroom in Moscow. As he lay on his backside, feet sprawled out upon the floor, he reached up into his shirt pocket and pulled out a pack of American cigarettes. His lighter, silver and tarnished, a gift of being ten years in the KGB, had fallen into the toilet.

He shook his head, an unlit cigarette in his mouth, until he rolled up his sleeve and fished for the lighter in the bowl. After washing his hands, sliding into his suit jacket, and straightening his tie once again, he walked back into the dining room of the T.G.I. Fridays, the bulky CIA man giving him a curious glance.

"Do not enter the premises," Vitaly said. "Much abuse to the toilet."

The man looked uneasy as Vitaly passed and rejoined the Rafferty table. Already the bounty of food had arrived, and he sat down to a steaming bowl of onion soup. The waiter brought him a tall glass of tea filled with ice.

"I'm sorry," Delores said, the waiter already buzzing to the next table. "I guess America will take some adjustment."

Vitaly smiled and waved his hand. "*Nichego*," he said. "It is not of a problem."

From the head of the table, Rafferty eyed Vitaly with all the doubts of Thomas. Vitaly took a spoon and pulled away the skin of white cheese to expose the onion soup. When he looked up, Rafferty brushed at his shirt collar and then motioned to Vitaly to do the same.

"You've got some dirt on your collar."

Vitaly nodded and brushed it away. Rafferty glanced down at Vitaly's hands and then back up at his face. Never had Vitaly seen a man more confused.

31

PETER

Connie Bennett drove a five-year-old Mazda RX-7, silver with a red plush interior scarred with cigarette burns. Peter used to pretend the car was a spaceship when he was a kid, his Buck Rogers phase, imagining his mom flying them from planet to planet, instead of just going to school or on boring trips to Marshalls for discount irregulars. His mom was a careful driver, always going the speed limit, using her blinker as she changed lanes, and rarely, if ever, did she lose her temper. Even if some bastard cut her off or flicked their high beams at her like they were doing now on the winding interstate home. Connie looked up at the rearview and then back over at Peter. "Why won't you talk to me, Peter?" she asked. "Please help me understand."

"I just wanted to see where you worked," he said. "We snuck out. We were just fooling around."

"Climbing a security fence and stealing my ID?" she said. "I can't imagine doing that when I was your age."

"Well," Peter said. "It's not all sock hops and milkshakes anymore. We were just driving and decided to look around."

"Mrs. Adams had no idea you were even gone," she said. "Scott didn't either. Do you know how bad that looks?"

No way Peter was going to rat out Scott or Brenda for being with him. When he didn't hear anything about them from Agent Weaver or the police, he figured Chad must've taken off in his shit wagon like a rocket. She'd asked how the hell he got all the way out to Lawrenceville and he'd just muttered "a friend." It was still raining that morning, windshield wipers tick-tocking like a hypnotist's medallion. Peter hadn't slept at all, and his eyelids were definitely feeling heavy.

"I don't like to even say it," Connie said. "But you might've been shot."

"Who would shoot a kid?"

"You were trespassing on private property," she said. "They take that all very seriously."

"Who is *they*?"

"The men who run the company," she said. "The partners. I had to go through hell getting that job. And now I might lose it."

"Who are *the partners*?" he said. "What do they do? I think it's some kind of military thing."

"Why would you say that?" Connie said. "Jesus. Do I smell pot on you?"

Connie looked wrinkled and exhausted when she'd first picked him up, wearing a slick leopard jumpsuit and trashy high heels. Her ash-blond hair pinned up into a bun. Her eyes seemed off, red-rimmed and unfocused. Obviously, it had been a long night out after the Barry Manilow show.

"What's all the interest in what I do?" she said. "You've never asked before. You could've just asked me."

"You just say you're a secretary."

"Wish it were something more exciting?" she said. "There's not much exciting in typing up letters, answering phones, and fetching coffee. If it weren't for your dad's pension, we wouldn't make it."

"Hooray for dead fathers."

"That's awful, Peter," she said. "I don't know what I've done to deserve you being so GD distrustful."

Peter stared straight ahead, head against the rest. "Gary isn't who he says he is," Peter said. "He's using you."

"Well," Connie said, hands tight on the wheel. Taking a breath, seeming to decide how to properly handle her newly juvenile delinquent son. "That's none of your business. Is it?"

"That's why I tried to break in," he said. "I wanted to know why Gary would want to date a woman like you."

Connie Bennett swallowed and nodded. Damn, Peter surprised himself, being such a son of a bitch. He knew he'd just torpedoed the hell out of Connie Bennett's famously fragile heart. She had to know she was too plain and basic for ole stud muffin Gary. Out of the corner of his eye, he could see his mom tearing up and then wiping her face as they took the off-ramp home.

Peter wanted to tell Connie he was doing all this for her. He was trying to protect his mother from this big Russian bastard. But all he could do was insult her for not deserving a man like Gary. He wanted to apologize, tell her what he learned from Hotch and Jackie, but everything just seemed so useless and empty right now. He wanted to make her understand. He wanted her to choose him over this random douchebag who was likely stealing from her company. Why couldn't she see it?

She parked in their little carport and ran inside. Connie seemed to be holding back the real emotion for when they got home. Peter walked around the house and down into their unfinished basement. He kept a little pad down there, as if it was his own private bar, with cardboard tacked up on the studs, a shitty old stereo, and a bench press with weights he'd filled with sand. A few castoff posters of Bruce Lee with nunchucks and girls in swimsuits lying on sports cars.

Peter turned on the stereo and sunk down into the beanbag chair. The record player came to life and landed on the flip side of the new Prince record. *Around the World in a Day*. He'd been so busy looking into his mom and Gary, he'd barely had time to listen to it. The flip side kicked off with a record starting, skidding to a stop, and then starting again with Prince playing his own take on "America the Beautiful" on electric guitar. Prince singing about a single woman making barely minimum wage. *She may not be in the black. But she happy she ain't in the red.*

He heard the door open at the top of the stairs. Connie called down to him.

Peter didn't answer. The door shut politely.

Connie's way. She'd just torture him later with more tears. Tears for Peter but none for goddamn Gary. Peter had replaced all the lights downstairs with red party bulbs and the soft light, music, and being up all damn night finally took over.

He fell fast asleep. Until at the edge of a dream, he heard a tapping at the basement window. Peter opened his eyes.

It was Ana.

• • •

"Where have you been?" Ana said. "Jesus. I've been trying to find you."

"How'd you know where I lived?"

"I asked around school."

"No, you didn't," Peter said. "You don't even go to my school. You don't go to any schools. Not around here, anyway."

She put her finger to Peter's lips and looked upstairs. They both heard the creaking of the crossbeams above them. Connie nervously walking back and forth over the kitchen floor. Peter had already screwed up so bad, there was no way he was letting some strange girl into their basement.

"Everything I told you was true," she said. "Is that why you didn't call me?"

"I didn't call you because your number rubbed off my hand," he said. "I tried to remember but then I heard you were lying to me, too. No one has ever heard of you."

Ana laughed, caught herself, and placed her hand over her mouth. She had such lovely, long fingers and short pink nails. And she smelled so damn nice, too. After the other night, Peter hadn't washed his EPCOT T-shirt, the sweet perfume still on it after she'd kissed him.

"Don't be mad at me because you're mad at your mom."

"I did something stupid last night," Peter said. "I'll probably be grounded for the rest of my life."

"Then one more thing won't hurt."

"Like what?" Peter said.

Ana leaned in and kissed him hard. He felt her tongue deep in his mouth. The floor tilted, and son of a bitch, time seemed to stop cold. When he opened his eyes, she smiled at the expression on his face. He must've looked like a lovesick nut. He could barely remember what Stacey even looked like. Fuck her and Mitch's moped.

"Come with me," she said. "I parked down the street. To hell with these stupid adults."

"Who are you?"

"I told you," she said. "My name is Ana."

• • •

She didn't stop talking all morning. The top up on her little white Rabbit, windows fogging up as she talked about moving to Atlanta a couple of years ago from California and how difficult it had been going to a private school. Pace! No wonder no one had heard of her. That was some serious money. She had an older sister who was a senior and a dad, an alcoholic architect back in Santa Clara who'd left their family for a waitress at Denny's.

"Sounds like your dad should meet my mom."

"I told you it's not your mom's fault," she said. "As gross as Gary is, he has some kind of weird hold over women. I don't get it at all. But he totally fooled my mom until she found out he'd been stealing money from her."

"What a douchebag."

"A total douche."

They crossed the river and climbed the long hill on Johnson Ferry Road, headed south to somewhere or nowhere. Peter didn't care much. He felt absolutely fucking terrible about what he'd said to his mom. And now Ana was telling him all about being a gymnast, breaking her left wrist, and how her mom still thought she could make the Olympics.

"Which is completely nuts," she said. "Once you get hurt, get pins in your arm, it's pretty much over."

"I basically called my mom a slut."

"So."

"I guess she can't help it," he said. "She picked me up in jail this morning. She was all dressed up from the night before. I think she came straight from fucking Gary's. I could smell his nasty aftershave on her."

"Jail?"

"Long story," Peter said, suddenly feeling a hell of a lot older then fourteen. "Shit. I'm sorry I'm being an asshole. Thanks for coming to get me."

"I missed you, Pete," she said. "Me and you have a lot in common."

"Like what?"

Ana snicked in the cassette of *Around the World in a Day*.

"I went to Turtle's after you said how much you loved it," she said. "I've been playing this song over and over."

The beat for "Raspberry Beret" started as it suddenly stopped raining. Ana put down the top of her convertible at a stoplight and smiled. "I left you a little rum," she said. "It's in the glove box."

"Then my mom would really be pissed."

"Jesus, Peter," Ana said. "Quit acting like a stupid kid. Fuck our parents. They obviously don't give a shit about us."

...

The last thing he remembered was heading uphill on Peachtree Dunwoody Road, rounding the turns and looking out at all the nice, quiet houses in the rain. At some point, he fell fast asleep again. When he woke up, Peter was staring into a white-hot light burning into his eyes. As he tried to move, he felt that his arms had been bound to a reclining chair. "Easy there, Mr. Bennett," a man's voice said. Serious Eurotrash overtones. But it was older, rougher. Definitely not Gary's.

Peter tried to ask what the hell was going on, but felt a long piece of plastic that had been set in his mouth, stretching his lips tight.

"Just relax."

"He's been relaxing for the last two hours," a woman said. Another Eurotrash accent.

"Do you want me to kill him?" the man asked. "I can only use the sedative so long."

"He knows nothing," the woman said.

"He knows something," the man said. "Now hand me my tools."

Peter's mind was finally coming awake; at the periphery of the chair he could make out pale yellow walls, a silver tray before him and the splashing of water into a bowl where you were supposed to spit. Son of a bitch, they had him locked in a goddamn dentist office. Ana had taken him to a fucking Russian dentist.

Some strange electronic music played from a circular speaker overhead, sounding like that kooky music from *Risky Business*. "Love on a Real Train" and all that. Where was Ana? Where had she taken him?

"Have you had these brackets on your teeth for long?" the man asked.

"They're called braces," the woman said. "*Braces.*"

"How long have you had the braces?"

Peter tried to answer but it all sounded garbled and nonsensical, the damn plastic thing making his mouth so dry that he wanted to puke.

"You will have to forgive me, Mr. Bennett," the man said. "I have great experience with the taking of the teeth. But not so much of the tightening. I will begin with removing the bands with these pliers. You may experience quite a bit of painful discomfort."

"Would you shut up," the woman said. "Ask what he knows. What do you know, boy? What did you tell the police? What did you hope to find at the scientific lab?"

Peter began to choke on his own spit, the man pressing the flat of his hand down on his forehead, his body convulsing until he could breathe again. The man congratulated Peter for being so brave as Peter stared directly into the light, so white hot it felt like the sun. The music, so odd and eerie. In his dim vision, he saw the silver flash of needle-nose pliers, and felt the plucking of rubber bands along all his top teeth. "Lay back," the man said. "No need for the struggle."

The man stabbed the pliers deep into his mouth, reaching for the wire at the back. Once he had a good hold, the man began to twist the pliers as if winding a watch. Peter screamed. The sound that came from him was something he'd never heard before in his life. Strange and primal.

The woman said something in Russian and Peter heard a door slam. The light seemed even brighter with the pain, and he could taste blood.

"So squeamish," the man said. "You do not like the music? Perhaps I might play something you like. Like the 'Invincible and Legendary,' the music of the unbeatable Soviet Army. Was this what alerted you to our agent? Or was it the gun? Surely not a gun. I hear all people who live in the American South carry them. Like John Wayne with the funny walk. Then, perhaps the radio you found? The shortwave?"

Peter didn't know what else to do. He was being asked a bunch of questions but couldn't answer with a pair of fucking pliers pushed down his throat. The man turned the pliers again like a key. Peter tried not to scream but nodded. The white-hot light appeared red, and he felt the thin wire poking into his cheek and then deeper into his mouth. He gagged even more.

"When I was a boy, I was taught not to pretend I was a man," the man said. "Not until I was ready. You are just a boy. Good boys tell only truth. Has this not been what your mother has taught you? Perhaps you need a hard, Russian upbringing. The firm hand of a father, the sting of a leather belt, to keep you from being like a cat filled with curiosity."

Peter was fully awake now. More than awake, filled with fear and adrenaline, straining at whatever was binding him to the chair. He pulled with everything he had but whatever restrained him only cut more into his wrists. *Where was Ana? Who was Ana? Where was Gary? What had the son of a bitch done with his mom?*

"Once more," the Russian dentist said. "But this time with more feeling."

The thought came to him so perfectly and detailed, he could almost see it on the yellowed pages of *Blues for a Bookie—A Bud Everett Adventure*. He recalled speeding toward the end, those two hoodlum linemen taking Bud Everett out of their dirty trunk and then going to work on him with a baseball bat. Everett, knowing he couldn't fight his way out of it, decided—as he explained in a funny interior monologue—to play a little possum. He drooped to the ground as if knocked unconscious until one of the trolls had walked back into the stadium. Everett picked up a tire iron from the trunk and swung for the other man's bad knees. Bud joking, *Never met a down lineman yet who didn't have shit for knees.*

Peter rolled his eyes back up into his head and held the frozen look as he made raspy breathing sounds. The man slapped his face several times. "Mr. Bennett. Mr. Bennett. Mr. Bennett. *Sukinsyn!*"

Peter figured that either meant "son of a bitch" or "Fuck!" with a capital *F*. He heard the man groan and walk off. He called out to the woman. "Motya! Motya!"

Peter worked his wrists back and forth until he heard what sounded like tape ripping. He knew he was bleeding, the tape slicing his skin, but he didn't care. If he didn't get out of there, he'd be dead and maybe his mother would, too. A damn filthy nest of spies. Jesus. Where had they taken him? He got one wrist free, blood spilling across his shirt as he tore into the tape on the other.

Unsteady on his feet, his eyes still blinded by that hot light. He looked around, slowly getting some focus to see he was in an oblong orthodontist office. A big poster of Snoopy on the far wall said, *It's Cool to Flash a Silver Smile*. Peter shook his head, walking toward it, trying to adjust to the dimmed light. Snoopy had on an orange turtleneck that read *Heavy Metal*. Jesus. He didn't see an exit and turned the other way, moving past a darkened receptionist desk and toward a big wood door.

A small, balding man walked in, still carrying his bloody pliers. Peter reached for the first thing he saw on the desk, a ceramic black cat candy dish. Filled to the brim for Halloween.

He picked it up and clocked the bastard right in the temple, butterscotch candy flying everywhere. The little man fell to the floor and Peter rushed into a waiting room crammed with shopworn furniture and piles of magazines. Overhead, that weird Eurotrash electronic music was breaking into a crescendo. (Peter's sixth-grade music teacher taught him that.) The door was locked with the deadbolt on the inside. He turned it and found himself in a long, dimly lit hallway.

Peter spit blood onto the floor and ran for the exit sign.

"*Ostanovis!*" the man yelled from the door. "*Sobaka!*"

32

HOTCH

After his shift at Oxford, Too, Hotch took a shower, changed into his orange terry-cloth robe, and put on the Falcons game. It had been 7 to 7, but damn if the Dirty Birds didn't just pull ahead. Al Richardson had blitzed and knocked the hell out of the Saints QB, leading to a fumble for big Mike Gann to scoop up for a TD. Hotch was so excited that he nearly spilled the Calvados. He sat on his couch, running a towel over his bald scalp, when someone knocked at his apartment door. It wasn't Jackie. Jackie was working tonight. "Nutbush City Limits" was the theme . . .

Had he paid the rent? Double-parked Big Bertha?

"Mr. Hotchner?" a female voice asked.

The Russians. It had to be the goddamn Russians. Hotch jumped up, limped over to the kitchen, and pulled his .38 Special from the cookie jar, a gnome standing guard by a mushroom that he'd bought at a yard sale last year. More knocking. "Mr. Hotchner?"

The kicker drilled the extra point, and all was well at Fulton County Stadium as the broadcast headed into a commercial break. *Your word's your word. A friend's a friend. And Miller's the beer!* Hotch stood at the wall beside the door. "Yes."

"I'm Agent Weaver with the FBI," the woman said. "I'd like to speak to you."

"Yeah, right," Hotch said. "Get lost, lady. Since when do the Feds hire women?"

"Since 1922," the woman said. "Alaska P. Davidson was the first. If you care to look it up."

"Alaska?" he said. "Really?"

"Really, Mr. Hotchner," Agent Weaver said. "Would you mind opening the door? Peter Bennett gave me your name."

"Peter," he said. "Jesus."

Hotch couldn't unlock the door fast enough, two deadbolts, a chain, plus a latch. He opened up to find a serious-faced Black woman who stood about his height and a tall, gawky white man. Both wore dark suits as was the custom with Feds and funeral directors.

"What happened with Peter?" he asked.

"May we come in?" Agent Weaver asked again. She didn't look pleased to be asking a second time.

"Peter gave *you* my name?"

The woman nodded. The white man stepped up beside her.

"Can I at least see some credentials or something?"

They opened up their leather badge cases. Hotch was no expert, but the IDs looked pretty solid. Besides, he had nothing to hide. All he'd done was try to help a kid root out some Russian spies in the wilds of East Cobb.

Hotch left the door open and walked over to turn down the volume on the TV. The white guy's name was Irv with a last name that sounded like *radish*. He'd been so focused on the woman, and a little taken aback with her also being Black, that he hadn't been paying attention.

Back when he was participating in sit-ins and marches in Chapel Hill, a Black female Fed was about the last thing he thought he'd ever see. The FBI wasn't exactly known as a progressive organization.

"What's the score?" Agent Radish asked.

"Fourteen to seven," Hotch said. "Falcons just scored on a fumble. It was that tough bastard Richardson from Tech. Man, that guy is good."

"May we sit down?" Agent Weaver asked.

"I'd offer you a drink," Hotch said, "but probably too early for Calvados and beer for you two."

Agent Weaver perched on a stray ottoman. Agent Radish found a seat on his comfy recliner. Hotch glanced around to see the latest issue of *Playboy* splayed out on the coffee table by his pack of Pall Malls and Zippo. Beelzebub launched through the sink window into the kitchen, took a look at the strangers, and dashed back out. No one paid him any mind.

"When is the last time you spoke to Peter Bennett?" Agent Weaver asked.

Hotch looked from Weaver to Agent Radish to see if something bad had happened to the kid. Weaver was staring at the cast on his ankle still covered in a taped-up garbage bag.

"How'd you get hurt?" she asked.

"I tripped and fell into a dumpster."

"I understand you were being chased," Agent Radish asked.

"If you knew I fell while being chased," Hotch said, "why did she ask how I was hurt?"

Agent Weaver leaned forward a bit on the ottoman and smiled. She had on a silk cream top under a well-cut black blazer, the butt of a big-ass pistol, a .357, poking out.

"Peter was concerned your life may be in danger," Weaver said.

"He's a smart kid."

"Is that true?" Agent Radish asked.

Hotch looked down at the last bit of Calvados, warm and

welcoming in the glass. He very much wanted to take another sip but didn't want the Feds to think he was a lush or, worse yet, nervous. If they thought he was nervous, they might start to think maybe he was a Russian, too, and fuck up the entire second half of the Falcons game and his grand and glorious plan to get shit-faced and go to bed early tonight.

"Peter Bennett trespassed on private property last night," Agent Weaver said. "He told me he was trying to find information to help you."

"Help me?" Hotch held up the flat of his hand. "Hold on a damn second."

"He says you believe a man Peter knows is acting as a foreign agent," Weaver said.

"Foreign agent?" Hotch asked. "You mean more like a KGB spy."

Irv had turned away and appeared to be watching the game. The Saints driving deep into Falcons' territory. The last thing the Falcons needed was a tied game going into halftime.

"Mr. Hotchner?" Agent Weaver said. "I understand you were once a journalist."

"Well," he said. "That's kind of like being a hooker. Once a hooker—"

"Peter said you and an associate witnessed this man Gary Powers making a handoff at a bar in Marietta?" Weaver asked. "Of some sort of contraband."

Hotch nodded, following the game over Agent Weaver's shoulder. The Saints quarterback scrambling, Richardson and Gann coming for his ass. The defenders knocked the crap out of the QB and Hotch couldn't help but clap.

"Is that why you rummaged through the apartment of Jenny Buckner yesterday?" Weaver asked.

Hotch turned from the television and back to Agent Weaver.

"I know who Jenny Buckner is," Hotch said. "But I didn't do any rummaging."

"Is that your baby blue Cadillac outside?" Agent Radish asked, standing up now and staring down at Hotch. "With the big fins? My uncle back home had one just like it. Only his was gold. He wore a captain's hat as he'd cruise around Coney Island like he was piloting a yacht."

Hotch didn't think the statement called for an answer. He waited for the Feds to just go ahead and get on with the show.

"But you were at the Woods yesterday," Agent Weaver said. "Way out in Vinings?"

Again, Hotch didn't answer. Okay. This was the point when the Feds turned from nice to supreme assholes. Hotch was a patriot, and sure, he wanted to help the kid, but nobody who wasn't a moron talked to the Feds without a lawyer. Unfortunately, he still owed his longtime personal attorney, Dickie Herzog, six hundred bucks for handling the divorce.

Agent Weaver nodded. "I guess you and Peter both do a bit of trespassing."

Hotch noticed his robe had started to droop open, and he cinched it closed. It was his lucky robe, orange with white piping. He'd gotten it at Brooks Brothers a million years ago. When Janet was good and pissed, she'd say he looked like a big fat grapefruit. Ah, memorable times.

"Is there anything you've come across that might help us?" Agent Weaver asked. "And Peter?"

"That there are fucking Russians running amuck?"

"Yes," Agent Weaver said. "Exactly."

Hotch hefted himself off the couch and pointed down at his left ankle. "Exhibit A."

"And how exactly did you know you were being chased by Russians?" Agent Radish asked.

"Well," Hotch said, shrugging. "Maybe because they spoke fucking Russian. Mr. Radish."

"It's Ravetch," the man said. "*Agent* Ravetch."

"And how would you know what Russian sounds like, Mr. Hotchner?" Agent Weaver asked.

"You do a little time on the 38th Parallel and you pick up a few things," Hotch said. "Those boys in MIGs were supposed to keep silent. But when things got tight, sounded like fucking Radio Moscow up there."

The phone rang in Hotch's bedroom, and he excused himself, hobbling past the television. He stopped momentarily to turn up the sound and closed the door behind him.

"Jackie?"

"Mr. Hotch," Peter said, whispering. "I need help. Please. I'm in trouble."

"More trouble?" Hotch said. "Right now, I got the GD FBI watching the Falcons game with me."

Peter ran down a crazy story about a girl with white hair, an evil Russian orthodontist, and fleeing for his life deep down below Lenox Square. Hotch told Peter he'd be right there, belted his robe, and returned to the TV room, where the FBI agents waited. He tried to appear casual, calm.

"I'm sorry," Hotch said. "I have to meet a friend."

Weaver and Ravetch were both standing. While he'd been gone, it appeared Weaver had been thumbing through his LPs. The woman studying the back of Linda Ronstadt's *Heart Like a Wheel*. "You into Linda?" she asked, nodding her approval.

"It belonged to one of my ex-wives," he said.

The FBI agent looked disappointed and slid the album back in among the rest. "I'd play straight if I were you, Mr. Hotchner," she said. "If those Russians found you the other night, they sure as shit know where you live."

"I'll try to keep that in mind."

・・・

Hotch let Jackie drive to Lenox Square, down to the lower-level parking lot and the food court where Peter said he'd be waiting. Hotch switched places with him and idled outside Annie's Santa Fe, where he could stay ever-vigilant for any Russian spies. The movie marquee over the mall exit advertised: WEIRD SCIENCE. CREATOR. SWEET DREAMS. SILVERADO.

He figured he could've been honest with the Feds, but he didn't know how much Peter had told the woman. And he didn't want to get his ass in the sling by breaking into the Buckner woman's apartment and then driving downtown to steal her fucking sable coat. He'd stuffed it in the trunk by the spare tire while keeping the computer disk in the inside pocket of his jacket.

After a few minutes, Jackie emerged with the kid, and Hotch made a sweeping turn down the aisle of cars to the food court and theater entrance. Jackie opened the big squeaking passenger door as Peter catapulted into the back seat saying, "Go, go, go."

Hotch mashed the accelerator and Big Bertha lurched forward. "Who were they?" he asked. "Where did they go?"

"It was two of them," Peter said. "A man and a woman. I lost them. I think. The man chased me out of an orthodontist office down below the mall. I found a staircase and came right up by the fountain. Jesus. I thought he was gonna kill me."

Hotch looked back in the rearview as he headed around the sprawling mall toward Peachtree Street. The kid had blood smeared across his cheek, his face a ghostly white, and looked wild-eyed and in shock.

"Jesus," Hotch said. "What did they do to you?"

"Some Russian put a goddamn pair of rusty pliers down Peter's throat," Jackie said. "If I find that motherfucker, I'm gonna chicken Kiev his ass."

"Damn, kid," Hotch said. "What the hell did they want?"

"I've got to find my mom," Peter said. "Please get me to my

mom. I have to warn her. I have to tell her I'm sorry. Jesus, I'm so sorry."

Hotch fishtailed out onto Peachtree and then turned north back toward the burbs. When he glanced back again, he saw Peter was crying and then wiping his face with the backs of his hands. He had blood all over his shirt.

Jackie had turned toward the back seat. "How exactly did those motherfuckers catch you, kid?" he said. "You seem too fast for that shit."

"They didn't have to chase me," Peter said. "There was this girl. I think she's one of them."

• • •

Peter had curled up in the back seat of the DeVille and fallen asleep as they drove him back home. It was dark as they crossed over the Chattahoochee, not far from where they'd found Jenny Buckner's body. The air crisp, the trees along the banks turning bright red and yellow.

"What if Gary is there?"

"I hope he is."

"You really mean that?"

"We got to talk to his mother," Hotch said. "They're both gonna need protection."

"What if she won't listen?" Jackie said. "We gonna have to take the kid with us. You know that, right?"

"That's called kidnapping."

Jackie was chewing gum and reached up with his left hand to straighten his blond wig. "Kidnapping for his own damn good."

Peter stirred in the back seat and popped awake as they passed the Kroger and took a turn onto Roswell Road toward the subdivision by the power lines.

"I won't leave my mom," Peter said.

"We found something," Hotch said, hands on the wheel, remembering what Agent Radish had said about his uncle's car. Big Bertha did indeed feel like he was steering a big-ass boat. "Yesterday, Jackie and I broke into that Buckner woman's apartment. But don't go blabbing about it to those Feds."

"I won't."

"That's where I came in like a big-dick Nancy Drew," Jackie said. "Found this little piece of paper that said Ms. Buckner put her sable coat into storage right before she gone and got killed."

"So?" Peter asked.

"You as bad as Hotch," Jackie said. "You know that? Women don't put a fur coat into storage in the fall. That's when they take that shit out."

Hotch looked up into the rearview, the kid not seeing where all this was headed until Jackie explained about going to the downtown Rich's. "She'd sewed something into the fucking armpit."

"What?"

"How much do you know about computers, kid?" Hotch asked.

"Nothing," Peter said. "But I know someone who does."

• • •

Peter's mother, Connie Bennett, wasn't exactly excited to see Peter show up in a big blue Cadillac with a portly, balding stranger and a Black drag queen. She met them in the driveway, rushing to Peter and wrapping her arms around him. The blood on his face and his T-shirt didn't help.

"Who are you people?" she asked. "What the hell did you do to my son?"

All good questions. And Hotch didn't blame the poor woman a bit. It wouldn't exactly help when he explained the kidnapping and torture up under Lenox Square. He was about to start when Jackie stepped up in front of him. "I know this is a lot, Mrs. Bennett," Jackie said. "But we think you may be fucking Ivan the Terrible."

Jackie.

"We don't want to scare y'all, but we think you're both in some danger," Hotch said. "Two federal agents just came to my apartment asking me about your boyfriend."

"Jesus Christ," she said, holding Peter tight to her chest. "Who the hell are you people to talk about my private life?"

"My name is Hotchner," he said. "And this is Miss Jackie Demure."

"Miss Jackie De-what?" she said. "I'm calling the police. What the fuck did you do to my son?"

Peter put his hand on his mom's shoulder and tried to shake her, breaking her from her spell. "Mom," he said. "You have to listen. These are my friends."

"Friends?" Connie Bennett said. "Where have you been? What happened to your face? I've been calling all over the place looking for you. The police were just out here. God, Peter. I thought you were dead."

"I don't think you're listening, Mrs. Bennett," Hotch said, stuffing his hands into his leather jacket. "Gary Powers is mixed up in some bad business. Your life is in danger. Peter's life is in danger. He came to us because he thought we could help."

"I know who you are, Mr. Hotchner," she said. "Some old washed-up private-eye writer who's been filling my son's head with a lot of lies and bullshit. And your deviant friend. What are you, anyway? You're not a woman."

"Baby," Jackie said, calmer than Hotch expected. "I'm not a woman. I'm not a man. I am something I'm certain you can never understand."

"I want you both gone now," she said. "I'm calling the police."

"Mom," Peter said, yelling. "Would you please listen to me? For once."

"Go inside, Peter," Connie said, pushing him forward on a cracked walkway toward the old ranch with peeling white paint. "Now. You are in so much trouble, I don't even know where to begin. I'm probably fired after what you pulled. All these lies you've been saying about Gary are awful. Go inside now."

"Mrs. Bennett," Hotch said. "Someone tortured your child. Doesn't that matter to you?"

Mrs. Bennett had her hands on her hips. Hotch knew he was going to have to reach out to Agent Weaver and get her to help. God, he hated to work with the goddamn Feds, but it looked like that might be the only way.

Hotch and Jackie walked back to the car and Jackie got in behind the wheel. Hotch slammed the passenger door and watched as Mrs. Bennett pushed Peter inside the house and slammed the door.

"You do realize the kid has the disk now."

"Fuck me."

"He said he could open it," Jackie said. "Maybe we trust the kid a little."

"It appears we'd be the first."

33

PETER

Peter hoped like hell his mother hadn't followed him after he'd hopped on his bike and sped away to Brenda's. He'd never been inside the Yees' house before. But he knew you had to take your shoes off at the door.

As he slipped off his Nikes and headed into the living room, he felt like he'd stepped inside a furniture showroom. Two white sofas with tropical patterns faced each other across a large glass coffee table. On the glass, there was a marble statue of an Asian warrior on horseback next to a tall, fresh display of flowers. He knew the warrior was Asian because he wore one of those pointed hats, but wasn't so sure about the flowers. They looked real but as he walked up and touched the petals, he realized they were made of silk. A mirror had been hung above a cold fireplace with more marble and jade figurines on the mantel. Nothing was dusty. Nothing seemed out of place.

"Hey, numb nuts," Brenda said. "Quit screwing around."

Peter turned to see her halfway down the staircase, motioning him upstairs. Peter followed, the carpet a plush white, again absolutely spotless. He figured it must be hell being one of the Yee children, living in such perfection.

Thankfully, Brenda's room was different. Her room was a collage of posters and magazine ads stapled to the walls. Some shirtless dude with a wolf. The band Loverboy. Peter really hated Loverboy. He tripped over a few stray stuffed animals as he sat down on an unmade bed, finding Brenda at her beloved Commodore 64, waiting for the system to start working.

"Where is it?"

Peter reached into his jean jacket and handed her the disk he'd gotten from Hotch.

"What the hell happened to your face?"

"I had my braces tightened."

"Yeah?" she said. "You look like shit."

"Thanks, Brenda."

Peter sat on the edge of her cluttered bed as she started to type. He wasn't sure he could go home after this. His mom was plenty pissed. Maybe he could sneak down to the Adamses' basement and camp out there for a while. He'd never seen Mrs. Adams journey downstairs. He could live hidden among their houses, like E.T. in the closet waiting for his daily feeding of Reese's Pieces.

Brenda snicked in the disk. There was a click and a whir, and then green text started to zigzag across the screen. Everything moving so fast, the computer seemed to be possessed by the disk, and Peter half worried it might suddenly self-destruct.

"What's this supposed to be?" she asked.

"If I knew I wouldn't have asked you to open it."

"You don't have to be a dick about it."

"What's that?" Peter said, standing up off the bed and pointing to a place that Brenda had just scrolled past.

She scrolled up. And Peter pointed again.

"Project Excalibur?" Brenda said. "I should've known. Typical pillow humper D&D crap. I'm not going to sit around all day and go down into Middle-earth to fight trolls and goblins. I have stuff to do."

"That's not what this is."

"*Project Excalibur,*" Brenda said, reading down over the screen. "*Top secret. Eyes only?* Whatever is on here is encrypted. Without a password, we're screwed."

"Isn't there some back door?" Peter said. "You're supposed to be smart. Can't you break the code?"

"I don't know," Brenda said. "I can try. Why? What's all this about?"

"Did you hear about that woman who got killed down by the Chattahoochee?"

"Of course," Brenda said. "Some psycho raped her and then ate her head."

"This is why she was killed, Brenda," he said. "Someone killed her looking for this disk."

"Oh, gross, Peter," she said. "You brought me some dead woman's stuff to look at? I always knew you and Scott were sick. But this is really disgusting."

Peter got down on his knees and waited for Brenda to turn her chair around.

"My mom's boyfriend killed her," Peter said. "If he knew I had this, he'd probably kill me, too."

"And you brought this crap to my house?" Brenda said. "My dad will shit a brick."

"Your dad can't know."

"What do you want me to do, then?" she asked. "This says *Top secret. Eyes only.* You nearly got me arrested this weekend."

Peter thought about it for a moment. "Do you have any extra disks I can borrow?"

• • •

Peter pedaled back home on his PK Ripper, Brenda's new disk in his pocket. The first thing he'd do was make sure that Gary was nowhere around. And then he'd talk to his mom and convince her to cooperate with Agent Weaver. If she wouldn't listen, he'd talk to Agent Weaver himself. Besides Hotch, she was the only person who was listening to him right now. Weaver would get her spy. Hotch would get his story. And he'd finally be rid of fucking Gary Powers.

He turned off the good road in Twin Lakes and into Woodland Hills, standing up off his seat to pedal on the incline. The dead leaves in the trees fell over him like a ticker-tape parade in those old films of the celebrations for astronauts and war heroes. Maybe he'd get some kind of reward, maybe a medal. "Teenage Boy Uncovers Commie Spy Ring."

Peter was nearly up to his street when he heard a car behind him. He looked back to see it was a white Rabbit turning the corner and speeding up toward him. Peter pedaled faster and zipped down his road to his house. There was no fucking way he wanted to talk to Ana.

Peter was sweating and out of breath as he coasted into his driveway and set the bike down in the grass. Connie's silver RX-7 had been parked half out of the carport. He sprinted for the door as Ana braked and got out of her car, calling to him. "Peter," she said, yelling. "Peter. We have to talk. You don't understand."

Peter tried the door, but it was locked. He banged on the door, then reached into his pocket for the key he kept on a shoestring but realized he'd left it in his room. The back door to the basement would be open. He ran around the side of the house, opened the door, and locked it behind him. He ran up the basement steps calling for his mom.

Maybe she wasn't there. God. Maybe Gary already got her.

"Mom!"

He ran into the living room and then the kitchen. He heard her bedroom door open and out came Connie Bennett in a knee-length gray wool dress. Black and white butterfly patterns. Connie was screwing an earring into place, looking startled Peter was back home. She had on brown pantyhose and nice shoes and didn't seem to be concerned about him in the least.

"Weren't you going to at least look for me?"

"What is it?"

"Where are you going?"

"I need a drink," Connie said. "I'm meeting friends."

"No," Peter said, feeling a big rock in his throat. "You're meeting him."

Peter ran to the window and pulled back the billowy curtains. He saw Ana standing beside her little white Rabbit and looking at her watch. Did she think he was that stupid? His mouth still felt like he'd been punched over and over.

He headed into the foyer and deadbolted the door, drawing the chain.

"Mom," Peter said. He grasped her shoulders. "You have to listen to me. Gary killed Jenny Buckner. His friends tried to kill Mr. Hotchner and nearly killed me."

Connie nodded. She reached out and touched Peter's face. "Oh, Peter," she said. "Not the killer orthodontist. You're just making up things to disguise what you did at my office. I spoke to my boss, and everything is going to be okay. But this lying has to stop."

Connie Bennett walked to their dinette set and picked up her purse and keys. "You're almost fifteen," she said. "I can't lock you up like a child. But you'd better be here when I get back, mister. You and I have a lot to discuss."

"Gary killed Jenny Buckner for this," Peter said. He reached into his jacket and showed her the disk. "What is Project Excalibur?"

Connie tilted her head. Her face went white. "Where'd you get that?"

Peter heard another car and walked back to the window. Connie trailed him, still talking, and headed to the front door. When she tried to open it, she noticed the deadbolt and chain. "Oh, God, Peter," she said. "What are you doing now?"

He watched as a second car pulled up behind the Rabbit, Gary in his 911. "I'm calling Agent Weaver," he said. "You need to see this."

"Who is Agent Weaver?"

"The woman who interviewed you," Peter said. "The fucking federal agent, Mom. I talked to her yesterday before they sent me to the jail. I told her everything. *I told her everything.* Don't open the door. Please don't open the door."

"Oh, God," Connie said. "*Peter. Peter.* What have you done now?"

Peter watched as Gary spoke to Ana. Ana nodded and walked back around her little car, climbed inside, and drove off. Gary headed up the driveway and back to their house. He had on his tight red Polo, jeans, and those stupid cowboy boots. He didn't just look mad. He looked like a stone-cold killer.

Peter ran for the front door and covered it with his back, refusing to let his mom open it.

"Call Agent Weaver," he said. "She left her card. Call her. She can explain."

Connie shook her head. She looked sad. She closed her eyes and touched her forehead with her fingers, a gesture of supreme disappointment and annoyance. Peter didn't budge. He waited for Gary to knock. He couldn't breathe. Peter couldn't fucking breathe.

The side door to the carport creaked open and he heard Gary calling out for his mom.

"Con?"

"Where's your gun?" Peter said. "Go get your gun, Mom. He's going to kill me."

"No one is going to kill you, Peter," she said. Connie Bennett offered a smile of sympathy and shook her head. "I'll keep you out of school tomorrow. We'll have a nice talk with Dr. Millhouse, okay? We'll talk about these fantasies."

"Con?"

Gary's hulking shape filled the doorframe from the kitchen, Porsche keys in hand. "What the hell's going on?"

"Let's go, Gary," Connie said. "Really, Peter."

Gary's face was red, his forehead sweaty. "Do you know where I've been? I just spent four hours downtown with the goddamn FBI. Your damn kid told the Feds I was a Russian killer. First, he breaks into my office, then your office, while trying to destroy my life. You've got to get hold of this little shit. He's making a mess out of everything. What's the matter with you, Peter? Are you on drugs?"

Gary walked up to Peter and grabbed him by the upper arm. The big man jerked him back from the door and then grabbed his other arm, shaking him. Peter waited for Gary to break his goddamn neck any minute. Connie was screaming and yelling. "Stop it," she said. "Gary. Stop it."

Gary stopped abruptly. He slowly let go of Peter. His normally perfect hair all crazy. He was breathing hard, and his eyes looked bloodshot. Peter's heart was beating so fast, he felt like it was about to explode out of his chest. He looked to his mother, completely frozen.

"Don't touch my child," Connie Bennett said. Something had changed in Connie's eyes. "Ever."

"I'm sorry," Gary said, catching his breath. "I just—"

Gary didn't finish. Connie stepped forward and snatched up Gary's forearm, quickly twisting it over her back, and tossing him hard over her shoulder. Gary landed with a heavy thud in the foyer. By the time he tried to get to his feet, Peter's mom had pulled a gun from her purse. Gary's mouth hung open in surprise as she fired three times into his chest.

Blood flew up into Peter's face as he screamed. He could taste Gary's blood in his mouth.

Gary lay toppled in a heap. Connie put away the gun and got down on her knee to check his pulse. She looked cool and calm before glancing over to Peter, an afterthought, who'd started to hyperventilate. Connie Bennett placed a single finger to her lips and stepped into the kitchen. Oh, God. Oh, God. She was calling Agent Weaver. It was done. It was finally done.

Peter stepped over the dead man and followed just in time to hear his mother on the phone. *"Ya ubil yego."*

His mother was speaking fucking Russian.

34

DAN

Everything seemed to be going well with Wanda now that her idiot boyfriend was dead. His body long gone, dropped into the Potomac or maybe buried deep somewhere out in the Virginia woods. Dan didn't know and didn't care what the Russians had done with the son of a bitch. All he knew is that he'd never seen Wanda healthier and happier. Her face glowed. She seemed more at ease. More confident with her performance. Dan had just enjoyed her spectacular lunchtime show at Joanna's, a real doozy celebrating patriotism in America. "Born in the U.S.A." Neil Diamond's "America." And closing it with a slow grind on the brass pole to none other than Mr. Elvis Presley. Anyone who didn't believe "An American Trilogy" could be sexy as hell had never seen Miss Trinity Velvet's interpretation. After lighting several sparklers in each hand, she performed a full split. An old man in an Omaha Beach mesh ballcap stood up to salute. Tears ran down his cheeks.

"Where would you like to go?" Dan asked, pulling on his seat belt and starting the car.

"Don't you need to get back to work, big daddy?"

"I told my supervisor I was ill," Dan said. "I said *I had the stomach pains. Much time in the bathroom.*"

"Are you imitating your little Russian friend?"

Dan laughed as the stereo played the classics. Dvořák's New World Symphony. The piece had been a favorite of his father's back in Chicago. An ordinary beat cop who used to love listening to classical and opera in his white undershirt, a blank smile on his face as he stared out the second-story window of their apartment. Dan enjoyed those rare moments of complacency. Too often it was a razor strop or a belt, a frying pan launched at his mother for burning the bacon. But that was another time. Ancient history that had nothing to do with this beautiful day.

Dan drove along the Rock Creek Parkway, the foliage nothing short of spectacular this time of year. The yellow, orange, and red leaves truly on fire across the rolling hills and over the black stone outcroppings. The kids' soccer balls and footballs rolled around in the back as Dan took on the turns, humming along with Dvořák. Everything was about helping Wanda. Even listening to the right music. She could become a lady. He just knew it.

"I wouldn't ever get you in no trouble."

"Of course," Dan said, ignoring her grammar for once. "I know."

"And you know you're my special friend?"

"And you are mine."

"But I need some help, big daddy."

Oh, no. Here we go. Just when he thought everything had returned to normal, finally an equilibrium with his family and the occasional dead drop, Wanda was having personal issues.

"I need some money."

"Oh, thank God."

"Really?"

"Last time, it was far worse," Dan said. "I just didn't want some new boyfriend or angry husband jumping out of the bushes."

"There's no one else but you, Winfield," she said. "I don't know what I'd do without you."

Wanda rested her head on his shoulder as he took the gentle turns along the parkway, cars speeding past them in the blossoming traffic. The cool air whooshed through his wife's LeBaron and the music played ever so softly. "I need twenty thousand dollars."

Dan about ran off the road and into a stone outcropping. He steadied his hand on the wheel. Good God, that was nearly half of his annual salary.

"Larry owed some money," she said. "Real money. Now those men are after me. He got in over his head with betting on the Redskins and a shit ton of cocaine. Larry wasn't exactly a stable person, and these men think I'm still his wife."

"Wait," Dan said. "I thought he was just your boyfriend?"

"Well," she said. "We got married last summer in Atlantic City. I was so drunk that I'd nearly forgotten about it. So, can you do that? Can you help me with these people? They really scare me, Winfield. They came to my show last night and started talking about breaking my legs so I couldn't hang upside down on the pole no more."

"Anymore."

Wanda looked up at him. Dan let out a long breath. Some things he just couldn't let go.

"So you couldn't hang upside down anymore," Dan said. "Remember?"

Wanda smiled. As she reached across to pat his leg, her hand seized his groin, and he felt a strong buzzing between his legs. *Traveling light today. In the eye of the storm.* Twenty thousand. Jesus. *Twenty thousand.*

Maybe his time with Vitaly would finally pay off. Vitaly proclaimed he'd betrayed the Motherland for love. But Dan didn't believe it for one goddamn second. No way Vitaly was doubled over in pain out of lovesickness for some woman in Atlanta. What else could it be but the goddamn CIA going behind the FBI's back and sending Vitaly off to search for that missing file?

What Dan and Wanda had going was bigger than anything in this lousy spy game. Something so powerful that it would make a man crawl a thousand miles on his hands and knees through deserts and broken glass. Dan had turned forty-five last year; how much more time did he have? Did God truly want him to be unhappy? To prostrate himself, wear the hair shirt for the side glances of Delores? The disdain of his children, who whispered he was a dork behind his back?

"Let me ask you something," Dan said. "If I ever had to leave Washington, would you come with me?"

"As your girlfriend, Winfield?" she said. "Or as your wife? Because I can't leave a good-paying job at Joanna's without a ring on my gosh dang finger."

"The course of true love never runs smooth."

Dan recalled the line from some summer stock he'd seen with Delores years ago, well before the kids. He believed it was Shakespeare but couldn't be completely sure. The leaves floated down from the trees, scattering upon the unwinding blacktop. *Twenty thousand.* Surely, there was more he could offer the fucking Russians.

Maybe he could deliver Vitaly and the missing file, but not in time to help Wanda with her problems. What else did he have?

Well, he did have access to some names.

• • •

It broke his heart to drop Wanda off at the crummy apartment she shared with another exotic dancer. A woman who went by the name of Chesty Larue and performed nearly naked stage shows, twirling six-shooters and a lasso. But Dan had to return to work, heading almost an hour out to the safe house to meet with Vitaly.

He wasn't exactly shocked to learn the Agency had approved

Vitaly's trip to Atlanta. Dan had been told all the talk about depression and stomach pains had finally worn them down. They needed a happy defector to freely give away information. Dan wondered exactly how much the security detail would be costing the American taxpayers. A joint operation with the CIA and a private plane to Atlanta. Charlie, the man from Langley, had called Dan earlier and said the Agency had even contemplated taking Yurchenko to Las Vegas, to let him *get laid and play fucking blackjack if it would make him shut up.*

Everyone lies.

The security detail met Dan at the mailbox before the big turn down to the lake. They knew Dan but he presented his credentials anyway, happy to be Daniel J. Rafferty again. He hoped he could tell Wanda the whole truth soon enough. Dan was sick and tired of this Winfield Legate.

He parked down by a row of dark boxy K-cars. The man Vitaly only knew as Charlie greeted Dan as he crawled out of the family LeBaron. His real name was Phil Thompson, an Ivy League ass who'd affected smoking a pipe as he'd lecture Dan about golf, sailing, and international affairs. Dan might've only had a degree from Knox College, but he knew a hell of a lot more about Russians than that arrogant prick.

"I had to take in some air," Thompson said, gesturing with the pipe. "The whole house smells of boiling meat and cabbage. Yurchenko's goddamn witches' brew of teas and potions. Where have you been, anyway? I thought you were coming an hour ago."

Thompson made the annoying gesture of tapping at his watch. Dan just stared at him.

"Something came up."

"I told your people that I want you in Atlanta, too," Thompson said. "Yurchenko listens to you. He trusts you. That's the only way I'll sign off on the goddamn travel. If he were to do something stupid, we'd all lose our fucking jobs. You can soothe him with all his bellyaching. Make sure to keep his leash tight."

"Of course," Dan said. "Glad to help."

Thompson puffed on the pipe, the smoke scattering into the wind. As the two walked back to the safe house, Dan spotted a bored Vitaly sitting on a stump at the edge of the lake and puffing on a cigarette while two CIA minders took turns knocking balls into the water.

"His friend is a cook at a place called Nikolai's Roof in Atlanta," Thompson said. "I guess they're old drinking buddies?"

Dan nodded. "Buddies."

"Why?" Thompson said. "Did he tell you something else?"

Dan shook his head. He watched the old Russian spy stand up off the stump to stretch, one of the minders slicing the ball far to the left. The ball landed with a solid *plop* into the lake. Yurchenko shook his head before spotting Dan and offering a wave.

"That's right," Dan said. "A cook. Old comrades in vodka."

. . .

The drive back home took more than an hour from the safe house. On the way, Dan stopped off at Manassas National Battlefield to use the bathroom and call the number he'd memorized. He parked at the visitors' center and found a bank of pay phones facing the sprawling battlefields and the lonely stone house that was now a Civil War museum. During the Battle of Second Manassas, the Union troops had used the house as their headquarters, the names of injured soldiers carved into the plank floors, Dan recalled from a field trip with his daughter.

Dan slipped in a quarter and dialed the number. The line rang three times and then he hung up. Exactly five minutes later, the phone rang again.

"Are we clear?" Dan asked.

"Be brief."

"We need to discuss our terms."

"Are they not satisfactory?"

"More is needed."

"And what do you have to offer?"

"Your man," Dan said. "He's being moved. Very soon."

"Yes," Dimitri said. "Atlanta. We are aware. Hmm. Perhaps you have something else?"

"Well," Dan said, hand sweating on the receiver as he glanced around the nearly empty parking lot and back across the endless rolling battlefield. "So much more, my friend. Pretty much everything you need."

"When can we meet?"

35

JACKIE

Charlie Tuna played piano as Jackie rehearsed the big "Proud Mary" number on the Illusions stage in a pair of raggedy gym shorts and a Falcons T-shirt with the sleeves cut off. The night was yet another AIDS fundraiser, too damn many sick and dying. At the end of the set, Jackie planned to shower the crowd in condoms and make them promise to suit up and protect each other. Maybe now with Rock Hudson gone, more folks would start paying attention. *The wrath of God, a biblical epidemic.* Jackie had heard it all. He closed his eyes to concentrate on the music and dance, Tuna banging on the piano. *Big swim. Right, left. Right, left.* "Take it from the top, Charlie." *Whip, whip, whip the wig. We're rolling. We're rolling. Tap, tap, tap those feet.*

"You okay up there, Jackie?" Tuna asked. Out of his wig and makeup, Charlie looked like any other short, fat Southern man. Really at home in a seersucker suit. But in drag, Charlie would become larger than life, known as the Bitch of the South.

"Shut the fuck up and take it from *big wheels keep on turnin'*," Jackie said, spinning his forearms over and over. And then there was the move, *rollin'*, like he was wheeling a goddamn wheelchair about the stage. *Throw your big leg back and drop the head. Tina step. Tina step.* The Tina step was damn near everything.

"That's it," Tuna said, a cigar clamped in his mouth. "That's it, bitch. Now you're cookin' with Crisco!"

Jackie finished up the number and Tuna did a big flourishing finish on the upright. He tossed a towel up to Jackie, who wiped his face. Getting ready for a drag show was almost as hard as the Falcons' two-a-days over at Suwanee. Back then, Jackie had been set to repeat as a Pro Bowl defensive end until he'd been caught in the team golf cart with the fella who played Freddie fucking Falcon. The golf cart hidden up under this giant-size red helmet that they believed shielded their activities. But when the equipment manager noticed that big-ass red helmet rocking back and forth, he called security. The next day, Jackie was out. On waivers. No one wanted to pick him up.

The Illusions stage manager, a kid they called Chachi on account of him looking like that kid from *Happy Days*, poked his head out from the curtains and told Jackie he'd missed a call from Hotch. Charlie walked up the little staircase onto the stage and said, "I don't know what you see in that old, bald-headed bastard. How'd the hell you two become such good friends?"

"You're one to talk," Jackie said. "Ever see that movie *Lawrence of Arabia*?"

"Damn right I did," Tuna said. "Peter O'Toole had the bluest eyes I'd ever seen in my life. My young pecker nearly popped out of my shorts."

"Remember when Lawrence saves that Arab motherfucker in the desert and then that man owes him a life debt?"

"Don't tell me you broke a nail saving Hotch's ass."

"No," Jackie said, thinking back on that night. Three peckerwoods coming at him with sawed-off metal pipes and chains. They said they wanted to teach that nigger queer a lesson. "Other way around. Old Hotch might be a heroic drunk but can still hold a pistol real steady."

Jackie walked down to the bar, found a pay phone by the bathrooms, and tried calling Hotch. The line kept on ringing and ringing, but the son of a bitch wouldn't pick up.

Jackie checked his watch, knowing he didn't have long until showtime.

He took a shower backstage and put on a flowing silk kimono, doing his eyes in a big round lighted mirror. The eyes were the most important part, making them all big and dramatic with dark liner and long spider lashes. Then came the contouring of the cheekbones. Jackie had always had nice cheekbones, so it wouldn't take too long.

About twenty minutes later, sweaty and out of breath, Hotch arrived backstage. Jackie wasn't sure he'd ever seen him at Illusions. Hotch had come to a Christmas party at Backstreet way back when with his last wife, Janet. Hotch got so drunk he fell off the barstool and Jackie had to carry him over his shoulder out to Big Bertha. But Janet had had a hell of a time, getting up onstage as Jackie let it all out as Gloria Gaynor. Goddamn right. *He will survive!* "Big Time" Jackie Johnson couldn't be stopped.

"I think I'm being followed," Hotch said. "Again."

Hotch looked a mess. He wore a fucking Hawaiian shirt with gray Sansabelt slacks and that ugly-ass leather trench coat. As Jackie finished brushing his cheeks with powder, Hotch reached into his coat for one of his fucking Pall Malls. Jackie remembered seeing Ronald Reagan shilling those cigarettes in one of his grandmomma's old movie star magazines. A cigarette dangling from the Gipper's mouth, *Its He-Man aroma WOWs the ladies . . .*

"You mean the Russians are coming," Jackie said. "The Russians are coming!"

"Maybe," Hotch said, spewing smoke from the side of his mouth. "Different car, not the Audi. Looks like one of those goddamn

K-cars Iacocca's been making. So ugly they got to wrap the insides in Corinthian leather."

"That's a motherfuckin' Cordoba, Hotch," Jackie said, widening his eyes. "They don't put jack shit in one of those K-cars besides a steering wheel and a gear shifter. Besides, what the hell you want me to do about it?"

"No one's answering at Peter's house."

"I don't think Peter's mom ever took to us," Jackie said. "Sad. Must be on account of your bad eye."

"And that FBI agent, Miss Weaver, has been calling me," Hotch said. "She won't stop. Left five messages on my machine."

"Look at it this way," Jackie said, reaching for his lipstick. The Tina wig proudly waiting cockeyed on a Styrofoam dummy head. "At least someone loves you, Hotch."

"I'm pretty sure I lost whoever it was," he said. "But maybe I could crash on your couch? I don't want to wake up with a knife at my throat."

"Fine by me," Jackie said. "I'm doing Tina for the big closer. And before you say a goddamn word, it's not gonna be from *Private Dancer*. I'm doing the queen of it motherfuckin' all, 'Proud Mary.'"

"The big Tina step and hair toss?"

"You know it."

Jackie studied Hotch in the mirror. The man looked more lost than usual. He watched as Hotch picked up a makeup-soiled towel to wipe the sweat off his brow and bald-ass head.

"Maybe we ride out to East Cobb after the show?"

"And get arrested by the redneck police?" Jackie asked. "No thanks. Peter's mom promised she'd call them if we came back. Just don't complain if you hear me knockin' boots in my bedroom later on."

"Fucking Russians," Hotch said, squashing out his cigarette. "They're fucking up everybody's life."

"'Big wheels keep on turnin','" Jackie said, singing and reaching for his wig. "Jackie Demure keep on burnin'. You're gonna love the big finish, Hotch. I swear the hair's gonna grow back on your bald-ass head."

"Spectacular."

• • •

The set would end with "Proud Mary" but begin with "River Deep, Mountain High." *When I was a little girl, I had a rag doll* and all that stuff. Well, that wasn't exactly true. When Jackie had been little, he'd had an old Wilson football. Dolls didn't come until much later. His older sister had one of those doll heads where you could practice braiding white lady hair and experiment with all kinds of makeup. Jackie had found the thing fascinating as hell but when his mother caught him playing junior cosmetologist one day, she'd whipped his legs bloody with a switch. She'd taken little Jackie straight to the preacher to figure out why exactly had the devil come and tempted her only son. Her little baby, Jackie. *What's wrong with my boy? Why's he want to be like a little girl?*

Up onstage and under the colored lights, Jackie gripped the mic and worked the stand back and forth. Jackie shook his shoulders and stretched out the mic, closing his eyes as he hit those high Tina notes. He had on a sparkly silver dress that really showed off his legs while he worked those shoulders just like Tina, walking up and back, owning that stage and wearing that cocky little smile.

Through the haze of smoke and bright lights, he saw Hotch saddled up (Hotch's phrase, not Jackie's) to the bar, with two empty martini glasses. On one side of him was Charlie Tuna in his massive bouffant wig and frog-green eyeshadow with big-ass Bertha Butts on the other. Bertha was the only other Black queen in the show, in his snug white dress and feather boa. Hotch didn't seem to be paying them any mind but instead pointed to the front door opening onto Peachtree Street.

That's when Jackie spotted two white men cut through the crowd in long gray overcoats and with mean-ass expressions. One looked exactly like a goddamn gorilla, tall and ugly, with an old-fashioned brush cut and a face that looked chiseled from stone. The other was short and wide, much older, scowling under his black fedora. In a sea of pastel tank tops and sequin dresses, these two stood out like a couple of dog turds on a wedding cake.

What about that puppy? That always followed your ass around? Jackie kept on with the show, careful not to cause too much of a stir. The last thing you wanted to do in a gay club was yell *cops* or *peckerwoods* to send folks scattering. Although lately there had been a different attitude, about standing their ground. *They were here. They were queer.* Even Ivan the Terrible and Joe Stalin couldn't fuck that up.

The big men shouldered past the audience, craning their necks, and Jackie just knew they were looking for Hotch. But Hotch had left the barstool and seemed to be trying to get backstage, the steps jammed with adoring fans. Jackie saw the whole thing play out from his peripheral vision; working a club wasn't a hell of a lot different than watching an offense develop after the snap. *Keep cool. Stay focused. Keep your eyes on the ball.*

The next song was gonna be "Honky Tonk Woman," and that's when Charlie Tuna would leave the DJ stand and bring Jackie his rhinestone cowboy hat. As the first chords started up, Jackie, by way of Tina, said, "We got a little something special for y'all tonight. Two sisters just flown in from Siberia, their peckers still frozen to their legs. How about a nice, hot, sticky, and warm Hot Lanta welcome!"

36

SYLVIA

The man Peter Bennett had known as Gary Powers seemed to have vanished. He lived in a two-story town house close to the new White Water Atlanta theme park, but according to people Sylvia and Irv interviewed, he spent most of his time at his soon-to-open gym called the Muscle Factory. The grand opening was a week away, according to the flyers, *Join Today for Your Best Tomorrow*, when they'd found the gym door unlocked. They'd sat in the nearly completed gym most of yesterday checking out the equipment. Sylvia and Irv may have also checked out Powers's office—just in case he left a Russian radio lying around—but despite finding some empty vials of what might've been steroids, the place seemed clear of Soviet activity.

Irv wanted to lean on Dennis Hotchner a bit. If Gary was in the wind, maybe he was still following Hotchner around Atlanta. Hotchner had claimed two Russians tried to run him down on the way home from a bar.

Sylvia sat in the back of a van with a three-person SSG team, a special surveillance group made up of some highly trained civilians working for the Bureau. The great thing about the SSG teams was they didn't all look like basic white guys. They could be grandmoms, scruffy kids right out of college, and in one case a midget named Poco who could hide cameras and microphones in the tightest of spaces.

The woman running the SSG team looked exactly like the woman who played the maid on *The Brady Bunch*. That woman, Sylvia remembered, was Anne B. Davis. This woman's name was Katie McNeil, but damn if Sylvia didn't want to keep on calling her Alice, wanting to know if she'd ever gotten around to marrying that Sam the Butcher.

"Hotchner left twice," McNeil said. "Once in his bathrobe to look for his cat. Later on he got a liquor store delivery. It was two o'clock and he was still in his robe. I used to be married to a man just like him. What a fuckup. I can smell the whiskey from here."

"Hotchner doesn't drink whiskey," Sylvia said. "Gin and something called Calvados."

"What is that?" McNeil said. "Brandy?"

Sylvia shrugged. She watched the black-and-white monitors running feeds from four different cameras. They'd set up two in his apartment, one in the stairwell, and one facing the parking lot. Her squad supervisor had secured a warrant by saying Hotch was the possible target of a foreign enemy. But watching him ramble about his house, the robe barely covering his T-shirt and boxer shorts, she figured the real enemy might be Hotch himself.

Hotch poured some more of that fancy brandy in a coffee cup and sat down in front of the television. Donahue interviewing Pete Rose.

"I'm going to start up the first report," Kathy said. "What do you want to call this thing for the official record?"

Sylvia thought on it for a moment. "Operation Sitting Duck?"

• • •

Hotch disappeared from the cameras for a short bit but returned a little later, presumably showered and dressed. The grown man now in a Hawaiian shirt and black leather jacket, heading into the hallway and locking the door behind him. Sylvia opened the sliding van door and headed back to her car, where Irv sat waiting with a burger he'd picked up from Hotch's hangout, George's Bar. She'd begged him not to add onions, but as soon as she crawled inside, she knew he'd gone against her wishes.

"Really?"

"You can play your own music," Irv said. "But a burger without onions is both lonely and sad."

Sylvia reached for a few stray napkins and wiped some mustard off his chin. Irv cranked the K-car as they both watched Hotch's massive blue Cadillac fishtail out onto the road. She could barely make out the first bit of "Ain't Too Proud to Beg." Irv waited a beat before he picked up his walkie-talkie. "Call me Ishmael."

In the passenger seat, Sylvia rolled her eyes and shook her head.

"See, his car looks like—"

"I get it, Irv," she said. "I took freshman comp, too."

...

Hotch was either drunk or taking them on a crazy tour of downtown and then midtown.

"How much you think that thing gets to a gallon?" Irv asked.

"Make sure you ask him."

"You know, I picked up one of his books at the store where he works," Irv said. "The guy behind the counter bragged he knew Hotchner but then told me I was wasting my money. He said it was complete crap and I really needed to get into some Philip Roth to explore my Jewish male identity."

"What'd you say?"

"Thanks, but no thanks," Irv said, keeping four cars back behind the blue boat. "I have to say the story really moves. In the first chapters, some broad is kidnapped and then this guy, Bud Everett is his name, is hired by the girl's father."

"Please don't say *broad*."

"Sorry," Irv said, taking a hard right back onto Peachtree Street. The way Hotch was driving, mainly swerving, Sylvia was pretty sure he was onto them. "*Broad* is part of my Newark Jewish experience and identity. Anyway, this Everett guy goes fucking blind in chapter ten. Some pimp throws fucking lye in his face and so for the next few chapters, he's trying to detect shit by feeling around and bumping into walls."

"Like us."

"Exactly," Irv said. "Jeez. What the hell? Where's he going? Does he know that's a queer bar?"

Sylvia looked up to see Hotch park the boat sideways and jump ahead of a line snaking into a place called Illusions.

"Have I told you about Hotchner's best friend?"

"Is it a big, badass Black guy named Brutus?"

"Almost," Sylvia said. "I'll let it be a surprise."

"I'm not going in there."

"Jesus, Irv," Sylvia said, the car slowing to a stop. "You afraid someone's gonna ask you to fox-trot? This isn't in the handbook, but I promise you're not gonna catch the gay from coming inside. We'll just watch unless something happens."

"Like what?"

"We'll know it when we see it."

Irv turned on the radio and began to wind the dial to 94.9 and his goddamn easy listening. She slapped his hand away.

"Don't even think about it," she said. "We made a deal."

• • •

Half an hour later, and halfway through her personal cassette of *Prisoner in Disguise* (Irv finally coming around to Linda after her badass version of "Many Rivers to Cross"), Irv nudged Sylvia and pointed to two men speaking with a bouncer at the entrance to Illusions. You didn't need much sense or Quantico training to know these two fellas sure as shit weren't locals. They were both white men dressed like it was 1956. One of them had on a hat; what did they call those things? A homburg? Little German-looking fedora with a tiny red feather in the brim. The other man was massive, with a black brush cut and a hard, mean face. Some words were exchanged, but then the shorter man slapped a wad of cash into the bouncer's hand. The small man nodded decisively. The bouncer, a muscle-bound white man in a *Frankie Say Relax* tank top, shrugged and lifted the velvet rope.

"What was that all about?" Irv said.

"Capitalism," Sylvia said. "Come on."

"Oh, Jesus," Irv said. "Do I have to?"

"Agent Ravetch made the decision to wait in the car and listen to easy-listening tunes while Agent Weaver took it upon herself—"

"Okay," Irv said. "Jesus. I get it. But I still don't like it. Goddamn commies and now queers."

• • •

The club was a sea of men, and maybe some women, although it was tough to tell, with the biggest Black woman she'd ever seen onstage. Or was it a man? The man was dressed up to look like Tina Turner, and two other drag queens joined him onstage as they launched into the first raunchy chords of "Honky Tonk Woman." One of the drag queens handed the Tina Turner a rhinestone cowboy hat, before moving in unison with Tina and a short, fat Black woman, acting as backup dancers. *What did Tina call them back in the day? The Ikettes?*

It took Sylvia longer than it should to realize that Tina Turner was none other than Jackie Johnson. She'd pulled a mug shot of him and Hotchner. Jackie had been arrested several times for assault and once for some trumped-up morals charge. And Hotchner had scored a few DUIs over the years. But it was him. No one had shoulders like that but a former NFL defensive end.

Sylvia looked out into the crowd of so many gay men laughing and dancing and singing along, most of them in colorful tops and spandex, until her eyes settled on Hotch in his black leather trench coat slinking toward one of the exits. The two foreigners they'd spotted saw him, too, and pushed and shoved their way toward him. Jackie Johnson, but on the marquee MISS JACKIE DEMURE, announced they had some real special guests. Jackie made a joke about some boys from Siberia with frozen peckers and soon the sea of gay men and tough-looking women were pushing the two Russians—well, goddamn, she knew they were Russians—up toward the stairs at the right side of the stage. Jackie started into a real hip-thrusting grind, singing about a barroom queen down in Memphis. Taking someone upstairs for a ride. Wouldn't that mean it was two women? Or was Jackie still singing as a man? Which way did Tina sing it? Did Jackie change the words?

The crowd of men catcalled and whistled, jostling the two men in heavy gray overcoats to the front of the club and finally pushing them up onstage. The short, stumpy Black woman lassoed the big one with the brush cut with a long, white feather boa, pulling him forward, inch by inch, as if a predator catching a late-night snack. The short man in the homburg did his dead-level best to get off the stage, even trying to make a break for the curtain, when the big white woman with the enormous blond bouffant jumped in front of him and bounced him straight back with her pelvis. All happening in perfect time to the music.

"What in the hell am I seeing?" Irv said.

"Art," Sylvia said. "Art."

"Never seen a collar like that."

The music slowed to a steady pace, a little of what the preacher would have called the spoken word of their program. Former defensive end Jackie Johnson, with the lacerated eye in the mug shot, disappeared from Sylvia's mind, and instead there was Miss Jackie Demure talking low and slow, enunciating just like Tina. Maybe with just a trace of the purr of Eartha Kitt?

She blew my nose. And then you know what else she blowed?

"Come on up here, comrade," Jackie said. "You two queens sing it with me. Nothing to it. You got this, baby."

The short man gave what a normal person might call a withering glance. His face the color of borscht. Sylvia knew how much those Russians loved their beets. She looked across the crowd at Irv, and both of them couldn't help but laugh. The short, white woman was now wearing the homburg on top of her blond bouffant. *Give me. Give me. Give me.*

And the little Black woman with the feather boa had jumped up on a barstool, wrapped her hands around the big Russian's neck, and then quickly, and without mercy, pulled his big Joe Stalin head right into her crotch. "Whew," Jackie Demure said. "That's it. That's it. I think I see the damn tip of the iceberg!"

"That's what I call a real bump and smile," Sylvia said.

"Should we intervene?" Ravetch asked.

"Why would we go and do a fool thing like that?"

Sylvia watched as Dennis Hotchner slowly snaked his way to the exit and disappeared out a back door.

The big Russian finally had enough and pushed the drag queen away and off the barstool. The other man snatched back his homburg before they both quickly made their way down the stage steps and back toward the front door.

Ravetch reached for his walkie-talkie to alert the SSG team, hoping they'd already set up the cameras to watch from the van. Sylvia would sure love to have footage of two KGB agents slithering out of Illusions nightclub.

She and Ravetch followed and headed out to their car, spotting the two Russians running down Peachtree Street. They jogged after them. Ravetch loosened his tie as they saw the Russians turn right on Eleventh. They jogged with purpose, careful to keep them in sight but not wanting to make any arrests. She mainly wanted to see just where the hell they were going, hopefully get a license plate.

They passed a chain-link fence around a construction site of an old, two-story brick house. A sign announced fundraising for the home of Margaret Mitchell, the famous author of *Gone With the Wind*. Damn, would this city never learn? She and Ravetch were catching up to the Russians surprisingly fast. Ravetch radioed the team again.

Sylvia nodded to Ravetch to go ahead and make the approach as the two men ducked down into a damn MARTA station. *Shit*. The two agents followed the men down the steps as they headed out onto the platform. The Russians jumped on a train just before the door snapped closed and sped away.

Ravetch reached for his radio. Sylvia bent over and tried to catch her breath.

"That man Hotch knows a hell of a lot more than he's telling us."

Sylvia nodded and they walked back up the steps to Eleventh Street. The van had stopped right outside the MARTA station, engine idling. She knocked on the door, hoping to circle back and catch up with Dennis Hotchner and his pal, Big Jackie.

This time, they'd take them both to the Bureau offices and get some damn answers.

37

PETER

He was in shock. Wasn't he?

It was hard to know, because Peter didn't really know what shock felt like. There was that time when he was ten and his mother got in a car accident; a pickup truck T-boned their station wagon and sent it careening out into oncoming traffic. Connie Bennett cut through multiple cars before slamming on the brakes up into a gas station parking lot. She'd done the whole thing steering one-handed while holding Peter against the passenger seat. He figured the other time he'd been in shock was when he'd fallen out of a magnolia tree, hit several branches, and broken his arm when he landed. The bone poked from his left forearm, but Peter remembered feeling only a wave of calmness. *Oh, that must be my bone. Isn't it supposed to be inside my skin?*

After his mom shot Gary, she'd told him, *Pack only what fits in this bag. Only take what you need. Go now.*

Peter didn't argue. The adrenaline rushed through his body, his heart beating so damn fast. He felt everything was going in slow motion, a washing machine whooshing in his ears. He could still hear the blast of the gun echoing from their foyer. Gary was dead. His mom, good old Connie Bennett, spoke Russian.

So who was Gary? Who is my mom? Who the hell am I?

Connie piled him and their stuff into her crappy RX-7 and sped away from Woodland Hills, Peter huddling down in the passenger seat as she drove. He didn't speak. She didn't speak. She flew in and out of traffic, across the river, across town. He wasn't paying attention and didn't really know where they were headed. *"Destination Unknown." Where do we go from here?*

They ended up in another suburban neighborhood, somewhere out of East Cobb, pulling up to a generic brick ranch house with a wide-open garage. Connie got out and Peter followed. Connie opened the hatch to the Mazda and carried both their bags. Two old convertible Mustangs from the sixties were parked in the garage, red and white. Each with Georgia tags reading *HIS1* and *HERS2*.

After Connie rang the doorbell, she turned to Peter and then pulled a handkerchief from her purse. She wet the handkerchief with her mouth and then dabbed it over his nose and cheeks. Gary's fucking blood. Peter thought he might puke.

They'd fled their own house through the kitchen. Peter wondered if his mom just left Gary on the foyer rug, a big crazy hole in his chest. His jaw gone slack, eyes turned to glass. It was totally gross.

A very tan woman, dark and leathery and wearing an odd blue dress, opened the door. The dress seemed like something women would've worn twenty years ago, with big white buttons and large pockets. Something he'd heard people call a housecoat. The woman's hair was stiff, bleached an ashy blond, and she had on lots of silver eyeshadow and bright red lipstick.

"This must be Peter," she said. The woman beaming.

Peter didn't answer. An older man in a brown cardigan over a checked shirt and gray pants emerged from somewhere, heading down the staircase. He was bald and had a pair of reading glasses hanging from his neck. He looked at Peter as if he'd known him his entire life, something like pride on his face, as he clasped Peter's shoulder and asked if he'd like a cold Coca-Cola.

Peter nodded. Sure. After watching his mom commit murder, Coke Was It!

His mother and the odd woman headed into the kitchen while he followed the older man into a basement. Halfway down, Peter looked back up the staircase; the length of it seemed to grow longer and longer as the man called him down. His mother wanted him safe. Right? That's why she'd brought him here. All of this would make sense. The judo. The gun. This weird couple with matching Mustangs.

The couple had a finished basement with blue-gray carpet and paneled wood walls. There were La-Z-Boy recliners with doilies on the arms, an old-fashioned crank telephone, and old-fashioned framed prints on the walls. Old Model Ts and women with parasols. The older man wandered into a far room with a pool table and a wood bar that matched the walls. He opened a cabinet and found one of those curvy green Coke glasses before bending down to open a small refrigerator. "One Coca-Cola coming up, sir."

The guy was completely weird. He was dressed like Mr. Rogers with the button-up sweater and the glasses, stiff gray polyester pants and worn-out leather slippers.

The Coke was served without ice. The man then asked if Peter would like some music. "Or perhaps the television," the man said. "You kids and your MTV."

Totally weird.

Peter took the Coke. The man kept on staring at him, smiling. He needed a shave, face all bristly, and there appeared to be more black hair in his ears than on top of his head. The whole house had a weird smell to it. Like boiling vegetables and meat. The man and the woman seemed way too familiar with Peter. And they seemed familiar to him.

He knew them from somewhere, maybe when he was much younger? It hung at the edge of his memory.

"I must speak with your mother," the older man said. "Please relax. You can just call me Mr. X. Names aren't so important here."

Sure. Mr. X. And Mrs. X.

"I want to talk to my mom."

"She'll be down in a jiffy, Peter," Mr. X said. "Just a little adult business first."

The man smiled and turned, Peter hearing him head up the stairs and then his footsteps above the finished basement. Peter wanted the Coke but then remembered what had happened with the spiked rum before the fucking crazy orthodontist. Wait. The man, Mr. X. Those were the goddamn people from Lenox Square. His mother had taken him back to the very people who'd tortured him. His memory was hazy and surreal, but he remembered the man's voice as he tightened his braces. It was definitely him. Peter's heart began to race again, and he was having a hard time breathing. He set down the Coke on a side table and bounded up the steps. He tried the knob, but it was locked.

He banged on the door. But no one answered. He put his ear to the door but heard nothing. Peter closed his eyes, swallowed, and tried to think what to do. He ran back down the steps and looked for a way to escape. But there were no windows, no doors in the basement. Again, he heard the footsteps upstairs. They were probably plotting to kill him.

His mother. Fucking Connie Bennett was the Russian. She probably wasn't even his mother. She probably only kept him around as cover. Peter walked behind the bar and started to look for anything he could use as a weapon, finding a corkscrew and then, in a side table by the steps, a screwdriver.

He slipped the screwdriver into the waistband of his jeans. He looked up as the sound of feet seemed to be getting closer. When the old man hobbled back down, he'd stab him right in the chest. Peter stayed put, hearing the door unlock and footsteps coming down the stairs into the basement.

Peter pulled out the screwdriver and held it unsteadily in front of him. His heart felt like it was up in his throat.

He stepped forward to stab the old man and bolt up the steps but instead saw Ana. She shrieked and lifted up her hands. "Peter, what the hell are you doing?" she said. "You nearly gave me a heart attack."

• • •

Peter sat in one of the La-Z-Boys and Ana sat cross-legged on the blue carpet. The stress and that smell of boiling meat making him lightheaded.

"It's not so bad," she said. "I promise you'll get used to it. I was ten years old the first time I returned home."

"To Russia?"

"Yes. At first it was strange," she said. "But somehow a part of me had always known."

Peter thinking he'd heard those words before. From his mother. Or Stacey. No, it was Princess Leia when she'd learned she was Luke's sister and that she'd also been born a Jedi. Did Ana have special abilities? Did he? He didn't want to ever be a Russian or to live in Russia. He just wanted out of this musty basement and out into the air, where he could breathe and think. He needed to find Hotch. Hotch would know what to do.

"I returned last year," she said. "We went in as visitors to Czechoslovakia. From there, Moscow isn't far. Have you heard of Odessa? There's a resort there and a wonderful beach. We start each day with ablutions and then some light gymnastics. Some healthy sunbathing with sports. Maybe even chess."

"I hate chess," Peter said. "Gary tried to get me to play with him."

"Poor, stupid Gary."

"Was Gary Powers his real name?" Peter asked. "Why'd my mom shoot and kill him?"

Ana shrugged. It would be so much easier to be mad at her if she wasn't so damn beautiful. Her face was thin, almost elfish, and today she'd worn her blond hair teased all wild. Like the girl from 'Til Tuesday. *Hush hush. "Voices Carry."* Brenda told him it was a story about dudes who beat up women. Brenda. *Jesus.* She had the disk.

"Peter," she said. "Why'd you break into Scientific Atlanta? What were you looking for?"

Peter laughed. "If I didn't tell those freaks upstairs when they were tightening my braces, why the hell would I tell you?"

"Those freaks are my parents."

"Bull crap."

Ana leaned forward and rested her chin on Peter's knee. He looked down at her and wanted so much to move his leg away but couldn't.

"Don't blame your mother," Ana said. "They're only doing what's best for us. Sometimes it's hard to understand. It took me a long time."

"And now you do all the dirty shit they do?"

Ana didn't answer. She lifted her head off his knee and looked up at him with sad eyes. She and Peter looked at each other for a very long time. Almost like staring directly into a mirror.

"Russia," she said. "It's not so bad."

"What is an ablution?" Peter asked.

"Washing," she said. "Like a ceremonial washing. Russians are different. But it's in us. You adjust really fast."

Even deep down in a stranger's creepy basement, the idea of Ana and the ceremonial washing made him just a little curious. *But Russia? Fuck that.* "Is that where we're headed?"

Ana looked at him, her eyes so clear, blue, and perfect. Her mouth parted slightly. But she didn't answer.

"I want to talk to her," he said. "Where's my mom?"

38

VITALY

He had had a fitful sleep.

And awoke at dawn to the sounds of toilets flushing from the agents in this new house in Atlanta. Another supposed safe house where they would sit and wait until it was time for the meeting.

Vitaly had been waiting on this day for many years. So much anxiety. So much worry about what he might say. He had unpacked his suit last night. Since arriving in America, the agents had bought him new pants, shoes, and shirts. But he still had the same navy jacket he'd worn when defecting in Rome. That seemed so very long ago, wandering in the heat up on top of Capitoline Hill to commune with Marcus Aurelius. He took a long shower and shaved carefully around his drooping mustache. More American products. Not just a razor but one made by Bic, the shaving cream from Barbasol, and the cologne called the Drakkar Noir. He had no idea what it meant. But he applied it to his freshly shaven face and neck, dabbed a bit under the arms.

He slid into his pressed dress shirt first, then socks (so much better in America, no garters!), then the pants, and then the shoes and belt. Should he wear a tie? It was so very American, relaxed and carefree, to go without, but he couldn't help but fix one around his neck like a noose. And then the jacket, custom-made for him many years ago by the second-best tailor in all of Moscow. A worker at the safe house in Virginia had mended the small rip in the front pocket and a small moth hole on the right cuff.

Vitaly Yurchenko, a man stripped of all accomplishments and titles, stood in front of a long mirror to admire himself. He sucked in his stomach and lifted his chin. Maybe not the same man she'd met so long ago. But perhaps she was not the same woman either, not that it would matter. He would love her still. His lovely Zoya, with her strong body, knowing eyes, and cunning mind. Yes, today they would be together again.

She would join Vitaly in this wondrous, crazy new life.

Someone knocked on the bedroom door. "*Da.*"

"It's Rafferty," the voice said. "We're all ready. How about you, pal?"

• • •

Ten agents from the CIA—ten!—drove in four cars from the safe house into the city of Atlanta. A city that looked somewhat futuristic, rising from its history of ashes, so many tall, mirrored buildings shining in the morning light. Dan sat in the back seat with Vitaly. He'd been explaining who in the detail was with the Agency and who was from the local FBI office. "You're big-time, Vitaly," Dan said. "They usually only offer this kind of protection to presidents and kings. Don't worry. You'll be very safe."

"I don't worry."

"You're sweating," Dan said. "A little. Would you like a handkerchief?"

"Daniel," he said. "It's been so long. I don't know what she'll think."

"You mean your friend, the chef," Dan said, nodding up to the men in the front seat. "From Nikolai's Roof? I know he'll be glad to see you."

"Yes," Vitaly said. He rubbed his fists over his eyes. "Yes. An old friend. Our love was so warm and tender. Can it all be gone?"

The FBI agent driving the car glanced back in the rearview mirror. Dan cleared his throat. Vitaly sat quiet, very alone with his thoughts of Zoya.

• • •

They'd agreed on a very public space surrounded by many people with several exits and a dining spot that would be sectioned off just for them. They called this place the Varsity. It meant something like "university athlete," Dan had said. A place for great athletes to eat. But as soon as they walked in, Vitaly realized this was no place for Olympians. The air smelled of much fried meat and potatoes. His stomach clenched and he felt sick. *Please, not today.* Please do not send him to the toilet before finally meeting with Zoya. What would she think? *Yes, Comrade Yurchenko is here but first he had to use the toilet.* Or what the agents jokingly called the little boys' room. No, Vitaly thought. He stood up taller. He took in much air and nodded, following Dan around a gathering crowd, as crowded as a Moscow breadline, to order hamburgers, hot dogs, fried potatoes, and onions. A sign even offered sweets that were fried. Fried peach and apple pies. Coca-Cola was everywhere.

The floor was terrazzo, like in the Russian embassy in Washington, and the whole space had the feel of a military bunker. Many of the agents had already taken their places, so easy to spot with their unsmiling faces and sunglasses. A rope had been drawn over a staircase leading up to a large, windowed dining room with many tables.

"Good luck," Dan said.

"You are not coming?"

"It's as you requested, pal," Dan said. "Just you and your special friend."

Vitaly nodded. He reached out and clasped Dan Rafferty in a tight hug. Dan Rafferty was truly a rare friend.

• • •

Vitaly sat at a small table in the center of the dining room. He adjusted his tie and straightened his posture. He imagined what he might say to Zoya as he arranged the salt and pepper shakers. A large bottle of Heinz tomato sauce. *My dear love. My darling. My heart.* Would he speak in English or Russian? Zoya had been speaking only English for so long. Perhaps in English, then. That would show that he was ready for America, ready to begin their new life.

He checked his Majak watch. The time had stopped at 6 a.m. *Fuck your mother!* Now it must be eleven. So much time wasted. Years and years. Where was she? Would she even come? She had been given the signal that few knew. *Sussudio.* Although Vitaly had no idea what it even meant.

Vitaly heard a discussion at the foot of the staircase and rose to see what was transpiring. Dan stood arguing with two men who'd flown down with the CIA. He couldn't hear everything but assumed he was trying to calm the men about the change in the meeting. Something was happening. Zoya had arrived. Vitaly walked toward the staircase as he heard soft steps and she emerged on the landing as Venus from the sea.

Zoya was more beautiful than he remembered. Her brown hair now blond, face finely made up with American lipstick and so much of the eyeshadow. She wore a simple red flowered dress and a smart white jacket. Her legs were as long and muscular as when she'd been an elite gymnast, so very close to the Olympics. Little accents about her. Red pumps, red belt, and big red hoop earrings.

She walked to him. Vitaly could not breathe. He clasped her shoulders like he would a comrade of vodka or war. He could hear Dan's incessant bickering downstairs. *Hey, pal. It's all fine. It's all fine.*

Her wondrous perfume cut through the smell of the fried meat and onions. Vitaly always knew that deep down, buried in his gut, he was a passionate man. Not being able to help himself, he began to cry. He would do anything for this woman. He would go to Rome. He would cross oceans. He would even betray his country.

"Zoya," he said. "My love."

She smiled. Perhaps even blushed. "Please," she said. "My name is Constance. Or Connie. Who are these men with you? You promised we would be alone."

Vitaly smiled, almost choking on his tears of happiness. "Come," he said. "Sit. Would you like a fried pie?"

"No, Vitaly," she said. "Why are you here? I was told you defected."

Vitaly swallowed and tried to project his pride. "Yes," he said. "For you."

Connie nodded. She took a seat at the small, insignificant table with the shakers, the tomato sauce, and the dispenser of napkins. It felt as if they were in the very center, the true heart, of the United States. Was there a better place to project his love?

"They will try to arrest me," she said. "What did you tell them?"

Vitaly laughed and covered his mouth with his fist. "I told them nothing," he said. "We are alone. I have their word. No listening devices. No cameras."

"Americans are liars."

"I told them you were a man," he said. "An old comrade who defected years ago."

"Clearly, I'm not."

Vitaly reached across the table and clutched Zoya's finely manicured hand. He held it and stared at her. "Come with me," he said. "I am promised a million dollars and a salary of forty thousand a year."

"You sold out your country for so little, Vitaly," Zoya said, shaking her head. "You're a fool."

Vitaly's blood ran very cold. He began to sweat. This was not something he had anticipated. He always knew this would feel right and that she would reciprocate. She'd only entered the Illegals program to please Vitaly. And to make things clearer while they figured out their delicate situations.

"Oh, Zoya," he said. "I want to see my son."

"You're a traitor," she said, speaking very low. She kept on glancing about the room, looking like a caged animal. "I have nothing more to say. Coming here was a mistake."

"Our son is not a mistake."

Zoya shook her head and took back her hand. "Oh, Vitaly. Is that what you thought? He's not your son. You didn't need to see me. This is a bad time. Really, the worst."

"I know," he said. "I know all about it. I know about the intelligence you have. What would that get you? An Order of Lenin. What about your family? Countries come and go. Empires crumble. But love?"

Zoya shook her head. She kept on glancing opposite the staircase to where the dining room turned to form an L. There was another agent waiting there. He'd noticed him through the glass windows as they'd walked up.

"I didn't believe it," she said. "The great Vitaly Yurchenko defected to America. No. He must be a double agent. He must be playing a spy game."

"We can live wherever we want," he said. "We can go wherever we want. Our son can finally meet his father."

"You are not," Zoya said, pounding on the table with her fist. Looking more like Khrushchev with his old shoe and not the beautiful woman he'd fallen in love with back in Odessa. "His father."

"Zoya," Vitaly said, choking back so much emotion. "We are all experts on lies. There's no time for these games."

Zoya looked down, clasping her purse, and then up at Vitaly. So much had changed in her. So much hate. He was about to tell her about the safe house in Virginia and this new doctor who had helped his stomach, when she got up and ran. Vitaly barely had time to stand, knocking the chair to the floor as he watched Zoya rush a CIA agent and punch him right in his nose, sending him to the floor. Men from the landing began to shout, four agents running up the steps, one asking Vitaly if he'd been injured. All of them running after Zoya. There would be more men outside, perhaps even police.

But Vitaly sat down again, like a decompressed balloon. They wouldn't catch her. No one could catch her.

That's why she was Lisica. The White Fox.

39

HOTCH

He knew it had to be Peter's choice, but damn if Hotch was going to abandon the kid. Too many had done that to Hotch and his sister over the years. Not to mention, Peter had been kidnapped by foreign agents and tortured, and those same agents, or someone working with them, had followed Hotch twice. The bastards had tried to run him down with an Audi and made him jump into a goddamn dumpster. Hotch could still smell the garbage stink on his clothes.

"Glad you put the top down," Jackie said, driving the DeVille. "You need to fumigate that damn leather jacket."

"What'd you do with the sable?"

"Took it to this tailor who makes my costumes," he said. "He said he could cut it up into a nice vest and maybe a cute little hat to match."

"That's what I call ingenuity."

"That's what I call my reward for saving your ass last night."

Hotch had his right arm hanging out the window as they flew

down I-285. He blew smoke from his Pall Mall into the open air. "Bullshit," he said. "Even if you didn't do your song and dance, I could've shaken them."

"Did you see the size of that big Russian?" Jackie asked. "Big as Mean Joe Greene, only white. But he ain't offering you no fucking Coke and a smile. He'd have broken you into so many pieces, all the king's horses and all the king's men couldn't do shit."

"We got to find the kid."

"What the hell you think we're doing?"

"Even if we have to make a ruckus with his mom."

"Good thing making a ruckus is my goddamn middle name."

"I thought your middle name was David."

• • •

They should've never given the kids the damn disk. Hotch could've found someone, somewhere to open the damn thing. But everything happened so fast with Peter's mother threatening to call the cops and the kid being so damn sure he could figure it all out. What the hell did Hotch know? He'd barely even seen a computer except in the movies. Maybe the kid had something by now, something from that neighbor girl Brenda that Peter called a genius. Or that guy at the army/navy store. Fat Sam?

Jackie parked the Caddy up in the driveway. They didn't see the mom's car, but when Hotch got out and headed to the front door, he noticed the garage door had been closed. Both times they'd been there before it had been wide open.

Hotch knocked on the door.

"Avon calling," Jackie said.

Jackie was in street clothes again today, jeans and a denim shirt. His relaxed hair slicked down on his head. No makeup, but still a little fancy in sparkly white cowboy boots and a brass belt buckle that read *Honky Tonk Freeway*.

"What are you going to tell the cops?"

"Everything."

"Maybe Peter's mom had time to think on things," Jackie said. "She seemed like a nice lady. I know she loves her boy. I just don't think she believes in these crazy stories. I mean, I seen this shit live and up close and I barely believe it myself."

"Ever dated a Russian before?" Hotch said, knocking again.

"Nah," Jackie said. "But I once fucked a communist. He'd been a teacher from Berkeley. Came to one of my shows and couldn't resist me."

"Warms the heart," Hotch said. He knocked again, now with more urgency. He moved over to one of the windows and peeked into the dining room. The windows and screen so dirty it was tough to see inside. All the lights in the house appeared to be on. He knocked again and then tried the doorknob. The door was open.

"You as bad as the kid," Jackie said. "I'll stay right here, if you don't mind. I'd just as soon not read about an Atlanta drag queen arrested in an East Cobb B and E."

"Might be good for your career."

"Shit," Jackie said, walking back to the Cadillac and leaning against the hood. "Jackie Demure is already internationally famous. I'm known from Paris to Mozambique."

"Mozambique?" Hotch said. "Show me on the map."

"Fuck you, Hotch."

Hotch shrugged and pushed inside, calling out to Peter. If the kid was here, he'd force him to come along until things got sorted out. They'd have to get Sylvia Weaver involved now, after she'd seen those fucking Russians chasing him at Illusions. Maybe she could talk sense to Peter's mother about Mr. Gary Powers, American hero and dead spy plane captain. The real man, the actual Gary Powers, the pilot of the spy plane, went through damn hell in the Soviet Union and a big-time prisoners swap, only to die in a plane crash back in California. Hotch had learned more than he needed to know about Powers while looking for Constance Bennett's Gary Powers, stud muffin and owner of the newly minted Muscle Factory. Jesus, what was with these people.

He didn't get far into the foyer when he spotted the blood. A lot of blood. It reminded him of being out in the woods hunting, the way the ground looked after gutting a deer or a turkey. The blood soaked into a broad circle on a cheap Oriental rug. Hotch bent down to touch it and the rug was still wet and sticky. The air smelled like old pennies.

"Jackie," Hotch said, calling out. The door was still ajar. "Jackie?"

Hotch stood and headed through the stale and airless kitchen, calling for Peter. He felt his adrenaline pushing that sense of fear he'd felt back in Korea and the other night after that Audi nearly ran him over. The rush had made him run around that church and hop in a damn trash dumpster. Survival was one hell of a motivator.

"Peter?"

He moved through the family room with sliding glass doors looking out onto a leaf-strewn deck. He followed a hallway and opened the first door to his left. It was obviously the kid's room, with a sloppy, unmade bed and a small desk crowded with books. The walls covered with posters of rock stars and athletes. William "Refrigerator" Perry, the new guy playing for the Bears. And then Prince. He knew Prince because of Jackie, although he couldn't name a single one of his songs. Some guys doing tricks on bicycles and then another shelf crowded with books. Hotch bent down on one knee to see almost all his Bud Everett series. They'd been neatly arranged starting with *The Atlanta Underground*. Then *Death of a Debutante, Swingers Lament, Blues for a Bookie, Gridiron Gamble, No Prayers for the Dead* . . . But his last one, *City of Ashes*, seemed to be missing. The last one he'd published before Popular Library decided not to renew his contract. *City of damned Ashes*. He looked around the shelves; lots of Ian Fleming, fucking Bob Ludlum, and some old Len Deighton. Hotch kind of liked Len's style. Not to mention Len once gave him a really nice blurb through his foreign agent.

Was Peter trying to tell him something? *City of Ashes*? What was the fucking thing even about?

Hotch walked from Peter's room, barely able to even remember the story. He did remember it had all ended in a tobacco barn in North Carolina. He'd imagined it as the same barn where he'd been forced to work in foster care. As large as an airplane hangar, with big spaces to breathe between the slats. Something cathartic about Bud and Brutus killing ten Klansmen there and then later setting fire to the place after dousing the curing racks in kerosene. Burn it all down. Maybe everything was autobiographical in some sense.

What was Peter trying to tell him?

He headed back out into the hall to check on the mother's room. The louvered doors of the closet were wide open and it appeared a large section of clothes were gone. He checked the woman's bathroom and several drawers had been pulled out, empty of basic toiletries.

Goddamn it. The fucking Russian had taken them both.

Hotch ran back to the front door, careful not to step in the pool of blood, and called out to Jackie. Then back to the kitchen, where he started looking around for anything that might tell him where they had gone. Did she take her own car? Hotch headed into the garage and hit the button to open it.

As soon as he walked into the space, something smelled very off, like someone had forgotten to empty the garbage. As the garage door slowly opened, light spilled into the crowded space. Hotch spotted the hump of a car under a tarp and reached for the material like a magician about to perform a wondrous trick. Jackie moved inside to join him.

"What you got, Hotch?"

"Do you remember the end of *City of Ashes*?"

"Bet your ass," Jackie said. "Bud and Brutus took out a nest of KKK bastards. Neo-Nazis and all that. I think one of them killed a fuckin' dog. Who'd do a thing like that except those motherfuckers?"

"What was the twist?"

"Fuck, I don't remember."

"Come on," Hotch said. "All my novels hit the twist at the end of the second act."

"The rich dude with the big plantation wasn't a neo-Nazi after all," Jackie said. "He was actually just a fall guy for his crazy-ass sister or some kind of shit. What the hell are you even fucking talking about? Come on. We need to go. Got us a goddamn Gladys Kravitz across the street staring down my Black ass. You know she's about to call the police."

Hotch pulled back the tarp to uncover Gary Powers's nifty little 911 Carrera. The ragtop and windows were up. The back plastic window fogged up as he touched the rear motor. The car was cool to the touch.

"I ain't stealing no damn Porsche," Jackie said.

Hotch opened the driver's door and a man fell flat the hell out onto the concrete. Goddamn Gary Powers with his eyes wide open, three holes in his chest. His purple tongue lolled from his mouth like a dog's.

"Oh, shit," Jackie said. He stepped back and covered his mouth with his forearm. "What the fuck? We better go on and call the goddamn cops. If we don't, you just put your fingerprints all over the house."

Hotch stepped back and walked out of the garage just as a tall Chinese girl pulled up to the house on a ten-speed. She looked out of breath and excited.

"Brenda?"

She nodded. "Where's Peter?"

Brenda could tell something was very wrong by the look on Hotch's face. Jackie walked from the garage with hands on his hips and shaking his head. He walked over to some shrubbery and began to puke.

"Oh, God," she said. "Where's Peter?"

"What happened to that disk?" he asked. "Were you able to open it?"

Brenda, still straddling her bike, tried to get a look at just what they'd seen in the garage. She shook her head. "We couldn't open it and then Peter disappeared and I didn't know what to do. I waited outside almost all night. Is someone in there? Who is it?"

"Maybe let us give it a whirl."

Brenda shook her head. "I couldn't break the access code," she said. "But my dad drove me down to Georgia Tech this morning. My cousin is a computer science major and kept on trying."

"What did you get?"

"I don't really know," she said. "My cousin got worried when he saw it was top secret. We printed it all out. I have it here in my backpack. I was bringing it back to Peter."

"We're working hard on finding him."

"He said I could trust you."

Hotch looked to Jackie. And then back to Brenda.

"Young lady, I don't know who to trust these days," he said. "But right now, we're as good as it gets."

40

DAN

Dan arrived on the fifth floor of the Federal Building in Atlanta looking for Jeremiah Sullivan. He and Sullivan had once been partners in New York, ten years ago, before they both became squad supervisors running their own agents in Washington and Atlanta. Sullivan was a legend in the FBI, working two high-profile civil rights cases in the late sixties. He was a ramrod straight–talking Texan, and Dan knew he'd get an earful from the man about what happened earlier at the Varsity drive-in. Luckily the news hadn't been tipped that an infamous Russian defector had met his girlfriend only to get rejected, with the girlfriend breaking the nose of a CIA officer and outrunning two men from the Bureau. *Who was this woman?* The truth was Dan didn't really know. Yurchenko only called her his lost love.

The office buzzed that morning, full of agents working phones and typewriters, cigarette smoke and stale coffee in the air. He went back to Sullivan's cramped glass office and closed the door behind him. "Good morning, Jeremiah."

"You want to explain why the fucking CIA came to take a dump in my city?"

Dan explained the best he could in the simplest terms. But he left out the fact Yurchenko had confided that he wasn't actually meeting an old comrade who lived legally in the States but an old girlfriend who might be—and probably was—part of the Soviet Illegals program. Dan leaned back in his chair, hoping to find out just how fast they'd try to get Yurchenko back on the plane to the Virginia safe house. And what Sullivan really knew about Vitaly's cockamamie deal with the CIA.

Sullivan tapped out a cigarette from a hard pack of Marlboros and set fire to the end. He shook his head, staring at a place just over Dan's right shoulder. Dan turned back to see a Black woman, one of their own, speaking with a skinny young white agent with black hair and a rumpled suit. They accepted all kinds these days.

"We had some Russian trouble last night," Sullivan said, drawing on the cigarette. "At a fucking drag queen show in midtown."

Dan didn't answer. Sullivan, with a lot more gray in his hair than he recalled, didn't appear to have slept in a while. "Descriptions match fucking Dimitri Kostov and his KGB thug Anatoliy Zub. Ring any bells?"

"Both are from our rezidentura."

"Correct," Sullivan said. "So what the fuck are they doing running around a goddamn queer club in Atlanta trying to snatch some washed-up old paperback writer?"

"Come again?"

"The Russians were observed tailing a man named Dennis X. Hotchner," Sullivan said. "I guess you're not a fan of pulp fiction. Ever hear of *Death of a Debutante*? No? Good, neither had I. They'd apparently already tried to run him over the other night in Virginia-Highland. Two of my agents had Hotchner under surveillance when they spotted the fucking Russians."

"Did you bring them in?"

"We tried," Sullivan said. "But they escaped down into the MARTA."

"Just like Yurchenko's girlfriend."

"Shit," Sullivan said.

"You mind if I speak to our agents who tailed the Russians?" Dan asked. "Can't be a coincidence that Kostov flew down with his ape, Zub. I think they're here to kill Yurchenko."

Sullivan reached over the desk to ash his cigarette in a Houston Oilers coffee mug. He shook his head. "A little more to it, Dan," he said. "We already got some Illegals trouble here in town. And one of our assets got killed two weeks ago. A civilian working at a tech facility out in Lawrenceville. You want a cigarette?"

"I quit," Dan said, lying.

"What exactly do you know about Project Excalibur?"

"You mean all that Star Wars stuff?" Dan asked. "But all that's out in California. Right?"

• • •

Dan didn't know Atlanta at all but drove his rental out from the FBI parking garage and found his way onto Peachtree Street. It seemed everything was some offshoot of Peachtree Street, and he needed a nice, cool, dark place to think. And maybe have something to drink. His head was absolutely spinning.

He parked outside a place called the Stein Club that looked pleasant enough, with a Miller High Life sign outside. It was dark and nearly empty this early in the day as a nice barman, tall, thin, bearded, and white, pulled him a draft. He had one. And then another. The man's name was Faulkner. With a *u*, as if that gave him some import.

This changed everything. The goddamn Atlanta office had managed to lose an asset and possibly blueprints to Reagan's goddamn wet dream, only weeks before meeting with the Soviets in Geneva. This had to be the file the Russians wanted and the real reason Vitaly was in Atlanta. He and Wanda could be set for life. No more cowboy stew from Delores. No more PTA meetings or having to prostrate himself each week with Father Rick, rolling pennies for Jesus. He could continue his good work with a new name, a fresh start, and a thousand ways to make a difference. But first, he needed to speak with Wanda.

He asked the barman to break two dollars and headed back to the pay phone. It was hard as hell to hear with the jukebox going at full blast. "Take Five" by Dave Brubeck filling all the space after two in a row from warbling Billie Holiday. It was a dive bar, but there seemed to be some snobbery here, probably a lot of professor types and graduate students from Tech. A wall over the liquor boasting hundreds of beer steins where ostensibly you could keep your own.

"Is that you?"

Wanda sounded very sleepy. Dan looked at his digital Seiko. Four twenty in the afternoon. But then he recalled the day and knew she'd had a late shift at Joanna's.

"I think I'm ready."

"Ready for what?"

"Living for myself," Dan said. "Something's come up. We'll be able to go where we want to. Do the things we discussed. We can travel the world and not ever have to worry about money. Have you ever dreamed about a sunset cruise on the Seine?"

"What about your family?"

"Oh," Dan said, feeling the second beer hit him. "They'll be fine. That relationship was severed years ago. She won't give a damn when I'm gone."

A long pause on the line. Dave Brubeck Quartet echoing in the cavernous, nearly empty old bar. The operator's voice asked for an additional fifty cents. Dan inserted the money. He recalled how his oldest son had once played alto sax and had practiced a bit of "Take Five" up in his room. The sound so grating, he'd never been able to enjoy it again.

"Winfield?"

"Yes, dear."

"Are you sure?"

"More sure than about anything in my life."

"You do love me."

"Yes, Kit-Kat," Dan said, loosening his tie. So ready to break free of his cage, his damn day-to-day existence with Delores and at the Bureau. He knew God wouldn't have presented such a gift as what he'd learned from Jeremiah Sullivan if He didn't want Dan to take it.

"This all is happening fast," Dan said. "I need you to start packing. And please don't ask too many questions. There'll be time for all that later."

"I have to work tonight."

"Call in sick."

"But I'm not sick."

"Then quit," Dan said. "Quit now. I don't want another man to be seeing your beautiful naked body but me. Have you ever been to Mexico? We could climb Mayan pyramids, for God's sake."

"Is that where we're going?"

"Maybe," Dan said. "No more DC winters for us."

The operator came on again, asking for money. Dan rang off with so much love for Wanda, the illustrious Trinity Velvet finally his. All these days pinching pennies for orthodontists, college funds, and poorly played saxophones would be over. Delores would be fine. She already spent all of her free time with Father Rick anyway. That smug little creep.

Dan started to walk back to the bar for another beer when he had a second thought. He punched in the new number he'd memorized. The line buzzed and buzzed until he heard a heavily accented voice answer.

"Tell your boss I need to meet," Dan said.

"Do you have jacket?"

"What?" Dan said. "Yes. Of course, I have a damn jacket."

"Await instructions," the Russian, the man he knew as Zub, said. "Jacket required."

• • •

The Hilton was a five-minute walk from his hotel. Dan didn't like the instructions and took precautions. He knew if these Russians were camped out in the Hilton, the Bureau had them covered. Despite what Jeremiah Sullivan had said or, in this case, not said. He slicked his hair back, then put on a black wig and mustache. As he studied himself in the mirror, he looked like Robert Goulet. "The Impossible Dream" came to mind as he slipped on the raincoat and donned a houndstooth hat. If he were to be stopped, he'd simply say he was following an important lead and there hadn't been time to check in with the home office. Under the raincoat, he'd dressed in a gray suit, white shirt, and red tie. He didn't know why the damn Russians were being so formal. Jacket required. In an Atlanta Hilton? Please.

The inside of the Hilton didn't look a hell of a lot different from the Hyatt, so much so he did a double take to be sure that he hadn't walked back inside his own hotel. It was an open atrium adorned with more plants than a tropical rainforest, walkways to rooms ascending around the atrium steadily up to the heavens. He took a glass elevator to the thirtieth floor, to the glass spaceship at the top and Nikolai's Roof.

It wasn't yet five o'clock. And as he stepped out, his ears still popping from the ride, he noticed the grand sunset coming from the west side of the restaurant. A placard by a hostess stand stated that the dining room was closed. A smattering of waiters—dressed as Cossacks in ornate robes and all—were setting linen-topped tables.

Dan stepped into the glass-walled restaurant and removed his hat and coat. Through 360 degrees of tall windows, you could see all of downtown Atlanta and miles and miles beyond from the top of the Hilton.

"Give them to me," said someone in a hard, Russian accent.

He turned to find the big man, Zub. Zub wore a gray suit bulging at the seams. His black hair and mustache looked freshly cut and very Stalinesque.

"Hold your arms out."

Dan held his arms out.

Zub patted down every inch of him, including a barnyard grope to the groin before he stepped back and nodded. "No wire. Mustache is crooked."

"Wire?" he said, adjusting the mustache. "Why would I be wearing a wire?"

"You wear wire," Zub said, motioning to the windows. "And only one way down. No elevator."

Dan nodded, about to pick up his raincoat and hat from the chair when Zub snatched them and pointed to a hallway away from the big open dining room. Dan followed the hall into a private room with wood-paneled walls and a long dining room table. The lights were dim, with candles lit across the linen, which was laden with platters of what looked like smoked salmon, a large bowl of red soup, and embarrassing mounds of caviar and toast. Three bottles of Stolichnaya sat in ice buckets.

Dimitri Kostov sat at the end of the table, chin resting on his hands, as Dan entered. "Daniel," he said. "Welcome to Atlanta. Did you know they call Atlanta 'the city too busy to hate'? I hope that is true for both of our purposes."

Dan planned to remain standing. But Zub came up behind him, pulled out a chair, and pushed him down by his shoulders. Without being asked, Zub reached for the vodka and poured a healthy measure into a wineglass.

"And this place not even owned by a Russian," Dimitri said. "Can you believe it? May I interest you in some borscht?"

"No, thank you."

"Caviar?" Dimitri said, the top of his bald head dull and white. "True beluga. As large as marbles. So very delicious with the sour cream on the toast."

"No, thank you."

"No borscht, no caviar?" Dimitri said. "I was hoping we might celebrate. Or did you come to offer something new?"

"Goddamn, Dimitri," Dan said. "Couldn't you people wait a few weeks before acting on my list? It wasn't twenty-four hours before the KGB snatched up those people and placed a bullet in each of their heads. Some of them I'm not even sure were spies."

Dimitri shrugged. He reached for a linen napkin and dabbed a bit of sour cream from the corner of his mouth. Zub walked to the door, closed it, and then stood to barricade the only exit with his back.

"You said you must talk," Dimitri said. "We are safe. This room is clean. Speak, Daniel."

Dimitri picked up a whiskey glass full of vodka and lifted it in his direction. "*Na zdorovie.*"

Dan didn't want to toast the son of a bitch. He wanted to talk. But damn, he needed a drink so badly. And he knew from the countless dossiers he'd read that if you didn't drink with a Russian, you didn't do business with them either. Would it be too much to ask for some vermouth, a shaker, and a bowl of Spanish olives?

"Cheers."

"Yes," Dimitri said. "The cheers."

Dan lifted the straight vodka and took a long pull. He watched, curious, as the Russian reached for a pepper shaker and doused the top of his vodka.

"The water in Russia not so good," Dimitri said, shrugging. "The pepper. It drags down the pollution."

Dan nodded. He felt naked without his gun. There was no way out—the door barricaded by Zub. But this was how deals like this were done, behind closed doors and away from prying eyes. Just a few more steps and he and Wanda would be lying on a beach somewhere in South America before Christmas. He had seen the perfect bikini for her last summer in Delores's Sears catalog. Hot pink with string ties.

"I will need two million up front," Dan said. "And safe transportation to Mexico City. I know that's possible. From there, new passports. New identities for me and a special friend."

Dimitri emptied the glass and set it back down on the table. He wiped his wet mouth, waiting. From behind him, Dan could hear Zub's heavy breathing, like a hibernating bear.

"Two million?" Dimitri said. "Ha. You promise me the head of the Gipper?"

Zub snorted and cursed in Russian.

"I have something better."

"We are listening," Dimitri said. Dan looked back again and Zub nodded.

"Vitaly Yurchenko," he said. "And a comprehensive file on Project Excalibur."

Dimitri's body stiffened and his right hand sent the empty glass rolling to the floor. He looked again to Zub and then back to Dan.

"Your people have less than a month to Geneva," Dan said. "How much is it worth to have a peek at the hand the ole Gipper is holding? I can get you that missing file. And I damn well know what it's worth to you."

"He's lying," Zub said. "Let me toss him from roof. It will be fun. *Whoosh* and then the splat."

Dimitri stared at him. He lifted the flat of his right hand and nodded to Zub.

"When?"

"Twenty-four hours," Dan said. "But then the money, Mexico, and a new life."

Dimitri nodded, stood, and picked up the Stolichnaya bottle. He picked up his fallen glass, refilled it, and then topped off Dan's. Dan reached across the table for some pepper. *The water not so good*. Wonderful. Dan would have to get used to that fact.

"There will be no going back, Daniel," Dimitri said. "Not now. Not ever."

Dan lifted his wineglass full of Stoli to both men. "That's the idea, Comrade Kostov."

41

PETER

He'd lost track of time.

Peter didn't know if it was day or night or how long he'd been locked down in Mr. and Mrs. X's basement. It felt like it had been days. At least there was a toilet and all the Coke and Sprite you wanted. A few wine coolers if he wanted to catch a buzz. But Mr. X had lied—what a shock—when he mentioned the MTV. Peter had found a television but it wasn't hooked up to a cable box and only produced a snowy screen. But after watching your mom judo chop a man and shoot him three times live and in living color, watching *The Fall Guy* or *Moonlighting* couldn't really compare. There was an older stereo and turntable and a row of records stacked in an otherwise empty bookshelf. The albums seemed like something you'd break free from a time capsule. Pat Boone. Glen Campbell. *Wichita Lineman*! And two separate sermons from Billy Graham. Also some kind of weird record of Chubby Checker performing a million different versions of "The Twist."

At some point, Peter fell asleep on a barstool, head down on the bar like an old drunk, and woke up to his mother's voice. He had lost his place in time, and for a moment thought he was back in his bedroom and it was time to go back to school. But when he opened his eyes, he didn't see Prince or Dire Straits, Carol Alt, Conan the Barbarian, or Roger Moore on the Golden Gate Bridge looking down from his walls. He knew he was back in the dimly lit basement with the light-colored wood walls and gray-blue carpet. Mr. and Mrs. X's house.

His mom was rubbing circles on his back.

Peter pulled away.

"You can keep sleeping," she said. "I thought you might be hungry. Would you like some chicken soup and crackers?"

"Soup and crackers?" Peter said. "Are you serious?"

She smiled and rested her hand on his back. Connie Bennett was back.

"I know this is a lot to take in, buster."

"Who the hell are these people?" Peter said. "Who the hell are you?"

"I'm your mother, Peter," she said. "And you need to listen to me. What you saw was just me protecting you from a very bad man. You were right. I'm sorry I didn't listen. I told the police everything I know about Gary. I never saw that side of him. When he grabbed you, I didn't know what else to do. I guess it was a maternal reaction. Just a big momma bear protecting her cub."

Peter looked at the woman he thought was his mother. He studied her concerned face and that deep crease between her eyebrows when she was worried. She smiled softly at him and looked as if she might burst into tears. Now he knew that every time she'd pulled that shit, like when he'd told her he was embarrassed for not having a father or not being able to afford to race BMX, it was all an absolute lie. *Parlor tricks, old-time manipulation.*

"Let's talk this out, Peter," she said. "It might make you feel better."

Peter shook his head and slid free of the woman's touch. He backed up and crossed his arms across his chest. "Ana told me everything," he said. "I know who you people are. You brought me into a goddamn nest of KGB spies. Mr. and Mrs. X? They're the ones who tried to kill me. Not Gary. I saw you change. I saw the real you when you flipped him over and pulled that goddamn gun. Just let me go. Leave me the hell alone."

The soft, concerned face changed again, and there was a harder expression on this woman's face. The woman, the former Connie Bennett, aka Mom, looked like she was considering Peter for the very first time. She pursed her lips and nodded. "It's too much," she said. "For now. I'll explain in time. But we can't let you leave. Too much is at stake."

"Like what?"

"Do you remember us talking about mutually assured destruction?" she asked. "MAD? After we watched that movie *The Day After* that made you have those horrible nightmares. You saw my face burning into a skull. You woke up crying for weeks."

"That was a long time ago," he said. "Let me go. I'm leaving."

"Where would you go?" she said. "What would you do? Live on the streets? You've had a very easy life. You couldn't last. Like it or not, you're safe here. We're all safe here until we figure out what's next."

"I know," Peter said. "Ana said we're all going to fucking Russia."

Connie shook her head and took Peter's spot at the bar. She sat up on the barstool and watched him for a bit, seeming to be thinking on the day's wonderful events. Not at all concerned or shaken, not after Peter called out her bullshit, that she'd just blown away her boyfriend. Her little stud muffin Gary. So long, Muscle Factory tank tops and big belt buckles.

"So Gary was a spy?"

She shook her head.

"Who was he, then?"

"Exactly who he said," she said. "Nobody."

"Why'd you kill him?"

"To protect you."

"Bullshit," Peter said. "You were protecting yourself from the FBI. Agent Weaver is onto you. She knows who you people are. I told her everything. She's coming to get me. You people are screwed."

"Think again," the former Connie Bennett said. "She's just some young policewoman with little experience. But I'm not leaving this basement until you tell me what you did with the real disk. The one you brought home was blank, so the real one is still out there. Tell me where it is. You weren't supposed to be part of this. Your life may be in danger."

"No shit."

"Peter," she said. "I'm still your mother. I'm doing everything I goddamn well can to protect our family. What did you do with the real disk?"

Peter shrugged. He walked over to the bar and picked up the rest of the warm Coke. He took a drink and shook his head. "I threw it away," he said. "It caused enough trouble."

"I know when you're lying."

"Did you kill that woman, Jenny Buckner, too?" Peter asked.

"Of course not," she said. "Now you're just being ugly."

Peter threw the Coke glass against the wall, shattering it. He ran past the woman formerly known as his mom and rushed back up the steps, trying the door again. When the knob wouldn't turn, he began to beat against it with his fists. And when that didn't work, he stepped back to kick it open.

"Okay," his former mother said. "Okay. You want to know? You want to know everything? Are you sure? Come with me. Because I promise you don't want to make Mr. X angry."

"Fuck Mr. X."

"Peter," she said. "Watch your language."

"Really?" he said. "You're a goddamn killer, Mom."

• • •

More time passed and then Ana appeared again. She had her delicate hand to her face as she walked up to the La-Z-Boy where Peter sat throwing a tennis ball over and over against the wall. He took some comfort in the steady rhythm, the screwdriver right beside him in case Mr. X returned to kill him.

"Are you okay?" Peter asked.

Ana smiled. But when she dropped her hand, he noticed a large red welt on her left cheek. "They're taking you somewhere," she said. "In the morning."

"Where?"

"I don't know," she said. "I'm hearing some things."

"They're liars," he said. "They're all liars and traitors."

"Don't say that," she said. "These people are brave."

"Your parents?"

"Those people upstairs?" Ana said, shaking her head. "They aren't my parents. My parents are back in Russia. I was honored to be part of this program. It is a gift for a Soviet to be selected so young."

"This is insane," he said. "Where are they taking me?"

"Downtown," she said. "To some hotel."

"To kill me?"

"Your mother wouldn't allow it," Ana said. "She's a very dangerous woman."

"No shit."

"Everyone is afraid of her," Ana said. "But they are all very upset. Important men from the KGB are here. In Atlanta and they've issued orders that no one likes."

"My mother said only I can help end nuclear war."

Ana tilted her head. The welt on her face made Peter sick. He reached out to touch it. She took his hand and held it to her reddened cheek. And then she leaned into him and kissed him softly on the mouth. Her entire body seemed to be shaking from fear.

Peter knew. He absolutely knew this was all part of their games. But he couldn't pull himself away.

"They say they are taking you to your father."

Peter leaned back. He just stared at her.

"Is that a problem?"

"My father's dead," Peter said. "He died fighting in the Vietnam War. At a battle in Laos."

Ana held his hand tight. And then rested her head upon Peter's knee. His mother wasn't his mother but a killer. His father wasn't an American war hero but alive and maybe another stupid Russian. The entire damn basement seemed to be spinning like a carnival ride. He imagined himself being pulled by centrifugal force to the paneled walls and sticking there, unable to move. Frozen in space and time.

"I hate them, too," Ana said. "And I hate what I've become."

"Would you do something for me?"

Peter knew, absolutely knew, this was a long shot. But what the hell did he have to lose? If he didn't try, he'd soon be in some goddamn gulag in Siberia pissing in the snow and eating boiled potatoes. He was still Peter Bennett, American. No matter what these people thought. He was an American. He'd never be a lousy lying Russian.

Peter stood up from the La-Z-Boy and walked over to the bag he'd packed back in his house. He reached into it and pulled out a paperback of *City of Ashes*. He flipped open the tattered back cover and showed her a photo of Dennis X. Hotchner. It had obviously been taken some time ago. Hotch looked much thinner, with darker hair. He cradled his head in one hand, a cigarette burning in the other.

"I need you to find this man for me," he said. "Can I trust you, Ana?"

42

SYLVIA

Coleman Vaughn agreed to meet her at a parking garage two blocks over from the Bureau office. He was waiting when she arrived down below West Peachtree, leaning against a spotless black BMW, in a navy blue suit with a navy blue turtleneck underneath. The man was handsome, she'd say that for him, and he damn well knew it.

"If Keyes finds out, he'll fire me."

"Probably."

"Is the Bureau hiring?"

"Maybe," she said. "But you're a little old to be run through Quantico."

"Damn."

"Just being straight with you," she said. "Did you bring it?"

Vaughn nodded and opened up the passenger door to the BMW. She watched as he pulled a legal-size manila envelope from his leather briefcase. He held it before her, waiting a beat, before handing it over. "Can we keep this between us?"

"Constance Bennett and her son seem to have disappeared," she said. "I'd think Scientific Atlanta wouldn't want a replay of what happened to Jenny Buckner."

He handed over the personnel file, light as a damn feather. Sylvia thought about taking it back to her office, but then worried if she had questions it might take some time to track down Vaughn. And next time, he might not be so helpful.

"What's that scent you're wearing?"

"Polo," he said. "By Ralph Lauren."

"That yuppie shit in the big green bottle?"

"Yes, ma'am."

Sylvia slit open the envelope with her fingernail and laid out the file on the trunk of Vaughn's car.

"Come on, now," he said. "Not here."

"Give me a second."

"Y'all got me paranoid," he said. "Saying Russians might be following my ass. Looking all over the damn place for men in fur hats."

"But I'm here, Coleman," she said. "To protect you."

Vaughn muttered something about being able to protect his own damn ass. Sylvia glanced up as a Chevy Malibu came squealing down into the garage, headlights shining up onto her and Vaughn. But the Malibu quickly passed them, and she continued to flip through Constance Bennett's résumé, application, and two performance reviews. From the handwritten notes, Xerox copied, Bennett seemed to be a real model employee. Smart, attentive, always on time. The résumé said she went to Oklahoma State for college and later a business school in Chicago. Going back to a high school in Tulsa where she was a cheerleader and on the debate team. Way back in 1965. Sylvia started to read through the performance review.

"Can't you do this later?" Vaughn said.

"Ain't nobody here but us chickens."

"You like Louis Jordan?"

"My momma did."

"'Caldonia.'"

"Uh-huh," she said. Running her finger over the handwritten notes. "What's this about Ms. Bennett turned down additional review for clearance and a possible promotion?"

He shrugged. "I guess she was happy with her job."

"Who the hell's happy with their job?" she said. "What kind of clearance?"

"Same as Jenny Buckner," Vaughn said. "She'd have to go through an extensive background check with you people before she'd have access to DOD files or get to work in the Vault."

"What's the Vault?"

"That's where the real shit goes down," he said. "I could tell you, but that's on a need-to-know, Agent Weaver. You understand?"

"Quit fucking with me, Coleman," she said. "Are y'all building space lasers and shit out there in Lawrenceville?"

Vaughn glanced around the parking garage. He nearly jumped as a door to the stairwell creaked open and a white man in a plaid suit came out and quickly got into a boxy green Buick. Vaughn waited until the car passed them, the white man eyeing them both, and headed back up the street.

"Keyes and his team don't make them," he said. "They study them. They were given a multimillion-dollar grant by the DOD to study the probability of SDI actually working."

Sylvia nodded. "And?"

"Well, Miss Weaver," Coleman Vaughn said. "That's the goddamn sixty-four-billion-dollar question, now, isn't it? Well above my pay grade."

• • •

"Fucking Jimmy Caruso can't quit talking about Mars," Irv said. "It's driving me nuts. We finally get a major Russian case down South and he's more concerned about colonizing the red planet. Jesus Christ. Anything new on those Russians from Illusions?"

"The boss was in with some guy down from DC," Sylvia said. "We know they're staying at the Hyatt. Apparently, the favored Russian hotel. But we're not really sure why they're here."

"I know why they're here," he said. "Fucking Vitaly Yurchenko. Can you imagine the bounty on that man's head? And then our friends at the CIA take him for two yellow dogs walking and a bag of stings."

"What you talking about, Willis?"

"Varsity lingo," Irv said. "I'm trying to blend in. You know, like a fucking local."

"Then why are the Russians following Dennis Hotchner?" she said. "He's got to be a big target to follow his ass into Atlanta's biggest drag party featuring Miss Jackie Demure."

"You know that guy was a hell of a football player," Irv said. "Jackie Johnson? Second round out of LSU. I remember him knocking Steve Grogan's helmet off during *Monday Night Football*. Cosell about lost it."

Just then Ella, Jeremiah Sullivan's personal secretary, walked up to Sylvia and Irv's abutted desks and laid down a stack of thin sheets. Hot off the fax.

"Here you go," she said. "Report on that woman Constance Bennett you requested. You sure you got the right social on her?"

"Got it from her personnel file."

"Looks like that social belongs to a girl from Minnesota who died in 1952," Ella said. "You want me to run that number again?"

• • •

Sylvia and Irv were leaving the office, headed back out to East Cobb, when she got the call from Dennis Hotchner. The team hadn't seen him at his apartment all day. She'd been worried the Russians had finally gotten his broke-down ass. "I'm calling as a concerned citizen," Hotchner said.

Sylvia waved off Irv and sat down at her cluttered desk. She cradled the phone closer to her face and said, "Where the hell are you? Been looking for you all over creation."

"Safe," he said. "And doing much better than Gary Powers."

"Peter's KGB agent."

"I don't know who he was or what he was," Hotchner said. "But the son of a bitch is dead. Someone shot him in the heart and stuffed him behind the wheel of his shiny new Porsche in Peter's garage."

"Shit."

"Smells like it."

"You there now?"

"Hell no," Hotch said. "But I figured you'd like to know."

"Goddamn right I'd like to know," she said. "Where are you now? Stay put. We're coming to you."

"Hold up, Agent Weaver," he said. "Peter Bennett and his mother are gone. A neighbor says they've been gone for a while. I'm pretty sure these people have 'em and plan to kill them."

Sylvia didn't say anything. She let the buzzing silence just land there between them. She looked over row after row of desks and out into the nighttime skyline. The lights of Atlanta twinkling in the darkness.

"And what do you think you can do about it?"

"I may have something those Russians want."

"Like I said, we're coming to you," she said. "Where are you?"

"They killed this son of a bitch Gary," he said. "They killed the Buckner woman. What makes you think they won't kill the kid and his mom?"

Sylvia looked up at Irv. He was already sliding into his overcoat and laying his rubbers over his tacky-ass black dress shoes. Fit in like a local? Mr. Newark. Come on, now.

"Here's the thing, Hotch," she said. "May I call you Hotch?"

Hotchner didn't answer.

"I don't think anyone took Peter and his mother," she said. "I think Peter and his mother are Illegals."

"What?"

"The real Constance Bennett died back in 1952," she said. "Fell into a frozen lake up in Minnesota. The kid's mom must've stolen her identity to get her a social security card. That's why she never applied for top-level clearance at Scientific Atlanta like Jenny Buckner. She knew it would set off alarms all over the place."

"Fuck a damn duck."

"You got that right, Hotch," Sylvia said. "Now, where can we meet?"

But Hotchner had hung up. A hard buzzing filled the line.

43

HOTCH

Hotch hung up and walked back to the bar at George's.

A half-drunk gin martini sat at his empty spot. He knew he better go ahead and finish it; the Feds would be along anytime. You can't just leave a dead Russian in a suburban garage and walk away. And you sure as hell couldn't find a top-secret, eyes-only security disk in the lining of a sable coat and pretend it never happened. Even if the only people who knew about it were kids and maybe the Chinese girl's cousin in a dorm room at Georgia Tech.

He'd spent the afternoon reading through printouts of the files, the vast majority not making a bit of sense to him, and he'd once taken a freelance job writing copy for medical device companies. Hotch had never heard of Project Excalibur but he sure as hell knew about the Star Wars concept. Ronnie Reagan's zany idea to launch laser-shooting satellites into space in case of a first strike by the Soviets. Reagan tried to sell it to the American people as a laser grid over the world that could shoot down intercontinental ballistic nukes before they reached their targets. But reading the report, giving it what Hotch called the Grad School Read, this damn thing didn't work worth a shit. The folks at Scientific Atlanta and a research facility near Los Alamos said the energy needed to run the technology was decades away. *Decades.* In his speeches, Reagan talked about the damn thing as if they were ready to deploy.

Hotch lifted the martini. It was no longer half full or half empty but completely gone. He looked up at the television playing over the bar. Dan Rather on mute, a clip of Gorbachev and then the Gipper. Lingering B-roll shots of lovely Geneva where, in less than a month, Reagan and Gorbachev would sit down to decide the fate of the world. And here sat Dennis X. Hotchner, once hailed as a "bold new voice in American noir," with a study that could knock the chess pieces off the board. *Would he live to tell about it? Would he save young Peter's life? Would he have a second martini?* Yes, to the last one.

Hotch nodded to George. He looked at his watch, another gift from his second wife. A really nice Hamilton she'd gotten from her rich daddy's estate. Maybe he should've stayed with her and finally written that great American novel he'd been thinking about. Something that would really make the snobby booksellers at Oxford, Too stick it up their ass. A critical take on the New South that would make *Deliverance* seem like goddamn Nancy Drew.

He weighed his current options. If he handed the disk over to Agent Weaver, they'd take it into evidence and probably destroy it. But he figured the longer the disk was out there, the safer Peter would be from the US government and the damn Russians. That's what happened to Gary. Jesus. The poor bastard had no idea what hit him. Maybe, if there was an afterlife, he was doing squat thrusts behind the pearly gates.

"This is the part when the bartender asks, 'Something troubling you, bub?'" George said.

"The weight of the world is on my shoulders."

"That's a bit dramatic, Hotch," George said. "Even for you."

"What do you think about the apocalypse?"

"I think it's overrated," George said, shaking the martini. He laid down another glass.

Hotch remembered a time, long, long ago, when the traveling preachers would talk about the End Times. It used to scare the damn piss out of him. The fucking Four Horsemen. The Antichrist. Then those training films at basic and warnings about the commies. A mushroom cloud. Mickey Spillane and that goddamn *Kiss Me, Deadly* glowing box. Did Hotch have something in his coat pocket that might change the course of human history? What would his ex-wives say now? What about Maury Brillstein of Brillstein and Associates? *I don't know, Hotch. Not sure anyone wants to think about nuclear war. It's the eighties. Let's party.*

"Mr. Hotchner?" a girl asked. A pretty blond girl. But way too young to be in George's Bar.

"Yes?"

"Dennis X. Hotchner?" she said. "The writer?"

"The *X* is fake," he said. "I made it up to sound fancy."

"Peter sent me," she said, tucking a loose strand of hair over her ear. "He's in trouble."

• • •

Hotch picked up Jackie at Illusions, Jackie already in costume for the opener. He looked like he was doing Diana Ross tonight with the wild curly wig and slinky white satin jumpsuit. "What happened to Tina?" Hotch said, Jackie taking the wheel after smelling Hotch's breath.

"Tina's on break," Jackie said. "Miss Ross is on deck."

"Never heard you do Diana Ross," Hotch said, holding on to the door as the Caddy lurched forward. "You any good?"

Jackie launched into a little of "Upside Down" as he wove in and out of cars along West Peachtree, heading straight toward downtown.

"I need Miss Ross to run a little interference at the Hyatt tonight," Hotch said. "You think she can do that?"

"Round and round," Jackie said. "You turning me, baby."

"Does that mean yes?"

"Is this for Peter?"

Hotch nodded.

"Then yes."

Hotch told Jackie about calling up Sylvia Weaver, Sylvia saying that Peter's mom was a suspected Russian and that made the kid Russian, too, and then having some crazy teenage girl showing up at George's Bar. She called herself a friend of Peter's, said her name was Ana, but the whole thing smelled like a setup. Even a bigger trap than the end of *Swinger's Lament* when Bud Everett had been kidnapped and taken to Mr. Big. Brutus had shown up at the exchange in an abandoned Underground Atlanta with a big suitcase presumably filled with the cash they'd found but instead opened it and snatched up a sawed-off shotgun. Mr. Big's henchmen were killed, Bud and Brutus escaped to fight another day, and the money was passed on to an orphanage. Or something like that.

"This girl told me the Russians will arrive at nine," Hotch said. "We should see them come in if we stake out the lobby."

"And then what?"

"I make the suggestion that they trade the kid for this goddamn disk."

"What if they tell us to fuck off?" Jackie said. "Only in Russian. Do we really know what all that shit is on the disk anyway? That shit was like five hundred fucking pages."

"I read most of it."

"Bullshit."

"Well," Hotch said, holding on to the dash as Jackie lurched up and around a Honda, nearly taking out a fire hydrant. "I skimmed the son of a bitch. I'll explain it all later, but yeah, this is some shit that some Russians would like to know. And if it gets the kid back, that's all that really matters. Fuck these people."

"Wouldn't that make you a traitor?"

"Sure," Hotch said. "But I'm already thinking ahead on this. We get the kid back and then the Feds can round up all these Soviet assholes."

"Did that FBI woman really say Peter was a Russian, too?"

"Says his mother's a Russian," Hotch said. "So that makes them all Illegals."

"Ain't no way that kid thinks he's Russian," Jackie said. "He's as American as apple pie and Marilyn Monroe's coochie."

"He asked for our help."

"Nobody helped me when I was a kid," Jackie said, holding on to his wig with one hand, driving with the other. "How about you, Hotch?"

"Nope," he said. "Never."

"If you get caught passing that disk, you know the Feds gonna send your ass straight to prison?"

Jackie glanced over as he drove. Hotch reached into the glove compartment to retrieve a pint bottle of Gordon's. He took a swig and then offered the bottle to Jackie. Jackie shook his head as they passed the bright marquee of the Fox Theatre. Lights flashing CAMEO LIVE! shone down into the white leather seats for a brief moment and then they were back in darkness.

"Prison can't be worse than stocking books at Oxford, Too."

"Ever been to prison?"

"Nope."

"Well, I've been to jail a time or two," Jackie said. "I checked too damn many boxes for the guards."

"The world is rigged," Hotch said. "The bastards run the show."

"You just figuring out that shit now?" Jackie said. "I've known that my whole goddamn life."

44

VITALY

"There's been a change of plans," Dan Rafferty said.

The federal agent said it more for the benefit of the two young agents in the front seat than for Vitaly. He and Daniel had already worked out this part at the safe house, Daniel complying with Vitaly's wishes after seeing him so glum. The love of his life, his wondrous little White Fox, had spurned him. He'd given up his wife, his daughter, his country for this woman and the son he'd never known. *What is it all worth, Daniel? Do I live out the rest of my days without meaning and purpose? Am I not entitled to meet my own child?* Daniel listened intently and then came to him later this evening. Oh, his aching stomach. The worst ever. This American Alka-Seltzer making things so much worse. The *plop-plop fizz-fizz* a torture to the senses. *What if there was a way, Vitaly? It can't be long. But I can set something up.*

How, Daniel? How is this even possible?

But Vitaly knew. Vitaly had known within the first days of

arriving in America that Daniel was a pawn of the Soviet Union. This was not so much the faithful offer of a friend, but perhaps Rafferty's chance to lead the bleating goat to the slaughterhouse.

"It must be public."

"Of course."

"And we must be watched by your people," Vitaly said. "No chances."

Daniel had arranged for special transport with two FBI agents, a man they called the Bulldog and one called Caruso, to accompany them to a place called Piedmont Park, the largest park in all of Atlanta. From there, Dan would make contact with the KGB, probably that madman Dimitri Kostov, and hopefully Vitaly's son. The meeting would not last long, shaking hands on a park bench, and Vitaly was to make no offers to the child about coming with him. Those were the terms, Daniel explained. But what was Daniel up to?

"Comrade Yurchenko is in danger," Dan said. "There's a mole in the CIA and they know all about the park. We've made arrangements, without the Agency's knowledge, with the local office to transport our man here via MARTA and then arrive at the Peachtree Center station."

"I do not like the sound of this," Vitaly said.

"Trust me, Vitaly," Daniel said. "It's all very public, open and safe."

The one they called Agent Caruso turned around in the passenger seat. "Excuse me, sir," Caruso said. "Let me get this straight: You want to move a high-level Russian defector on the MARTA? No disrespect or anything, but I don't think it's a good idea. If your man doesn't get kidnapped, he'll probably get mugged."

"Jeremiah Sullivan made the plans," he said. "If you don't agree, you can take it up with your supervisor, Agent Caruso."

Vitaly may have been KGB, but he understood the FBI chain of command. The rolling of the shit down the hill. And in this car, Daniel

Rafferty, friend and quite possibly traitor to America, was temporarily in charge of this elaborate show. Daniel had seemed very jumpy and nervous at the safe house, like a man who'd had too much caffeine or had been zapped by electricity. Vitaly had seen many men take the shocks to their body, quivering and wild-eyed, jumping from subject to subject with few thoughts of coherency. He seemed to view Vitaly from a distance from behind his very thick, smudged golden glasses.

"Special Agent Sullivan planned this?" said the thick American agent they called Bulldog. "After all that mess at the Varsity?"

"Well," Daniel said. "You're not making the decisions, are you? Aren't you both still on probation as rookie agents?"

Caruso muttered something unpleasant under his breath. Vitaly was almost sure he'd said something like *fuck your mother*. But it was changed a bit. Saying something about Daniel perhaps fucking himself? Either way, Daniel didn't appear to be listening, watching out the rear window for this train that would take them into the city of Atlanta and this big hotel where he would finally meet his son.

Vitaly might have been scared, if he hadn't been aware that he'd been on his own mission for some time. And it was Daniel and even these Illegals in Atlanta who had no idea of his real purpose. The thought gave Vitaly his first smile since defecting in Rome and coming to America.

His son. Peter. How wondrous.

"Mr. Yurchenko," Agent Caruso said. "Did the Russians know there might be water on Mars?"

"No," Vitaly said, wondering why the man asked such trivialities. "That was a scientific matter. Not for KGB."

Vitaly saw the squat concrete bunker of a train station coming up on his right. He watched as a subway train shot from the platform and headed toward the tall sparkling buildings of downtown Atlanta.

• • •

Vitaly had memories of an Italian-made Western he'd seen long ago. It had been showing in Moscow at the Khudozhestvenny; the big faces of Charles Bronson, Woody Strode, that one actor with the wild eye named Elam on the screen. Always playing the drunk man. So concerned with the irritating fly on his neck. He recalled Bronson arriving on the train, playing the harmonica on a platform made entirely of railroad ties. There was so much eeriness and buzzing of flies, the thrilling anticipation of the battle that was to come. *"Looks like we're shy one horse."* The quick draw, the shootings and violent deaths. Blood the color of icing on cake. Is this what Daniel expected? He'd already disobeyed his own orders and lied to his own people. Where did he expect to go? Surely not to Russia? Only a madman defected to the Soviet Union.

Vitaly waited as the agent parked the car and then opened the door for him. The big man, Agent Bulldog, who drove, had already moved ahead into the empty station, Daniel trailing them as they headed up and around the stairs to the platform. He could hear Bronson's seesaw harmonica music in his head. He didn't know if it was the threat of an immediate death or the thrill of seeing his son for the first time that scared him more.

But Vitaly would not die. Russia needed him.

• • •

There was no shooting or problems at the train station, just a long boring ride into the city on this subway. So much cleaner and more efficient than the Metro in Moscow. But there was no art in the subway stations of Atlanta, no grand golden chandeliers, frescoes, and bronze statues. The Soviet ideal to bring art to the people in everyday life. But then came the graffiti and the defacing. The flyers taped to the stained-glass images of forgotten war heroes.

The train car was empty except for Vitaly, Dan, and the two young handlers. Or were they just young agents? Daniel had spoken down to the young men, Jimmy Caruso and the Bulldog, so very American, about being on the probation. The seats were a bland orange with city maps and advertisements between the windows. Marlboro cigarettes. Colt 45 malt liquor. McDonald's. Coca-Cola. The commerce of America was their art.

"Just a few more stops, Vitaly."

"Where is my son?"

"Soon."

"Here?"

"Just wait," Daniel said.

They stopped off at a large shopping mall, the car suddenly filled with shoppers laden with bags. As the doors were about to close, Vitaly scanning every face in the car, he watched as his Zoya, Lisica, entered the end of the train with a young boy. At the doors closest to him, he saw Daniel Rafferty step off onto the platform.

The doors shut and the car jolted forward to the lights of the city.

45

PETER

Without a single word, Mr. X bounded down into the basement and pointed a gun at Peter. Peter stayed put on a barstool and just stared at the old man. Even with the gun, the man didn't look threatening; he looked like someone's grandfather or crazy old uncle. *Would you like a warm butterscotch candy from my pocket? How about a hug?* Could you really be afraid of a guy in a moth-eaten cardigan with hair in his ears? He motioned to the stairs with his chin and spoke to Peter in Russian.

Peter still didn't move.

"Now, boy," Mr. X said. "It's time you learn your mother tongue."

"Eat me."

The man looked confused, as if he was the one who didn't know the language. Although Peter was being pretty clear in his directions to the old fuck. The man reached down and grabbed Peter's arm and yanked him from the barstool. The man was surprisingly strong, like the way Peter had heard elderly chimps could rip your damn arm off.

The old man smelled funny, too. Old beets and cabbage, his breath like a thousand ashtrays. "We go."

"Easy, man," Peter said. "Jesus Christ."

He dragged and pushed Peter down the hall and up the stairs, back up into the all-American ranch house. Peter spotted his jean jacket by the door, a Rude Boy pin proudly displayed on the pocket. Peter still not knowing what it really meant, only that he'd seen Prince sport one on his trench coat once.

"You are not to speak," he said. "You are to do as I say."

"Or you'll tighten my braces?"

The man laughed. He smiled at Peter. The man's teeth were awful, yellow-stained, sharp, and crooked. Definitely not the mouth of an orthodontist. Before Peter could say another word, the man slapped him hard in the face. "Now."

Peter knew as soon as they hit the door, he'd sprint as far as he could away from this man. And if this man wanted to shoot at him, all the better. He remembered his kid safety from back in elementary school. You had a better chance running from a kidnapper than going quietly with him. Also run in a serpentine pattern. *Serpentine.* Yeah, he could do that. Just open the door, you old fucker, and he'd be long gone.

"If you try the funny stuff," the man said, "it will be the last you will see of your mother."

"Whatever," Peter said. "She's not my mom. My name is Peter Bennett. I'm a goddamn American citizen and the FBI knows all about you pillow humpers."

The man looked confused. He lowered his gun for a moment and tilted his head. Peter thought about Chuck Norris in *Invasion U.S.A.* and figured he'd kick the man hard in the nuts and take his gun. That's what Chuck would do. Maybe then he could get the keys to his car and drive right to a police station. It might take a while for them to listen. *The KGB has been holding me hostage!* But he'd tell them about Agent Weaver. Agent Sylvia Weaver of the FBI.

"What is this 'pillow humper'?"

"You fuck pillows," Peter said. "Because you're a total loser."

The man snatched up his arm with his left hand and unbolted the door with his right, pushing Peter through the threshold and out into the night. Peter had absolutely no idea of the time. Maybe it was midnight, maybe it was right before dawn. He looked across the street at the similar ranch houses all around them, his eyes adjusting to finally getting out of the basement. Peter started to yell and the man pushed the gun into his ribs and said, "I shoot you in the spinal cord. You might live but you will break. Never walk again."

With the gun barrel in his back, Peter decided not to run. He walked down the path to a blue Volvo parked behind a closed garage where he'd seen the old Mustangs. He moved toward the passenger door, but the man yanked him toward the trunk, the keys rattling in his hand. "In you go, Peter," he said. "In you go."

• • •

Where had he come from? Where had he been? Peter's earliest memories were of New York City and his tiny room in a tiny apartment. They had a television on a rolling cart and that television had been everything. *Sesame Street. Batman.* Man, he loved *Batman. The Electric Company.* "Hey, you guys!" And Spider-Man swinging in to save the day. His mother was gone a lot, and there had been an older woman, Mrs. Lombardi, who'd fed him breakfast and lunch. He remembered the smell of her cigarettes and the way she cut the crusts from his PB&Js.

Peter could see inside the cluttered trunk from the dim red of the brake lights. It seemed to him like Mr. X was taking on every curb, every pothole for calling him a fucking pillow humper. For some reason the insult had really stuck with the old son of a bitch. Peter moved from his back to his side, feeling around in the dim light for something. Another screwdriver or maybe a tire iron. Yeah, a tire iron would be nice. He could clock the bastard in the head and run the hell away.

But then what? *Who was he? Where had he come from? Where had he been?*

New York had been all gray skies, black slush, and snow. And then it was on to the endless golden sun of California, where he and his mother lived outside San Francisco. He went to school but was left to fend for himself for days on end. He climbed orange trees and learned to swim in the apartment pool. The smell of chlorine and oranges still brought him back to those times. He cooked hot dogs in a little portable oven and watched television for hours. This time *The Lone Ranger*. He'd been the Lone Ranger in a Halloween parade once. His mother had bought him a hamster, his first pet, and he'd named it Tonto.

Another fucking pothole. Peter bounced up and knocked his head into the trunk. He reached up and felt blood in his hair. Where were they taking him? What had they done with his mom or Connie or whoever she really was? Were they just going to kill him? Surely, they'd just kill him, as he knew everything about who they were. But nothing about what they wanted beyond the computer disk found on the dead woman. Jenny Buckner. Did they put Jenny Buckner in a trunk?

His mother became a secretary at Ford Motor Company in Detroit and she'd bought a house. She'd loved that house and so had Peter. He remembered it was full of mirrored walls and how his mother had hated them, using a crowbar to break them into shards and paint the walls a bright yellow. Peter had been a good student. He played soccer. He had a lot of friends. He ate pizza, rode bikes. He was in a symphony. He played the bass. His mother cried when she saw he had some musical talent. *Like your father.* The dead Vietnam War hero. A man whom he'd only seen a few times in photos. A handsome young man with lots of brown curly hair in his army uniform and cap. A military man. Peter had never met his father's family. His mom abruptly ending any questions. *They are horrible. They hated me. They did not want you.*

Peter felt sick, being jostled in the trunk. He rolled around the musty carpet, the red light making things worse. At one point, he hoped Mr. X would just pull off the road and shoot him. Be done with it. Go ahead and finish things.

Then they were gone from Detroit. An overnight trip, so fast to pack. He had to leave everything and never questioned why. That was normal, right? Getting off the bus, coming home, and finding your mother packing the Country Squire station wagon. *Get in, I have a new job.*

On to St. Louis. The Arch. The Mississippi River. His mother worked at McDonnell Douglas out by the airport. There were no symphonies or music. But they seemed to have money. For the first time, Peter got new clothes, not ones picked up secondhand. He got his first BMX bike and traveled endlessly among all the suburban neighborhoods, finding his way around lakes and getting lost in cul-de-sacs. He and his friends once found an abandoned golf course, churned up by earth movers and erosion, and they used to play war with toy guns and slingshots. He kissed a girl at twelve. They'd gone into a photo booth, and as the first picture was taken, he leaned in and kissed her on the mouth.

He was in love. Two weeks later, they'd moved to Atlanta.

This time they brought all their furniture and all their clothes. And he was in seventh grade in a new city and a new school and all of it had seemed so damn familiar. Late nights for his mother. More than usual. Or maybe that's just when he noticed all the men. So many goddamn men.

He started to hate her a little.

Even before he knew she was a spy.

Peter curled up into a ball. It was so damn cold back in the trunk. He wrapped his arms around himself and closed his eyes. And when he thought the trip to hell would never end, the car stopped, and Mr. X turned off the motor.

He hadn't found a tire iron or anything behind the pile of old clothes and shoes. Empty packs of cigarettes and a woman's wig. Who were these people?

The trunk sprang open. Mr. X loomed over him. He stood there in the bright lights of a parking lot. Peter's legs had cramped, and he wasn't sure he could move.

"Come."

Peter reached for the edge of the trunk, staring up at Mr. X, until he saw his mother joining the man. She had on a black raincoat, her hair tied up in a scarf. "Yes, Peter," she said. "Come, now. You have someone to meet."

• • •

They pushed Peter up the steps of a MARTA station and his mother slipped three gold tokens into the turnstile. As they got onto the platform, he saw he was at the Lenox station. What was it with these Russians and stupid Lenox Square? He figured they must've kept some kind of office or secret spy base below the mall. Probably near where Mr. X had played sick orthodontist with a pair of pliers, asking him questions about the disk. Had his mother been there the whole time, sitting in the waiting room and flipping through old copies of *Us Weekly* and *People* while Peter screamed his lousy head off?

Two trains appeared, stopped, and then left. Mr. X stood right next to Peter, close enough that he could still feel the gun in his ribs. His mother stood several feet away, checking her watch and watching the trains come and go. She'd stepped onto the last one and then hopped back onto the platform at the last minute. Again, checking the time. She didn't seem concerned in the least about what she'd done to Gary. Who the hell was this woman?

When the third train arrived, his mother looked to Mr. X and nodded. Peter caught her eye and his mother stared back with such a hard, unblinking intensity that he felt as if his blood had started to freeze. Mr. X gripped his arm again and marched him forward. Nothing to see here, just a teenage boy and a creepy old man in an old tweed flop hat and trench coat. Could he yell? Would the man really just shoot him?

They all stepped into the train, and Peter watched as his mother nodded to another man, a geeky-looking guy with a mustache in a Members Only jacket and Coke-bottle glasses. He looked like the kind of guy who'd hang out by the ball fields and offer kids candy to come into his van. He had a really weird vibe about him.

The creeper sat next to a sullen-looking, heavyset man with a big walrus mustache. The man looked deep in thought, maybe a bit sad, and even more confused as the creeper geek quickly left the train, brushing right past Mr. X and his mother. Peter watched as his mother handed the creeper a thick leather satchel of some sort. What in the fuck was going on?

Mr. X marched him down the aisle, most of the seats taken with shoppers from Lenox Square, until they got to the sullen man in the big mustache. Mr. X told Peter to take a seat and then wandered toward the center door, Peter's mother covering the front of the train. The rear doors were open if Peter wanted to make a run for it. And he would as soon as he got a chance.

Peter sat down, closed his eyes, and placed his head in his hands. He still felt sick from being stuffed in that nasty trunk. He could still feel every pothole and sharp turn of Mr. X's crappy old car.

"Peter?" the sad-eyed man with the big mustache said. "It is so very nice to see you with my own eyes."

Peter raised his head and looked at the man. The man smiled so big at him and shook his head as if in amazement.

"We haven't much time," the sad-eyed man said. "But I've come very far to meet you."

Peter shrugged.

"My name is Vitaly Yurchenko."

Peter shrugged again.

"I am your father, Peter," he said. "We have much to discuss."

46

HOTCH

The first gin martini was for courage. The second was a little indulgent.

But damn it, he'd been waiting at the Hyatt's Parasol Bar for more than an hour, and so far, not a Russian in sight. Jackie had overwatch, although that's not what Jackie would ever call it, up on the fourth floor. The levels seeming even more dizzying with the little balconies and philodendrons trailing down into the open space. Great glass elevators shooting up and down from the giant lobby. Hotch looked up to Jackie.

Jackie nodded down to him. From the distance and well into the second martini, damn if he didn't look just like Diana Ross. There'd been a little trouble with the security guard earlier, but Jackie said he'd be performing jazz standards later at the Parasol Bar and the guard believed him. The guard put in a request for "Summertime" and Jackie said he'd try and be sure to slip it in.

Hotch plucked an olive from the glass as a woman sat down next to him. He didn't give it much thought as he scanned the lobby for the Russians he'd seen at Illusions.

"Bad idea, Hotch," Sylvia Weaver said. "Nobody wants to see one hair harmed on that kid. But I might remind you that knowingly passing along government secrets is a little thing we in the FBI call treason."

Hotch nodded. He finished the martini.

"Where's the kid?"

"I have a working theory."

"How'd you find me?"

The Weaver woman gave Hotch a look like he'd gone simple. She shifted her weight on the barstool, to show off the gun under her black blazer. "Do I need to remind you I'm a federal agent?"

"You were following me?"

"Everybody was following you, Mr. Hotchner," she said. "We have a whole goddamn team in a van following you and Mr. Johnson."

"When he's in costume, he prefers to be called Jackie Demure," Hotch said. "His stage name."

"Is that what this is?" Sylvia said. "Y'all performing a stage show? I see a once-famous writer consoling himself with gin. And goddamn two-hundred-pound Diana Ross up on the fourth floor about to sing 'I'm Coming Out.'"

"Oh, Jackie came out a long time ago," Hotch said. "About the time he got caught fucking Freddie the Falcon."

"Please tell me y'all got a plan."

"How about you?"

Sylvia Weaver nodded. The other agent he'd met, the tall guy named Radish or something, stood over by the elevators. He glanced across the lobby, obviously looking for the same Russians who'd taken Peter. Hotch still had a hell of a hard time believing Peter's mother had thrown in with them or was a Russian herself. Even though he'd written a pretty accurate assessment of how Russians could indeed be living next door. East Cobb was a hell of a long way from the Caspian Sea.

"Are you sure about the mother?"

"Pretty damn sure."

"You know what this is all about?"

"I think it's all in the family, Hotch."

"The US government was paying Scientific Atlanta to study SDI," he said. "You know. Star Wars? Strategic Defense Initiative? Laser beams and satellites. More peace-through-strength bullshit."

Agent Weaver leveled another gone-simple look at Hotch.

"So what?" she said. "I don't give a good goddamn what they were doing. I just want you to hand over that disk. And keep your ass out of federal prison."

"I'd probably get a lot of work done," Hotch said. "Finish up this project on Russian spies."

"You can't write this," she said. "Not now. Not ever."

"Says who?"

"Uncle Sam."

"Fuck Uncle Sam," he said. "And fuck Ronald Reagan. And fuck Bonzo his stupid chimp. This is nuts. All of this is nuts. No matter what happens, these assholes are going to figure out a way to blow us all up. They've been itching to do it since after the war. I got frostbite in Korea over this bullshit and nearly got my eye shot out."

"Always wondered about the eye," she said. "How about that disk, now?"

Hotch shook his head. "Do you think I'd be stupid enough to walk into the Atlanta Hyatt with it on me?"

Sylvia Weaver let out a long breath and shook her head. "You really want me to answer that question?"

"If Peter's mom is a spy, then it's not his fault," Hotch said. "He just got born into a crummy world where adults don't give a shit about kids. Other than to use them up for cover or just plain use them up and work them to death. You blame the kid for the sins of the mother? He didn't ask for this. He didn't ask for any of this crap."

"You talking about Peter?" she said. "Or your own self?"

"Oh, hell." Hotch motioned to the bartender. "Who are you, Dr. Joyce?"

"I wouldn't."

"Well, you're not me," Hotch said. "Either arrest me or leave me the hell alone. I'll handle this the way I see fit."

"May have to wait, Hotch," she said. Sylvia wasn't even giving him the respect of looking him in his good eye. She was watching some kind of commotion in the lobby. "Our Russians are just coming on the scene."

Hotch glanced over his shoulder. *Well, fuck a duck.* Instead of the two Russians from Illusions, it was an older guy who looked like a medieval professor by way of Mr. Rogers. And then Hotch saw Peter with his mom. But she didn't look like nice Connie Bennett. Dressed in a black trench coat and dark scarf covering her head, she looked like a woman on a mission.

"What's wrong?"

"Well," Sylvia said. "This ain't Piedmont Park."

"Piedmont Park?" Hotch asked. "What the hell? They were always coming here. Let me approach 'em. I make the trade and then you people do whatever the hell you want."

"You saying you want to be an asset?"

"Sure," Hotch said. "It will surprise the hell out of my ex-wives."

"Uh-oh."

"What do you mean, uh-oh?" Hotch said, laying down a generous ten-dollar bill.

"Means we're fucked."

As the group turned, Hotch saw Peter's mother had left the group and a new man stood speaking with Peter. Hotch glanced over, looked back to Sylvia Weaver, and then glanced back again. The man looked like a stockier version of Lech Wałęsa, with graying hair and a big, droopy mustache. "Holy crap," Hotch said. "Is that fucking Vitaly Yurchenko in Atlanta?"

"And it looks like he lost our agents."

"Uh-oh," Hotch said.

"Goddamn right."

. . .

Sylvia rushed toward the elevators, where she met up with her partner, the man she called Agent Ravetch or Irv. Ravetch, of course. Like the guy who wrote the movie *Vengeance Valley*. How fitting. The guts of the big hotel looked like a wide concrete valley. Hotch cut through the open lobby looking up at all the glass elevators. He spotted Peter in one with both hands pressed to the glass and looking down to Hotch. He was saying something, breath fogging the glass. *Help me?* Or perhaps *Oh, shit*. Either way, Peter was trying to tell him something.

Hotch reached into his leather jacket and touched the edge of the disk. If he could just get a message to the damn Russians, maybe they'd free the kid.

Sylvia and the other agent ran past him toward the front desk. Hotch looked up at Jackie and shrugged and then motioned for him to come on down. *Why the hell not?* Something was happening and he knew Jackie Demure would want to be part of the show. Diana Ross! Writer Dennis Hotchner! Defector Vitaly Yurchenko! How about Telly Savalas? Or Charles Nelson Reilly? Nothing would surprise Hotch at this point.

Sylvia had walked ahead of a line of guests checking in and was currently having a heart-to-heart with the woman behind the desk. The woman looked icy and cold, lots of eye makeup and frosted hair. "Their elevator stopped at the twenty-second floor," Sylvia said.

"We don't give out guest information," the icy blonde said. "If you'll just step back and get in line, ma'am. And wait your turn."

"Wait my turn?" Sylvia Weaver flashed her badge. "Lady, y'all about to have a goddamn international incident. My partner needs to use your phone. I just need to know who in the hell is staying in the suites on the twenty-second floor and get me your security. No one is leaving this castle."

Hotch stepped back in time to see Jackie round the corner from the stairs. Hotch looked around for the house phones and found a neat little paneled cove by the gift shop.

"Did you see Peter?"

Hotch nodded.

"And his momma?"

Hotch cradled the phone between his ear and shoulder, and punched up different variations of rooms on the twenty-second floor. On the fourth try, a man with a noticeable Russian accent picked up. "Yes."

"I have something you want, Ivan."

"I'm not Ivan," the man said. "Who is this on telephone line?"

"A friend of Jenny Buckner's."

The line went silent for a moment. Hotch heard men conversing in Russian before a woman with an American accent picked up the phone. "What do you want?"

"Mrs. Connie Bennett, I presume?" he said. "Dennis X. Hotchner. How about you send Peter down and I'll send up that disk that's caused all that trouble."

"What disk?" the woman said.

"Or I could hand it over to the Feds right now," he said. "I only want to see Peter safe."

The line was quiet again. This time for even longer. More arguing in Russian. This time between the woman, Peter's mom, and two men. From the cover of the house phones, Hotch watched Sylvia Weaver and her partner speaking to two armed guards. Agent Weaver was pointing upward into the atrium, beyond the endless philodendrons, high up to the twenty-second floor.

"You want to sit this one out, Hotch?" Jackie said.

"I would," Hotch said. "But my ass has grown sore."

Hotch patted the right-hand pocket of his jacket and motioned to Jackie to sneak around the atrium toward the elevators. They got onto a glass elevator without being stopped but when Hotch tried to mash the button for the twenty-second floor, it wouldn't light up.

"You need a key."

Hotch pushed the button for the twenty-first floor and the same thing happened. Jackie shook his head, pressed the button for the doors to open, and stepped off the elevator. "Only one of us is going to be able to hike on up there. And ain't your broke-down ole ass."

"Bring down Peter," Hotch said. "When I see you two coming down safe, I'll ride up with the disk."

"But you don't have a key."

"Let me worry about that," Hotch said. "Just get the kid."

"So that's it?" Jackie said, shaking his long Diana Ross locks. "We gonna just sell out motherfuckin' America?"

"Damn it, Jackie," Hotch said. "Didn't you ever read *The Peterson File*?"

"Is that the one where they exchanged the thingy with the whosis?"

"Exactly."

47

VITALY

"Peter," Vitaly said. "Our time together is quite short. You must listen to me and decide for yourself."

Peter, just a boy, stared at him. When Vitaly was that age, it was during the Great War. He had to care for his entire family in Leningrad while his father was in a U-boat patrolling off the coast of America. A miraculous day might produce a potato or a beet. He had to scrounge for wood and trash to burn. He once found a live chicken—a miracle!—and clubbed it to death with a brick. Such a feast at their house. His mother broke into tears when he set it upon their empty table.

"You're not my father," Peter said. "My father is dead."

"No, no," Vitaly said. He tried to summon a sympathetic smile. He'd been trained extensively in building rapport with enemies. But his son was not his enemy. The boy in front of him in the jean jacket was his own child, born to a conniving, beautiful, and athletic new recruit brought to the Yurlovo facility so many years ago. "Lies from your mother."

"Is she even my mother?"

"Yes," Vitaly said, patting Peter's knee. He flinched and Vitaly noticed the cut on his head. What had these animals done to his son? Would he now be faced with watching a father he'd never known receive a bullet in the back of his head? "I came for you, Peter. I came here to find you."

The boy didn't look like he knew what to say. Zoya and her two Illegal handlers were in another hotel room with that bastard Dimitri Kostov and his ape, Anotoliy Zub. They were discussing a plan to get Vitaly to the port at Savannah and on a freighter bound for Gdańsk in Poland. He was to be sedated and bound. His superiors in Moscow wanted him alive to face his country in person. All at once, the days of watching the CIA men play golf and grill steaks in Virginia seemed pleasant. So many talks with the man they called Charlie. An alternative to the madness.

"I will help you, Peter," Vitaly said. "You must trust me."

The boy shook his head. "I don't trust any of you Russian bastards," he said. "Let me go."

"Peter."

Vitaly smoothed down his mustache. He stood up and walked close to the doorway where he could hear Zoya arguing with that maniac Kostov. A man named Hotchner had called and he had brought a computer disk. A disk? What was this about a disk? Suddenly there was great confusion and worry, the man threatening to give it to the FBI if they didn't listen.

If he could subdue Zub, they could escape. Even Zoya wouldn't stop him. She knew it was the best thing for the boy. His heart broke that she wouldn't follow. But he always knew that was the way of his little White Fox. She would disappear down the hole and be gone forever. But his Peter was right here. If he would just trust him and listen.

Vitaly took a seat again across from Peter. The floors were thick with rich, brown American carpet, walls covered in metallic gold wallpaper. The city lights twinkled beyond the great windows. He clasped his hands together and spoke in a whisper. "What do you know of a disk?"

"My mother killed a woman for it."

"Yes," Vitaly said. "She does such things."

"And she killed a man named Gary Powers."

"From the spy plane?"

Peter shrugged. Vitaly noticed he wore a small pin on the pocket of his Levi's jacket that read *Rude Boy*. Vitaly motioned to the pin.

"It means not to take any shit."

"We must escape," Vitaly said. "Or we die."

Peter shrugged again. "Whatever."

"It is the only way."

48

PETER

His father left the massive hotel room, and his mother replaced him. Without a word, she took the very same seat occupied by the man called Vitaly Yurchenko and reached out to touch Peter's hand. He pulled it back and shook his head. "You're all crazy," he said. "You're all a bunch of liars."

"Did he ask for you to return to Russia with him?"

Peter shook his head. His mother, holding herself in quite a different way than good ole Connie Bennett, nodded and cocked her head to the side. "That is good," she said. "Your father, Peter, is a traitor. He sold out his country for a million dollars and forty thousand dollars a year. What kind of man does such a thing?"

Peter didn't know. It sounded like a crap ton of money to him.

"When he returns to Russia, he'll no longer be a man of position," Connie Bennett said. But not sounding much like Connie Bennett anymore, her soft, sensitive way of speaking now harder and much more direct. But still without a trace of an accent. "Your father will face a tribunal and will be executed. I know you just met. But life is hard, Peter. It's better for you to know these things."

"I'm not going to Russia with him," he said. "Or with you. I'm getting the hell out of here."

"First, there's something you must do," Connie said. *Connie.* It was best just to think of her as Connie. Not his mom or fucking Olga or whoever she really was. She wasn't so scary. She was just a crazy lady with a flowery scarf over her head. "You should've never trusted this writer. He's followed us here and he has something that was stolen from me."

"And you killed the woman who stole it."

Connie shrugged. "It wasn't hers."

The direct coldness, and the way Connie just stared at Peter as if he was far too bright to be questioning her motives, made him uneasy. In the next room, the Russians were arguing in—what else?—Russian. He heard the word *police* and *FBI* and then the man—his *father*, Vitaly—raised his voice in English and said, "Fuck your mother."

A print of an oil painting hung over the super-king-size bed, a young, muscled dude in a toga flying past the sun on large, feathered wings. Even at the moment, Peter found the art to be odd inside the Hyatt. The toga dude looked to be falling from the sky but raising his fist in triumph.

"Very soon a man will knock on the door," she said, pressing a room key into his hand. "I want you to take the elevator down with him. But as soon as you can, I want you to go to the stairs and come back."

"Bullshit," Peter said. "I'm running away."

"To where, Peter?" she said. "Where would you go? You come back here and we can leave together. We can start over in a new town with new names. You're almost old enough to have a car. I hear it's very nice in Arizona. No more cold winters."

"You people are absolutely nuts."

"Or," she said, "if you don't go, one of the men will put a bullet in Dennis Hotchner's head."

Peter stared at her. He was so angry, he wanted to slap his own mother. He swallowed and stood up, walking over to the wall with the framed print. As he got closer, he could see something melting off the dude's wings. He was absolutely coming undone and falling to the earth.

• • •

It wasn't Hotch. It was Jackie.

But Jackie didn't look like Jackie or even Tina Turner tonight. He had on a very slinky, sparkly pantsuit and a long, black, curly wig. He sported dangly diamond earrings along with his deep blue eyeshadow and bright red lipstick. In the hotel suite foyer, Jackie stood toe to toe with a huge Russian with a buzz cut. Both men were about the same height and weight.

"You dress for the Halloweens?" the big Russian said.

"I'm dressed to celebrate Diana Ross," Jackie said. "Do you know the name of her new album?"

The big Russian looked over to the shorter, older Russian in a funny old-fashioned hat and tan jacket, and shrugged.

"*Eaten Alive*," Jackie said. "Don't go and fuck yourself, big man. I been up against Stan Walters with the Eagles and put his damn dick into the dirt. Six feet six and two seventy-five. Don't let these high heels make you stupid."

"This woman who is man," the Russian said, "he make me laugh."

"Laugh all you want, Ivan the Terrible," Jackie said, looking over at Peter. "Here's how it's gonna go. Me and the boy are going to get on that glass elevator. As soon as my associate sees we are safely on our way, he'll come up and hand-deliver the disk. After that, y'all can dance the fucking Kalinka and pull each other's peckers. But if you harm my man, Hotch, ain't a rock in Siberia that won't be finding your ass."

"I don't Kalinka," the big man said. "How about you, Vitaly? Perhaps you learn the Kalinka when you go back to Moscow. Before your execution."

The shorter Russian in the old-fashioned hat and coat nodded to the larger Russian. "You see this is done properly. Yes?"

Peter's mother put her arm around Peter and marched him toward the door. Just then Peter's newly found father, the infamous Vitaly Yurchenko, came out of the bedroom. He told the other Russians that he didn't want his son going anywhere.

"Don't worry, Vitaly," his mother said. "Don't worry. He's loyal. I'm the one who trained him. Not you."

• • •

Peter and Jackie were on the elevator. The big Russian had come with him, using his key to make it all work, and soon they were descending fast into the lobby. "I don't think I gotta tell you to get the fuck out of here," Jackie said, whispering to Peter. "This place is crawling with cops and motherfuckin' FBI. Those Russians won't know what hit them."

"And my mom?"

"Be quiet," the Russian said. "No discussion."

"I don't know, kid," Jackie said.

Halfway down, Peter caught sight of Hotch. He waved as they descended, and after they stopped and the doors slid open, Hotch walked up to the elevator. He looked over at the big Russian and shrugged, not at all surprised by an armed guard on the way back up.

"My mom said if I don't come back to her, she'll kill you."

"Shut up," the big Russian said. "You must be quiet."

"Russians are big jokers," Hotch said. "Your mom must be a real riot."

"I promise," Peter said. "They'll shoot you. They're taking my father somewhere near Savannah and then back to Poland. To face a tribunal and then an execution."

"Be quiet, boy," the Russian said. The big ugly man pulled a pistol from his belt and pointed it at Hotch's midsection. The gun was long and skinny with a silencer pipe on the end. Russian assassins fucking loved their silencers.

"Wait," Hotch said, holding the door open. "Your father?"

"My father," Peter said. "Vitaly Yurchenko."

Hotch stepped onto the elevator, but before the doors snapped shut, Jackie stepped inside with him and held the doors open. He looked out at Peter.

"Go get Sylvia," Jackie said.

Peter ran out into the sprawling lobby and craned his neck up to see Hotch, Jackie Demure, and a massive Russian ascend up into the ceiling. It felt like they were traveling so fast the elevator would break free and rocket into space like in *Willy Wonka*.

49

HOTCH

The big Russian tried to shoot them both before they even reached the tenth floor. Jackie saw him raising the pistol and knocked it free from his hand. The Russian reached out and ripped off Jackie's wig and Jackie hit him with a hard right. The Russian shook his head and wiped his mouth with the back of his hand. "I never fought woman before."

"We even," Jackie said. "I never fought a Russian. Let's go, bitch."

Hotch stepped out of the way as the Russian knocked Jackie against the glass. Hotch on his hands and knees looking for the gun and finding it. He stood up and aimed it as the men fought, moving the barrel from right to left, afraid to shoot and hit Jackie in the tiny space. The men thudded against the glass again and then the elevator suddenly stopped, all of them tumbling out onto the twenty-second floor. Hotch fell onto his back and was trying to stand when he felt a shoe on his hand that held the gun. He looked up to see Peter's sweet mother, Connie Bennett, in her *Ninotchka* getup with the headscarf and black raincoat.

She pulled the gun from his hand and then kicked him in the face. He tried to get to his feet when she aimed the gun and shot him. The woman fucking shot him. She shot him right in the stomach. The strange thing was that there was immense pain and then damn well nothing. Just like the time with his eye. Only this time he didn't lose consciousness. If anything, he was more awake than ever.

Jackie was bareheaded now in a rhinestone jumpsuit, high heels kicked off, in a fistfight with a big, ugly Russian. The Russian tried to kick out Jackie's legs but Jackie was too damn fast and sidestepped him. Jackie lunged for the man, stepped back, and then stepped forward with a hard punch to the gut. It must be hell getting your ass handed to you by Diana Ross.

Hotch was on his back and pushed himself against the wall. He opened his leather coat to see the wound and it wasn't pretty. Some internal stuff, besides the blood, that was probably best kept inside the body. As Hotch tried to close the coat, Peter's mother reached inside and extracted the disk from his inner pocket.

He closed his eyes and then opened them again. Peter and goddamn Vitaly Yurchenko stood over him. The man he'd seen in *Newsweek* and *Time* yelled for towels and then began pressing the towels hard against Hotch's stomach.

Peter was on his knees beside Yurchenko trying to help Hotch, while down the hall, Hotch saw Peter's mother step onto a service elevator. He tried to speak but couldn't say a stupid goddamn word. Hotch pretty damn sure he saw a smile on the woman's face as the door snapped closed. She had no idea the disk was a fake. A *Mad* magazine *Spy vs. Spy* game Peter's friend Brenda Yee had passed along.

More Russians yelling. The older man in the cardigan, the one he'd seen in the lobby with Peter, stepped out in the hallway and yelled for Jackie and the big Russian, the man he called Zub, to stop. But neither of them listened, both battered and bloody, Jackie's right eye swollen closed, blood pouring from the big Russian's nose as they circled each other. The old man in the cardigan yelled again for them to stop and then pulled a gun. Great, another fucking gun. Hotch's eye drooped. He thought of Slim Pickens in *Pat Garrett and Billy the Kid*. That Dylan song about knockin' on heaven's door. Yes, he'd done it. He'd helped save the kid and Jackie was about to finish off Ivan the Terrible. *Where you headed? Nowhere special. Always wanted to go there . . .*

"Stay awake," Vitaly Yurchenko said. "Stay awake."

The Mr. Rogers Russian aimed his gun at Jackie, but before he could shoot, goddamn Vitaly Yurchenko bodychecked the son of a bitch and sent him flying over the barrier and down twenty-two floors into the mouth of the lobby. Hotch couldn't see it but damn well heard the glass breaking. He was pretty sure the bastard had gone through the umbrella roof of the Parasol Bar.

The big Russian didn't even stop. He lunged again for Jackie, and Jackie shook his head. He stepped back and lowered his fists, crouching into a defensive end stance. The Russian smiled and rushed him again and "Big Time" Jackie Johnson took out the man's legs and knocked him hard into the concrete barrier. Hotch thought he was about to send him over into the lobby, too, Jackie lifting with his legs. But instead Jackie dropped the beaten man in a big heap in the hallway.

Jackie, trying to catch his breath, had seen something across the atrium. Hotch turned in the opposite direction to see two security guards and Sylvia Weaver's partner hauling ass down the long hall. The federal agent had pulled his gun, holding it in both hands as he ran.

The shorter Russian from Illusions raced over to help the big Russian off the ground. Like rats, they did their best to scurry toward the exit to escape. *Good luck with that.*

"Best seat in the house," Hotch said.

Jackie walked up beside Vitaly Yurchenko. "Okay?"

Vitaly shook his head.

"You could at least lie," Hotch said. "Christ. Can't a KGB agent just lie?"

"Save your strength," Vitaly said. "You may die later. But now I must have your help."

Hotch nodded, eyes fluttering closed, hearing Dylan's song. What a great send-off. Killed by a Russian assassin! He'd definitely get a *Times* obit. They whole staff at Oxford, Too could suck it. His backlist would be in print again. Maybe a television deal.

Jackie leaned over the banister and looked down into the lobby. He shook his head but wore a big grin. "FBI snatching up all those fools," he said. "I'm going to get some help, Hotch. Stay cool. And don't die. That's the important part."

"Peter's mom?" Hotch asked.

"I don't see her."

"And you never will," Vitaly said. "*Whoosh*. She is a little white fox."

The last thing Hotch remembered before passing out was Jackie down on one knee and looking over at the great Russian defector. "Yup. Chasing tail been the downfall of many a man, Vitaly. Hotch? Come on, now. Hotch?"

50

DAN

Atlanta had not ended well. An Illegal killed as he dropped through the glass ceiling of a Hyatt bar, the number two Russian at Washington Station arrested, and a suspected KGB assassin gone with the goddamn wind. The boys at the FBI annex had a lot of fun with the whole *Gone With the Wind* thing, calling the unknown Soviet Illegal, known as Constance Bennett, the real Scarlett O'Hara. *"After all, tomorrow is another day."* Dan Rafferty didn't think it was funny at all. The Russians had fucked up and now had fucked him. His plans with Wanda had to be put on hold and it had been ten days since he last saw her. Ten damn days until it was okay to meet up again, at midnight in the lonely parking lot of a Safeway in Bethesda.

Dan arrived first and Wanda a few minutes later. He was shocked to see her driving her late boyfriend's—perhaps husband's—baby blue Pontiac Firebird. As ostentatious as it was inappropriate.

"How's tricks, daddy?" she said, sliding into the passenger seat of his dull silver Citation. Compared to the Firebird, he looked to be driving a bread box on wheels.

"You look wonderful," he said. "You smell wonderful. My God, Wanda. This has been such a mess. Such a mess."

Wanda had on a pin-striped suit with big shoulder pads and a cream silk top that offered a generous display of her lovely assets. A strand of pearls Dan had bought for her some time ago dropped nearly down to her navel. She looked like a true fashionable lady. A woman who could join him at fine restaurants across the globe once their new life began together. He wasn't sure when that would happen. After Atlanta, the Russians had been a bit cagey about coming around to his terms. Especially Dimitri Kostov, who was picked up in Atlanta and spent a week in jail. At the moment, the paperwork was being filed for him to be deported as an undesirable. But the Russians would make good. And Dan had already been laying the groundwork with Delores, tipping her off that life was about to change for the Rafferty family and to pray for new beginnings for them all.

"It won't be long," Dan said. "How did your manager at Joanna's take it when you quit?"

Wanda had her short hair poofed up with a lot of mousse, the tips frosted and bold. Her earrings looked like those triangle badges the crew on *Star Trek* wore on their chests.

"Oh, I didn't quit," she said. "That's the best job I ever had."

Dan felt the blood rush to his face. Did everything he planned have to fall apart? He'd told this woman time and again what she was supposed to do, and still she wouldn't listen. It was that hard, hillbilly brain of hers that couldn't conceive of a life where she didn't get by showing her damn tits.

"I told you to quit," he said. "You've got to be ready at any moment for us to leave."

Wanda reached into her purse for a paper receipt and spit her gum into it. She closed up the paper and stuck it back in her purse. "Daniel," she said. "Dear Daniel. They will never let you leave."

"What did you say?"

"I said, you can never leave," she said. "I can never leave either. We are doomed to walk the earth in their service."

"You called me Daniel."

"Yes," she said, the hillbilly shuck gone now. Now he heard more Warsaw, or Odessa, than Wheeling, West Virginia. "That is your name. Daniel Rafferty. Second in command of counterintelligence at the FBI annex. No?"

"Wanda?"

"Sure," she said. "Or you may still call me Trinity Velvet. I quite like that name. So wild and fun. But you are not to leave your post. You're too important to us, Daniel. You have brought so much wonderful information to the people of the Soviet Socialist Republic. You are my comrade now."

Dan looked out onto the Safeway parking lot, all the empty spaces under the lights. The Safeway sign missing lights in a few of its letters. It looked to be spelling "Safe." *Safe. Sure.*

"Do you love me?"

"Of course, Daniel," she said. "Why not? You buy me many gifts and bring me much pleasure."

"And your husband?" Dan asked. "That guy Larry?"

"Oh," she said, grabbing his knee. "So fun. The fake blood from his mouth. You were so scared. Perhaps we do it again."

"I can't stay here," he said. "It's only a matter of time until they blame me for Atlanta. There's already an investigation. I've already taken cash out from my pension. I plan to leave my wife and family. All for you."

"That wasn't so smart," she said. "Was it?"

"Wanda," he said. "Why?"

"Am I not now the woman of your dreams?" she said. "Do you wish to unbutton your fly? I'll make you happy. This one last time."

Dan looked down at his crotch. Not feeling a thing below the belt. Not even a pleasant stirring.

Wanda smiled. "This is what I thought."

She shrugged and climbed out of the modest Chevrolet. A middling bureaucrat's car.

Dan sat frozen as he watched her cross the empty lot and get into her baby blue Firebird, blazing bird decal on the hood. She revved the engine before screeching off into the night.

• • •

A day later and it was Halloween. Vitaly Yurchenko was back at the safe house with the CIA and locked down so hard, they barely let Dan back into the compound. He was shocked to know that the CIA okayed him having dinner with Vitaly before Vitaly would be moving to somewhere in the Midwest into much safer keeping. Dan offered the Mayflower for dinner. Vitaly said he preferred something French. They decided on the Au Pied de Cochon in Georgetown. Only a few blocks from Joanna's 1819 Club, which put him in a glum mood.

"Daniel," Vitaly said as they sat across from each other at the white linen–covered table. "We have lived to tell the tale. So much excitement."

"Perhaps for you."

"But for you, too," Vitaly said. He was dressed the exact same way as he had been when he'd stepped into the first safe house in Virginia. The tattered white dress shirt, navy sport coat, and gray slacks. Even his shoes seemed to be his old Russian shoes. Was he trying to make a point?

The restaurant was old-school French with copper skillets and pots hanging from the dark wood walls, brass banisters across the bar. The waiters wore white aprons and your glass of wine never seemed empty. So far, Dan had had three glasses of a passable Côtes du Rhône that was less exotic and more reminded him of communion. *Oh, God. Communion.* So much he'd have to explain to Father Rick.

"I must know, Daniel," Vitaly said, smoothing down the edges of his ridiculously long mustache. "How is it that you talked your way out of this one?"

"What do you mean?"

"Oh, please," Vitaly said. "Only comrades here. More wine?"

Dan shrugged. Vitaly reached over and refilled his glass.

"You changed our meeting at the park," Vitaly said. "You disappeared off the train so that the KGB could evade those two young federal agents."

"You're the one who lost me," Dan said. "You're the one who insisted on the train because you thought you'd be killed in the park."

"Interesting," Vitaly said. "You are such a robust liar, Dan. You are a fine asset to the Soviet Union."

"Excuse me?"

"Was it for love or for money?" he said. "Or are you a truly committed communist?"

Dan just stared at Vitaly. He breathed in and out. Dan Rafferty was completely exhausted, turned inside out. A strong Christian man, a man of faith and conviction, who'd been completely played by a fourteen-year-old kid, a hack writer, and a fucking transvestite. This was exactly the kind of world that had scared the hell out of him.

Vitaly leaned into the table and smiled. "I have a secret, too."

Dan raised his eyebrows. He took a large swallow from his glass of wine.

"It was all a ruse," Vitaly said. "A game. I return to Soviet Union soon."

"You faked it?"

"Yes," Vitaly said, stroking his mustache. "We both played our hands, Daniel. What fun. I commend you on your work. You will be rewarded in time."

Dan let out a long breath. At least this was something. At least he'd be recognized for all he'd done. He reached for the wine and finished it off. Vitaly poured more. Everything was so festive. Such a relief to know he and Vitaly were working together.

"Do not be upset with yourself," Vitaly said. "About the woman. Your handler is quite good. You should see the wondrous intelligence she gleaned from the Japanese ambassador. He was ready to sell Tokyo to this woman. She's very, very good."

Dan closed his eyes. He breathed again. "I loved her."

"Ha," Vitaly said, lifting his glass. "Such fools are we."

"But you had a kid."

"To meet him once," Vitaly said. "This was all worth it."

"There were other things," Daniel said, not able to stop talking. "I gave the KGB other things. Names of people in Moscow who reported to us. They were killed, Vitaly. Not even a tribunal. I gave them names. Your little friend, hotfooting out of the hotel with a disk with Star Wars secrets. I gave away the world for love. Where does this get America at Geneva? We have nothing."

"You gave the USA away for yourself, Daniel," Vitaly said, standing and placing the napkin in his lap upon the table. "My stomach again. If I don't come back, you must not blame yourself."

"Excuse me?"

Vitaly walked away as a half dozen people surrounded their quaint, quiet little table. One of them was the Black rookie agent from Atlanta. Agent Weaver or some other thing.

"Is there a problem?"

"Yes, sir," said the Black woman. "You're being arrested for espionage, Mr. Rafferty."

"Special Agent Rafferty."

"Not anymore," Weaver said. "We got everything you just said on tape. As clear as Maxell and Ella Fitzgerald breaking that glass. Now come with us, sir."

As they marched him out of Au Pied de Cochon, Dan yet to touch the poached salmon they'd both ordered, he caught a glimpse of Vitaly Yurchenko walking away. No handlers, hands in pockets, and blending into the Halloween revelers.

Where was he headed?

51

VITALY

If he could not be with his love or his son, perhaps he could be the man who saved the world. Vitaly walked with purpose down M Street, in and out of Halloween frivolity. So many masks of the aliens, monsters, and men dressed as exterminators of ghosts. A drunken woman in a mask bumped into him and asked him if he'd like to phone home. *Phone home?* Yes, he would. Vitaly was exhausted and would very much like to return to Moscow to his boring wife and indifferent daughter, his job of much bureaucracy and the dacha that needed much work. The windowsills were rotting and letting melting snow inside. But it was home. He was tired of the fast food, the shopping malls, and so many traitors. Dan Rafferty was supposed to be a friend but instead turned him over to KGB to receive the bullet reward. No more.

Vitaly would return home a hero. Already there would be talk of the Order of the Red Star. How could this be? How could a lovesick man wander the streets of Rome and turn himself over to the CIA and still be a hero? Because Vitaly was returning home with a prize, a reward from his time in America, a locked computer disk—not even seen by Lisica herself—that contained so many secrets on Reagan's Star Wars. Gorbachev and Reagan at the Fleur d'Eau château on Lake Geneva. Perhaps this little disk could help the Russians decide their own fate. The horrors of a mutually assured destruction finally averted.

He could only imagine the wondrous lies the disk held. But the CIA man called Charlie had called it a game changer. It had been Charlie who'd orchestrated the meeting with Dan and the letting go of the Big Fish. Vitaly Yurchenko would walk the two miles back to the Soviet embassy and declare a Russian victory. A false defection. His mission complete.

According to the disk the CIA gave him, Reagan's dream was a reality. For now. Space lasers could exist. Russia could not compete. The Americans could make a first strike with little retribution. It was time for the madness to end.

Vitaly enjoyed his final night free in America. He lifted the collar of his coat and blew on his hands. It would be so much colder in Moscow. He saw Halloween revelers dressed as Frankenstein, the Dracula, and men made up to look like women. And women, men. But also the rubber faces of Reagan and Gorbachev. Even a Fidel Castro or two. Merely players. Was that correct? The world a stage full of men dressed as women and spies masquerading as heroes. So much madness.

Before heading into the embassy, he stopped off at a small drinking establishment. He ordered a Jack Daniel's and smoked a cigarette from a pack Charlie had given him. Above the bar on a small television played a movie about the end of the world. Spaceships and laser beams. Perhaps a time when the nations would need each other.

Maybe someday. He finished the whiskey, stubbed out the cigarette, and walked across the street and back into the old, drafty mansion that was Mother Russia.

"Fuck your mother."

52

LISICA

It had been 1975 or '76 and Lisica had been tasked with planting bugs inside the United Nations and a suite at the Waldorf where the American ambassador often stayed. A glorious time. The Soviets had antennae on rooftops all across Manhattan. Lisica had so many contacts and so many lovers, an encrypted notebook was kept with names, occupations, and proclivities. Lisica broke into secure facilities, cultivated assets, and made dead drops and brush passes throughout the city. All of this while raising a child and keeping a respectable job at the FAO Schwarz on Fifth selling Barbie dolls and teddy bears. The job was a wonderful cover and a delight to Lisica's young son, a bright, mischievous boy whom she called Peter. Named for the Prokofiev composition.

They had a helper, a kindly neighbor woman named Mrs. Lombardi, who not only walked Peter to and from kindergarten but would brighten their dull apartment with the smell of boiling tomato sauce on cold winter evenings. Lisica had never had such wonderful food and despite slipping out in the middle of the night and the odd two-day assignment, life and the mission were in harmony.

Lisica had never wanted a child. The entire affair had been a mistake, a folly of youth and arrogance while training at the Yurlovo facility in a thick forest outside Moscow. Vitaly Yurchenko had been a powerful man, a party elite who'd come to speak to their classes. He'd been taken with the young, beautiful, and ambitious Lisica. And Lisica had responded as any orphan child from East Germany might. Lisica showered Yurchenko with adulation and much physical attention. He was so stable, so clear-eyed in his purpose for Mother Russia. Yurchenko's personal tutoring sessions soon took place in Moscow hotel rooms and once in a great sauna where they were alone except for a bottle of vodka and many birch branches. Before each ending, he would say *my dear little fox*.

Lisica thought the special mission, special purpose, was over after becoming pregnant. Lisica even arranged for a termination at a special government clinic. Ending a pregnancy was neither legal nor illegal then. Like much of Russia, it was something that happened while other people counted their rubles and looked the other way.

It had been the great Vitaly who'd begged—no, ordered!—her to keep the child. He, of course, could not take responsibility. But the child would make a fine cover in America. *Who would suspect a young mother and her delightful child being Russian spies?*

Peter had been born in America, at a hospital in Buffalo, New York, the birth only solidifying Lisica's cover story as Constance Bennett. The New York days had been Lisica's happiest, living in Manhattan while infiltrating the UN and spying on those who might prove themselves disloyal to the Soviet Union. Lisica recalled when one low-level KGB agent working as a reporter with TASS, the Russian state news agency, had started to turn against them, meeting with known FBI agents in Central Park. Lisica had been running late from the Christmas rush at FAO Schwarz. Besides Barbie, there was the Six Million Dollar Man (a favorite of Peter's, especially his battle with the evil Bigfoot), and even the King Kong who'd climbed his way to the top of the Empire State Building once again.

Lisica had met with another agent, another Illegal known only as Doug, at the golden monument to the most American of all lies, the blowing up of the *Maine*. Lisica and Doug took turns tailing the traitor through the park. Through the tunnels and under the arches, Christmas lights in the trees, all the way to the carousel. They watched the KGB agent make a brush pass, a thick envelope given, and then wander across Sixty-Fifth toward the Tavern on the Green.

Lisica had stopped the young man. *What was it now? Did she ask him for a cigarette? Perhaps a comment on his smart suit?* Lisica was young then, quite beautiful, and as the TASS man fumbled in his overcoat for a pack of cigarettes, Doug pulled over in a sedan with two more men. They took the traitor to an abandoned warehouse along the bay. She recalled the fabulous view of the Statue of Liberty from a broken window as they beat the man while a transistor radio played music of the holidays. *Do you hear what I hear!*

The torture took a long time. Lisica did not have time to wash or change, just put a coat and gloves on over her bloody clothes and hands and returned to her apartment. The KGB would later note in the report that Lisica's youth and inexperience led to a lengthy detention of an innocent TASS reporter. Of course, it was all a lie.

The apartment was quite dark when Lisica entered. Mrs. Lombardi up watching Johnny Carson. Carson had brought on the funnyman Don Rickles, inexplicably dressed in a military uniform, to explain why he'd broken Carson's cigarette box the night before. Mrs. Lombardi laughed as she stood, offering Lisica a light, sleepy kiss on the cheek. Not even noticing the splatters of blood across Lisica's clothes. She left with a soft click of the front door and Lisica turned the four locks behind her. You could never be too careful in this city.

Lisica walked into Peter's darkened room. Looking down at the sleeping boy, Lisica recalled a song from long ago, before the Great

War, when Lisica had a family, before the bombs fell and her world caught on fire. *Schlaf, Kindlein, schlaf. Sleep, little child, sleep. The father watches the sheep. The mother shakes the little tree. At that, a little dream falls here* . . .

When Lisica bent down to kiss Peter, a spot of the tortured agent's blood imprinted on the boy's forehead.

All these years later, driving across the Arizona desert to a town called Bisbee, Lisica could not forget the image. As the sun rose in the rearview mirror, Lisica knew the boy was much better off without her. He would grow strong.

He was Russian.

53

PETER

Two weeks had passed before the memorial at George's Bar. So much for Peter in between: endless interviews by the FBI and a handoff to a social worker, who brought Peter to a crummy house out in Tucker. Two FBI agents kept watch on him in case his mother came back. But Peter, sitting in a back booth of the bar with Jackie and Hotch's ashes in the coffee can, had tried to explain to the agents that it would never happen.

"Maybe I can put some of these ashes in a bottle of Gordon's," Jackie said. Jackie wore a black tuxedo with a black bow tie. His straightened hair slicked back like an old-time movie star's. He'd even penciled in a little mustache. "That would've made Hotch happy. Just a touch of vermouth and extra olives."

Peter nodded. The can was for Maxwell House. *Good to the Last Drop!*

The whole mood at George's was depressing as hell. Hotch didn't have too many close friends. There were some indifferent coworkers from the bookshop. One ex-wife, her name was Janet, showed up. She hugged the bartender and Jackie but didn't stay more than ten minutes. They played some of his favorite 45s on the jukebox. "Good Golly Miss Molly," "Shout Bamalama," and some of that old Motown crap, "Dancing in the Street," "Stop! In the Name of Love." Peter had watched the big reunion of those old singers on television but only really paid attention when Michael Jackson did the moonwalk to "Billie Jean."

"My mother killed him," Peter said. He said it suddenly, the shame of it building up ever since Hotch had died at Grady Hospital. Somehow, he was responsible for all of this.

"I'm sure your momma killed lots of folks," Jackie said. "Kind of her thing. She's a motherfuckin' Russian assassin and now on the Ten Most Wanted list. Listen to me, baby. Hotch made his play. And that play made him happy as hell. Man spent most of his life playing hero and then finally got to be one. Shit. I don't think it gets much better."

"Won't you miss him?"

Jackie didn't say anything. But Peter saw the sadness well in his eyes. After a few moments, Jackie tapped on the plastic top of the coffee can as if it was a conga drum. "Hotch never judged me," Jackie said. "He liked my authentic self. Man never gave a damn for phonies. People pretending to be someone they're not."

"I'm sorry."

"Don't be sorry, Peter," Jackie said. "Hotch wouldn't be."

Peter stood up and walked back to the bar, where the owner had made him a bacon cheeseburger. The owner thought, as did most of the people at the memorial, that Peter was a relative of Hotch's. Maybe a nephew or something. The owner was a bald Middle Eastern guy in a striped shirt and wore an apron over his dark dress pants. "I'm sorry for your loss," he said. "And sorry Hotch never finished his book. It was a hell of a story about a French freedom fighter who kidnaps Hitler. Maybe you can finish it one day?"

Peter took the bacon cheeseburger back to the booth, apparently Hotch's booth, where they kept the coffee can surrounded by cards and flowers. He didn't want to think about what would be coming next: foster care, more interviews with the FBI, never going back to his house, his school, and his friends. Sylvia said the social workers would do their best to keep him at the same school but that there were security concerns. That sounded like witness protection to him.

He'd talked on the phone a few times to Brenda, who'd kept what she knew to herself. Sylvia had arranged a meeting with Scott Adams and his mother. None of the truth of what happened at the Hyatt had made the news, thankfully. But everyone knew about Gary's body being found at Peter's house. It had been described in the *AJC* as a domestic incident, meaning that everyone knew Peter's mother had killed Gary and then gone on the run. Nothing about deeply embedded Russians and missing secret files.

Peter spoke to a few people from the bookstore where Hotch had worked. A guy with long, stringy hair and glasses said he appreciated Hotch for unflinchingly and unselfconsciously delving into the storied history of pulp. Peter had no idea what he meant. A heavyset woman in weird cat's-eye glasses said she'd worked with Hotch at the newspaper. She said she'd never seen a man who could drink whiskey while smoking and typing one-handed.

Soon Sylvia Weaver walked back into George's. Apparently, she'd been sitting outside the entire time. Peter said goodbye to Jackie and hugged his neck. Jackie said something about maybe going out for a ride in Hotch's Cadillac sometime. "You can have the goddamn thing when you turn sixteen. Okay?"

Sylvia drove Peter back to the foster house. She didn't speak for a long time. But then suddenly said, "Not a lot of this is sitting right with me."

Peter didn't say anything. He just stared out the window and looked beyond the interstate to a mess of construction where I-85 and I-285 met up. His mother had said she didn't believe they'd ever complete the massive interchange. Peter let himself think for a moment about his mother, wondering what happened to her and if she ever made it back to Russia. But he'd decided to hate her, and for now, that made everything easier to handle.

"You saw in the news that your father defected back to Russia?" she said, both hands on the wheel of a K-car. "I don't know if you call that redefection? I was there, Peter. I knew he was having a sit-down with a traitor working for us. He helped us get what we needed to get the guy. But after it all went down, the CIA was supposed to pick up your father. Instead, they let him walk all by his lonesome to the Soviet embassy. That doesn't make any sense."

Peter shook his head.

"The Kremlin awarded him something called the Order of the Red Star," Sylvia said. "For what? Changing his damn mind? Coming on a fool's errand to see some old flame, no offense, and the son he'd never known? No. Your daddy brought something back. He was too smart to arrive empty-handed."

"My mother left with the disk."

"She left with some bullshit Hotch brought her," Sylvia said. "A silly-ass video game called *Spy vs. Spy*. Hotch's idea of a joke."

"You think my father got the real one?"

"Nope," Sylvia said. "Your friend Brenda gave us the one Jenny Buckner had taken from your mother. I still don't know what's on the goddamn thing. Between us, I think the CIA loaded up your daddy with a buttload of phony intel and sent his ass straight on back to Moscow."

"He'd do that?"

"Everybody's got a purpose, Peter," Sylvia said. "Don't let who your momma is mess too much with your mind. I think your daddy just might be the real deal."

"But I can't talk about him," he said. "Or any of it."

"Nope," Sylvia said, navigating all the construction. The highways looping high up in turns and circles like strands of spaghetti. Just looking up into all the concrete twists and turns made Peter dizzy. "Never. But I figure we'll know soon enough. Hold up, now. Do you mind putting on your seat belt?"

54

THE GIPPER

He was annoyed the fish was dead.

Ron and Nancy had been staying at the Aga Khan's château, Maison de Saussure, when he'd found the note. The Aga Khan's son Hussain had asked the American president to please feed his fish while he was away. Ron had been using young Hussain's bedroom as a study to prep for this morning's meeting with Gorbachev. *Was it his fault?* He'd told his chief of staff to please take care of the fish. *Had the fish been fed too much? Or too little?* Was the dead fish a bad omen for meetings that might just stop the world's superpowers from blowing themselves up?

"Can we replace the fish?" Reagan asked.

"How about two fish," his chief of staff said. "To make up for the one."

"Why'd the goddamn fish have to die?" Reagan asked. "On today of all days."

Ronald Reagan looked out the window of Château Fleur d'Eau to where Gorbachev and his team would arrive any minute. The skies were dark and cloudy, and there was talk of snow. His chief of staff and Dutch Shultz had been discussing whether he should wear a coat or not. Let Gorbachev arrive all bundled up in an overcoat and hat. Maybe no coat was a sign of strength?

"Stick with the script," Dutch said, his hooded eyes serious. "He'll try to get you talking about SDI. He's obsessed with it and won't be swayed."

"I know, I know, George."

"The Russians weren't expecting Project Excalibur's success."

Reagan turned. This was something new. The Gipper was no longer thinking about young Hussain's dead fish or whether or not to wear an overcoat. He was thinking of satellites, laser beams, and a beautiful protective grid over America the Beautiful.

"Like *Smashing the Money Ring*?"

"Just like *Smashing the Money Ring*."

Reagan had made the picture in '38 during his time at Warner Bros. He'd played Secret Service Agent Brass Bancroft trying to take down a two-bit hoodlum counterfeiter named Dice. Bancroft had to pose as an inmate in the prison to get the secret workings of Dice's operation. Much like their man Vitaly Yurchenko. His sacrifice for the balance of the superpowers and world peace would probably never be known. Bill Casey had run over from Langley to the White House and given him the full rundown personally. The son of a bitch Yurchenko actually brought back some good old-fashioned counterfeit intel to Gorbachev. Star Wars was real, and if he didn't sit down and deal with the Gipper in Geneva, the US wouldn't be so eager to talk next time since they had the upper hand.

Reagan smiled to himself as his chief of staff let him know the Russians would be there any moment. The guards opened the front door to the château and Reagan said, "Oh, hell," shed his overcoat, and headed to the top of the staircase. The two-story château fashioned of stones with a stellar view of Lake Geneva faced a horseshoe drive filled with small pebbles.

At precisely 10 a.m., not a second before, Reagan spotted the big, ugly ZIL limo pull into the drive. Tiny Soviet and American flags fluttering. Reagan had been briefed that the passenger seat next to Gorbachev was inhabited by a fifty-caliber machine gun. He watched as an agent opened the passenger door and then opened the door for Mikhail.

Gorbachev emerged from the back in a black fedora and heavy black coat, adjusting the scarf worn loose around his neck. Reagan decided to go off script and walk down the steps and meet the man. He heard his chief of staff cursing as he walked down the staircase.

Gorbachev smiled and removed his black fedora, revealing the trademark red birthmark on his bald head. The men shook hands as cameras whirred and clicked upon the momentous moment.

Reagan pointed up the staircase and the waiting doors of the château. "Shall we go inside?"

Acknowledgments

Special thanks to Frank Figliuzzi, former FBI assistant director for counterintelligence, for answering my endless protocol questions about working as a rookie agent in Atlanta in the 1980s. And for sharing his stories about KGB agents passing through the "city too busy to hate."

Thanks to author Lee Goldberg for his infectious passion for all things Ralph Dennis. Thank you for bringing Ralph to my attention and providing the inspiration for Dennis X. Hotchner. Please check out Ralph Dennis's Hardman series. It's terrific.

Perennial thanks to my pal Jack Pendarvis for early readings of my manuscript and sharing his fuzzy memories of the Atlanta bar scene and life down on Ponce and Highland.

And a big heartfelt thanks to my true pals Brenda Yee, Scott Adams, and Stacey Brand Ostervold for returning to our childhood in 1985 Atlanta with me. You all were special friends whom I've never forgotten.

About the Author

Ace Atkins is an award-winning, *New York Times* bestselling author of more than thirty novels and numerous short stories. A former college football player and newspaper reporter, he's a recipient of the Richard Wright Literary Excellence Award and a member of the Alabama Writers Hall of Fame. He lives with his wife, Angela, and two children in Oxford, Mississippi.

Elke Neumann Taylor

Elke's Memoirs of Hamburg 1941

The heartwarming story of a little girl born during WWII

By
Elke Neumann Taylor

Bloomington, IN   authorHOUSE   Milton Keynes, UK

AuthorHouse™
1663 Liberty Drive, Suite 200
Bloomington, IN 47403
www.authorhouse.com
Phone: 1-800-839-8640

AuthorHouse™ UK Ltd.
500 Avebury Boulevard
Central Milton Keynes, MK9 2BE
www.authorhouse.co.uk
Phone: 08001974150

© 2006 Elke Neumann Taylor. All rights reserved.

No part of this book may be reproduced, stored in a retrieval system, or transmitted by any means without the written permission of the author.

First published by AuthorHouse 4/17/2006

ISBN: 1-4259-1607-4 (sc)

Printed in the United States of America
Bloomington, Indiana

This book is printed on acid-free paper.

I dedicate this book with love, to my husband Jerry, who encouraged me, my two sons Jeffrey and Randy who never tired of my stories, and of course, Mama.

Dear Reader,

The first couple of years of my life are from the stories that my Mother and grandparents had told me so many times over the years when we lived in the Quonset hut. Mama had encouraged me for years to tell our story; sadly, she passed away in 2002, before I could finish the manuscript. This is our story, to the best of my memory. Mama this is for you, I hope I did you proud.

Prologue

The year was 1941, the day I was born; the hospital was getting bombed again. Out of necessity, the operating rooms that were on the first floor were already set up in the basement where everything was running on generator power, due to the constant outages. Whenever a bomb made an indirect hit near the building, it would cause a jarring explosion, the percussion of it would loosen the plaster that would fall from the ceiling, windows shattered and exploded, and light fixtures fell while others remained, flickering and swinging. The staff already pushed to the limit of exhaustion was working around the clock.

There were doctors shouting orders and nurses dropping instruments as they cringed when a bomb found its mark. Grandma said it would have been safer to deliver me at home; it was not such a big target. The hospital was filled with war casualties, but some were already beyond help. While others were dying, Mama brought a new life into the world; the cycle of life goes on.

Chapter 1

Our house was nice and spacious, Mama had crocheted me lacey layettes and pram covers. Mama's friend was a tailor and she made me ruffled little dresses with bonnets to match, I was quite the little fashion plate.

Father was a pilot in the Luftwaffe, and when he came home, Mama would greet him at the door and he would hand her his briefcase, unload a bouquet of flowers in her arms and ask for me. Then he would head for the nursery, pick me up and carry me around until Mama told him that it was time to eat.

We would take outings to my grandparents' farm. The farm was a nice retreat from city life, and with the war going on and the shortages and rationing of food, it was a treat to go to the peaceful farm.

Safe in my parents arms I delighted in watching the sheep grazing in the pasture, chickens strutting around the berry vines, looking for a morsel of dropped fruit and the hogs rooting around in their enclosure. There was an apple orchard, plum trees, berry bushes and a large vegetable garden. Grandma would put the ripe fruit and vegetables into cans, place them in a basket and walk to the cannery, where they would heat and seal the cans for a small fee. Grandma would take them back home and put them on shelves in her cellar, so we could enjoy them through the barren winter months. Grandma commented that she never had so much company as when the fruit and vegetables came in. She never sent anyone home, without giving them bags of produce to take back with them. Mama helped Grandma to make jams and jellies from the plums, currants and gooseberries; they would cover the jars with paraffin and tie them off with waxed paper.

Grandpa was tall and thin, he always wore a fisherman's cap. He came from Denmark originally and was a seafaring man. He had brought home china, cloth and furniture from different countries around the globe, and the farmhouse was comfortable and a joy to visit. No farm is complete without a cat to get rid of the vermin, and Grandma always had a black cat.

It was a good life, for a while. Then in 1943 when I was around twenty months old, Father's plane was shot down over France. He survived the crash, but died during surgery on the operating table. That is when our life turned upside down.

Hamburg was in flames; our house was no safe haven, as we got bombed out along with our neighbors. To make matters worse, the government drafted Mama into the Army. She received training as a military radio operator, after basic training the Army sent her to Italy in 1944. Mama worried about leaving me in war torn Hamburg and took me to a convent where the nuns took care of me in her absence.

Mama missed me so much that in order to see me she volunteered to return several German girls back home after they became pregnant in Italy. She delivered the girls back to German soil and picked me up at the convent on the way to my grandparents.

After a week of staying home, Grandpa asked Mama when she was going back to the front, to which she responded that she was not going back. Grandpa told her that she had to go back or the whole family will be shot for treason. She explained that working as a telephone operator, she was privy to a lot of information, and one thing she knew for sure is that no one knew what they were doing since the country was in such a mess.

Not only did she not go back, but she did the unthinkable, after a few weeks, she packed up her uniform, put her return address on the parcel and sent it back to her post. To make a long story short, they never came after her and she received her Army check for several years afterwards.

We stayed at my grandparents' farm until they also were bombed out and then we were homeless.

During the day, we walked the streets, looking for wood, twigs, string, and paper, anything we could use to make a fire. In the evenings, we searched for soup kitchens or a handout. This was no easy task as hundreds of other people were doing the same thing. At nights, we looked for a safe place to sleep, usually churches, schools and bomb shelters. Here we would take refuge for the night, sleeping on sacks filled with straw. Sometimes they would turn us away, because there was no room, and then they would tell us where else we might try to find shelter.

Our little family consisted of Grandma, Grandpa, Mama and me. After a miserable day of looking for food and shelter, we finally found the school we had been looking for that day. It was already dark when we came to the entrance. A woman met us at the door, telling us that they were already overcrowded, but took pity on us, but told Grandpa that he would have to stay outside on the stoop. Mama said that she would change places with him but Grandpa said that I would need her, and shoulders stooped, head cast down, he went back outside. The school had the usual blackout curtains on the windows, but when a bomb hit you could see lights flash and the brightness of it would light up the gymnasium.

Even in the darkness, you could make out dozens of forms lying on the straw filled sacks, laid out in rows, side by side, like so many sardines in a can. Mama and Grandma put me between them, but it was hard to sleep. There was so much noise, although most were sleeping, there were so many people tossing, turning, coughing, snoring and babies were crying it seemed more like a subway station then a house of refuge.

Whenever a bomb dropped from a plane, you could hear the whistle as it hurled toward its target, and when it exploded, the sky would light up through the black out curtains and would illuminate the room with an eerie light. People that were still awake would cover their children with their bodies, until the ground stopped vibrating.

Grandma was worried about Grandpa sitting in the entrance to the school, and got up to join him. Mama told her to stay with me and she would go out to him, but Grandma said that if we are hit by a bomb she wanted to be with him, also that if I woke up and saw the old hag that was lying beside her on the other side, I would scream my head off. Therefore, Grandma left the sanctuary of the gym floor, and joined Grandpa on the stoop, sitting side by side, holding each other for comfort and warmth from the cold of the night, and out of pure exhaustion, they too fell asleep.

Chapter 2

Each day seemed to get worse instead of better and Mama and Grandma made the decision that we needed to get out of Hamburg. Grandma was going to sell her wedding band so we could buy train tickets with the money it would bring to go to Bavaria, but when it came time to do it, Grandma could not get her wedding band off, and Mama made the sacrifice and sold her wedding band. This was about 1944 when I was three years old. Surely, it must be better and safer out in the country.

After arriving in Bavaria, Mama asked about for shelters and someone told us to go to the castle, that it had many vacant rooms.

We found the castle; it was big, gray and cold. It looked very imposing, with a high wall around it, rounded turrets, many windows, which must mean many rooms.

The castle seemed deserted since all the young men were fighting at the front. An elderly proprietor and his family met us, telling us that we could not stay there, but had to move on. He had never dealt with Grandma, she had a lot of backbone and never took no for an answer. She told him that this was wartime, and if he had room he was obligated to take in refugees, grudgingly he gave in, showing us a room that we could use. The room was big, with a high ceiling and a tall window; there were a couple of cots with blankets on them. The room was cold and damp.

When Mama asked the proprietor about food, he said that we could forage in the woods for berries and mushrooms, that he had barely enough food for his own family. We saw milk cows on the property, and knew that he had milk and was holding out with the food.

Grandma started going out in the woods searching for anything edible. She had no trouble finding things. There were blackberries, brambleberries, hazelnuts, several different mushrooms, blackberry leaves, and the mint found along a streambed made a tasty tea. When I got tired of walking I would just sit down on the ground, until Grandma and Mama had finished foraging and collected me to go back to the castle. Grandma and Mama would take me to the woods to teach me the edible mushrooms and berries, and in short time I was a pro at foraging the woods for food as I joined Grandma and Mama.

Much to the proprietor's dismay, another family showed up asking for refuge. Since he knew that Grandma already talked to them, he thought better of it to give them a hard time, and put them in a room opposite ours.

When they asked about food, Grandma told them to take me to the woods, that I would know what was edible. They looked at me as if I had grown another head, but decided that I was their only choice, and off we went. After a few outings and me showing them what was edible, they became more confident and started foraging for themselves.

One day, when it was just Grandma and me in the woods, I had wandered away from her, heading toward a berry bush that caught my eye. When I came to the bush,

I saw something behind it, and parting the branches, I saw a small airplane in between the trees with brush growing around it. It was so small, that at first, I thought that it was a toy. I called Grandma and she came over. I pointed to the plane, and started going toward it, when she grabbed my arm telling me not to go near it, as it might be booby-trapped. I could tell that she was afraid, and we just looked from the distance at the little plane with the broken windshield and one little seat. Grandma told me not to tell anyone about what we saw, that it would be safer that way.

The daily routine of foraging took its toll, and we had to go out farther and farther to find anything, until one day we came back empty handed.

Mama had asked the proprietor, several times, if she could get some milk for me. He would always refuse her. She tried one more time and again he refused. Mama waited until the family got together for their evening meal, and as they were sitting on benches around their long table, filled with food and pitchers of milk, Mama sat me square in the middle of the table. The proprietor jumped up yelling at her, asking what she was doing.

Mama replied, "This is Elke, I have no food or milk for her, you do and you can take care of her." He sent her back to our room with a pitcher of milk and me in tow. Every day after that, a pitcher of milk was sent to our room by one of the family members.

I remember the day that the American soldiers came, Mama said that every time I saw a soldier in uniform I would run up to him and call him Daddy. A couple of the soldiers also came to the castle out of curiosity. When they met us, they tried talking to us, using a few German words and a lot of sign language. A couple of them came back, bringing oranges and a couple of Army blankets. One soldier came every weekend, he would bring me an orange, put my shoes on, and holding my hand, he would take me for walks around a pond where the swans were and he would talk in English to me.

Mama said that he had a little girl like me in America and he missed her. One-day Grandma, Grandpa and Mama went to forage for food; they left me asleep on the cot. My soldier friend came with a couple of friends to visit. Finding me asleep, they did not want to wake me. Mama said when they got back I was still asleep. They knew that I had company, because there was a ring of oranges around me like a halo.

In 1945, our Americans friends came with the big news that the war was over, so we packed up and made our way back to Hamburg.

Chapter 3

The city was completely in ruins, streets lined with mountains of rubble, where buildings used to be. Men, women and children were sifting through the bricks and rubble, trying to salvage what they could.

We moved into a tiny one-room apartment on the second floor of an apartment house. We were practically on top of each other; the tenants shared bathroom and kitchen privileges. There was a list posted when to use the kitchen. Food and personal items came up missing, bickering was constant, and it was not a pleasant place. It was November 6, Mama's birthday. Grandma had traded some ration stamps for extra sugar to bake Mama a birthday cake this was such a treat. Just when we were ready to cut the cake there was a knock on the door, scrambling, Mama shoved the cake under the bed.

It was a man from the government or state. He is sent around to the people to see what they needed. He would question us about what we had, and what we needed, as he filled out a form. Grandma said that we could use an extra blanket. He looked at the cots, and saw that we had a blanket each and that it was adequate. Mama mentioned the lack of pots and pans. He said that he was in the kitchen and saw pots there. Mama and Grandma exchanged helpless looks, since those belonged to the landlady. All of a sudden, the landladies' cat came out from under the bed with whipped cream around its face and whiskers. Everything got quiet, then the man started to laugh, and Mama reached down and salvaged what was left of the cake. Grandma tried to explain that we usually do not have cake, but that this was a special occasion as she handed him a slice.

With the cake plate carefully balanced on his knee, he got out his papers again and said, "Those blankets are worn out, you could use about four more, and I see you need pots, and how about a couple of chairs and a few dishes? I am sure you can use them as well." When he finally left, Grandma said that she never would have thought that a cat could save the day.

I remember one day in particular, when Grandpa and Mama were out working and Grandma had to run down to the store. She left me alone and the last thing she said was, "Elke, I don't want you shoving any dry beans in your ears while I'm gone," I did not quite understand this, but I thought it must be something that you do, if she told me not to. I had to hunt up the beans. With the stealing going on what little food we had was hidden away. When I found the beans, I tried to see how many of them I could shove into my ears.

When Grandma came back, I was laying in the hallway at the top of the stairs screaming in pain, as several of the women held me down and pried beans out of my ears with bobby pins. Grandma stood over me, hands on her hips and said, "Didn't I tell you not to put beans in your ears? Where do you get such ideas from?"

Chapter 4

Mama came rushing home one evening; she was very excited saying she heard they were setting up Quonset huts along the Alster River on the Winterhuder Kai. It was for homeless families that were bombed out, but they just put up so many and it was on a first come, first serve basis. Mama and Grandma were delighted to leave the apartment and have a home of their own again, even though it was a Quonset, anything would be better this.

It was not that far away from the apartment, and we rushed over to get on the list. Winter was on its way and the days were getting shorter now. It was already dark by the time we got there.

A couple of men showed us into a Quonset, it was a big, hallow half moon of a metal shell. The whole hut was illuminated by two light bulbs that hung from the ceiling in the center of each half of the hut. Since it was completely empty, it seemed huge, and it echoed as they talked. When asked how many were in our family, and Mama told him just the four of us, we were told that we were just entitled to half the Quonset, that we would have to share it with another family. We would also have to wait for the workers to put up the dividing wall in the hut. Since they were busy on the other Quonsets, it was hard to say when we could expect the workers or when we could move in. Grandpa told them he was a mason, and if they supplied him with the bricks, mortar and trowels, he would go ahead and do it himself. They were pleased of the free help and gave permission to proceed; telling him everything he would need would be there in the morning. They told him to measure the building and put the wall across the center.

The next morning Mama went out looking for work, and Grandma and I went with Grandpa to watch him build the wall in the Quonset hut.

The Winterhuder Kai looked a lot different in daylight. The Alster River was within yards of the long row of Quontset huts. The Alster had a slight curve as it went upstream, and the Quonsets mimicked the curve on the land. Behind the Quontset huts was a row of beautiful vine covered brick villas, between them and us a narrow lane. How they must have despised the building of the barracks, spoiling their view of the beautiful Alster and the park on the other side of it.

Grandpa took off his coat, rolled up his sleeves, and set to work. Grandma and I would hand him bricks, and in between, Grandma swept, keeping the cement floor clean. At noon we ate buttered bread, Grandpa kept working, trying to be done as fast as he could. The men from the council came to check on the progress, and told Grandpa that he was doing a good job.

There was a potbellied stove in the living room of the hut, but we had nothing with which to make a fire. When I got tired, I would sit on a pile of bricks and rest.

It took Grandpa about four days to finish the wall. He then build another wall in the back end with a doorway; this was to be our bedroom and for lack of a door, Grandma hung a curtain for privacy. Another short wall from the front door toward the back was build; this was dividing the kitchen part from the living room.

There was also another door as you came in, a small vestibule. The partition walls inside our part of the hut just reached about three quarters of the way up to the ceiling. That way what little heat there was would go in the other rooms, and the one light bulb in the center could illuminate the other rooms. Our new home was ready for us to move in.

The move did not take long. All our belongings amounted to the two chairs we received, our blankets, a couple of pots and a few dishes, and a trunk, with some clothes and towels in it. These items were stacked on a little wagon Grandpa had made from scraps; the wheels to the wagon had once been on a baby carriage. Grandpa pulled the wagon as we walked beside him. We looked like so many other homeless people, but we were heading for our new home.

At the corner where Hudtwalcker Street intersected with the Winterhuder Kai, was a famous landmark, the Winterhuder Fahrhaus, it was build in 1895, and was a fancy restaurant and ballroom. Around 1948, they built a second open-air restaurant across from the first one along the Alster side, with about three rows of forty tables. That was open just during the spring and summer months. This was about two hundred yards from where the Quonset huts started.

I was in the original Fahrhaus once, about two years after we moved into the Quonset hut. After Mama and Grandpa got jobs and regular pay, Grandma sent me with two plates to the Fahrhaus, she told me to ask for two specials. The restaurant was big and elegant with many tables occupied. Several people stared at me as I came in carrying our plates, a few smiled kindly. I went up to the counter and asked for two specials. With a polite nod, the waiter took my two plates, and put them on a dumb waiter. It was the first one I ever saw. He opened up a little cabinet, stuck my two plates in, and they went down to the kitchen. In a few minutes, he opened the cabinet again and pulled out our plates filled with food, I was in awe. I hurried with the food to the Quonset to tell Grandma about what I saw. I was going on and on about it, that Grandma had to tell me to eat my food before it got cold.

As we ate, Grandma reminisced about the old days, saying that when Kaiser Wilhelm was ruling Germany a mark was still worth a mark, and how the late Otto van Bismarck, the first chancellor of Germany, would not have gotten Germany in the state it was in now. When I asked about von Bismarck, she told me how one of the greatest battleships, named after him, was build right here in the Hamburg seaport.

Chapter 5

However, our excitement was short lived, as we were facing one of the coldest winters in years. Without fuel and little food to sustain us, I am sure that Mama must have wondered if she had made the right decision. We were back to sleeping on straw sacks on the living room floor. It was so cold, we were told to keep the radio on at night; that someone in the family was to stay awake to make sure that everyone made it through the night. Sometime during the night we would hear an announcement to be vigil; that someone in another barrack froze to death.

Mama and Grandpa kept me in the middle while they slept, Grandma would take the first two hour watch, then Grandpa and Mama had the last. What little bit of fire material we found had long been burned up by now, and the interior of the Quonset and the two windows had a glistening sheen of frost on them.

Within a few days, we gratefully received three cots, a table and two chairs. Grandma scrubbed and cleaned them, anxious to make the hut a home.

Grandpa lost his job, and while he was out looking for work every day, Mama became the sole provider for all of us.

When Mama received her pay packet she would hand it over to Grandma, because she took care of all the shopping and the bill paying, and in return, Grandma would give Mama a few Marks, to last her to the next payday.

While Mama was at work, and Grandpa was out looking for a job, Grandma and I would walk the streets, looking for paper, sticks, or anything we could burn in the pot bellied stove. Whatever we found, was always saved till they came home, so we could all enjoy the warmth while we ate. Then we hurried to bed before it got too cold, because without any insulation, when the fire went out, the metal building became a deep freeze in mere minutes.

It got so cold that the water froze up in the wash house, which was our only means of getting water. Everyone was gathering outside the wash house with their empty buckets, and all were in loud discussion that something needed to be done. The man that was in charge of the barracks went to the villa behind our hut, explained the situation, and asked if we could get water from them.

They gave us permission, and we were to line up at the back door. We were not to enter the house, since the maid would take and fill the buckets, and then hand them back out to us. I stood in line with Grandma, it was cold and the snow was still coming down. The walk was getting slippery, as people were spilling some of the water as they turned to leave with their filled buckets.

When it was our turn, I saw the young maid in her black and white uniform, she did not look pleased. She must have been freezing without a coat on, filling and carrying bucket after bucket to the door. While she took our bucket, I craned my neck to see the inside of the beautiful villa, but the maid shut the door, as she went to fill up our bucket and Grandma told me not to be so nosey.

The men worked at thawing out the water pipes, and got the water running. The next day, there was a notice at the washhouse door, that when it was very cold, to keep the stove going in the laundry room with tubs of water on it to produce steam to keep the pipes from freezing. That was the only time I remembered about the water freezing up so bad that we had to get it from the villa.

No matter how cold it was, Mama and Grandma were firm believers of fresh air, and every night before we would go to bed, dressed in our nightclothes, we would open the door, step outside and take several deep breaths of fresh air. Grandma said this was good for the lungs to help us sleep. I don't remember Grandpa taking part in this ritual.

Things got a little better when Mama got a job in a hospital. She worked where there was heat and food, but she worried about us all the time. Leftover food and scraps were carelessly tossed in the garbage while we were slowly starving. Even if you had money, food was rationed and hard to get, due to the many shortages. The workers were not allowed to take any scraps home, to make sure of that, they were searched as they left the hospital at night.

Mama tried to take a couple of fresh eggs home, which she hid under her cap. After a guard checked her pockets and purse, he patted Mama on the head and said, "Good night, Blondie." Mama said that it cracked the eggs and she hurried on before he could see them running down her head. When she arrived home that night after ten, she had to wash her hair out in cold water.

Mama figured a way to get food out without being caught; by tying a stocking on a string around her neck and letting it hang under her dress.

Mama did not come home until 10:00 p.m. and Grandma would get the plates out hours ahead, waiting in anticipation, and hoping Mama would not get caught. Grandma would try to get me to go to sleep on the sofa, with the promise she would wake me as soon as Mama came home with the food, but I always stayed up, afraid that I would miss out on the food.

When Mama finally came, she would hand the stocking to Grandma who would put it on the table and empty it. Everything was always mashed down to the foot of the stocking, a pat of butter, part of a jelly container, half a slice of bread, and if we were lucky, a piece of fish or part of an egg, sometimes we went by smell to figure out what it was…fish or fowl? We did not care, it was food. We would oh and ah over the feast before us and comment on every bite. Everything was divided up evenly, a piece of this and a scrap of that. And late on those cold winter nights when the rest of the people in the Quonset huts had their lights out and slept with empty bellies, thanks to Mama, we dined like kings.

At noon, for the lack of something better, our meal mostly consisted of bread spread with lard and salt.

Grandma worried about me being in the cold Quonset all day and Mama decided to take me to work with her at the hospital. She hid me in the broom closet. Here I would spend up to 10 hours at a time in complete darkness. Mama would smuggle me leftovers of patients' food trays. I was content; I had food to eat and a warm place to sleep.

One night I thought that I had overslept, I peeked out and no one was there, the hall was completely deserted, I thought Mama had forgotten about me. All of a sudden, she and a doctor came out of the ward, happy to see her;

Elke's Memoirs of Hamburg 1941

I forgot about hiding and ran to her. Mama tried to fend me off; as I wrapped my arms around her legs the doctor grabbed me, pulled my clothes off, picked me up and ran with me in his arms into a room that had a bathtub in it. He ran hot water into the tub, put me in it and he and Mama used stiff brushes and scrubbed me so hard that I cried with pain. They had to do this because they had just come out of the diphtheria ward. On our way out to go home, I remember the doctor telling Mama, "If she gets sick, let us know right away."

I was not feeling well, going in and out of a dream, just a couple of nights later the bright lights of the ambulance were shining outside our hut. They carried me out on a stretcher, like the people that died in the night, but I was still living. I did not know that I had diphtheria.

I vaguely remember being in a ward full of cribs filled with children, there were bright overhead lights that hurt my eyes, and several doctors and nurses examining us. Then I was put in another ward, here little cots were lined up along the interior walls of the building.

The next morning the nurses were to wash us. A big nurse set a bowl of water by my bed and handed me a washcloth, and told me to wash myself, that I was big enough. I was too weak to wring out the cloth, and I just laid there, with the wet cloth dripping on me. I felt sad, thinking that if I was home, Grandma would wash me. When the other shift came in, we got a young nurse that was very kind and she washed me properly. It seemed like I was in the hospital forever. At first I was so weak that I did not know what was going on around me.

A lot of oatmeal was served, which the big nurse placed beside my little bed. Too weak to feed myself, she would tell the other nurse that I was not hungry. Thank goodness, after a few days I was moved to a different floor, and put in a crib. The younger nurses were in charge here and I was properly fed and bathed.

Chapter 6

I was in the hospital for weeks. There were no visitors allowed since diphtheria is very contagious and life threatening. Every Sunday Mama would come and stand on the lawn and wave at me. I was on the fourth or fifth floor; the nurse would take me to the window to let me wave back. Mama looked like a little fly, so far away.

When I got a little stronger, they would put blankets around us for lack of coats, and walked us in the woods for fresh air and to heal our lungs; it was nice, but very exhausting. The evergreen trees were so dark green that they looked almost black, and the forest floor was soft from the moss and pine needles. Once we came to a little clearing; there was a little pond surrounded with moss; it looked so beautiful.

The weather was getting really cold, with a chill in the air. I did not enjoy our outings so much anymore, as they left me feeling weak, and I wanted to be strong so that I could go back home.

Mama would always buy me a chocolate bar when she came to see me and hand it to the nurse to give to me. There was a little boy in the crib next to me and he had a teddy bear that I coveted. He told me that if I give him my chocolate bar, he would let me have the teddy bear. I agreed and handed him the candy as he handed me the bear. What joy! As soon as he ate the chocolate he started to cry. The nurse came and asked him what was wrong; he said that I took his teddy bear. She made me give it back to him despite my explanation.

He tricked me like this every Sunday, and I kept falling for it because I wanted the teddy bear so bad. I never got to eat any of the chocolate bars. Wonder what Mama would say if she knew that she was buying it for that little lying brat all this time.

Chapter 7

I came home Christmas Eve. I was afraid that I would miss it as that is the day we celebrate Christmas; when the wise men brought gifts to the baby Jesus. Every year the people that were well to do and living in the villas would invite a poor child to spend Christmas with them, which would mean a big meal and gifts. I was invited and Mama and Grandma were ecstatic; perhaps they thought, I would get a new coat or new shoes. I would not go; I cried to stay at home. Grandma reminded me that St. Nickolaus does not come to the Quonset huts, but I did not care, I was home. They were really disappointed with me, for the things that I was missing out on, but I was happy. I got to stay at home.

That night Grandpa got a Christmas tree from his friend, the Christmas tree vendor. He always told

Grandpa to wait till dark on Christmas Eve and if there was a tree left, he could have it.

The tree was decorated behind closed curtains. I stayed out in the little kitchen and when I was called in I stared at the beautiful tree, illuminated by slim white candles in their clip holders attached to the branches and heavy silver icicles flickering in the candlelight.

I said my verse that I had been practicing and went to the tree for my gifts. There was a little parcel from the Red Cross with a dress that was too little and too thin for winter. At the base of the tree trunk was a golden orange, and hidden in the trees branches, a matchbox. When I opened it, there was the tiniest pillow and blanket Grandma had made and a little cut out doll from black paper lying underneath the cover. I was so delighted with my present that I carried the matchbox everywhere, showing my friends. I'd take the doll out and put it back under its covers so many times, until the little paper cut out doll finally disintegrated.

Karin, my best friend came over the next morning; she lived next door. They got a whole Quonset hut to themselves, since there were eight people in their family.

They had a front and back door and windows at each end. She had received a doll carriage from St. Nicolaus and we put her old dolls in it, and played with it endlessly.

Chapter 8

The convent had their annual Christmas party for the poor and homeless children, and Grandma took me to it. All the way to the convent, she had preached into me that when St. Nickolaus asked me what I wanted for Christmas, to be sure to tell him I needed a winter coat. Since we were going to the party, where there would be food, we gave Mama and Grandpa our share for the day.

By the time we got to the convent, we were both very hungry, but excited about the meal we would receive.

When we finally arrived at the convent, a nun led us into a big hall already filled with dozens of parents and children of all ages. The room was set up with many short, round tables, surrounded by little chairs. We were supposed to get our meal in here, but the parents were to wait out in the hall. Grandma told me to sit at the table and she would be right outside waiting for me. I started to cry because I knew how hungry she was, because we had just talked about the meal.

The nuns got impatient with me, not realizing it was about the food. They thought I just did not want to be apart from Grandma. When they saw I would not be consoled, they told Grandma that she could stand inside against the wall, where at least I could see her. I will never forget, as we sang Christmas carols and said grace, a nun came out from the kitchen, making her way to our tables carrying a huge oval tray above her head, piled high with link wurst, and the Mother Superior said, "Look children, hot dogs from heaven!"

When I got my share, I asked if Grandma could have some of mine, and the nun told me to eat and behave myself, that I should be grateful. I looked over to Grandma and she smiled at me and motioned for me to eat. We had always shared whatever we had, and as little as I was, I could not enjoy eating this food by myself, knowing Grandma was hungry too.

Afterwards, with much anticipation, came Saint Nickolaus. Mother Superior called out the names and children went up to receive their gift. When it was my turn, very quiet and shy, I told St. Nick that I needed a coat, while he pressed a package into my hands. I took it over to Grandma and she opened it and found a gray pleated suspender skirt and pink sweater inside, it was the prettiest outfit I had ever seen.

Yet, the entire way home Grandma admonished me that I had not asked for a coat as she told me. She did not realize that the gifts were sorted out ahead of time.

Grandma took me to the outdoor market a few days before Christmas. The sights and smells were wonderful to the senses. There were all kinds of booths set up and vendors hawking their ware. There was Grandpas' friend at the Christmas tree lot, selling trees.

People in booths were selling beautiful Christmas ornaments; one stand had marionette puppets and wooded soldier nutcrackers while another had dolls and handmade wooden toys. My favorite booths' were the candy ones. I could look at the displays forever, especially the Turkish delight candy, and how the man in the turban would shave, the big creamy blocks down with a huge cleaver and put the candy on paper squares ready for purchase.

There was a booth set up with huge naval oranges and tangerines, walnuts and filberts were set out in crates. Everywhere you looked, there was Christmas in the air.

The popcorn booth always smelled good. This popcorn was sweet, sort of like caramel corn. There were the meat booths, chickens and ducks hung from hooks, and skinned rabbits hung around one booth by strings for a Christmas roast.

I asked Grandma if we could have a rabbit for Christmas dinner. She said, "Those are not rabbits, those were poor cats." I asked her how she knew that and she told me to look at where they had cut the tail off, she said, "Do you see that big stump? A rabbit has a tiny skinny tail, and a cat has a fat tail that leaves a stump." Grandma was the smartest person that I knew. I thought about all the poor cats that they had butchered, and the dumb people that bought and ate them.

Chapter 9

Before we knew it, spring was on the way. The willows put out their yellow whips, and long green leaves emerged from them. They swayed to the warming breeze that drifted across the Alster. We took our hard bread crusts and fed the swans along the shore line and watched as they took the bread and held it under the water with their long orange bills to soften it.

On the other side of the Alster there were children flying kites, and I watched as the colorful kites circled above. At the noon meal, I asked Grandma if I could have a kite and she said that Grandpa could make me one. I was so excited, that I could barely wait for him to come home.

I ran toward him as he walked up the lane and told him of the project. Grandpa took the axe to a little board and cut narrow pieces of wood. He then asked Grandma for some string and waxed paper and the glue. While he was making the kite, he told Grandma and me to tear up little pieces of rags to tie to the tail of the kite. Finally it was finished. It looked awful small and seemed very heavy for its size, but Grandpa said that the tail made up for it.

He attached some string to the cross pieces and he told me to hold the kite while he ran to get it off the ground. I then was to release it when the string got taut and it hit the ground like a rock. We tried it again and again. Grandpa and I ran till we were exhausted, but my little kite never got airborne.

Grandpa claimed that we did not have the right material for the tail and that was the problem with the kite.

Chapter 10

Our barracks were set out in a row along the Alster River bank. One day we noticed a lot of activity going on, they were constructing a small building with drive on scales below our barrack next to the river bank. Workmen poured a cement pad for the drive on scales, as other cement trucks came and poured another big pad, close to the river edge and directly in front of our barrack. This was followed by putting a round track, which was like a train track on the pad. We wondered what was going on and the excitement was mounting as they brought in a huge crane and set it on the platform track, so it could make a complete circle.

The coal barges started to dock right below us as soon as the construction was completed. Big dump trucks came, the crane man would scoop the coal out of the barges and fill the trucks, then they would drive onto the scales, to be weighted, documented and then the driver would sign for the load. This was repeated all day long, until the coal barges were emptied.

Everyone from the barracks stood around the truck with a bucket, in anticipation. Grandma always sent me as I was faster, and she had trouble bending over. We had a semi circle around the truck, everyone vying for the best position. When some of the coal would roll off the loaded truck, there was a big scramble to see who could reach it first, old and young alike.

The crane operator was a kind man who knew how hard up we all were, and he always filled every truck to the brim, spilling lots of coal ensuring that we all get at least a bucket a day. The truck drivers and the scale man kept complaining and trying to hold us back, but to no avail. One day, we came out with our buckets and there was a new crane operator, and we were given a warning not to go near the trucks. Our fuel supply had come to an abrupt halt.

With the old crane man gone, our coal supply had dwindled down to nothing, and our little wall of security was coming apart at the seams again. The coal barges came, one after another and unloaded their precious cargo, with the scale man watching over every load, making sure not a scrap would overflow the coal trucks.

The flat barges had a small narrow walkway around their circumference where they could walk. The crane bucket could not reach underneath this lip, and the bargemen have to shovel the rest by hand into the crane bucket. There was always a little left in the crease around the inside of the barge where the shovel would not fit.

The coal barges had the living quarters down in the front bow, a small cabin where the engine room was. One of the coal barges belonged to a young couple that had a little girl about my age; they would come every few days with a load of coal. They were not allowed to leave the barge, and after they were unloaded, and pulled up out of the way of other barges, I would go to the river edge and talk with the little girl. One day her father asked me if I would like to come aboard to play with his little girl. I was glad to, as I always wondered how they could live in that tiny bow on the barge.

I remember that the cabin was very tiny, it made our Quonset hut appear huge. Bunk beds were built in on each side of the triangle of the bow. There was a little kerosene stove in the center and a bare bulb hung from above, the low wattage bulb, run from a generator gave a hazy, orange glow to the kerosene smelling cabin.

That night, after dark, and all the other barracks had their lights out, there came a knock on our door, it was the bargeman. When Grandma answered the door, he told her to turn out the lights, for fear someone should see him and told her to send me down to the barge with a bucket.

Grandma got me out of a sound sleep, grabbed a bucket and took me down to the barge, where the bargeman took my hands, lowered me down into the barge, dropped the bucket and told me to stay on the inside edge, go clear around and pick up any coal that I could find and not make any noise.

Here I was in the middle of the night, crawling around on my hands and knees in complete darkness groping for coals. I kept thinking of my girlfriend, Karin, next door sound asleep in her bed with her sister, and I could not even tell her about tonight.

When my bucket was full, he would take it from me and hand it to Grandma, and she would take it to our barrack. On a good night, I could get two to three buckets of coal. This routine was repeated often, whenever our barge friends came to the Alster to unload their coal.

When I had gleaned all the coal, he would pull me up from the barge; Grandma would wash my face and hands in cold water and send me back to bed. I would be so tired that I was almost asleep before she got me cleaned up.

Chapter 11

Grandpa started coming home with a few bricks every evening that he picked up from the rubble of the bombed out buildings. On his day off, he would take the little wagon and fill it with bricks to bring home, and pile outside the hut. In the evenings, he would take a little hammer and knock the cement off them. Finally, he had enough for his project and started building a little shed against the side of the barrack, complete with a wooden door and a roof from a piece of salvaged tin. Inside he made a bin to hold coal or wood, and he kept the little wagon in there.

By this time Mama got a job at the Post Office as a mail carrier, she really enjoyed her job. Over a period of time, with Mama and Grandpa both working, we accumulated a few necessary household items.

There was the set of bunk beds against the dividing wall in the bedroom. I slept on top and Grandpa on the bottom. On the other side of the wall toward the living room was a wooden wardrobe, and Mama still used the cot from the state for her bed. Grandma slept on the sofa in the living room. In front of the sofa was our dining room table, and the two odd chairs. In the kitchen part was a small table used for preparing food, and a small electric plate for cooking, two water buckets which we filled at the washhouse, and a little cabinet with a screen door to keep the flies out of the food.

There was a wide space between our barrack and the next barrack, because the power pole was there. The next Quonset was the washhouse which included the latrines. You entered the washhouse from the front, the lane side. As you went in, the left side had been partitioned off with toilets for the barracks; each one had a door with their barrack No. on it and a lock. This was one of three wash houses, evenly distributed among the Quonset huts.

The back of the washhouse was portioned off and had a laundry room in it. There was a big woodstove to heat water, big tubs to boil the laundry, every barrack had a certain time and day to do their laundry, and usually two families went together. If they took longer then their turn, and there were always some, it run into the next person's laundry time and cut them short. Then there would be a loud exchange of words that were anything but ladylike. On the front right side were the sinks and clotheslines.

This was a good place to go to in the winter, as the steam from the laundry heated up the whole barrack. When it was Mamas' turn to do the laundry, I would head there after school to talk to her and get warm. I remember we were in the washhouse when I asked her why I don't have a middle name, and she said that Grandpa had several names and when Grandma got mad at him she could never think of his first name, so she called him all his names. She said, "That's when I decided if I ever had a child, it would have one short name."

Sometimes I would go to the washhouse to use the bathroom and forget to bring the key; then I would try all the other toilet doors. There was usually one or two that were not locked, and hope I was not caught using someone else's toilet.

Grandma dreaded the harsh winter time, not only for the cold, but once the Alster froze solid, it would mean the end of the coal barges, till the weather warmed again.

Chapter 12

The fire was lit more sparingly now, trying to conserve the ever dwindling coal supply. Wrapped up in a bib apron over her dress, sweater, head scarf, and heavy stockings, Grandma would hold off lighting the fire till close to supper time, so that the barrack would be warm when Grandpa and Mama came home from work. By that time ice had formed on the inside walls and windows and hovering under a thin blanket on the sofa brought little relief.

She would keep an eye out on the Alster, waiting for an early thaw, and once in a while was rewarded by the crunching sound of the Coast Guard Ice Cutter, slicing the ice in front of it, allowing ships to pass, and in its wake would be coal barges with their precious cargo, ready to be unloaded. Of course it was no help to us, unless one of the coal barges belonged to our friend. Then I knew to get to bed early, as Grandma would wake me in the early hours with the coal bucket at the ready.

There were nights when the wind whipped harshly at my thin coat, and I dreaded going out in the pitch dark, thinking of Karin and Heidi sound asleep in their beds, but once I was lowered into the coal barge which broke the wind; it did not seem bad at all. I could hear the water lapping on the sides of the barge. The only thing to worry about was the temptation to crawl under the ledge of the barge curling up, and going to sleep, but I knew that while I was sheltered, Grandma was standing on the shore freezing, waiting for a bucket of coal to be lifted up and handed to her to be emptied.

It was pitch dark and impossible to see down in the barge, I would scoot on my hands and knees and run my hands along the crease of the ship, feeling for the coals.

The faster I could get around the circumference of the barge, the sooner I could get back in my cot and sleep of what was left of the night. In the morning there was school.

Karin and I shared many secrets, but this one I had to keep to myself, for fear of getting the barge man in trouble and spoiling it for Grandma and us. In the mornings I would look inside the little shed to see how much coal I had gathered, and I was always proud to see the little pile of coal in the bin.

I don't know which was worse, the fuel shortage or the lack of food. The best and the most of the food supply went to the front for the soldiers. At one time we could not get any wheat, because the white bread went to the soldiers. For a brief period the bakers could just get cornmeal, unaccustomed to it, they used it like flour. It made the worst bread; it would crumble to pieces before you could eat it, and tear if you tried to spread margarine on it. I disliked the flavor and the texture of it.

Ration books were used and stamps were traded around the neighborhood. Those with larger families got more stamps. Grandma always traded soap stamps for extra sugar stamps with Karin's mother, as they had six children and never enough soap.

It was on one of those frosty mornings, when Mama set off from the Post Office with two big mailbags crisscrossed over her shoulders, when she slipped on the ice and broke her nose. She came home early and was in terrible pain.

Chapter 13

Grandpa had fought in WW I; he was a horse soldier, or Calvary. During one of the worst winters, Grandpa and a few of his men got separated from the rest of the battalion. Freezing, and with their provisions gone, they were forced to draw lots to see whose horse would be shot in order for them to survive. Grandpa lost the draw and he never got over it. He would always tell Grandma never to buy horsemeat, although it was easy to get and much cheaper than the other meats that were send to the soldiers. Grandma would tell Grandpa that in France it was very fashionable to eat horsemeat. Grandpa turned a deaf ear to her.

Going after groceries one day, Grandma finding she was short of money again, and after swearing me to secrecy, decided to buy horsemeat.

That evening she busied herself in the tiny kitchen fixing a delicious stew, consisting of the meat, potatoes, carrots and onions. Grandpa had two helpings and ate with gusto. When he finished, Grandma said, "See, I knew that you could eat horsemeat!" Grandpa never made it to the slop bucket; I can still see him retching to this day. Grandma felt so bad about spoiling his supper and seeing him go to bed with an empty stomach. She never bought horsemeat again, but Grandpa never trusted her again when it came to meat on the table, he would corner me and ask me what kind it was.

One morning, after inspecting the food cupboard and finding a tin of fish, Grandma said she would go to the bakery for some rolls. She left me at the hut, because we had an electrician working on a faulty electric line. Grandma told me to watch him to make sure he didn't steal anything. For lack of something to do, I set a couple of plates on the table; in anticipation of the lunch we would soon be eating. The electrician asked where Grandma was and I told him she went to get rolls for the tinned fish. I hung around till he left. When Grandma returned to fix our noon meal, the tinned fish was gone!

She was mad at me, saying she had left me in charge to make sure this wouldn't happen. It was back to rolls with lard and salt.

Grandma was always concerned about my weight, always giving me extra of her meager ration, telling me that she had no appetite. I wound up with jaundice anyway.

Chapter 14

Grandma took me to the Red Cross where I lined up with about twenty other children to be examined. After the examination they told Grandma that I had jaundice and malnutrition. They told her to bring me back every other day at 10:00 a.m. which was for the girls. The boys had a different day and time.

When Grandma took me the next time, there were several girls there already, and I was told to take off all my clothes. The nurse gave me a pair of black goggles to put on and told me to lie on a blanket under a sunlamp for a certain amount of time. I did not mind, as it was nice and warm under the lamp. It was always a disappointment when they told me to get up and get dressed. Before we left, we lined up again, and every child got a tablespoon of Cod Liver Oil. I could not help but make a face each time as the thick, fishy, oily liquid went down my throat. For a reward, and to wash the taste away, we were given a small piece of hard candy.

Then we were ready for our walk home. We started this routine when there was still snow on the ground. Before I knew it, springtime had arrived. It was such a joy to walk and talk with Grandma, hand in hand, under the flowering chestnut trees that lined the streets. Grandma would tell me that I was getting brown as an Indian and that always made me smile. Soon after that, the nurse told Grandma that I was doing fine and did not need any more treatments. I was disappointed, as I was getting used to the routine and I would miss the warm naps and the hard candy, not to mention the walks with Grandma.

There were plenty of things that took my mind off the treatments. Spring was on the way. Even around the barracks, clumps of grass and buttercups emerged, adding color to the drab metal Quonset huts. It was as if God used a paintbrush to make everything pretty, even here. The limbs on the willow trees were turning yellow and leafing out, and their long branches swept in the Alster below with the breeze. The beautiful swans came back with their little ones trailing behind.

I will have to tell Karin that I don't need to go for treatments anymore, so now we will have more time to play.

Chapter 15

As I said before, Grandpa divided the Quonset in half because of the size of our family. In the front half, facing the lane lived a widow and her son, about my age. She invited me in one day shortly before Christmas. Their side was clean and tidy. After asking how we were doing, she put two pieces of paper on the table with three short crayons and two pencil stubs, and said that we could draw. I still remember drawing a pine bough with a candle on it, in anticipation of Christmas, and she said how pretty it was. The boy drew a Christmas tree with balls and we kept passing the crayons back and forth, as we colored our pictures.

His mom said that I could take the picture home with me. On leaving, I turned to them and said that our house was larger than theirs was. She said that it was impossible, since all the Quonsets are the same. I shrugged my shoulders, saying that I was sure that our half was bigger.

I told the boy to come outside with me and I would go inside our hut, next to the partition and bang on the wall. I ran past Grandma into the bedroom part and started banging away. Grandma came in the bedroom and asked me what I was doing. When I told her she about keeled over. She grabbed my arm for me to stop. She said that Grandpa had given us a few extra feet, and he would get in big trouble if they found that out. I went immediately into the living room, shortening the distance, and pounded away.

When I went outside and asked him if he could tell where I pounded. He said yes, and that his part was actually bigger than ours was. I just shrugged my shoulders, with that out of the way; we started talking about Christmas again. We never discussed that matter again. I felt that Grandpa did the right thing, since the Quonsets are according to family size. There were four of us and only two of them; our part should be bigger.

Heidi wanted me to sleep over, which I always enjoyed. Her mom preserved elderberry juice in bottles and always gave us a little glass before bedtime for our health. The bad part was, when we washed up at night, she would clean our fingernails and push back our cuticles. Mine were always in bad shape and she would push them so hard my fingers would be sore all night.

When Heidi asked me to stay over after a couple of days, I would always make up an excuse. I loved staying there, but I remembered my painful, throbbing fingernails. I needed at least a week to recover and forget the pain.

Heidi always wanted to play beautician. She combed my hair before bedtime, trying out different styles on my short hair, which felt so soothing and relaxing. Heidi had an older sister, who had a job and helped contribute to the family's income

Chapter 16

Heidi and I woke early, and rushed through our milk and bread. Then we walked along the barracks to the other end; the way we would go to school at Alsterdorfer Street. Here were the regular houses and one in particular was a little Tudor style house. It reminded me of the Hansel and Gretel house. The old woman that lived there had a big German shepherd named Fritz.

On certain days, she would let him outside, hand him a basket with a cloth in it, and Fritz would take the handle in his mouth and walk toward the train tunnel. This was the way to school, but instead of turning right toward the school, he crossed the street where the shops were located.

This was not the street where Grandma shopped, this was further away and the opposite direction from Ludolf Street.

The routine was always the same. First, he would go to the butcher who would greet Fritz by name, give him a scrap of meat, while he took the note out of the basket. Then he would put a package of wurst or whatever was on the list, take out money and make change, cover everything with the cloth and tell Fritz to go to the Bakery. Here was the same routine again; the baker checked the list, added the rolls to the basket, and took out his fee. Customers would gladly wait and give up their turn in line to let Fritz shop, as he always went straight to the counter and received immediate attention. If that was everything on the list, the baker would tell Fritz to go home, but Fritz was smarter then that. He would always double back to the Butcher Shop for another meat scrap, which he always received.

Sometimes Fritz would make a mistake and go to the wrong store, they would read his list and tell him where to go next, and so he would always get his shopping done.

When finished, he would walk home, put the basket on the stoop and bark, the woman would come out, pick up the basket, pat Fritz on the head and they went back in the house.

It was always a treat to be able to follow and watch him. We ran many a day when there was no school following Fritz around, and I wished that he was my dog. I never did find out if Fritz's master was blind or lame. She did come to the door with a cane, but they must have made those trips every day for years, for him to know the routine so well.

A family of eight came up the lane one day. Grandma was outside and they stopped and asked if there were any Quonset huts available. They told her they had nowhere to go and needed a place to stay. Grandma told them she thought they were all occupied. She told the man who to see about them, in case there was one available. She also said they should check out the last eight Quonsets, as they were set up for larger sized families.

The next morning, as I was going on my way to school, nearing the last of the Quonset huts, there they were; laying in a row, all bedded down on sacks outside the Quonsets, the parents and their six children. It was freezing and the blankets had a dusting of frost on them. At first I thought that they had all committed suicide, but then I saw them breathing and moving slightly. They were still asleep, and I walked by softly, not to wake or embarrass them. On my way home, I looked for them, but they were gone.

I told Grandma about what I saw and asked if we could not put them up in our hut. Grandma said we did not have the room and since they had already gone, it did not matter.

Chapter 17

Of course, not every dog was as well behaved as Fritz. For instance, I was always afraid of the walk to school, I had to go all the way to the end of the barracks, to get to the street, where my school was. Toward the end of the barracks was a woman that had a big shepherd with a wicked personality. He was on a chain, but it was long enough to reach across the path. I always had to make sure I got way out of his way, because he would show his teeth, growl and jump, straining on his chain.

One morning I was still eating my bread with butter and sugar on it and not paying attention. I was right in the dog's path, and he scared me so bad I threw my bread at him, thinking he would eat it and I could get by him. When I threw the bread, he jumped up, and standing on his hind legs with his front paws on my face, he stuck a big claw on top of my nose. I was screaming out of pain and fear as the blood ran down my face.

The woman came out of the hut and asked me what I had done to her dog to provoke him. She threw a dirty kitchen rag at me, told me to hold it on my nose, and go to school.

When I got to the school the rag was soaked in blood and dripping on my dress, after hearing my story the teacher send me home. I walked back home and told Grandma what happened. She went to the woman and let her have it with both barrels. I do not know what she said, but after that, the dog was on a shorter chain. After that, the woman always looked out and gave me a mean look as I passed by her hut.

One day, coming home from school, I saw a cat lying between the washhouse and our cabin, it was very sick, with yellow stuff coming out of its mouth. I felt so sorry for it, I ran to tell Grandma. She was in the washhouse with a neighbor doing laundry, and they both came running. They said that the cat must have gotten into some poison. There was a rat problem and the people, in the villas behind us, had put out poison to get rid of them.

Several people came to look at the poor cat and Grandma asked if there was a man around that could put it out of its misery. They were all at work, and the poor cat had to suffer for hours before death finally relieved it.

To get my mind off the tragedy, one of the teenage girls volunteered to take us out in the country to a farm and pick apples. Grandma was pleased, she wanted to make applesauce and can it, as she used to do on the farm. We left the next morning on the streetcar, there were about five of us all together. Grandma packed me some butter bread in my rucksack, which she hoped I would fill with apples on our return.

When we arrived in the country, we asked for directions to the farms. When I asked how she knew if they would have apples, she said all farms have apple trees on them. We arrived at the first farm and the proprietor told us to get off his property. It was the same with the next farm. We covered a lot of territory, watching the kilometer signs go by as we trudged on. We had been singing, but that had come to an abrupt halt after the second farmer turned us down.

It was getting dusk, and she decided we would try one more farm. The farmer told us to go ahead and pick what we wanted, as long as the apples were on the ground.

We were delighted, it was getting hard to see, but we grabbed what apples we could find in the grass, trying to fill our rucksacks. I just thought how happy Grandma would be having all these apples, and I picked as fast as I could. Finally, we stopped, trudged the long way back to the train station, and when the streetcar finally arrived, we sat down and relaxed. Everyone was hungry so we decided to eat an apple, when we noticed the apples were full of worms. It was not just the apples, but also our rucksacks were crawling with them as well. We let out squeals, and took our rucksacks and dumped the apples out behind the train along the tracks.

When I got home, Grandma asked for the apples. When I told her, what happened she got mad, saying how much she had looked forward to the apples and that she could have cut the wormholes out. Now she had no apples and was out the train fare. I felt bad and went to bed right away after washing my hands. I was so exhausted;

I did not remember ever walking so much or Grandma being so mad.

The next day Grandma was still upset, so I asked her if she would teach me how to knit, to get her mind off the apples. She brought out her knitting needles and some yarn. She taught me how to make a potholder. It took me a couple of days and I finally finished it. I gave it to Grandma, who said I did a good job, and I ran out to play as if I had been on home confinement.

Karin had not been to school for several days. When I went outside, I saw her near her hut. I went over to play with her and she told me not to get near her as she had whooping cough. I told her that was neat, telling her to cough in my face so I could catch it, we could both stay home, and play, but she would not do it. I hung around her, but never did catch it.

Chapter 18

Fall was setting in; the days were getting shorter and colder. Instead of spending our spare time swimming, we made do with other recreations.

We drew chalk marks on the truck scales and played hopscotch. When we tired of that, we played marbles, or jump rope. We held races and played dozens of outdoor games. Whenever it got dark, the parents would call us in for supper. After dark, we usually stayed inside.

These were good times too, because Mama would reminisce about the past. When she was a teenage girl, she had a mandolin with ribbon streamers on it. She and a couple of her friends would play their instruments on the street, for anyone who would listen, and how, before she met my father, she was engaged to a young man in the Navy.

The Navy was to test out a new U-Boat (submarine). All the families and girlfriends of the sailors went to the docks to see them pull out to sea. He gave Mama his wallet and said to hold it until he returned. Mama said she waited until after dark but they never came back from the sea.

I found out that although she was an only child, like me, that Grandma and Grandpa had adopted a little baby boy from a mother who did not want him because he was sickly and had tuberculosis. He thrived on the farm, with the good food, and plenty of milk. Grandma would bundle him up and lay him out in a lawn chair for the fresh air. When she took him back to the doctor, he was in perfect health. He was a happy and loving little boy.

After a year, the mother stopped by, saw how healthy and happy he was and wanted him back. Grandma did everything she could to keep him but to no avail. In less than three months, the little boy died. Mama said he died of a broken heart, and Grandma and Grandpa never got over their loss.

She also told me how crafty Grandma was. When Grandpa was out at sea, Grandma ran the farm single handed, watering all the vegetables, harvesting, canning, pruning berry bushes and fruit trees, washing of the hogs, tending to the chickens and sheep. One Christmas she took a little hand saw and made me an entire zoo, with all kinds of animals and fences.

She also told me that I should be a ballerina, that ever since I started to walk, I would walk on my tiptoes. Mama had already signed me up for ballet classes. When I asked why I was not a ballerina, she said that because war broke out, and now we did not have money for the classes.

I also learned that as a baby, Mama gave me beer to drink, she did not have any milk and it was next to impossible to get any because of the war. When I asked her if it did not make me sick, she said, "No, but you slept a lot."

I could listen to Mama forever, but with bedtime nearing, all my requests for just one more story were ignored, and finally I got up in my bunk. Below me Grandpa was already sound asleep.

Grandma suffered from migraines, which usually happened at bedtime. I always knew when it happened, because she would turn the light on in the living room to take a couple of aspirins. She would then try to do a crossword puzzle or read a magazine trying to make herself so tired that she could sleep. When I asked her once why she had so many headaches, she said that it was from being cold, damp and hungry for several years, and she hoped it would never happen to me.

Grandma had a habit of misplacing her glasses, since she just needed them for reading. She would ask me if I saw them, I would look at her and burst out laughing, because she usually just shoved them up on her head, there they set, like a crown in her hair.

Chapter 19

All year Grandma saved her pennies and nickels for the fair, which always came in the fall. I was so excited when the big day came.

When she took me to the fair, there was so much to see I did not know where to look first. I wanted to see all the animals but mostly I loved to watch the elephants. I watched kids get on the rides, we checked out all the booths and vendors. One had balloons, and I just stared at them, they were so pretty. I asked Grandma if I could have one and she tried to talk me out of it, saying that I might want something else instead, but I held firm and decided on a green one. I could not keep my eye off that green balloon. They did not have the helium-filled ones then, but where they tied a knot in the balloon, they would attach a two-foot stick, so when you hold it, it would be up in the air.

We ate a sausage, Grandma put me on a ride, and we walked and looked at everything. What a day it was! We even brought a little bag of sweets home to Mama and Grandpa, since they had to work and could not go with us.

It was dark when we arrived home. There was a chill in the air but I was warm with all the excitement of the day.

Grandma had a passion for crossword puzzles, and she was very good at it. In hard times, she would erase all the pencil marks and reuse the book until the pages wore out. She slept in the living room on the sofa, and those many nights that she could not sleep, she would be working on her crossword puzzle.

She asked me to go with her one evening to the tobacco woman for a new crossword book. As we walked down Ludolf Street, and were ready to cross over to her store, Grandma pulled me back on to the sidewalk and said that we could not go to her store today. When I asked why, she told me to look at her door; someone had painted a big white swastika on her dark brown shop door. Grandma said that it was not safe and she hoped that her old friend was all right.

Next grocery day, we noticed that the swastika was gone and her shop door was open. When we entered, Grandma asked her what had happened. She said that some young hoodlum boys did it and she had lost quite a bit of business since everyone was afraid to enter her shop. The big shepherd lay behind the counter in his usual spot. After petting him, I went to the window, got a cartoon book to look at while they caught up on the latest gossip and news.

After a while, Grandma told me to put the book back as we were ready to go home. On the way back, I noticed the dry grocer had decorated their storefront window for Christmas and had a little grocery store on display. It was just my size and so cute, I was glued to the window, and Grandma finally had to pull me away so we could go home.

The wind was fierce as we crossed the bridge over the Alster, and Grandma said it wont be long till it froze over, cutting off the coal barges till spring. I looked across the bridge toward the Quonset huts and I could see the silhouettes in the dusk and wisps of smoke coming out of the chimneys.

When we arrived at the hut, Grandpa was in his chair reading his beloved newspaper, "Das Hamburg Abendblatt", checking for the latest soccer scores. Grandma brewed them a cup of coffee and started on her crossword puzzle, while I colored a picture until it was bedtime.

As I lay on the top bunk I was telling Grandpa, who slept below me, about the little grocery store that was complete with a counter and shelves with tiny cubbyholes. Grandpa finally told me to go to sleep, that he had to get up early to go to work. I asked Grandpa to rock me to sleep. He would raise his legs and push my mattress up and down with his feet until I was tickled, and we would both be laughing until Grandma yelled at both of us to go to sleep.

Our class was to put on a Christmas play this year at the Opera House. Grandma and I passed it every time we passed the bridge to shop, but we had never been inside of it. When there were activities going on there, you could see people all dressed up, getting out of cars and taxies, and going up the steps of the big fancy building. After a while, you could hear the sound of beautiful music emerging from within.

Our teacher held an audition; we had a pantomime act of a man with a toothache, sitting in a dentist chair getting his tooth pulled, and the story of The Little Match Girl. There was solo singing and a chorus singing beautiful Christmas carols. Those with no apparent ability became dancing flowers…....I was a flower.

The flowers had to wear a gathered pink skirt, with suspenders, and a white blouse. Since material was too costly, the teacher decided that our skirts would be made of pink crepe paper by our parents.

After school, I headed home, armed with instructions for Mama on how to make the crepe paper skirt. Mama did a fine job; she even reinforced the suspenders by sewing them on strips of cloth so they would not tear.

A few nights before Christmas came our big day. Grandma, Grandpa, Mama and I walked across the bridge. The wind blew icy cold on my legs through the paper skirt, but I did not mind at all. I was in costume and so proud of my big moment.

There were parents and children coming from all directions, as other grades had programs to perform. The Opera house was gilded on the inside and all dressed up for the Christmas holidays with candles, pine boughs and red ribbons. Christmas music filled the air, different choruses sang, children danced and performed their plays, proud parents applauded, and all too soon, it was over. I wish we could have stayed longer in the beautiful warm building, and as we left, Grandma commented on the comfortable red velvet seats.

My seat hit the floor during one of our dance numbers and I got a big rip in my beautiful pink crepe skirt. Mama told me to quit sniffling about it, because I could not wear the skirt to school, even if I had not ripped it. In that case, I did not care, and so much for my stage career. There was not time to dwell on it, Christmas was in a couple days, and that was far more important right now.

This would turn out to be the best Christmas ever. On Christmas Eve, as I stood behind the curtain, trembling with anticipation, I heard the front door open and Mama coming in from work. She was making a racket and there was a lot of whispering going on. Grandma came in the kitchen, got a rag and went back into the living room, telling me to be patient just a little longer. I was rehearsing my verse I was going to say, and then Mama told me to come into the room.

There, in front of me was the little grocery shop I had been admiring at the dry grocers display window. I could not believe my eyes. It had a little scale and tiny cone shaped bags. Grandma went into the kitchen, put some rice, and dried beans in the containers, and Mama had got me some penny candy to put on the counter. I was ecstatic. Forgetting my verse, I ran over to Karin's and we played grocery store until bedtime, with Mama, Grandma and Grandpa joining in and pretending to be customers as Karin and I took turns taking their orders and weighing and bagging their purchases.

Mama told me later on, how she had asked the shopkeeper, every week, if she could buy the display. They always told her that it was not for sale. She tried one more time on Christmas Eve, and they relented. Mama was ecstatic. I have no idea how she managed to carry the bulky display across the bridge and bring it home for me.

Chapter 20

Father and his family lived in East Germany which is the sector that was under Russian control after the war. The Russians wasted no time building a barbed wire fence around it, complete with guard towers. This was in prelude to the concrete wall that followed. This was done to prevent people from leaving, dividing family and friends.

Father had a sister named Helga. She was married and they both wound up in a Russian concentration camp, working underground. Aunt Helgas' husband died while in camp, and she was released after several years of hard labor.

One night there was a knock on the door, it was Aunt Helga. She took a terrible risk going under the barbed wire, but she wanted to see me. She had brought a shopping bag with her, and reaching her hand inside of it, she had pulled out a beautiful white dress that she had made me, embroidered with wild flowers, and a little pocket that was on cords hanging from the waistline. It was the prettiest thing I had ever seen. Although she had to guess at the size, it was a perfect fit.

She had also brought me a peach; I had never seen one before. Everyone told me to eat it, that it was good, but every time I brought it up to my mouth, the peach fuzz would tickle my lips, and I could not bite into it. Finally, Grandma had to peel it for me, saying I was wasting the best part. I noticed as she was peeling the peach, she was eating every scrap of the peel, so I did not feel so guilty. They were right, the peach was wonderful, without it's little fur coat.

We all had a lovely visit, and Grandma filled up aunt Helgas' bag with some extra food, realizing they had a lot less than we did. Mama begged her to stay in Hamburg, but my other set of grandparents were still over there, and she said she would have to go back to take care of them. She was afraid they would be punished if she did not return. She stayed till midnight, telling Mama to turn out the lights so no one would see her leave. We watched out the little window as she faded into the night.

We never heard from her or my other grandparents again. It was like they disappeared from the face of the earth.

Chapter 21

Grocery day was always a big event that we all looked forward to. This was always on Fridays, when Mama and Grandpa got their pay packets at work. Grandma would get out the two big shopping bags, wind a scarf around her head, turban style, and wardrobe complete, we would walk up the lane across the bridge. We were on Hudtwalcker Street and turn right to enter Ludolf Street where all the shops were located. I loved this street.

The first store was the dry grocer, one of my favorites. There were several clerks working behind the counter. Grandma would pay a little on her bill, the clerk would get out the big ledger with what seemed hundreds of names, deduct the amount paid, and put a new total down. Grandma would then hand the clerk the list of items we needed. He would get them off the shelves for us behind the counter. Grandma would take the items and carefully place them in her shopping bag.

I loved to check things out while Grandma was being waited on. On the shelves were all kinds of canned goods and boxed food items. The applesauce always caught my eye, as it was canned in tall green jars and looked so appetizing. Fresh vegetables were in front of the counters in wooden crates, such as potatoes, carrots, cabbages, turnips, onions and apples. Oranges and tangerines would just come in at Christmas time.

The next store up was the butcher. Grandma always got two different kinds of sausage for our evening open faced sandwich; the main meal was eaten at noon. Before we left, Grandma would always ask for dog bones and scrap meat. I am sure they knew we had no dog, but they would always wrap up some bones in the crisp white butcher paper for her. Sometimes a young girl would work the counter and would always include some bones with a good amount of meat on them. She would cut off the ends of several sausages, which Grandma would turn into a tasty soup.

The next stop was the Dairy. Here we handed over the tin pail with a bail handle and purchased a liter of skim milk, it was cheaper, and half pound of butter. The milk was in a steel vat with a hose on it and the lady would stick the hose in the milk can, turn on the switch and fill up the can. There would be an inch of foam on top from the pressure and I loved to spoon it off, it tasted like whipped cream. There was no refrigeration and milk was purchased as needed. We then crossed the street, directly across from the Dairy which was the Fish Monger. The items here were usually pickled sour herring, or smoked fish. Grandma also asked for fish scraps for our non-existing cat. Grandma would take the heads, tails, and bones and turn them into a delicious soup.

We then made our way back toward Hudtwalcker Street where the next shop was Grandma's favorite, the Tobacco Shop. It was owned by an old Jewish woman and she and Grandma became good friends. They would spend some time visiting with each other. She had a big, gentle shepherd dog that always lay behind the counter to keep her company. Besides tobacco wares, she sold newspapers, puzzle books, magazines and comic books.

While they got caught up since their last visit, I would get a comic book that lay in the front window on display and look at the pictures in it. I remember it was Donald Duck.

The next shop was a Stationary Shop. They sold writing paper, envelopes, pens, pencils, ink, cards, and scrap pictures. We went in here very seldom. I remember going in just once, Grandma got a card there. The last shop on the corner was the Bakery, another one of my favorite stores. Behind the long counter were shelves along the wall with cubbyholes, or dividers that held different shaped rolls and a variety of loaves of bread. It smelled wonderful in there. They would come in at 2:00 in the morning, and bake until at 6:00 a.m. The doors would then open for business and workers would go in to get a fresh hot crusty roll for their breakfast.

I would hold the handle on one side of Grandma's shopping bag, as we headed back across the bridge, and she would always tell me what a big helper I was getting to be.

We always had the best meal of the week on Friday evening, that consisted of cold cuts on fresh bread. Mama,

Grandma and Grandpa then had what they called their "good cup" of coffee. After the third day, the grounds were boiled over until the next Friday, with the coffee getting lighter and lighter every day. Coffee was still rationed, much to their dismay.

Grandma supplemented our food larder by befriending the fishermen along the Alster. She would give them a cigarette or two and they would bring us a fish every now and then.

Chapter 22

The winter time was all consumed of food and fuel. Springtime had a completely different atmosphere. Nothing could seem bad or hopeless when the sun was shining, and flowers were blooming. Even the barracks got a new look. Grandma planted asters outside, and a lilac bush that grew along with me. She planted fava beans outside the kitchen window, tied strings up, and had them climb the strings as they grew. This gave her a little enclosed privacy fence.

My friend Heidi lived on the other side of the wash house. Her father was a big seafaring man. One summer, when I was about six years old, he decided that he would teach all of us kids to swim, before one of us drowned, since we were always around the water. He lined the five of us up, and started with Heidi. He tied a rope around her waist and lowered her into the water, telling her to move her arms and legs, supporting her by the rope. In no time she was swimming with the rope trailing behind her.

Next was my turn, I could hardly wait, it was a little scary being lowered into the water as the rope cut under my arms, but once I hit the water it was so nice and refreshing. Heidi's father was booming out instructions, leading me back and forth with the rope. As he was still talking to me, I looked up at him, and saw there was no rope in his hand. It was trailing like a snake behind me and before long; I was swimming after Heidi with the rope trailing along my back.

He had taught us all how to swim that summer, much to our delight and pleasure. How we would look forward with much anticipation to the hot days of summer after that. I wonder if he ever realized how many hours of pleasure he gave us with that simple act of kindness.

After that, there was not a warm day when we were not in the water. Heidi, Karin, and I were named the water rats by the neighbors, as we were in the water constantly, coming out only at mealtimes or when it was getting late in the day.

It was years later Mama told me that Heidi's father had never learned how to swim. I always wondered what would have happened if the rope broke or he accidentally let go of it too soon, but I guess he knew what he was doing, a born teacher.

With the weather getting warmer, the Shore Patrol made the daily rounds up the Alster to make sure no one was swimming in the polluted water. They would test the water till it was safe to swim in and then post a sign. We got wise to their routine and would time the Shore Patrol boats and know about when it was safe in between checks. If we were caught, we would be reprimanded for swimming in polluted waters and taken to our parents for further punishment.

Once the water was marked safe, there was no holding us back. First thing in the morning, Mama would put on her swimsuit and swim across the Alster, for exercise as well as a bath. Then she would dress and head for work. There were several adults that had the same routine. After rising, I would put on my bathing suit and go swimming until Grandma got me out to eat a piece of bread. She would then tell me to stay out an hour, so I would not get cramps. I figured out that this was just a ploy to keep me out of the water, so I sneaked back in the water after a few minutes, without any ill affects.

Chapter 23

Rowboats and canoes, with families, made their way down the Alster. In the boats were picnic hampers, women and children laying on blankets and pillows, while the men rowed or paddled. It looked so wonderful. At nighttime there would be boats on the Alster with strings of lights clear around them, and you could hear music on the shore. It was very festive.

One day, as I was watching the boats go by from the shore, two young men rowed by and asked me if I wanted to go for a ride and have a picnic with them. Against Grandma's warnings, I quickly said yes, as they helped me down into the boat. I sat on a cushion as they paddled along the Alster to a wooded grove, where the willows made a wispy screen. Here, they pulled the boat ashore and we got out. It was cool here, as the willows shaded us from the sun.

They introduced themselves and asked my name. Then they spread out a blanket and got out a basket filled with sandwiches and fruit, it was wonderful. Then we laid back and rested and enjoyed the beautiful spring day in the filtered sunlight of the willows. I found out they were University students. They asked me about life in the barracks, and after about an hour told me they had better get me back before my Grandma started to worry. I was sorry to leave, but I could not wait to get back and tell Grandma, Heidi and Karin about my outing.

Grandma was not impressed and was really mad at me. After all she had taught me, how I could be so irresponsible as to go with two strangers. They could have cut my body up and buried me under the willow tree. I took this advice with a grain of salt, and waited patiently by the shore for my two new friends to show up and give me another outing, but I never saw them again.

I came close to getting into big trouble, one day in late spring, Karin and I went swimming, before they removed the polluted sign. We were having a good time, not paying attention to the sound of an oncoming boat. Then we saw it was the Shore Patrol and they were heading right for us. We scrambled out of the water and I hollered at Heidi not to run to our huts.

We went past our homes, ran up the alley, and into the basement of a villa. It was the furnace room, and we surprised the janitor as he was putting coal in the furnace. Here we stood, dripping wet in our bathing suits. He asked what we were doing here, and we told him that the Shore Patrol was after us for swimming in the Alster. He told us to come closer to the furnace to keep warm while he went out to see if they were still there. When he came back, he told us that the coast was clear, they had moved on with the boat. We thanked him and he told us to come back and visit him, as he got lonesome down there. I told him I was surprised that he was still keeping the furnace up, as it was springtime and warm enough to swim. He said, "You know what rich people are like, spoiled! I have to keep a fire almost the year around".

Chapter 24

Friday was payday for Mama when she worked at the Post Office, delivering the mail. It was particularly exciting during the first part of summer, because of the short, fleeting cherry season.

Karin and I would be outside playing, but keeping a watchful eye out down the lane towards evening, knowing that Mama would be coming soon, with two paper cones, filled with dark, plump cherries, a bag for each of us. As soon as we saw her we would run to meet her to relieve her of our precious load. If we were lucky, we would find "twins" that were attached by a stem, these we would wear "for a little while" like earrings. The darkest cherries were rubbed across the lips to mimic lipstick. Oh, how we enjoyed every last morsel, spitting out the seeds of that precious fruit of summer

Chapter 25

Karin was telling me that her little brother, Dieter, seemed to have an endless supply of cookies all of a sudden. Since sugar, flour and butter were being rationed, cookies were as scarce as hen's teeth. Yet, every morning we would see him walk around with a cone shaped bag full of cookie pieces and crumbs, taunting us, but never sharing. Karin and I asked him repeatedly where he was getting his bounty from, but he remained stubborn, unwilling to divulge his source.

After several days of this torture, we finally told him that we would not play with him anymore if he did not tell us where he got the cookies. He finally gave in, and told us he went to the Bakery before daylight every morning and they gave him all the broken cookies and crumbs for the asking.

Karin and I devised a plan to beat Dieter to the Bakery the next morning. We took a long string, ran it from the outside window into our barracks, across the partial wall to my upper cot. From there I tied the string around my big toe. In the morning, when Karin saw that Dieter was getting out of bed, she was to tug on the string for our signal to get me up and we would outrun Dieter to the Bakery.

In the morning, when Karin pulled on the string, the whole thing went out the window. Grandma had seen it and removed it from my foot while I was asleep, saying that I could have gotten hurt.

By the time we ran across the bridge, there came Dieter with his cookie bag. Needless to say, we tried several schemes, close to locking him up in the wardrobe, but it was not to be for us.

We did find things to eat in late spring and early summer that Mother Nature supplied us for the picking. There were wild berry vines before you get to the Quonsets near the Alster. Gooseberry bushes with fruit as big as quarters, the deep maroon red and the glassy yellow ones. They were sweet as sugar when they were ripe. Hazelnut bushes were also abundant and every child picked to their hearts content.

Someone had a rhubarb patch and would share their harvest with us. Heidi's mother planted sunflower seeds and we ravished the ripe seeds out of them before the birds beat us. I found that in time of need, the poor are the most generous. I guess they know what it's like to do without. Grandma could never turn a beggar down, always giving, even when it was just a slice of bread.

Chapter 26

In the living room, was a small trunk that contained clothing. I never paid much attention to it; it was just a fixture against the wall facing the kitchen. One day Grandma opened it up and took out my fathers Luftwaffe dagger. She said that we were probably not supposed to keep it, and we might get in big trouble for having it. She handed it to me and told me to wait till it got dark, go up the river and throw the dagger in the water as far as I could, and make sure no one saw me.

That night, Grandma turned out the lights, looked out, to make sure all the other lights were out and no one was outside. She then sends me out on my mission. It was cool out, but I felt warm from the excitement, and my mind raced wanting to go against Grandmas' wishes and bury fathers' dagger somewhere. Years later, I could dig it up and retrieve it. Yet, Grandma was always right, and I could get us all in trouble by disobeying her. So with one quick look around, I slung Fathers dagger as hard as I could from the shore and heard the little 'plop' it made as it found its watery grave.

I remember how sad and empty I felt going back to the barrack, with the only possession we had of Father gone.

It was daylight when I woke up the next morning. I heard a trawler on the river and men talking loudly. I dressed quickly and ran out to see what was going on. Several men were on the trawler with grappling hooks, picking up metal from the bottom of the Alster. As I looked down on the trawler bed, I saw hand guns, iron crosses, knives, and daggers, which were mostly rusted. Whenever they got hold of something, they would yell at each other of what a fine catch they made, and stop to inspect their find.

Slowly the trawler made its way toward the bottom where I was last night. I kept saying. "Please don't find it." About that time one of the men let out a big yell. "Look at this! It looks brand new! It could not have been in the water long." He pulled the dagger out of its sheath. As he held up the dagger for the rest to see, the sun caught the blade. The bright light that reflected from the blade brought tears to my eyes, as I stood there and watched helplessly.

I was raised to be resourceful and to find solutions to solve most problems at my early age, but I was brought back to reality. I was just a little girl, without voice or action. When I did find my voice, I yelled to the men on the trawler, "What do you do with all the stuff you find?"

"Sell it," someone yelled back, "there is good money in metal, they melt it down, and we made a good haul today."

So now I knew the fate of Fathers dagger. Maybe it would wind up as a knife and fork in someone's kitchen. When I went back to the barrack, I confronted Grandma with it and quarreled with her, telling her that we should have kept it.

Karin and Rita, another one of my friends came in about then, and we changed the subject fast. They were all excited, both talking at the same time. Finally, when we got the story straight, we found out they were going to have a talent contest at the Alsterhaus. All the children were to be there at 5:00 that evening and sing in front of microphones. They were looking for new talent and the lucky one or ones that were chosen, were to have a part in a movie, and be on their way to fame and fortune.

Chapter 27

We discussed the song we were going to sing, with great anticipation and skipped our supper that evening, much too excited to eat. We ran to the Alsterhaus ahead of time, stars in our eyes, dreams of riches in our heads. When we arrived, we came back to reality; there was every mother's pride and joy lined up to use the microphone. They had them lined up on a long stage that encircled two sides of the building, with microphones set up every few feet, and children belting out the latest songs. I did not know there were so many kids in the world. Where did they all come from? The closer I got to the microphone, the dryer my mouth got, my legs felt like they were made of rubber. I would be too weak to walk up on the stage when my turn came. Was that my heart beating out of my chest or was that the drum beat to one of the songs.

The competition was fierce; this was not a done deal as we were hoping for. When it was finally my turn, my legs turned to jelly, and my stomach was churning, whose voice was that coming out of my throat? Someone kept yelling to sing louder. As I was close to bursting a lung already, how much louder did they want? With a short "Thanks", I was whisked off the stage. Karin, Heidi and Rita all suffered the same fate. We compared our songs and techniques going down the lane, and decided it was all rigged anyway. We raced home, hoping we did not miss supper.

Rita told us to come to her house the next day. She lived close to the Alsterhaus. Her father was a doctor, and he kept his outdated medical books in the cellar. We would go down in the cellar and peruse the human body, illuminated by a 15 watt light bulb, till her sister yelled for us, wondering where we were . Rita would pull the light cord and we would run like rats out of a hole.

Chapter 28

We had to wear knee socks till May Day it was our tradition. In other words, Grandma and a lot of parents believed you would get sick with all kinds of ailments if you did not wait till then. It was a big deal to wear short socks in the spring. Some girls got to wear them earlier to school, to the envy of the rest of us. Soon as the weather warmed a little, and I was out of Grandma's sight, I would roll down my socks, now I was right in style.

The Alsterdorfer School was a long brick three story building build in 1906. It had 30 classrooms and was divided in the middle. There were two entrances in the front, the girls side was on the right and the boys side on the left, even the school yard was divided.

My class was on the second floor. After going up the wide staircase I turned left. Coat hooks were along the wall of the hall. Everyone had an assigned hook to leave their coats on before entering class.

The girls were let out five minutes earlier, to get home safely before the boys were let out. This did not help in the mornings, especially in the wintertime. We had to pass a barricade of snow, where several of the older boys had built a snow fort. They had a bunch of snowballs formed ahead of time, working them in their hands until they were hard as ice, just waiting for us girls to pass by. They would aim them at our faces, bare legs, and when we ran toward the school, the back of our neck. The snowballs would break and slide down our coat collars and necks, making us cold for the rest of the day.

I was born left handed, and at the time, this was not accepted in school. I was told in no uncertain terms to use my right hand when writing. As hard as I tried, it was so awkward for me, and without realizing it, I would switch hands. I believe my teacher had eyes in the back of his head. One minute he was up front by his desk, and the next minute he was behind me rapping my fingers with a ruler. It would hurt so bad, that I could not use that hand for a while, it would make my fingers numb, but almost daily for weeks on end, this would be repeated, till gradually, I became right handed.

The one thing I did not like about school, was that we had too many kids in our class. The school had two shifts, a morning and an evening one, and my best friends, Karin, Heidi and Rita were on a different shift from mine. That is why I was always so happy when school was out so I could play with them.

One evening after I got home from school, I saw Grandma waving for me to hurry to her. I ran to her, thinking something was wrong. She told me there had been an American Red Cross truck down at the Alster all morning and they were giving away hot chocolate to the children. She pushed a cup in my hand and told me to hurry up, that she did not know if there was any left.

I ran toward the truck, soldiers were sitting in the opened back end of the truck smocking cigarettes and playing cards. I saw two large kettles with ladles sticking out of them, I could smell the cocoa, and so I knew there was some left.

I held my cup up to the soldier, and he told me that I already had my share, one cup per person. I told him that

I just got out of school, but he did not believe me. I was about to cry, and he handed me two cigarettes, which I gave to Grandma, who in turn gave them to a fisherman for a fresh fish.

This episode happened more then once; I never did get any hot chocolate. My friends said that it tasted wonderful. The soldiers did not understand that we had two shifts at the school, and I was in the second one, which made me come home later than the other kids. I quit trying after a while, I thought that they just did not like me and I avoided the truck with the Red Cross and the big kettles of hot chocolate.

Chapter 29

When the boys tormented us girls in the winter, it was a whole new ballgame in the summer. Before you reached barrack #1, close to the Alster, there was a hedgerow of wild roses. After they bloomed, they got rosehips on them. The boys found out if you split them open and got to the seedpod, they had tiny hairs on them that make us itch worse then fiberglass insulation. As we would pass them, they would grab the back of our dress and put the seeds down our back, it was pure agony. I would run home as fast as I could, pull off the dress, and Grandma would have to wash my back real good with soap. Then I would have to get the dress washed as the little hairs would be in the material, and you couldn't shake them out. Grandma would get mad at the extra work, and I was mad at the boys.

Karin and I were playing between our hut and the washhouse, digging in the dirt, when we came across a bunch of dead snails. The state had build steps up the slope going by our cabin, to get to the lane, and we thought maybe they got buried and died. I ran in the house and got one of Grandpas' cigar boxes; we put them all in it and had a fine ceremony as we buried them in the freshly dug earth.

A week later, for the lack of anything better to do, we dug the box up, opened it and to our surprise the box was empty, except for some slimy trails and a few empty shells. We really felt bad about what we did, luckily the dirt was loose enough that they could move the lid and get out. When we told Grandma, we got another lecture to leave living or dead things alone.

I was playing outside one fine spring day, when a big dump truck full of manure backed up to Grandmas' aster bed and was getting ready to dump his load. I yelled at him to get away from my Grandmas' flowerbed and not dump that stuff there. He told me that he was supposed to bring it here and unload it. There I stood, eight years old, one hand on the hip, with the other, shaking a finger at the trucker, daring him to try and dump it. About that time Grandma came with the milk pail from the dairy. The driver told her what I said, and she got all over me.

She had talked to this farmer and got him to give her this fertilizer from his farm. How was I supposed to know, Grandma usually kept me abreast with things. Not only that, but she made me apologize, and curtsey to him. Ugh!

Karin, Heidi and Rita and I spent our time playing jump rope, marbles, hide and seek, but my favorite past time was taking our old school notebooks that were filled up with writing, fold the pages in half down the middle, and in some of the folds hide some scrap pictures. Karin would do the same with her book, and then with another scrap picture we would stick the picture between the pages of each others book. If there was a picture there, you got to keep both of them; if the fold was empty, you had to leave your scrap picture in its place. We usually decided to put in ten pictures apiece, some were favorites, but more were ones we did not care about. We could play this game for hours.

There was a little boy who had a scooter about eight barracks down from us. When we saw him coast down the hill, we asked if we could have a turn. What fun it was, but other kids soon came and the line was so long, that he had to wait longer and longer to ride his scooter. After a while, he said none of us could ride it anymore.

Ever inventive, Karin and I tied two of her brothers little wooden cars to our shoes for roller skates. As you may have thought, the little wooden wheels did not hold up.

Karin was one of six kids; the two oldest, a brother and sister, had jobs already and could help out with the income at home, which was needed to feed that many mouths. Sometimes Karin would come out of her barrack with a bowl of raw oatmeal with a sprinkle of sugar and eat it as we played. I asked her if her mother did not cook it for her and she said she liked it as it was. She told me to try it, but I did not care for it uncooked, this must have been the first granola.

Karin went inside her hut to take the empty bowl and I followed. Her older sister was washing up the dishes. They did not have much either, but I was always fascinated they had a true kitchen table. It had six legs, two on one side and a double row of legs on the other. That way, you could pull the table out, with the two legs and extension, and inside was a hole with a dishpan. On the other side of the table, was a built-in drawer for the silverware. Karin's sister asked us to go to the Dairy and get a liter of milk; she wanted to bake a cake. After giving us the milk can and money, we ran outside.

As we went back out, Grandma told us to watch where we were walking as she had planted a row of fava beans along the edge by the kitchen window. She did this every spring, to make her a little gazebo. Grandpa had done some masonry work for someone, and instead of money, which was scarce as hens' teeth; he got an old rattan easy chair for Grandma. She put it outside in the summer and would sit behind her bean vines that provided shade and privacy.

As we crossed the bridge, Karin started to swing the milk can over her head, by the bail, in a big circle. I told her she better not do that after we get the milk, or she would spill it all. She said she did it all the time, and when you swing it around over your head, the milk would stay in, and she never lost a drop. Of course, I did not believe her. After the milk purchase she started swinging the bucket over her head, and sure enough, the milk stayed in. I could not believe the talent of my friend.

Needless to say, I could not wait to get sent on the same errand, which happened the very next day. I ran all the way to the Dairy, anxious to try out Karins' trick. I waited till I got off the main street and started across the bridge, and sure enough it worked. When I came home and told Grandma, she told me to never to do that again, because the milk was too expensive to spill, so I promised. The next time she sends me to the store with a little basket, after six eggs. On the way home, I thought about the milk trick, and decided that it should work for eggs too.

I swung the basket over my head, and sure enough, the eggs stayed in. I thought I would try it one more time, but slower, so I could see what was happening. Before I knew it, two of the eggs flew out of the basket. I just barely managed to catch the other four. What was I going to tell Grandma, after I promised not to do it again? Of course, that was milk, but I don't think the difference in food mattered. What was I going to say?

Grandma took the basket and asked where the rest of the eggs were. I told her that Karin carried the bucket and swung it and the eggs fell out. To my horror, she went straight next door and confronted Karin. When she found out she didn't even go with me, she came back and walloped me good. Grandma never had spanked me before, and I think she had it all saved up till now. I did not know that she could hit so hard.

I went outside crying and Karin jumped on me for telling such a lie on her. I told her that I was sorry, and after promising her my favorite scrap picture, she forgave me. I learned fast that lying does not help, it just makes matters worse. As Grandma told me, she did not spank me for breaking the eggs, she spanked me for lying. So I got a whipping and almost lost my best friend all for just not telling the truth. This was one lesson that I would not soon forget.

Chapter 30

After a few months, Grandmas' sister, Aunt Lotti, started to come see us every Friday evening, to go grocery shopping with Grandma. She was my favorite aunt and I always looked forward to her coming. She was tall, thin, dark complexioned. Her hair pulled back in a bun, and with her hat askew, she seemed to have a permanent twinkle in her eyes, and a constant grin on her face. She always entered the room with her familiar salutation, "God be with you!" She always had a little piece of candy for me.

After they were fortified with a cup of brewed over coffee and exchanged the latest news and gossip, they would be off to Ludolf Street after groceries. They would each have two big shopping bags, the shopkeepers would place the selected items on the counter and then Grandma and Aunt Lotti would arrange them in their bags. The newer shopping bag was for dry goods, the older one for potatoes and vegetables.

On their return, the table was set and they emptied their shopping bags and sorted out the items. The first thing they had was a good cup of coffee, followed by a quick meal of rolls, bread and cold cuts on open faced sandwiches. Aunt Lotti lingered over another cup, discussions of family and friends followed and too soon the visit ended, with the promise of coming back next Friday.

It was during one of Aunt Lottis' visits that a traveling salesman stopped by. With few jobs available, the traveling salesmen were on the rise. This one was selling big leather shopping bags, guaranteed to be sturdy enough to outlast both women. They looked over the samples he carried, and decided to get one apiece. He came by every Friday for a partial payment, until the bags were paid for.

He became such a fixture in the household that he also had to have a cup of coffee first. Then he would tell us who bought what bag in the neighborhood, followed by what Grandma and Aunt Lotti deemed as a lot of good gossip.

He would still stop in long after the bags had been paid for. Grandma had a gift of making people feel welcome. He played the harmonica, and we would sing together and have a good time. Other times, they would all play cards at night. Grandpa enjoyed these visits immensely, giving him some male companionship.

Several times a year we would hear the knife sharpener man cry out his profession, yelling out as he was going up the lane, to bring him our dull knives and he would sharpen them like new for a penny apiece. Grandma would get her paring knives and a butcher knife and hand them to him. He would put them against a wheel called a grindstone, then he stepped on a wooden peddle to make the wheel go around, holding the knife blade against it. Then he would test it by carefully running his thumb against the blade. When he was done, he would strap the contraption to his back and move on to another location.

We found out that the man in barrack #1A had a tiny chest freezer in his hut, and was selling ice cream bars. Karin and I asked him if we could look in his little box freezer, as we had never seen one before. He obliged, showing us the content. The ice cream bars were small, the shape of a Popsicle.

We hung around and watched to see who would buy the ice cream bars, for lack of something better to do, but his business was so slow, we tired of that game fast.

Chapter 31

It was around 1950-51, that the dry grocer had a new promotion, when you bought the brand name margarine, you could choose a hand colored picture. As soon as Grandma asked for the margarine, the grocer would hand me a box to choose my picture. They were all different prints from Africa, the animals or different tribesman.

It told the story of a young man who traveled to Africa, and of his experiences. After I had collected most of the pictures, Grandma bought me the album the pictures were to go into for two Marks. The pages told of his travels, and each page had a place for the numbered picture. That was my first album. In 1952, another brand of margarine came out with the same idea. This album was on animals from all over the world, the pictures were illustrated so beautiful making it hard to decide which one to choose. I would go home and look at each picture, and read the short outline of the animal on the back. Grandma also bought me that album to put the pictures in; a third album followed this.

I spend many wonderful hours reading the story and looking at each picture as if I saw it for the first time.

Chapter 32

Grandma was anxious to make the hut our home and got a purple lilac slip from Aunt Lotti's yard to plant by the hut; she also got some aster seeds and sowed them below the lilac. Grandma turned an old tablecloth into little curtains; there were just the two windows in the front of the hut facing the Alster.

Aunt Lotti came to visit and to see how her lilac slip was coming along. Grandma told her that it was thriving and never even wilted. Aunt Lotti was not feeling very well, and Grandma told her to go inside and she would make them a cup of coffee to perk her up. She no sooner finished her cup than she ran to the "slop bucket" and everything came back up, including her dentures. There they lay, at the bottom, topped with our nighttime visits and her vomit. Grandma told her she had better get her dentures out and she said that she could not bear to reach down into the bucket, so Mama did it for her, and washed the dentures off. Even though she was sick, we all got a good laugh over that one. Years later when someone said, "Do you remember when your dentures went into the slop bucket?" of course she did, and we were bound not to let her forget it.

It was not to long after that incident, that Grandma went with Aunt Lotti to help her shop for a new hat. While Aunt Lotti was trying on hats, Grandma decided she would also try some on. They were in the shop for a while, and after trying on different styles, Aunt Lotti finally found what she wanted, made her purchase and came home. As soon as they entered the hut, Mama started laughing. Here was Grandma, sporting a new hat with the price tag hanging down on the side. She was so embarrassed she grabbed Aunt Lottis' arm, and back out the door, they went, back to the store, except this time the hat was in her hand. She was berating Aunt Lotti all the way to the store as to why she did not see her wearing the hat and the price tag hanging down. After this, whenever Aunt Lottis' denture incident came up, she was quick to point out how Grandma was the one that walked out of the store with the unpaid hat on her head.

Chapter 33

Our little radio was the only entertainment that we had; which we used sparingly for the news in the evening and maybe a program through the day. The radio fascinated me, and one evening, while everyone was outside, I took the back off the radio, turning the screws with a butter knife. I was looking for the little people that did the talking and the singing, but could not find any, just a lot of wires and metal and glass tubes. How disappointing! I even shook the radio out over the table, thinking if they are hiding, some will fall out, but no luck.

When Grandma came in to check on me, she saw what I had done. I told her why I did it and she tried to explain to me how a radio worked, her explanation was more far fetched then mine.

Chapter 34

Mama was laid off from her job. This would have been a disaster, but she was able to draw unemployment from the state. We went to the city, twice a month, for her unemployment pay.

The train would have been the fast way, but we would take the riverboat for a special treat. I loved this time together with Mama and we talked a great deal of where we were going and what we would do and see in town. We enjoyed the beautiful scenery as the boat made its way down the Alster. There were beautiful brick villas partially covered with ivy vines, and the graceful weeping willows dipping their swaying branches into the waters edge. Near the shoreline we were rewarded with the white swans that graced the Alster in the summertime.

We would meet and pass other boats and wave at each other along the way.

As we embarked at the Pavilion, we looked up to find the Michaelis Church steeple to get our bearings; the courthouse was up the side street from it. The streets here were cobblestone, so old that the edges were gently rounded with wear. On the way, we passed a booth with a canopy over the top. This was a banana vendor. I eyed it longingly. Mama told me that we had to pick up her pay packet first, and then we would come back and we could get some bananas to take home.

True to her word, we stopped at the canvas covered stand on the way back; bananas were hung all around the framework, and laid out on the table in front of us. I chose a nice big bunch to take home. We ate one right away to fortify ourselves for the day.

The next stop was my favorite, the Stationary Shop. Mama let me get two pages of Victorian scrap pictures. The lady would put several sheets on the counter for me to choose from. I would agonize over the sheets, since they were all so beautiful and it was so hard to choose, but eventually I made up my mind, and armed with my new scrap pictures and the bananas, we went to the Fish Restaurant for lunch.

It was a workmans' restaurant, very large and crowded, and in order to save room and serve more people they did away with the chairs. There were just little round tables where two to four people could stand and eat. It is also a good way to get rid of loitering. With the shopping bag between Mama's feet, we had our hands free to eat. It was not too comfortable, but the food was delicious.

After that we window shopped, got a few food items to take back home and went back to the pier, to board the riverboat, for the ride back home.

The way back was always more quiet, as we were lost in our own thoughts of the wonderful things we had seen in town, and I tried to memorize everything, so I could tell Karin when I saw her.

When we arrived home, Mama gave Grandma the food items that she picked up and they busied themselves fixing supper in the little kitchen, as Grandpa sat in his chair, smoking his pipe and reading his newspaper.

Chapter 35

Grandma had two passions, one was her crossword puzzles, which she was very good at, and the other was playing cards, not only playing card games, but also reading cards. Whenever Mama or Grandpa would look for a job, Grandma would lay the cards out on the table to see if it was a good day for it or not. If it came out that it was not a good day, she would say, "Let me try it just once more to make sure." I used to think she had the gift, because she would tell me how she was the seventh daughter of a seventh daughter, and once in a while she told me how she was the queen of Sheba. I was so impressed, but later I found out that was Grandma's way of keeping me amused. We never tired of her telling our fortunes by reading the cards.

Neighbors, fisherman, salesman and Aunt Lotti would stop by on some Friday nights, and they would get into a card game, followed with much laughter, singing and reminiscing. I would be long asleep, and the card games would still be going on, and slowly one by one, they would depart, as the door would open and close on their leaving.

Then Grandma would get out her crossword puzzle book and work at it a while to unwind, before she made up her bed on the sofa and finally go to sleep.

Mama and Grandpa were always the first ones up, as they had to go to work in the mornings. In the summertime, Mama would get up even earlier, put on her bathing suit and swim across the Alster and back for exercise, and then she would hurry and change into her work clothes. There were several adults that followed Mama's lead and did the same thing.

Chapter 36

It was wintertime again, we kids enjoyed it and our parents despised it. Our minds were on the winter pastimes, while our parents had the worries of keeping the hut warm and the socks darned and dried. Mama put an extra layer of cardboard, in the soles of all our shoes to keep our feet warm and dry. Grandpa always had big holes in his shoes, and nothing kept out the rain and snow for him.

Mama always wore an Army greatcoat in the winter; I do not know where she got it, since she had mailed her uniform back to her post. She probably received the coat in a care package. Grandpa had an old overcoat that not only had seen better days, but better years. Grandma had a thin gray cloth coat, worn over layers of sweaters and scarves, and I had a little coat from a Red Cross parcel that was already worn out before I received it. Karin was outside rounding us up, Heidi, Rita and I. When one of us decided to play, we would always get the others to play with us. Our project that day was to make an ice slide. We would form a line, run as fast as we could and then slide on the snow, till it formed a long, slick sheet of ice, then you had to keep your balance and slide as far as you could. The boys always got the farthest. They would also take over our slide, after we worked on it and got it ready. They would try to make it so slick that none of the girls could stand on it. By evening you could slide for a couple of minutes, it would be so long and smooth. If you fell on it, it was almost impossible to stand up, as it was so slick. Some of the girls had muffs to keep their hands warm, which looked so cozy. Karin and I just dug our hands deeper into our pockets and stomping our feet in place to keep them from freezing, as we waited in line for our turn to slide.

The Shore Patrol made its rounds checking the thickness of the ice on the Alster. When it was thick enough, they would put up signs to show that it was safe to walk and skate on the ice. We always looked forward to that event. You could walk across toward Ludolf Street without crossing the bridge. Kids and adults from other streets would come with their ice skates and put on a show. However, like anything else, wintertime always brought its own tragedies. They come along when you least expect them.

The Shore Patrol had put up signs that the ice was safe to walk on. The areas that were not solid enough got warning signs, Danger Thin Ice.

Everyone was out on the Alster; we barrack kids working on making our ice slide and the town people were ice-skating. The very young and the older people were walking on the ice, for the sheer pleasure of it.

It was very festive on this particular day, and quite crowded on the Alster, when we heard someone shouting. Karin and I looked in the direction of the commotion as we saw a little girl about our age on ice skates, wearing a brown coat with a scarf around her neck, mittens on her hands with her arms outstretched, heading toward the thin ice sign. Now other people joined in the shouting for her to stop, she seemed not to notice and kept on going. As we watched, she disappeared through the ice.

The men and older boys ran toward the hole in the ice, the first man there lay on the ice, yelling for someone to grab his ankles, while he crept closer. Someone else held the ankles of the second man until they had a living chain going. The first man reached through the hole in the ice and every time he tried to grab her, more ice broke around the hole from his weight and the little girl went deeper under the ice layer. It was a horrible sight as you could see the back of her brown coat, through the ice, going further out of their reach.

Finally, someone came with a ladder, and laid it on the ice. One of the men got on it while others held the ladder in case it broke through the ice. He crawled toward the girl, furiously chipping a new hole where they saw her, but by the time they finally got her out, it was too late.

They carried her small lifeless body to a waiting ambulance; she would never feel the warmth of the blanket they wrapped around her.

Karin, Heidi, Rita and I went back across the Alster to our side, silent for once, deep in thought, and making wide circles around the thin ice signs that we used to ignore and were so careless about. After all, that could have been one of us.

I told Grandma about the girl, and got a sermon right on the spot about the dangers of the thin ice, and she hoped that it had taught us all a lesson.

For a long time after that, when I closed my eyes at night, I could see that brown coat, spread out like the wings of a butterfly floating under the ice.

The weather got worse, snowflakes, big as saucers, twirled toward the ground, covering it in a foot of fresh snow. Grandma needed milk. Usually she sends me with the liter milk can to the Dairy alone, but with the bad weather, she worried about me, so we both went. Just before we started to cross the bridge, we noticed a man on a bicycle having a hard go of it in the snow. All of a sudden, a big truck came along and struck the man. He lay in the road, evidently hurt, and the bicycle was laying close by all bent up with the wheels twisted.

The truck driver was trying to drive off when the pedestrians all gathered around the truck to stop him. Grandma told me to stay on the curb, and off she went into the fray. One hand on her hip the other shaking a finger at the driver telling him to pick up the poor soul and take him to a hospital. When he relented, several men picked the injured man up, set him up in the truck seat, while someone else picked up his twisted bicycle, and put it in the back of the truck.

As he pulled off and we continued across the bridge, I asked Grandma if he was going to take the man to the hospital. She said, "No, he will probably dump him out as soon as he gets out of town." When I asked why, she replied, "So he won't get into trouble with the authorities." We went on in silence.

Chapter 37

If I did not like going to school in the summer, because it cut into my swim and play time, I loved going in the winter. The building was warm, we got warm vegetable soup for lunch that had tiny bits of beef and barley in it, and it was getting closer to Christmas. We had an Advent Wreath hanging in our classroom suspended from the ceiling with red ribbons and four fat creamy beeswax candles on it, it was so festive, and the room smelled of pine boughs and the scent of the candles.

The teacher told us he had a surprise for us; a man was to come to our class and cut out paper silhouettes. He explained to us what that was, and we were very excited about our visitor.

We were not disappointed. When our guest came, he took out a sheet of paper, folding it several times, and with a tiny pair of scissors, he proceeded to cut away portions of the paper. He then held his work up high so we could see what he was doing. Upon completion, he unfolded it and like magic two beautiful swans with a tree in the center appeared, we were just spellbound. He cut several different pictures, reminding me of a magician performing his act in front of a captive audience.

Later on, he took us one by one, stood us sideways and cut out our profile out of black paper and slipped a white piece of paper behind it. The likeness was perfect, better then any picture could have been. I wore my hair in a short bob. Grandma kept it that way, telling me that my fine hair tangled so when it was longer. I always envied girls like Heidi that had long, fat braids, but my bob showed up really well in silhouette.

It was especially exciting, as it was close to Christmas and I did not have a gift for Mama and Grandma, this would be just perfect. I hid the silhouette in one of my workbooks so they could not see it and waited with anticipation for the big day. This made it so exciting, now that I had a present to give.

I knew Grandma had gotten a parcel from the Red Cross for me. They always asked her if it is a boy or girl, and what age and size. I also know that it was used clothing and it was always too small and worn thin, way before I would receive it. I was right about the clothes, but what I did not know was, that this time the parcel included a raggedy Teddy Bear that would steal my heart.

Chapter 38

On one of these cold winter mornings, Grandma had to run some errands. We did not go across the bridge to Ludolf Street. Instead, we turned left, at the Fahrhaus Restaurant and walked up Hudtwalcker Street, past the Underground Railroad. It was a very cold day and the wind was blowing hard. Some of the people passing us were holding on to their hats, and others were holding their parcels in front of them to block the biting wind.

These days were especially hard on Grandmas frail body, with little food to warm her body and the thin, worn cloth coat was not much in keeping out the cold. There was a restaurant across the street; we had never been in it. Grandma got out her coin purse and checked her change. Then we crossed the street, heading toward the restaurant. Grandma said there was enough money for two bowls of soup to warm us, and we would eat slowly and take our time, so we could stay inside a little longer until we thawed out.

As we entered people stared at us, or at our shabby clothes, but the waiter came, led us to a table and helped Grandma off with her coat, as if she was royalty. The tables covered in white tablecloths looked quite elegant. On it were cups turned upside down on saucers. The waiter handed Grandma a menu and she ordered two bowls of soup. In a few minutes, he was back, placing the bowls in front of us.

A man was in the restaurant playing a violin at different tables. He came over to our table as we started to eat, and serenaded us. Grandma reached in her coin purse, took out the last two coins, and gave them to him. I could not believe my eyes. I was quiet, as Grandma had taught me, but when we finally left the restaurant, fortified with the warm soup, I asked Grandma why she had given that man our last money. She said that he needed money too, and probably had a family to feed, and that might be the only money he got that day.

Chapter 39

It was our turn in the washhouse laundry room, and Mama called me over to help with the sheets. We would hold the sheet on all four corners and pull it flat, and then she would hang it with the others on the clotheslines in the washhouse. Mama had more whites boiling in a big pot on the stove. She would take a big wooden stick, stir them around, and fish up apiece of laundry with the stick, wring it out and hang it up. It was hot and steamy in there but a good place to be in the winter.

While we were in the washhouse, neighbors came by to use their toilets, wash up at the sinks, and stayed to gossip awhile.

This was Friday, and I was anxious to get back to the barrack, as Aunt Lotti would be coming soon. We met her coming up the lane as we were leaving the washhouse. She waved at us and I ran to hug her. She seemed preoccupied as she entered the hut with us. Grandma had coffee ready, and after handing Aunt Lotti a cup, she told us she would not be seeing us any more. We all stared at her in disbelief.

She said she was going to America. Aunt Anne and my Uncle Helmut had moved to America years ago. I really did not know them. My uncle had passed away and Aunt Lotti said Aunt Anne needed her, as she was all alone. Grandma was one of twelve children, and Aunt Lotti and she were always together. I could not imagine her leaving us. She brought us a few things to remember her by, a vase for Grandma, a scarf for Mama, a new pipe for Grandpa, a sweet and a picture of her for me to remember her by.

This was not the day I was waiting for, no usual shopping trip, no happy laughter, everyone was solemn and in thoughts. I cried and Aunt Lotti tried to console me, with the promise that she would write often plus saying how she would miss us too.

I fell asleep on the sofa, and drifting in and out heard them talking about the trip. I did not want to hear it;

I wanted to wake up and find out that this was just a bad dream. I heard the door open and shut, Grandma and Mama sobbing, and I knew she was gone out of our lives.

The next day, after Mama and Grandpa went to work and Grandma was cleaning the hut I tried talking to her about Aunt Lotti but she did not seem to hear me. She was shaking out the rug, washing windows, and mopping. She looked so sad I went out to play, because I think she wanted to cry.

We got a letter several weeks later from Aunt Lotti, saying she arrived safely by ship. That made Grandma feel a little better, but our Fridays would never be the same again. What we did not find out until years later, was that Aunt Lotti said she had made a big mistake. She missed Grandma and Germany so much; she never did learn to talk English, except for a few words. She was very homesick for Hamburg and us.

Chapter 40

When Mama came home from work on Friday, she said that Karstadt had their Christmas display up. Karstadt was a big shopping emporium like Macy's, with five large picture windows in front displaying the latest fashions and wares, but at Christmas time, it became magic.

Draperies were in place while they worked on the window displays, to hide what was going on inside. When the storeowner opened the curtains in December, every child and adult for miles around would stand out in the freezing weather to look at the display.

There were animated figures, so lifelike you would think that they were real. There was St. Nick's workshop, complete with real dwarfs that the store hires for the Christmas season, working on a toy assembly line. Another window surrounded with snow and multicolored lights, reflecting on the snow, and animated boys throwing snowballs at little girls. Another window showed parents decorating a Christmas tree while another window showed the children asleep in bed dreaming of sugarplums. One window showed the forest at night with all the animals gathered around a little Christmas tree that had lights on it.

The streets were crowded. Fathers were holding their little ones on their shoulders for a closer look. Then there were the lucky ones that were close enough to the windows to see. All the while, the Christmas music played through hidden speakers. It was pure magic. No one wanted to leave, but slowly, the cold got the better of us. Grandma had asked me a couple of times already if I was ready to go home. I did not want to, but the wet snow was seeping through my shoes freezing my feet, and I knew Grandma was cold as well. Mama and Grandma took me by the hand as we walked briskly home, talking all the way about the beautiful window display.

We were so cold, by the time we got home, that the barrack felt warm, because we were out of the wind.

Grandpa was still reading the sport page, and I told him all about the Karstadt window display.

As I went to bed that night, I felt like the children in the window, dreaming of sugarplums and Saint Nickolaus.

The Red Cross was collecting for the poor again. No matter how poor you are, there is always someone worse off than you are. Grandma put together a few items, my all too short dresses and a pair of shoes that made more blisters than I care to remember…and Teddy!

I did not have a clue until I came home from school and asked where he was. Grandma told me she sent him off to a poor child, that I was too old for a teddy bear. I cried, telling Grandma that I loved the bear, and that was the only toy I had. She turned her deaf ear; she did not want to hear any more about it.

Chapter 41

It was around this time that our teacher told us we would be going on a vacation trip next fall. We would take the bus and go to Niendorf, by the sea, and spend a week at the Hamburg Children's Home. We were so excited! However, in order to accomplish this we had to save to pay our way. We all got little bank savings booklets and were told to bring any change to school. We would then get a stamp from our teacher to put into our book, and when we had them filled up, we would have enough money to go.

I ran home with the big news, and between Grandma, Mama and Grandpa, I got one Mark. The next day I took my money to the teacher and got the appropriate stamp to put in my book. About every one brought some money; we were off to a good start.

Our teacher would talk about our upcoming trip, and encourage us to keep bringing any money that we could, and discouraged us from buying sweets with the odd pennies.

We met in front of the school on the second day of September. The bus came on time, and our baggage and sand shovels were stored in a compartment underneath the bus. Parents hugged and kissed their children one last time, before the bus pulled out. We sang, ate our fruit and sandwiches along the three-hour trip. The bus passed farmland and rolling hills until we finally got a glimpse of the blue green waters of the Ostsee.

The children's home was beautiful. It was a multi-level Tudor style building, and our bedroom was on the top floor with a glorious view. Our dining room was in another building adjacent to the main building. It was also in the old Tudor style complete with thatched roof, and eyebrow windows. It was a big, long building set up with long tables and benches to accommodate many children. We had the most wonderful meals here.

The cots in the bedroom had sheets and blankets folded on them. The teacher assigned us each a cot with a demonstration on how to make up the cot. Two women teachers came with us on the trip to help watch over us. They were very nice, and we all liked them. They, and our teacher, showed us how to make up our cots, complete with hospital corners. We all paid attention, and then they paired us off to make our beds.

Some of the girls cried the first night away from their parents, but the teachers came in and consoled them, telling them that their parents would want them to have a good time while they were here.

We had a schedule to follow, outings to the beach, a sailing trip, walking to the town, sight seeing, and a special day of games on the beach.

That was the most wonderful week of my life, and it ended all too soon, but I was looking forward to seeing Grandma, Mama and Grandpa. I could not wait to tell Karin, Heidi and Rita about this wonderful trip.

Chapter 42

When I was around nine years old, we started getting letters from America. Mama had a married cousin, Aunt Ella, who lived there. She planned on coming to Hamburg in the summer to take Mama and me back to America to live. The only one not excited about this news was I. How could we leave Grandma and Grandpa by themselves, without anyone to take care of them? How would they survive without us? Mama was the main breadwinner in the family. Besides, I could not think of leaving Karin, Heidi and Rita.

This was about the time that I started getting nightmares, always waking up in a sweat, sometimes sobbing. Mama and Grandma could not figure out what was wrong with me. One of them would always get up to console me. It got so bad that I hated going to bed at night, knowing that I would have a horrible nightmare.

Aunt Ella came at the end of summer, because she wanted to miss the heat. I thought it was funny that she and Mama had the same first name. She was very kind and went to take me shopping one day, but as we left too late, all the stores had closed already. She said that in America the stores stayed open at night. We came home empty-handed and disappointed. She said we would go shopping again, but it never happened.

She did not feel well and rested a lot. Finally, Mama took her to the doctor. She wound up in the hospital, needing surgery, and passed away.

Mama, Grandma and Grandpa were at a loss. They wired my uncle. The hospital expense and shipping of the body to America for burial, took most of Aunt Ella's money. My uncle told us to come also, since that was what she wanted, but by then, most of the money was gone, and there was just enough left for Mama.

She decided to go and find work and send for me as soon as possible. Mama packed her meager wardrobe and a few pictures in a suitcase, and got ready for her journey.

Grandpa told her to look up his old friend in America. He was a butcher, and had gone to America, several years earlier to start his own business. Grandpa said that she would be sure to get a job from him. Mama told him that she did not want to work in a meatpacking place. Years later, she would laugh at herself for missing the boat, when she saw his meat products in all the stores.

She promised to send us care packages as soon as she got there, and a letter every week. I had to promise her to take care of Grandma and Grandpa. When the day finally came, the house was quiet. Seemed like we had said so much, there was nothing left to say. When Mama told Grandpa good by, he pulled out his big handkerchief, it was the first time that I saw him cry. It was so sad.

Grandpa stayed home and Grandma and I left on the streetcar with Mama. From there we took the underground train to the Hamburg seaport, to see Mama off on the ship that night. We went onboard to see the ship. They called, "last call for supper," and Grandma told Mama she had better go eat, so she would not miss it. Mama did not want to go eat without us, so we left. As we were leaving, Grandma asked Mama if she had enough money, of course, she said yes. Grandma opened her coin purse and gave her a few marks.

Chapter 43

Grandma said that we had to hurry, after we waved at Mama from the shore, if we were to make the last U-train home. It was wintertime and getting cold out in the night air. When we got down the steps into the train terminal, it was like a deepfreeze, but at least we were out of the wind. The platform was deserted, and I wondered if we already missed the train. Grandma asked the clerk and he said the train should be here in a few minutes. She got in her coin purse and realized that she did not have enough money left for both of our tickets. Therefore, she told me to get a ticket, get on the train, and tell Grandpa to come first thing in the morning when the train ran again, with some money for her to come home.

I asked her where she was going to sleep and she told me that she would lie on the bench, that she would be fine. I looked at the long, narrow wood bench, and grandma's frail body. With her migraines, I knew I could not leave her there. The cold air rushed out of the train tunnels sending chills up your spine. I told her that I was not leaving without her. She could buy the ticket and I would sneak by the ticket booth. She said we were the only ones in the terminal, and the clerk had already seen us together. I told her to go, but she would not hear of it. I told her there was no use in both of us staying; one of us had to go to Grandpa. I fianally convinced her to go after promising I would not leave the bench, until she came back for me in the morning.

Grandma got her ticket and waved at me as she passed through the turnstile. As the train was coming, a handful of young people came running up to the ticket booth talking and laughing. I rushed up to them, and ducked behind them past the ticket booth, and under the turnstile, I went. Grandma was making her way down the track to the train, as I came up behind her and took her hand. I will never forget the look of relief on her face. We boarded the train hand in hand, and she did not let go of my hand until we got home. Then we told Grandpa about our big adventure.

Mama was on her way to a new beginning; all too soon, it would be my turn.

My nightmares continued. Mamas' ship did not dock on the specified day, and we were all scared that something had happened to the ship. Grandma and Grandpa listened to the radio news constantly, and learned that her ship was in trouble. It was battling high winds on the ocean, and running low on food. Finally they arrived, a week after they were supposed to dock. We knew, from the news broadcast, that her ship arrived safely after being lost at sea for several days.

We got a letter from Mama telling us about her ordeal, but she did not mention about the ordeal she was facing in America. Grandma and Grandpa never found out about this.

We wondered why we never got the care package Mama promised us. Grandma said she was probably saving every penny so she could send for me sooner.

Karin asked me if I wanted to go to the Hagenbeck Zoo with her, and we would need some money, to get into the zoo and for the streetcar. Grandma figured a change would do me good and gave me some money. She told us to be careful, and not come home too late. She also gave us some sound advice, telling us to stay away from the camels, that they were nasty animals and would spit on us. It seems that she had been to the zoo with Mama, when a camel had spit on her.

The zoo is one of the largest and finest ones, with thousands of animals, a rainforest and Japanese garden, complete with koi ponds. It was magical. We tried to see every animal there, and bought breadcrumbs to feed the fish and birds. Time passed too quickly, and before long, we heard the announcement they were closing for the day.

By the time we got to the streetcar, we realized that we had spent all our money, forgetting about the trip back. It was dark and we were hungry. We were alone, far from home, and I got scared and started to cry.

Karin tried to console me, when a man came by and asked what was wrong. When we told him, he said to come with him. He led us across the street to a hot dog vendor and bought us both a hot dog. When we had finished he gave us the fare money, took us back across the street, and waited until our streetcar arrived. He wanted to make sure we got on all right. He told us his name and said to tell our parents that we were in safe hands. I never was so glad to get back home as I was that night. Karin and I never told about this, as we knew we would never be able to go by ourselves again.

Time passed, life went on. Funny, I remember people dying in the Quonset huts, but I do not remember any births. In the years that we lived there, I do not believe there was one new birth.

Almost two years had passed since Mama left us, and about February, in 1953 her letters became more frequent. She instructed Grandma to get a passport and the required shots for me. She hoped to send for me in April. Time was of the essence, since my 12th birthday was on the 24th, after which she would have to pay full price for my trip.

Chapter 44

The paperwork took some time, and while that was going through, Grandma took me shopping. Grandma wanted to get me a pair of new shoes. We went to the shoe shop on Alsterdorfer Street. I sat in a chair, while they measured my foot; the shoe sales clerk brought several boxes over for Grandmas' inspection. At the end, we settled on a beautiful pair of brown shoes, and on the inside sole was a picture of an elephant. That was the shoes logo. Grandma let me wear the new shoes home, to break them in. Grandma had a saying, when shoes squeak, that meant they have not been paid for yet. Mine did not squeak, so I guess the saying was true.

She also got me my first wristwatch, and said that was an early birthday gift, so I would have something to remember her by. As if, I needed anything for that. I was so excited about my watch; every time I met someone walking toward me, I would look at my watch, hoping that someone would notice it. My hope was that someone would ask me for the time, and I could show off my watch, but no one ever asked me.

One day as I was making my way home from school, coming out from the train tunnel, a woman asked me if I had the time. Hallelujah!

I made an exaggerated motion to look at my wrist, and was dumbfounded. There was nothing there! I had forgotten to put my watch on that morning. Trying to regain my composure, I went up to her and said, "No, I do not know what time it is because I left my watch at home, but I do have a watch and can prove it." I showed her my white line around my wrist where the watchstrap kept it from tanning. The woman had a very strange expression on her face.

I never forgot to wear my watch after that, but no one ever asked me for the time again. Maybe that woman spread the word about me, odds are, someone else should have asked.

Then it was time to pack a little suitcase for me, which Grandma received from Karin's mother. Grandma packed a sweater that Mama had knit, a couple dresses that were already too short, and a pitiful few other items. She packed my doll in the center so it would not get broken. The doll had on a long white christening dress that Mama had embroidered, also a couple of extra dresses Mama had made for the doll from my cast-offs I had little roller skates for the doll, and Grandma told me to put the skates on the dolls feet. I told her it did not look right with the long dress, so I had to change the dress.

Then she showed me a ring, it was a topaz ring, Mama's birthstone. Grandma wrapped the ring in tissue, stuffed it into the dolls roller skate shoe and put it on the doll. She told me when I went through customs; they would ask me if I had any gold or silver to say no, that she could not afford the duty on the ring.

Since I was to go by plane there was a weight restriction on the luggage. I was sure I was way under, but to make certain, Grandma got out Grandpas' famous wagon that moved us into the Quonset hut, and had me pull it over the bridge to Ludolf Street. There I was to ask the dry grocer to weigh it for me, as they had big scales. Karin came with me on this momentous occasion.

Grandma had already told the shopkeepers about my upcoming departure. They were glad to help and placed the suitcase on their scale for me, and as suspected, I was underweight. They wished me the best of luck and told me not to forget them....how could I ever do that.

Chapter 45

As the day finally came, two days before my birthday, it was time for me to leave home. I had already said my goodbyes to all my friends and neighbors and the shopkeepers. Karin, Heidi and Rita were already in school. As usual, Grandpa stayed home, he seemed to cry a lot more than when Mama left, but he did not hide it as well this time. As I left the Quonset for the last time, I turned around and Grandpa had out his big white handkerchief, wiping his eyes. He looked so pitiful.

I could not help but look back at the Quonset, that familiar half moon building that had been the only home I would remember, so clearly, over the years to come. From the day, we moved into the cold shell of a building, to the summer days when I ran in my bathing suit toward the Alster.

Memories flooded back of the nights waiting up for Mama to come home from the hospital, waiting on the food she smuggled out in a stocking, and Grandma laying her cards to read our fortunes. The crane came to my mind and the scurrying to get the coal. Grandpa would never rock me to sleep again, or ask me what kind of meat is on the table. How I would miss the walks across the bridge to our wonderful grocery shops, and the anticipation of Aunt Lottis' visits on Fridays. Heidi and I would never follow Fritz again, the friends I was leaving behind, and the games that we played. Would I ever feel so loved and needed again?

Grandmas' lilac was budding out, and would be full of flowers this year, I wished I could stay and see it bloom. I kept looking back afraid that I would forget where I came from; my mind could not yet comprehend that I would never see this place again. I was not just leaving my home, no matter how humble; I was leaving my world, as I knew it.

Grandma was trying to make small talk on the train to the airport; I could tell she was sad too. I wished that I could stay, but I had to go to Mama. Grandma said

Mama had missed me and was lonesome for me. It was finally time to board the plane, as a flight attendant pinned a nametag on my coat. Grandma loosened my grip from around her neck, and a flight attendant took me toward the plane. Grandma had given me a package that I knew was a book I loved, but she said not to open it until we were off the ground.

The plane was not very full; I looked around the other seats. The flight attendant put me by the window so I could look out, and I had both seats to myself. Finally, the plane started up, a humming sound of the engines, and then we were rolling down the runway. I wondered if we were just going to roll to America, whenever, so gently, the ground below left us.

I settled back and decided to read my new book. As I opened the cover to the front page, Grandma had written:

A great bird is taking you to a far off land. However, you are flying to Mama so we are not afraid. Now we are all alone, but our thoughts will always be with you both. Have a good flight and much happiness in the future.

        Grandma & Grandpa

I closed the book just before the tears hit the page.

My last thoughts, before I closed my eyes, were what if they find the ring. Moreover, why did Mama never send a package? I guess that I would find out soon enough, as I too was heading for a new beginning.

Printed in the United States
64072LVS00001B/10-15